GONE FROM THE GAME

Also by Christopher Fahy

Novels:

The Christmas Star
Red Tape
Chasing the Sun
Breaking Point
Fever 42
The Fly Must Die
The Lyssa Syndrome
Eternal Bliss
Dream House
Nightflyer
The Compost Heap

Short Stories:

Matinee at the Flame
Limerock: Maine Stories
Greengroundtown

Poetry:

The End Beginning

Nonfiction:

Home Remedies

GONE FROM THE GAME

Christopher Fahy

LIMEROCK BOOKS

Limerock Books • 15 Mechanic Street • Thomaston ME 04861
limebks@gmail.com

The characters, events and locales in this book are fictitious or used fictitiously.

Gone from the Game: novel / Christopher Fahy

ISBN: 978-0-9746589-7-1

Cover art and design: Cortney Skinner

Printed in USA.

For Greg and Ben

1

THE HUNS SPOKE PERFECT ENGLISH. Nick had never quite gotten over that. All of them, every last one of them, all of the weeks he had been in this camp, had perfect American accents. They even used slang right. Impressive.

The Huns were vicious and heartless people, but one thing they weren't was stupid. As much as he loathed and despised them, he had to admit they were smart. Not smart enough to win the war, but smart.

Two of them lounged by the doorway, smoking. No accents at all, not a trace. They were talking about Christmas presents.

"I got her this bracelet, it's turquoise and silver, made by the Navajos out in New Mexico."

"Hey, that sounds swell."

"My nephew, he went there this summer and brought back a whole lot of stuff."

"Can you get one for me? Daisy would love it."

"I think he unloaded them all, but I'll check."

And that's how they spoke. As if they'd been born here, had lived here for all of their lives. As if they had never seen Mannheim or Darmstadt, the Rhine, the Black Forest. As if this was Jersey or Maryland.

A man in the corner, hunched up in a ball on the floor, began screaming. Nick covered his ears. "I can't do it!" the man was shouting. "Don't make me, don't make me, I can't!" Then he started to sob. The Huns in the doorway ignored

1

him. The taller one smiled. The shorter one said, "See you later," and walked away. A man at the table across from Nick said, "Shut up! Did you hear me? Shut up!" He was beating his head with his fists. The tall Hun came over and said, "Stop it, Leonard." The man at the table wailed.

Nick leaned forward, both arms on the table, and looked out the window. Something else that he couldn't figure was how they had turned off the colors. The world was all shades of gray, like a picture show: gray sky and gray buildings, black trees with no leaves, and prisoners wandering aimlessly, wearing gray. They'd been poisoned, of course. The Huns had drugged them senseless with potions much stronger than Johnny's pills. They'd tried many times to drug him too and so far he'd outfoxed them.

But he hadn't been able to stop them from putting things into his head. They put pictures and words and songs in his head and he didn't know how they did it, probably through his food. *Oh Johnny, Oh Johnny, how you can love,* went the song again and again and again. While they were watching, he'd never let on that they'd gotten to him, but back in his room he would clench his jaws and cover his ears and whisper harshly, *"Stop, stop, stop!"* but it wouldn't stop unless they told it to.

Outside, near the brick-lined walk, a babbling man on his knees was eating grass. The trees were bare but the grass was thick—though gray—in this part of Germany. If this indeed *was* Germany. What if the Huns had already won—and this was Belgium? Or France?

No, they weren't that good at war. They loved war, loved to kill, but they weren't that good.

The man on the floor had stopped his sobbing and lay curled up, dead still. The man who'd been beating his head was now staring blankly at the wall. A few other prisoners wandered around spouting nonsense, and some of these others were spies who'd attempted to make him talk, but he hadn't been fooled.

2

"Hey, pal, got a smoke?"

The man sat beside him. He was heavy, with rheumy eyes and a growth of black whiskers. He wore the same prisoner outfit that all of them wore, but he was a spy.

"Pay you back, swear to God."

Nick ignored him and looked out the window.

"You son of a bitch," said the man. "All I want is one smoke, one goddamn smoke."

Nick kept looking outside. The man was still eating the grass out there.

"One smoke!" said the heavy man, pounding the table.

Nick narrowed his eyes. He hadn't talked to the spies, but he'd fought them, he'd fought them good.

"Okay then," the heavy man said with a suddenly wary look, "I'll write it down." He took a pad out of his pocket. "I'll write it down and remember, you son of a bitch." He frowned. "You got a pen?"

Nick pretended he hadn't heard. The man grunted and went to another table. "Hey, pal, can you loan me a smoke?"

At the doorway, a guard was pushing a cart. His shoulders were broad and his neck was thick. He stopped, took a tray from the cart's top shelf and placed it in front of a thin gray-haired man with no teeth. "Okay, Harry, eat up," he said, but the man simply stared at the table. The guard moved on. "Over here!" yelled a bald-headed man with a patch on one eye. "I'm starving, goddamn you! You trying to starve me to death?" "You'll get some, just wait your turn," the guard said sharply.

He stopped at Nick's table and set down a tray that was holding a dish, a fork, a spoon and a cup. All were made out of metal. He said, "Your favorite, Speedball—shepherd's pie. And chocolate pudding for dessert."

Nick looked at the food. Gray meat, gray peas and carrots and mashed potatoes, all clearly poisoned with words. The pudding was almost black with songs. They'd have to do better than this if they wanted to fool him, much better. They weren't so smart after all.

"Well, take it or leave it," said the guard—and the way that he said it so angered Nick that he slammed down his fist on the table and swept it clean. Plates and trays and cups hit the floor with a tinny racket and food flew everywhere.

"Goddamn!" said the guard, and a man at the next table cried out, "Traitor!"

Nick scooped a spoon off the floor and threw it. It missed the man's face by an inch. The guard yelled, "Hey! Goddamn you, Speedball!" and started for Nick as Nick picked up a fork. *Oh Johnny, Oh Johnny, Oh Johnny, Oh Johnny... Stop!* Nick screamed in his head and then hit the deck as the first of the shells went off.

Johnny huddled against the side of the trench, his rifle tight in his hands. He'd taken the pills, but even so, he was shaking. The pills used to calm him down but now they just seemed to confuse him. His pale face was spattered with mud as he said, "Jesus Christ!"

"That's as close as they're going to get," Nick said.

"Come on, do you really believe that?" Johnny said. His eyes were wide from fear and the pills.

A shell went off down the line somewhere and Johnny ducked. The air above his head went black. "And what if they use the gas?" he said. "The gas, Nick, what about that?"

"That's why we have masks."

"But they don't always work, and you know it. You don't get them on fast enough—I mean Ellis and Smith—"

It had burned out their eyes. Nick said: "Stop it, Johnny."

A screaming sound, another, another, and Johnny was quivering. Black clots of mud hit his helmet and shoulders, rats ran through the slime at his feet. "Jesus Christ!" he yelled again.

"Shut up!" Nick said.

"It's insane!" Johnny said. "It's all a mistake, why the hell did we ever—"

4

"Because of our mothers. And Alice and everyone else we love."

"You're wrong!" Johnny said. "We're fighting for Ford and Rockefeller, that's what this war's all about! We're fighting for rich people, Nick!"

An explosion so loud Nick's jawbone shook. Johnny's voice sounded thin in the bright ringing noise: "I can't take it!"

"You have to!" Nick said, and his own voice was dim in his ears.

"I can't!" Johnny said. "I'm a coward, that's all there is to it!"

"I don't want to hear any talk like that," Nick said. "It's the pills that are talking, not you."

"The pills?" Johnny said. "If I didn't take pills I'd go out of my mind!"

"No!"

Another loud burst and a scream down the line.

"A hit!" Johnny said, and his eyes were frantic. "They got somebody! Let's go!"

He was suddenly climbing the wall of the trench. Nick watched him, stunned. He lunged for his leg, but too late. "Johnny!"

Johnny was gone and Nick scrambled after him. Smoke and bright flashes, a line of barbed wire, the clack of machine guns and Johnny was running through craters of mud and the shattered raw stumps of trees.

"Johnny, no!" Nick yelled, and a shell went off and he dived to earth as the stones stung his shoulders and legs. He was deaf and through teeth full of bitter wet grit he cried, "Johnny!"

A wooden cart lay on its side with a spoked wheel spinning. The horse was dead with its stomach wide open, its dark entrails giving off steam. The thick smell of feces, then Nick saw a soldier, limbs twisted—a corpse from a previous battle blown out of the earth, its head missing.

Then Johnny. No arm and no leg, and half his face gone.

5

And he said, "I'm okay," then he died.

"Your brother was brave, a true hero," Nick said.

"But he suffered so horribly," Alice said, and her blue eyes were bright with tears.

"He was gone in an instant. He felt no pain."

Alice looked down at her slender hands and Nick loved her with all his heart. "Poor Mother," she said. "She will never accept it. Never."

"Please give her my love," Nick said. Blood was soaking his uniform sleeve from elbow to wrist, but Alice didn't notice. She shook her pale head. "I'm so lonely," she said. "Please come back."

"Soon," Nick said. "They can't last much longer, they're on the run."

"I saw Helen and George last night," Alice said, and her eyes were blue, black, green, he couldn't tell. "We went out in their motorcar."

"I don't want you to do that!" Nick said.

"But I'm lonely. You've been away so long."

"George is not to be trusted."

"He's married."

"It doesn't matter."

"He's fun."

"He's a coward, he's yellow, he wouldn't join up! He's a German, too!"

"He was drinking and went off the road."

"Stay away from him, Alice!"

"Don't talk to her in that manner!" his mother said, and he turned to her, frowning. "Mom...what's wrong?" She was deathly pale.

"I'm just tired and hot, that's all. Such a long trip, and nothing to drink."

"Try this," Nick said as he unscrewed his canteen's cap. "Go on." But the fluid was foul-smelling, fetid and dark as it filled the tin cup.

"Oh Nicky, not that," his mother said. "I'm not ready for that."

He looked at the cup, puzzled, shaking and hot, his left arm dead, and Alice was saying, "When are you coming back to stay? Nick, darling, you have to come back. You have to come back right now, you've been gone so long—"

He sat at the window and watched the snow, white fragments of time falling out of the sky, erasing green grass and the redbrick paths. A man dressed in blue was walking by. The world was brilliant with color again. Nick was startled, amazed. He felt his face; he had a beard. He said, "What month is this?"

The man in blue stopped short. "Speedball," he said. "You *talked.*"

"My name is Nick."

"It certainly is. Nick Hutton."

"No," Nick said. "Not Hutton. Hudson."

"Your charts say Hutton."

"Charts?" Nick said. "Is this a hospital?"

"Of course."

Nick frowned. "You called me 'Speedball.' Why?"

"Well everyone calls you that. You throw stuff."

Nick looked at the window, the falling snow. "Throw stuff," he said, and images flooded back. He saw a ragged baseball field with weatherbeaten stands that quickly changed to Fenway Park, smooth bright green grass, the towering left field wall. He said, "It's winter now."

"December," said the man.

"I've been here since the fall."

The man gave a little laugh. "You've been here lots longer than that, my friend."

"How much longer?"

"Well, longer than me, and I've been at this job for five years."

"What?"

7

"That's right, and this is the first time you've talked."

The colors: brown tables, green paint on the window trim, tan walls, and all of it so bright it made Nick squint.

A man in a chair near the door to the hallway was chewing the palm of his hand. Another one stood with his arms clasped behind him and rocked back and forth, softly moaning.

Alarmed, Nick said, "What kind of a hospital is this, anyway?"

"Insane asylum," said the man in blue. "St. Luke's, in Baltimore."

Nick frowned again. "What year is this?"

"It's 1927, almost 1928."

"My God," Nick said.

2

THEY DROVE HIM TO TOWN in the hospital's van. He was wearing a dead man's trousers, shirt and shoes and an olive drab army overcoat. He had shaved and no longer had a beard.

There were cars all over the place in the Baltimore streets, banging over the cobblestones. Most of them were solid black and closed against the weather, like the van.

The driver, whose name was Jack, brought the van to a sudden halt. Looking up, Nick said, "You have to stop for that?"

The top of a metal post held two circles of glass, one red, one green. The red one was lighted.

"You bet," Jack said, "and they're everywhere."

A black horse-drawn cart with "Coal and Ice" on its side in red and gold script crossed in front of the van. The horse, in blinders, snorted and tossed its head.

"So many automobiles," Nick said.

"Yeah, more every minute."

Nick looked at the horse as it clopped away and a memory came back: a horse, a cart, an explosion, a spoked wheel spinning—

"Hey, look!" Jack said, "It's a Model A!"

A trim blue car whizzed past the horse. "The roadster," Jack said. "Niagara Blue, brand new from Mr. Ford!"

A voice inside Nick's head said, *Ford. We're fighting for Ford and Rockefeller, fighting for the rich.*

What a beauty!" Jack said as the light turned green. He

9

stepped on the gas.

Nick looked through the window at rows of brick houses with white marble steps, at a boy in a mackinaw holding his hat on against the stiff wind. On the corner, some signs on a drugstore: "Western Union" and "Bell Telephone." He wondered what they meant. "Beauty parlor," he said, and Jack said, "What?"

"That place is a 'beauty parlor.'"

"Yeah, the babes like to get dolled up, all right," Jack said. "Well, here we are."

He pulled up to the curb and stopped. "Good luck," he said. "Happy New Year."

"Same to you," Nick said. He opened the door and got out.

The van moved off. Clutching the neck of his overcoat, Nick mounted the wide granite steps and went into the station.

It looked pretty much the same as the first time he'd seen it in April of 1914. Alice had come from Philly to watch his first game and he'd met her right there by the doors that led to the platforms. She'd looked so beautiful with her auburn hair and bright blue eyes and her cheeks flushed red with excitement. They'd taken a trolley straight to the ballpark, and four hours later he'd pitched for the Providence Grays, beating the Baltimore Orioles, and Alice had been so proud.

But now something was wrong with his pitching arm and he didn't know what. It felt dead, detached from him. At St. Luke's he had gone outside one day and made some snowballs and thrown them as hard as he could at a tree, but the throws had no power behind them. He hadn't been hurt in the war or at St. Luke's, so what was going on?

After he'd woken up from his long mad dream he had seen a psychiatrist more than an hour a day for two weeks—or maybe three, he wasn't sure. The guy had said something that made Nick remember a soldier who'd suddenly lost his vision but didn't have anything wrong with his eyes. Maybe the same kind of thing had affected his arm. Maybe not. Maybe

10

with time and exercise his arm would get better. He hadn't thrown a baseball in more than ten years.

He went up to the ticket counter. "Philadelphia, one way," he said, and slid all his money, the sawbuck they'd given him, over the smooth brown granite. Behind the bars the clerk took the money and reached for a ticket and wrote something on it, then pushed it across to Nick with some bills and some silver. Nick thanked him and shoved the change into his pocket, keeping the ticket in his hand. He went to a bench and sat down and looked up at the clock.

It was five after twelve. Twelve hours from now a new year would be born. Another one, when he'd already lost so many.

Across from him, a young woman of shocking appearance sat down. Her hair was cropped close to her head and her cheeks were rouged and her lips were a cherry red. Then she shocked him still further: she felt in her handbag, came up with a cigarette and lit it with a silver lighter. She tossed her head and crossed her legs, displaying her calf all the way to the knee, and from where Nick was sitting it looked like she wore no stockings. No, wait—she wore stockings, but they were the color of flesh.

Nick sniffed. Her chances of drumming up business around here at noontime seemed mighty slim; she'd surely do better on Baltimore Street, at night.

His train was announced and he went to the platform. The black steam engine rumbled by, the dark green cars slowed down and stopped, and he got on board.

The car looked familiar, with brown plush seats and a metal rack for your luggage. But Nick didn't have any luggage. All that he owned in this world was a pair of blue trousers, a trifle too small, with a shiny seat and shiny knees, an overcoat with a hole in one pocket, an old pair of black wing-tipped shoes, a white dress shirt with a fraying collar, a handkerchief, and the change from a ten dollar bill.

He sat by the window. Outside he saw several dead shrubs by the tracks, a couple of rusty cans and an old newspaper, a

11

thin film of snow on them all. On a billboard, an ad for "Glostora," a product he didn't recognize.

The woman who'd smoked in the waiting room walked past and through to another car. Then another young woman came in and sat down on the other side of the aisle. She too had the same sort of close-cropped hair and rouged cheeks. So this was the style now? Then a couple of men and two women—quite young, maybe college kids—took the seats near the door. These women, mere girls, wore coats with fur collars, small hats that were close and tight, and again, that lipstick and rouge. They laughed and joked around as they stowed their belongings. The train started up. Nick looked through the window again.

As far as anyone could recall, he had never received any mail. He had been in St. Luke's for over nine years and had never received a single card or letter: from Alice, his mother, from anyone. Of course not: they had his name wrong and nobody knew where he was. The man who had run the asylum during the war had died in 1924, his replacement had lasted for just ten months, and the current director knew nothing about Nick's case. They had lost him. He'd been lost in his mind and they'd lost him. For nine long years that seemed to him now like a single colorless day, he'd thought he was a prisoner. Caught in a void of confusion he'd hoped for the Allies to end the war and free him from the camp. And then he was back in the real world again, just like that.

In the real world the Allies had won. But Johnny was dead and Alice was certainly married by now, and nine years of his life were gone.

As he looked out the window, war memories came back: The arguments among the troops, the illnesses and injuries, the infections and blood and pain, the nerve-wracking groans of the wounded who lay in the trenches beside the dead. All of this came in fragments, like splinters of broken ice, then melted and slipped away with quicksilver speed.

In his mind he could see Johnny searching the corpses for

12

opium pills, how he tore at their knapsacks and uniforms desperately, cursing. Liquor was always passed around before combat but wasn't enough for Johnny, he had to have opium too. It had mixed up his mind and he'd run to his death. Nick remembered his face as he'd said his last words, "I'm okay." His teeth were gone and his tongue was exposed and one of his eyes had been blown away, but his tone had been peaceful and calm.

Nick had fought in more battles after that and had seen more buddies die. He pictured a German charging, screaming; he'd shot the man right in the face and felt good about it. He'd thrown a grenade at a house somewhere and blasted its top windows out and then…he couldn't remember. He knew that he'd never be able to throw a grenade like that now, not with this arm he had.

He still couldn't believe he'd gone crazy. He had seen it happen to others, but couldn't believe it had happened to him. He'd been strong, not like Johnny, who'd suddenly broken and run to his death, or like others who'd burrowed inside themselves and sat like stones when orders were given or curled up whimpering. Some of them turned their guns on themselves. But his mind had been perfectly sound in all of the chaos. And then, somehow, it had failed.

What remained to him now from his years at St. Luke's was a jumble of images, tattered and dreamlike: a shaft of bright moonlight dissecting a peeling gray wall, a cat with three legs falling into a sewer, a man on his knees eating handfuls of grass, and none of these scenes could be trusted. The real and the unreal were fused in a seamless haze.

In Wilmington a fat ruddy man got on, and a prim-looking middle aged woman. The kids in the seat by the door were still horsing around. The girls had their hats and their coats off now, and their dresses were flimsy, their bodies as slender as boys'.

Then from somewhere outside, a loud noise and Nick

13

flinched. In his mind's eye the burst of a shell threw black mud in the air and Johnny was running, running. The train started moving and Nick feeling numb in his chest saw a man in a motorcar pulling away. Again the car backfired and bucked. Nick felt cold and his throat was tight. The psychiatrist said he was normal now, but Nick didn't believe it. There were things the psychiatrist didn't know, things he hadn't been told.

The conductor took tickets and once he had gone, the kids near the door passed a small paper bag. A blond-headed boy with tortoise-shell glasses caught Nick looking at him and said, "Happy New Year!" and lifted the flask. The girls giggled, teeth flashing. They seemed like some new kind of people to Nick, something he'd never encountered before. The one with the coppery hair was chewing gum.

As the train slid over the Chinese Wall, the viaduct that cut Philadelphia in two, the sky was a smooth slate gray. Nick looked at the blocks and blocks of brick row houses stretching away to the south, his stomach tense. He thought, *It looks the same.* But he knew that once he was actually down in those streets it would all be different.

One thing was already different: Broad Street Station's glass-roofed train shed, said to be the largest in the world, was gone, replaced by a series of smaller sheds. Nick wondered why.

He walked through the cavernous waiting room. He'd last seen it in 1917, when he left for basic training—more than ten years ago.

Outside, a banner above the archway to City Hall's courtyard proclaimed "Happy New Year!" and piles of dirt lined the sides of the street. As Nick stood on the corner, watching the laborers deep in the excavation, a stout man wearing a gray fedora and smoking a stogie said, "They claim they're gonna finish this job by next fall, but I don't believe it."

14

"Finish what job?" Nick said.

"The Broad Street subway. You ain't heard about that?"

Nick shook his head.

"I guess you ain't from Philly, then."

"I am, but I've been away," Nick said, and thought of his subway ride twenty years ago on the brand new Market Street line. He and his parents had taken it to its end and back, marveling at its speed and comfort. That was the only time he had been on a subway train. Or was it? He seemed to remember another time, but where? And when?

He looked at the trench again, and now he saw rats down there, big gray ones, almost black. And Johnny was down there too, dead, half of his face gone, and one of the rats was gnawing—

Suddenly light-headed, Nick quickly turned to the man beside him and asked, "What happened to the big train shed?" His voice didn't sound quite right. *No rats*, he told himself. *There are no rats.*

The man blew smoke. "Burned down in 1923. I seen it. Quite a blaze."

The trolley came, and Nick rode north to Spring Garden and then walked east. It was late afternoon and very cold, and he walked with his hands thrust deep in his pockets, his breath making puffs of frost.

He stopped at a tall brick row house with wide marble steps and a front double door with long panes of etched glass. Its trim had been freshly painted ten years ago when he'd stood on these steps and said goodbye, but now it was badly faded.

In the vestibule he checked the mailboxes. Box number 2 said, "Hodges." He felt a quick twinge in his stomach and pressed the button and heard the bell ring inside.

Nobody came, and he rang again. The door to the hallway had frosted glass and he couldn't see through it. He rang again, then the door opened up just a crack.

The woman was gray-haired and bent and wore slippers.

15

"I'm looking for Mrs. Hudson," Nick said. "My mother. She lived in apartment two."

The old woman looked puzzled. She shook her head. "I'm sorry," she said, "I don't know her."

Behind her another voice deep in the hallway said, "Mrs. Hudson? Gloria Hudson?"

"Yes," Nick said. He could just about see the woman down there; she was lost in the shadows.

"She died," the voice said, "right after I came here in the fall of 1918. The Carmichaels took her apartment, then four years ago they moved and the Hodges took it."

The woman behind the door asked, "Is that what you wanted to know?" She looked worried and cold.

"Yes. Thank you," Nick said.

He walked south, toward town, his grief muting the cold. He passed a few restaurants and corner cafés, but none of them advertised beer.

When he played in the minors he'd had an occasional beer and in France he'd had wine and rum. He rarely got drunk, but he needed to do so now, the quicker the better.

At the corner of Sixth and Market he stopped in a steamy luncheonette, went up to the sad-looking man who was wiping the counter and asked, "Say, where can a guy get a beer around here?"

The man kept on wiping without looking up. Tossing his rag in the sink, he said, "Can't tell you, pal."

"There must be some place close by."

"I'm sure there is, but I wouldn't know."

"Down on Dock Street, maybe?"

"Could be."

"Thanks a lot for your help," Nick said, and went outside.

Stopping a guy who was wearing a cashmere overcoat, he said, "Say, buddy, where I can get a beer?"

"Your best bet's Germany," the man said, moving on.

Nick thought: *You jerk.*

On Chestnut Street he went up to a hotel doorman.

16

"Pardon me, where's your bar?" he asked.

The doorman, whose face was puffy and pale, raised his eyebrows. "Get outta here, bud."

Nick's stomach tightened. "Hey."

"Come on, bud, I don't want trouble."

"Tell me where your bar is, then."

"It's in 1919, I guess," the doorman said. "Yeah, back in 1919 somewhere."

"You closed your bar?"

"Pretty hard to stay open when all of the others were closing, wouldn't you say?"

Nick remembered now. During the war there'd been talk about banning alcohol. But those kids on the train had been drinking, so you could still get it. Nick mumbled, "Right," and walked off.

It was dark now and street lamps were on and all the big stores were closed. Nick wandered around for a while then stopped in a café on Chestnut Street and ordered a donut and coffee. He sat in a booth feeling blasts of cold air as customers came and went, and everything seemed too quick, too loud, too bright.

His poor mother. He'd been dying to see her again, had hoped he could stay in his old room until he got back on his feet, and she'd help him catch up on things. He wondered where all her possessions had gone—her furniture, clothing, jewelry—all of it. And all his possessions too: his books, his clock, his pocketknife, the model planes he'd built... All gone. He'd been erased.

He swallowed the last of his coffee and walked down Chestnut Street. Two young couples went by, the women all painted and looking cheap. Dim trolleys slid past taking breadwinners home to their families, to dinners and New Year's Eve parties without champagne.

At the Rose Hotel at Eighth and Vine—Skid Row—he paid a man in a wooden booth fifteen cents. The man had a box near his elbow, and out of the box came music, a jerky disjointed frantic sound that grated on Nick's frayed nerves.

"Radio," Nick said. The man in the booth ignored him.

Nick mounted the sour-smelling stairs in the light of a naked filament, found his cubicle, 26, and sat on the edge of the torn stained cotton pad. It was hot in the tiny space and he took off his coat. As he spread it across the pad he remembered his mother and thought: She never even knew I was sick. She thought I was dead.

He sat in the weak yellow light with his head in his hands and a man lumbered up the steep stairs making wheezing sounds. When he got to Nick's doorway he held out a brown pint bottle and said, "Happy new year, pal."

"Where'd you get that?" Nick said.

"Private stock," the man said. "Have a taste."

Nick considered the offer a moment then said, "No thanks." The neck of the bottle was slimy with spit.

The man lurched to his left. His face was a reddish purple; his nose was black. "It'll bring you good luck," he said with a grin, and he lifted the pint up high. "To 1928," he said, "and more unparalleled prosperity." He took a long pull on the neck of the bottle and said, "I'll be lucky as Lucky Lindy this year, I can feel it."

"Who?" Nick said.

The man spread his arms and pretended to fly. "Ba-room," he said, shoving the bottle at Nick. "Come on, take a pull."

"No thanks."

"Go to hell then," the man said, his sloppy lips shining. He moved down the row.

"Happy New Year," Nick said.

3

"GET OUTTA HERE! Get outta my space, you son of a bitch!"

Nick woke with a start, his heart beating quickly, his skin soaked with sweat. He was startled to see that he'd punched through the flimsy partition beside his pallet. He'd used his left arm, his pitching arm.

"I'll break your goddamn thumb, you son of a bitch!"

Nick pulled his arm back; his hand was throbbing. A series of sharp popping sounds came from somewhere outside and he clutched his chest, his throat tight.

He remembered now: it was New Year's Eve. He was hearing firecrackers, not guns.

In his dream he'd been charging the Hun trench with Johnny and one of the bastards had come out of nowhere and Nick had slugged him a good one right in the mouth. But this was a real dream, not like the frightening daytime dream he'd had two weeks ago.

He was taking a walk on the hospital grounds when he heard a loud noise and instantly found himself back on the battlefield shooting at waves of advancing enemy troops. The episode lasted no more than a minute but left him dizzy and shaken. To think that something like that could just come out of nowhere; it meant that he still wasn't thoroughly healed, and he feared that it might be a doorway back into his madness. He didn't tell anyone what had happened, afraid they would keep him locked up if they knew he had dreams like that.

19

Now his knuckles hurt and his shoulder hurt too. He lay on his back looking up at the stained raw ceiling in light from the streetlamp outside. "Crazy son of a bitch," said the man on the other side of the hardboard partition.

Crazy, Nick said in his mind, and his heart was still beating too fast as firecrackers popped and popped and he thought of the night sky in France and the mud and the screams.

And now there were horns outside that sounded like lonesome geese, and people were shouting, so glad that another sad year was gone. Then after a while the ruckus died and Nick heard nothing but snores and a dripping sound.

When he woke again the room held cheerless light. He had dreamed he was back on the troop ship writing to Alice. His mouth tasted bitter and now he was shaking with cold. They had turned off the heat in the night.

He had slept on top of his overcoat so that no one could steal it and now he stood up and put it on. When he looked at his shoes the openings in them seemed to be mouths that were silently screaming. A couple of times these past few weeks he had heard a loud voice in his ears shouting something he couldn't understand, pushing against his temples, making them ache, and then suddenly it had stopped. He couldn't make it stop, he just had to be patient and wait.

He put his feet into his screaming shoes and walked across splintery boards past cubicles empty and occupied. The window above the rusty toilet was thick with swirls of patterned frost; his breath was visible as he relieved himself. He went down the hallway and stairs to a bleak New Year's Day.

A clock above a watchmaker's shop on Market Street said ten of ten. The street was dead. An empty trolley rattled by. Nick began walking east, and soon he was shivering, blowing white breath. He passed some clothing stores, a stationer's and stores where paint, cigars and shoes were sold. Most of the places were new to him. He passed a dentist's office and barbershop, both closed.

He came to a large familiar store, Strawbridge & Clothier, and stared at the displays: manikins dressed in fashions like those he had seen on the train. He wondered if Alice wore clothes like that now. It was here that he'd spent all his savings on her engagement ring. He remembered her tears of happiness as she slipped it on, but surely she was married to somebody else after all this time.

At the Reading Terminal, the ground floor coffee shop was closed. Nick mounted the wide smooth granite steps, grateful for the station's heavy warmth. A handful of people were sitting around on the waiting room's benches, looking lost.

The barbershop across from the men's room was dark. In the men's room itself, no attendants, no bootblacks: Nick was alone in the huge tiled space. In a marble urinal, water trickled.

He went to a porcelain sink, ran water and splashed his face; in the mirror his cheeks were hollow below his eyes, which were rimmed with dark. No attendants and therefore no towels, so he wiped off his face with his shirttail. He remembered the shock he had felt the first time he looked in a mirror after his return to sanity. *My God*, he had thought as he stared at his beard and his hair, the touch of gray at his temples, *I'm thirty-three.* He'd noticed a jagged scar above his right eyebrow and wondered how he'd received it.

Now he rinsed out his mouth, ran his hand through his hair and tucked his shirt into his trousers again. No way he could shave and he looked like a bum, and maybe he ought to hold off till tomorrow. But he knew that he couldn't.

He sat on a bench and waited awhile, absorbing the warmth. Across from him, a withered old woman in black with bowed legs and thick stockings sat clutching a canvas bag and muttering to herself. It made Nick think of Baltimore, St. Luke's. When the hands of the huge clock reached eleven, he stood up and went down the stairs.

The day was brighter now, not quite as cold, and people

21

were out on the sidewalks, heading toward Broad Street, the Mummers' parade. Nick walked past a prosperous-looking couple with two small kids. The girl held the hand of her father, the boy ran ahead. The mother was wearing a long fur coat and holding a black leather purse. Nick wondered how much money that purse held.

He went down Twelfth Street, barely noticing the stores and offices. He had eaten nothing but wasn't hungry; his stomach felt cold and tight.

At Catherine Street he turned east, walked two more blocks, and then went south.

The house was just like all the others in the row: brick, three stories tall, without shutters. Shutters were for the prosperous places on Locust and Spruce and Pine. Some of the trim on this block was black and some was brown. The trim on this house was black, and peeling badly.

He mounted the marble step and rang the bell and went suddenly weak inside. He touched his chin, the stubble there, and blew on his hand. Behind the glass the curtain moved and the door opened slowly.

A short gray-haired woman with glasses looked up at him. "Yes?"

"Mrs. Hill," he said. He could scarcely believe that's who it was, she had changed so much.

She looked worried, afraid. "Yes?"

"It's Nick. Nick Hudson."

The old woman drew in a breath and went "Oh!" and covered her mouth with her hands. Then she broke into tears.

Nick stood in the cold as she wept. "It can't be true," she said in a small choked voice. "It's impossible...impossible." Then wiping her eyes with her fingers she said, "Come in, come in, my God..."

He stepped inside. She closed the door and then gave him a hug, her arms so frail and thin. When he'd seen her last her hair was brown and her figure full. "Oh, Nick," she said, and took a handkerchief out of her sweater pocket and wiped her eyes again.

He followed her into the parlor, which was just as he remembered it: the same blue easy chairs and davenport, the same brown flowered rug. Ten years had passed since he'd seen this room and it hadn't changed.

"I just—" said Mrs. Hill. "I can't—" She looked confused, almost despairing. "Sit," she said. "Sit down and I'll get you some coffee."

"No, please," Nick said, "Don't trouble yourself."

"I have some made, I'll get you some." She bit her lower lip, then left the room.

He took off his coat and folded it up and sat on the blue plush davenport. One of the chairs held a needlepoint pillow, Alice's work; some pink and red roses against pale gold. On the table beside the chair was a photo of Johnny in uniform, smiling. *So young,* Nick thought. *We were all so young.* He remembered the last time he'd looked at Johnny with half his face gone.

On the brown marble mantel a cast iron frog and a picture of Alice—an old one, he knew it well. He felt something give in his heart.

He looked at the carpet, its flowers and leaves, he looked at his hands, he looked at the picture of Alice again. He heard Mrs. Hill in the hallway.

She crossed the room and set the cup and saucer down on the table in front of the davenport. "You take it black, don't you?" she said.

"You remember."

"Of course." Mrs. Hill sat down across from the table and said again, softly this time, "Of course."

"You'll have to excuse my appearance," Nick said. "The barbers are closed today."

Mrs. Hill didn't seem to hear. She said, "We thought you were killed—with Johnny."

Alice, Nick thought, and again, in his heart, a shift. "I was shell-shocked," he said. "I didn't know where I was for the last nine years."

Mrs. Hill didn't speak for a moment then said, "Oh Nick, how horrible."

"They kept me in this place in Baltimore, St. Luke's. It was like I was sleeping, some kind of a dream. Then a couple of weeks ago, I woke up. But sometimes I still think I'm dreaming."

"The war—" Mrs. Hill began, and her mouth was quivering now.

Nick looked at his hands and took a quick breath and said: "He was terribly brave. He died fighting beside me, a hero."

Tears came to the old woman's eyes again and she took out her handkerchief.

"It was all very fast," Nick said. "He felt no pain."

"Thank God," said Mrs. Hill. Wiping her eyes again she said, "It's been so long, and I ought to accept, but..." Shaking her head, she looked down at the carpet.

Nick wanted to say something, something to help, but he'd never been good with words. "I'm so sorry," he said. "And Alice—"

"She's dead," Mrs. Hill said, not meeting his eyes.

Nick stared at her, feeling a pressure expand through his chest. A high whine began in his ears. He thought of Johnny, he thought of his mother, he thought of Alice in Baltimore, when she'd come on the train to watch him pitch for the Grays. His mouth felt numb as he tried to speak.

Before he could find his voice, Mrs. Hill said, "Consumption. We learned about Johnny and thought you had also been killed and she took it so terribly hard. She didn't eat right, she just didn't take care of herself. When the Spanish Flu hit, she caught it. It killed Mr. Howell and both of the Porters and all of the Riley boys on this block alone. And it killed your mother."

"So that's how she died," Nick said. He had seen the disease at work in France. It made your lungs gush bloody froth before it took your life.

24

Mrs. Hill shook her head again. "What a terrible time it was," she said. "Alice did volunteer work at Pennsylvania Hospital, that's where she caught the flu. I cared for her here at home and it passed, but she never was right again. She kept coughing and coughing and couldn't sleep, and she got so thin... And then she found out that she had the consumption. The doctor said maybe if she could get out of the city, go west, to Arizona or California... I begged her to leave, but she wouldn't listen. 'Maybe Nick's still alive,' she would say. 'Maybe some day he'll come back, and I have to be waiting here for him.' She kept getting worse and worse..."

Mrs. Hill wept again, holding her face, and Nick clenched his jaw. He remembered an incident—where, at St. Luke's or in France?—when enraged he had lashed out at food and utensils, sweeping the table clean, and then started to throw things. He sat there not moving and stared at the floor. How much would it take to return him to madness, he wondered, this time for good.

Mrs. Hill dabbed her eyes and breathed deeply. "So hard," she said. "I lost my husband long ago, then Johnny, and then my dear Alice. She went to her grave with your ring on her finger, Nick."

His stomach cramped. He felt empty and drained and his hands were shaking. "When did it happen?" he asked.

"In 1921. July."

"I was only a hundred miles away," he said. "In Baltimore, St. Luke's. If only someone—"

"She tried not to give up hope, but the years went by—"

"And I was right *there.*"

Mrs. Hill raised her head. "Nick, where are you staying?"

"I have a place."

"You can stay here. Why don't you?"

Nick felt suddenly short of breath. "That's kind of you," he said, "but I have a place."

She was biting her lip again. "I'm so sorry," she said. "So sorry to have to tell you—"

"I thought she'd be married," Nick said. "I wouldn't have interfered in her life, I just had to know."

"I understand."

"And I wanted to see you and talk about Johnny."

"Yes."

No air, and the parlor looked flat and dim. He reached for his coat and stood and said, "I have to go." As he put on the coat he felt giddy.

"You didn't touch your coffee, Nick, and now it's cold. I'll get you a fresh cup."

"No thanks, Mrs. Hill, I have to go, but...where is Alice's grave?"

"In Monument Cemetery. Do you know where that is?"

"On Broad Street. Across from Temple College."

"Yes." Mrs. Hill shook her head. "To think of Johnny laid to rest so far away from home."

"His grave in France is beautiful," Nick said. He had no idea where Johnny was laid to rest.

"Oh, that is so good to hear," said Mrs. Hill. "You'll come back and see me again sometime, won't you, Nick?"

"I will."

She went with him to the door. He looked at her eyes and took her hands. Then he turned without saying a word and walked away.

He walked for hours through nondescript treeless streets, dull redbrick blocks. Windows held cutouts of Santas and snowmen and doors were hung with wreaths. He felt no hunger, felt no cold, just anger and sadness.

Since it felt as if only weeks, not years, had passed since he'd fought in the war, he had clung to the hope that Alice might still be waiting for him. But he hadn't expected that. He'd expected to learn she was married—but never that she was dead, and he still couldn't quite believe it. He wondered now why he'd ever come back to this world where nothing was left for him. At an alley he stopped and held his head, then savagely kicked a garbage can.

And then he heard music, the faint tinny sound of a banjo, and looked down the alley. At its end, a flock of excited children went past on the street, walking backward. They shouted and laughed as the banjo grew louder. Nick walked down the alley and out to the street.

The banjo player was wearing a white satin jacket and trousers and shiny white shoes, a gold crown and a blue velvet cloak. He capered and grinned as he played, and children and grownups alike marched beside him.

More Mummers began to appear. The formal parade on Broad Street was over and now they were back in their neighborhoods. A beefy man dressed in a sparkling white gown pranced over the cobblestones, lifting his skirt high, revealing white stockings and hairy thighs and a flash of white underwear. Another man in a fabulous circular headdress of gold and white feathers dipped forward then backward, forward then backward. He drank from a brown quart bottle.

Nick entered the crowd and went up to the man in the headdress and said, "Where'd you get that stuff?"

The man just kept dancing.

"Come on," Nick said.

The man simply laughed.

"Come on."

"What's it worth to you, pal?" said the man as he drank.

"For what?" Nick said. "Information?"

The man laughed again. "For this bottle," he said. "It's almost full."

"Four bits," Nick said.

"Four bits!" said the man, "what year are you livin in? I want a buck."

"Jesus Christ," Nick said.

"You can take it or leave it."

Nick felt in his pocket and brought out a bill.

"Good deal," said the Mummer. Taking the money he handed the bottle over.

27

Nick stopped and the crowd swirled past. He wiped off the lip of the bottle then drank, twisting his head to the sullen gray sky. The beer was strong and bitter.

This was the first hootch he'd had in nine years. It was hard to believe. He drank again. More Mummers came playing their banjos and xylophones, trailing loud spectators shouting and jeering.

Nick went to the alley and drank half the bottle. The music began to fade and soon it was gone.

He walked to a little park and sat down on a bench. Candy wrappers and newspapers clung to the barren shrubs. Some oval red berries still hung on the shrubs, and a small brown bird ate a few. Nick wondered if berries like that would kill people. The bird seemed to love them. It ate a few more and flew off.

Nick was feeling the beer and he thought: If a man were to kill himself, what was the best way to do it? Jumping in front of a train or out of a window would make a big mess that someone would have to clean up. So would slitting your wrists or shooting yourself in the mouth. Hanging was quick and neat if you did it right, but hootch was even better. You drank enough liquor fast enough, you'd just go to sleep for good. But maybe the best thing of all was to go to the bridge that had just been built on the Delaware River not far from the Rose Hotel, walk out to its center and jump. Your body would probably never be found, but if it was, at least you'd be nice and clean.

It was spitting wet snow and getting dark and he got up and started to walk. He'd had nothing to eat all day and the homebrew was hitting him hard. He walked past the houses with Santas and lights in their windows and thought of the families who lived in those rooms. He thought of the picture of Alice on top of the mantel in Mrs. Hill's house and remembered a summer day, a lake, a canoe ride with Alice up front. How she turned to him smiling and lifted her paddle, its blade streaming water bright with sun, and they coasted in silent warmth, their hearts filled with gladness.

He tilted his head to the hopeless sky and finished the last of the beer. Then, placing the empty bottle with care on the redbrick sidewalk, he covered his face with his frozen dead hands and wept.

4

NICK WAS SURE THAT HIS MOTHER was buried beside his father but didn't know where that was. He'd been fifteen years old at the time of his father's death. He remembered quite clearly standing beside the descending coffin with tears in his eyes but he never knew the graveyard's name or what part of town it was in. When his mother placed flowers on the grave each year, he never went along with her because it would make him too sad.

So now he went to City Hall to find what he needed to know. The clerk he dealt with was heavy, with folds of fat at her neck. She took forever at one of the many file cabinets against the wall, then returned to her desk. As she squinted through silver-rimmed glasses she said, "This must be the one you're looking for," and gave him the death certificate.

"It is," Nick said.

He read it: Gloria Hudson. Date of Death: October 14, 1918. Attending Physician: Dr. Meade. Cause of death: Spanish Influenza. Interment: Mt. Vernon Cemetery.

October, 1918, the month when he'd lost the world. They'd shipped him stateside during that month, when his mother was dying—or already dead.

"Thank you," he said to the clerk, and handed the paper back. "Now I'd like you to look up another one for me."

The clerk had a slightly annoyed expression. "Name?"

"Alice Hill."

The clerk wrote it down.

"Date of death?"

Nick's throat was tight. "July, 1921." He still couldn't accept it.

The clerk rose heavily and walked away. Nick looked at the ceiling, the dull brass chandelier, the peeling paint up there. He looked at the rows and rows of file cabinets in this spacious room. So many dead. He thought of St. Luke's and he thought of the war.

The clerk was back. She gave him the paper.

When he looked at the name, once again he felt weak all through.

Alice Hill. Date of Death: July 18, 1921. Attending Physician: Dr. Keller. Cause of Death:

Nick's heart seemed to stop. He stared at the paper. *Childbirth,* it said.

"It is the right person?" the clerk said, sounding impatient.

Nick looked at the date of birth: May 22, 1896. He nodded, and numbness spread over his shoulders. He handed the paper back.

"You don't want a copy?"

"No," Nick said.

On the street, in the shadow of City Hall, he took deep drafts of the cold raw air. It was late afternoon, with a thin copper sun, and the storefronts looked blank and dim. Quickly he spun on his heels and headed south.

He stood on the marble step of Mrs. Hill's house and rang the bell, blowing white breath, his heart beating quickly. No movement behind the curtain, no sound inside. He pushed the black button again.

At last he gave up and walked back to Broad Street. A drug store there had a telephone and he looked in the book that was hanging on a cord. He found the "Hill" he wanted and put in a nickel and dialed. This was the first time he'd ever used a dial phone and he hoped he was doing it right; it seemed strange not to talk to an operator. He listened, hearing his breath, then the ring on the other end began—and just kept going. He hung up, cursing through bitter teeth as his coin came back. "You lied to me, Mrs. Hill," he said. "I lied to you, but you *really* lied to me." Then he thought: *Maybe she doesn't even know. Maybe she doesn't know who got Alice pregnant and talking to her will only stir things up again and increase her pain. My God, the poor woman's lost everybody—her husband, then both of her children...*

His hands were cold but his chest felt hot. He looked through the telephone book again, and there, thank God, was the name he wanted: Harriman, James. The book said he lived on Girard Avenue, of all places—right up the street from where they had gone to school.

Nick raised the coin to the slot again and then had second thoughts. What if Jimmy said no, he wouldn't see him? What if he just hung up? It was better to go there. He absolutely had to see Jimmy, so yes, he had better just go there. He left the drug store and walked to the trolley stop.

After his father suddenly died of a heart attack in the summer of 1909, Nick and his mother were instantly poor. His mother sold their house to get some cash and looked for housekeeping work. Nick said he would drop out of school and find a job, but his mother wouldn't hear of it.

Since he no longer had a father and got good grades, he qualified for the free residential school for fatherless boys, Girard College. To go there would mean that his mother could take a smaller apartment and not have to pay for his board.

He entered the school that fall, and that's when he met Johnny Hill and Jimmy Harriman, whose fathers had died years earlier. The three of them became fast friends, spending a lot of time together on holidays and playing on the baseball team.

One Christmas vacation Johnny invited Nick to his house for dinner, and there he met Johnny's younger sister, Alice. Her beauty and manner enthralled him. Every chance he got,

32

he'd visit her, subjecting himself to Johnny's merciless ribbing.

After they graduated from Girard, Johnny worked in an office and Jimmy enrolled at Penn to study economics. Nick, whose pitching had caught the eye of a Boston baseball scout, signed a minor league contract and ended up on a team down South. He wrote to Alice at least twice a week, and as soon as the season was over he went to see her—even before he went to his mother's apartment, where he would stay.

He found off-season work at Frankie's Garage, which was owned by a guy his father used to know. It was only a couple of blocks from his mother's place. At Frankie's he learned how to fix transmissions and engines and brakes and exhausts. He was sure that the automobile was the wave of the future; if his baseball plans didn't pan out he would have a good trade to fall back on. He gave nearly all of his pay to his mother.

On Sunday afternoons he went to see Alice. They took long walks, skated on the rink in the park near her home, and drank hot chocolate together in her mother's kitchen. Because Nick was hanging around all the time he saw Johnny a lot. The two of them got together with Jimmy sometimes, but not very often.

And now, as he stood in the cold on the wide brick sidewalk and looked down the street at the school where he'd first met Jimmy, Nick tried to remember the last time he'd seen him. After his graduation from Penn, Jimmy had landed a job at a brokerage firm and had gone with a pretty girl named Rachel Pierce who came from a Main Line family. His life had been smoothly humming along back then, and to judge by the mansion he lived in, it still was.

Nick mounted the brownstone steps and rang the bell. He waited, feeling a tension in his chest. He heard some sounds behind the door, then it suddenly opened up and there was Jimmy, ten years older.

He looked it; his hair was still black, with no traces of gray, but had thinned considerably. He parted it on the side now, not in the middle. He had put on some weight and it seemed that his chin had receded a bit.

For a moment he just stood motionless, then a look of astonishment crossed his face. Astonishment and something else—was it fear? Nick had gotten a haircut and shave this morning but knew that he still looked rough, and he suddenly felt self-conscious.

"Impossible," Jimmy said. "I'm seeing things."

"No, Jimmy, your eyes are fine."

"But how —?" Then Jimmy broke into a hesitant smile and shook Nick's hand. "My God," he said, "come *in.*"

They went through the vestibule, into the hallway. A woman was standing there and Nick felt self-conscious again.

"Jane, this is Nick Hudson," Jimmy said, and his right eyelid twitched. "I've mentioned him many times. We went to Girard together, played baseball together... Nick, this is Jane, my wife."

Nick nodded and said hello, and Jane returned the greeting. She smiled, but it seemed forced.

"Nick, this is incredible," Jimmy said, and his eye twitched again. "It's some kind of *miracle.*"

Two little children came up now, a boy and a girl. "Kate and David," said Jimmy.

"Hello," Nick said, and the children just stared.

A moment of awkward silence and then Jane said, "All right, children, let's leave Daddy alone with his friend," and she herded them up the stairs.

"Come with me," Jimmy said.

As Nick followed him down the hall he noticed that Jimmy's limp was more pronounced than it used to be.

The library was dimly lighted, warm, with black leather armchairs, brown velvet drapes and a small crisp fire in the fireplace. Closing the wide paneled door Jimmy said, "Here, give me your coat."

Nick removed it, exposing his well-worn clothes, and felt embarrassed. Jimmy was wearing sharply pressed dark blue trousers with black suspenders, a starched white shirt and a patterned blue silk tie.

He hung Nick's overcoat on a stand near the door, then crossed to a cabinet and poured two snifters of brandy and gave one to Nick—who sensed a wariness about him. "Sit down, sit down," Jimmy said, as he waved at one of the chairs. The gesture was hesitant, stiff.

They sat in the armchairs and Jimmy said, "Nick, I don't get it, we thought you had died in the war. But here you are, with so many years gone by, and you never called? Never dropped me a line? Never stopped in to see me before?" When he lifted his glass to his mouth his hand was shaking.

"I couldn't do any of that," Nick said. "I was shell-shocked, Jimmy. I wasn't in Philly, they stuck me away in a Baltimore nuthouse. I didn't know where I was for the last nine years. And nobody else did either. They had my name wrong and they lost me."

"My God."

Nick took a drink of the brandy; it tasted wonderful. "My mind came back a few weeks ago, but before they'd let me out of the place they made me see this doctor. He said I was lucky. He said that most people who go as far down as I went never find their way up again."

"A psychiatrist?"

Nick suddenly felt ashamed. "That's right."

"You lost nine years of your life and he said you were lucky?"

Nick sniffed. "I didn't trust the guy. I wasn't sure if he really wanted to help me or just examine me under a microscope like some kind of exotic bug." He looked at the Oriental carpet, its red and blue and tan design. He drank again.

"We heard about Johnny, of course," Jimmy said. "Then they told us that you were missing, and time went by—"

"Jane's beautiful," Nick said.

35

Jimmy smiled, but still seemed uneasy. "She certainly is, she's a wonderful woman."

"But you were engaged to Rachel when I left."

Jimmy looked at his glass. He was silent a moment then said, "She died. Spanish Flu in October of 1918. Nick, it was ghastly, so many dead, you can't imagine—" He shook his head. "Of course you can, the things you must have seen... I begged the recruiters to take me, but this damn leg... Who ever thought when I hurt my knee it would keep me from serving my country?"

"Crazy the way it happened."

"A perfect slide, and then that rock...and that was it—for good."

"Just crazy," Nick said. "What the hell was that rock doing buried right there in the base path? But at least you got out of the war." He drank. "So what are you doing now?"

"I'm a stockbroker."

Nodding, Nick said, "Of course. And you must be a good one, Jimmy. It looks like you've done very well for yourself."

"It doesn't take too much skill in this economy."

"So times are good."

"The best. They've been great for years and there's no end in sight."

Nick drank. "That's wonderful, Jimmy." He looked around. "When we were students down the street I always wondered what these houses were like inside."

"Me too. I always wanted to live in one but never imagined I'd actually do it. I feel so fortunate. My wonderful family, this beautiful house on this beautiful street, a great job..."

"It's pretty fantastic."

"We got one heck of a good education, thanks to old Stephen Girard."

"Yes, we did."

Light fell in a yellow cone from the lamp on the table beside Jimmy's chair. A gilt picture frame held a photo of Jane and the children. Jimmy drank. His eyelid twitched. "So what are

36

your plans? Will you play ball again?"

Nick looked at his glass, at the clear amber brandy. "No, Jimmy, my arm's no good."

"Oh, terrible. Was it hurt in the war?"

"I guess, but I don't know how. I wasn't shot or anything. So much goes on in war that you can't remember. I just know I can't throw a ball with anything on it anymore."

"What a shame, you were great. That time you struck out twenty against North End..."

"Just sandlot ball."

"Even so, North End was good. One of their guys had played for the Cubs for a couple of years. And you did pretty well in the minors, too, didn't you?"

"Yeah, I did."

Jimmy frowned. "Has a doctor examined your arm?"

"They gave me a full exam before letting me out of the nuthouse. I told them my arm felt weak but they couldn't find anything wrong with it—not that they tried real hard."

"I think you should see a specialist."

"Yeah, maybe." The brandy and fire had made Nick feel warm all through. The room, with its brass and leather and ceiling-high bookshelves was calming, and now he could smell something wonderful cooking. "Alice died too," he said.

Jimmy nodded. "You know about that."

"I talked to her mother yesterday."

"You did."

"Yes. She told me that Alice died of consumption."

"Yes."

"No, Jimmy," Nick said, "she lied." He stared at Jimmy, who didn't speak. "I know how she died."

"You do."

"She died in childbirth, Jimmy. Did you know that?"

Jimmy let out a breath. "Yes, Nick, I did. But who told you about it?"

"City Hall."

"I see."

"Who was it, Jimmy?"

The room was filled with the smell of good food and the clock on the mantelpiece measured out time with contented thin strokes. Jimmy looked at his glass. "I don't know," he said. "Nobody knows."

Nick scowled sharply. "What do you mean, nobody knows? *Somebody* knows."

Jimmy shrugged, and his eyelid twitched again. "Well, yes, I guess somebody does, but I don't. And no one I'm friendly with does."

"Not even her mother?"

"That's right, she didn't even tell her mother." Jimmy looked into his glass for a couple of seconds, then drank. He said, "There were rumors, of course."

"What rumors?"

"Well, one of them had to do with your old roommate. He adopted a baby not long after Alice died."

Nick frowned. "Eddie Winters? Did he get married?"

"Not Winters, your other roommate. George."

Nick's jaw went tight; in his chest he felt quick sharp pain. "George," he said.

"Yes, he and his wife adopted a baby girl."

Nick stared at the books on the shelves behind Jimmy. Their covers were blurred, melting into each other as Jimmy continued, "It made all the papers."

Nick in his mind saw a man on all fours, raving, stuffing his mouth with grass. "What?" he said, blinking hard, and his voice was soft in his ears.

"Yes, no one was sure where the baby came from. George said one thing, his wife said another."

The room seemed suddenly brighter to Nick and he squinted. "But why did it make the papers?"

"Because papers are rags, they're trash, they thrive on sensation. Anything to do with George—"

Nick was shaking. "That lousy jerk!" he said, and the pain

38

in his chest expanded. "George the German," he said. "The man who got out of the war because he was married!"

"The German?"

"Oh yes, he's a German, all right! Where is he? He's still playing ball?"

"He sure is, he's the game's biggest star."

"Biggest star! He's a no good bum!"

"Bum or not," Jimmy said, "he's world famous—and rich as a king."

Nick remembered that when he was fighting in France he had heard that the Red Sox had won the World Series again and that George had been great. "I have to admit that the bastard can really pitch," he said, "but the game's biggest star..." He was holding his glass with both hands and his knuckles were white.

"He isn't a star because of his pitching," Jimmy said. "He was sold to the Yankees years ago and they turned him into an outfielder. Nick, he's transformed the game. Last year he hit sixty homers."

"Get out."

"He did."

"Impossible. When Harry Davis led the league with twelve in '06 we thought it was fantastic."

"Especially because he had gone to Girard and played for the A's," Jimmy said. "But back around 1919 they changed the ball. They say they didn't but they did, and they shrank the ballparks too. Shibe Park's outfield walls are fifty feet closer to home than they used to be. Plenty of guys hit thirty homers now, and George hit more than fifty twice before he hit his sixty. The right field wall in Yankee Stadium's a joke—less than three hundred feet down the line—and built that way expressly for George Ruth." Jimmy laughed. "Remember Fred Castle?"

"The English class whiz."

"That's right. He became a sports reporter. I see him around sometimes. He was in the Yankee clubhouse last year after

39

Ruth hit his sixtieth homer, and you know what Ruth's comment was? 'Let's see some other son of a bitch match that.'"

"At least he knows he's a son of a bitch," Nick said.

"But the public adores him. They call him The Sultan of Swat, The Bambino. He's a God in New York—and a villain in Philly, of course."

Nick stared at his glass. In his mind he saw Ruth take a swing at a pitch from a tall grinning black man—and miss. "So he was the one," he said.

Jimmy shrugged. "That's what some people thought at the time. It made sense. It was rumored that Ruth's wife couldn't have children, and then all at once she had a baby and nobody knew where it came from. Ruth had been seen with Alice—"

"Where?"

"At Shibe Park. She went to the Yankees games."

Nick looked at his glass, at his quivering hands. He remembered a time when he'd gone to a game with Alice and Ruth had tipped his cap to her. And he thought of a Ferris wheel.

"Have some more," Jimmy said, and again his eye twitched. "Here—" He reached for the crystal decanter.

"No, Jimmy, no thanks, that's all," Nick said. "It's late, I have to be going."

"You'll join us for dinner."

"I can't."

"Come on. Sophie, our cook, is a gem."

"I can't," Nick said, and set his glass on the table beside the chair. When he stood, his legs felt weak.

Jimmy stood too, saying, "Nick, you okay?"

"I'm okay."

"You can stay here tonight if you want."

"No, I have to get going."

"We have lots of space, we'd be happy to—"

"Jimmy, I can't," Nick said. He took his overcoat from the

40

stand, put it on. Jimmy opened the door and the two of them went to the hall.

"You take care of yourself," Jimmy said. "Are you going to stay here in Philly?"

Nick shrugged. "I don't know. I've been thinking of going out West—to Montana, maybe. A buddy of mine in the army lived out there."

"He's still alive?"

"I don't know."

As they went to the vestibule Jimmy reached into his pocket. "Now listen," he said, "you've got to come back again soon—real soon. You'll come for dinner."

"Swell," Nick said, and Jimmy pressed paper into his hand.

Nick looked at it. "I can't take this."

"It's a loan," Jimmy said, "till you get on your feet. No, I'm not going to take it back, I'm not."

Nick needed it badly. Because he'd been labeled "cured" he couldn't get disability benefits. Putting the bill in his pocket he said, "I'll pay you back, Jimmy, as soon as I get a job."

"Take your time."

"Thanks, Jimmy."

"It's starting to snow, are you sure you won't stay?"

"I'm sure."

"Well give me a call when you get a chance."

"Okay."

"And take care of yourself."

"I will," Nick said, and he shook Jimmy's hand. It felt clammy and soft and warm. "Thanks again, Jimmy."

"You stop by again real soon."

Nick nodded and went down the brownstone steps. The door closed behind him softly, with a gentle click. He went down the sidewalk, the bricks dusted thinly with powdery snow, and he knew he would never call Jimmy. He'd pay him back, but he just couldn't bear that contented home, that reminder of all he had lost.

He stood there and looked at the walls of Girard College

41

fading in snow. It was cold but he didn't feel cold, he felt hot all through—and as if he were coming apart, dissolving. A hard dark knot was lodged in his chest as he thought: *I risked my life for my country and lost my mind while the greatest danger that George Ruth faced was a fastball thrown at his head. And while I was fighting he took advantage of Alice. Now he's famous and rich, and does he deserve it? Does he? For what he did to Alice he deserves to die! He deserves it more than the Germans I shot in the war!*

He was shivering now, but not from cold, from heat. Head bowed to the wind, he walked in the snow toward the trolley stop and the ride to the Rose Hotel.

5

AT THE END OF THE HOTEL Majestic's hallway a shaft of Arkansas sunshine sliced through a window and brightened the dark red carpet. Nick could hear laughter in one of the rooms up ahead—not the room he had been assigned to, his room was number 12. He stopped in front of it, set his bag on the floor, put the key in the lock and twisted, then turned the knob.

The tall paneled door opened smoothly. A muscular young man, stark naked, stood smoking a fat cigar near an open window. "Jesus, keed," he said with a grin, "you caught me bareass." Tipping his ashes onto the rug, he laughed, then smoked again. "Hey, I know you. So you're my roomie."

"Looks that way," Nick said. He lifted his bag, brought it into the room and closed the door.

"Yeah, you was in Providence, right?"

"You got it," Nick said. He placed his bag at the foot of the bed that stood near the bathroom door. The other bed, beside the window, was torn apart, covered with rumpled sheets and soiled towels. Its pillow was on the floor. A baseball glove was perched on one of its bedposts.

"A pitcher, right?"

"That's right," Nick said.

"Yeah, I remember you, you had that cute little girlfriend, what was her name?"

"Her name is Alice."

"Alice, yeah. Nice ass."

Nick said, "Look, Ruth, let's get this straight right now—no

43

remarks about Alice."

The big man grinned again. "She's got a nice ass, that's all I said." He smoked, and a thick wreath of gray floated out of the window. "You think I'm after your girl, rook? Hell, I'm a married man now."

"You're kidding."

Ruth smoked. "I got hitched in October. I think it was in October, the leaves was red." He set his cigar in the heavy glass ashtray that sat on the table below the window and put a leg into his baseball pants.

"No underwear?" Nick said.

"Hell no," Ruth said. "It's hot as a son of a bitch out there by noon. These goddamn woolen uniforms..." He put his other leg in his pants, yanked them up, and broke wind. As he buttoned his fly he said, "Ahh, that was a healthy one."

"Ruth, you're disgusting."

Ruth put on his shirt. It was gray, with BOSTON across the front. As he buttoned it up, he smoked. "Scared shitless, ain't you, rook?"

"Who the hell are you calling 'rook'?" Nick said. "You were up for exactly one month last year."

"That's one month more'n you were, keed, an' you're shaky, ain't you? Scared you won't make it, right? Well me, I already made it. I mowed all them hotshot old suckers right down when they called me up. And once they seen how good I was, they sent me back to help you guys in Providence. You sure as hell needed the help, all right, you and what's his name—Summers."

"Winters," Nick said.

"Right," Ruth said. He was seated now, pulling a stocking on. "You needed the help, all right, without me you wouldn'ta won no pennant. I seen him yesterday."

"Who, Winters?"

"Yeah. He learn how to throw a fastball yet?"

"He's a control pitcher."

"Yeah," Ruth said, "me too, but I got some speed to go

44

with it. And I don't need to spit on the ball the way he does to make it hop." He stood up and tipped his cigar at the ashtray; the ash hit the table instead. "Christ, just finished buttonin up my pants and now I gotta shit."

Still smoking, he went to the bathroom and left the door open. Nick heard him grunting and heard all the sounds that went with it, and then Ruth returned. "Better get dressed, rook, Rough don't like late birds." He squashed his cigar butt into the ashtray and reached for the glove on the bedpost. "See you there, rook."

"Hey."

"Hey what, rook?"

"Didn't your reform school teach you how to flush?"

Ruth laughed. "It bothers you, rook, you flush it," he said, and went through the door.

"...Four, five, six, seven..." Ruth was counting the whores in the bleachers. A player standing beside him said, "I didn't know you could count."

"Goddamn it, you made me lose my place," Ruth said, and started all over again.

The field was fenced with chicken wire and ringed by garden plots. The stands were weathered, sagging planks. Wash hung on a line that stretched from the backstop to the nearest house, which was little more than a shanty.

"Twelve," Ruth concluded, "that's more'n last year. It's enough for me, I guess, but what are the rest of you guys gonna do?" Then, looking at Nick: "What about you, rook, what are you gonna do?"

Nick was having a catch with Eddie Winters and paid no attention.

"Big man," said a tall gangly player with prominent ears as he spit a thick stream of tobacco. "I thought you was married now, Ruth."

"What's that got to do with it?"

"Nothin, I guess, far as you're concerned."

45

Ruth grinned. "See that little one there on the end? The one with the yellow hair? When you poke her she goes 'Eek, eek,' like a mouse. So that's what I call her, Mouse. An' that big one beside her, the one with the long black hair and big tits? I stuck it up her ass last night."

"You'd stick it in anything with hair on it," the gangly player said.

Ruth responded by breaking wind.

Suddenly a gruff voice shouted, "Hey, what's goin on out here?"

Bill Carrigan, the manager, nicknamed "Old Rough" although he was only thirty-one. His face was red, and not from the heat. "What the hell do you think this is, a vacation? Ruth, warm up, you're startin today."

"Hot damn."

"Hudson, you warm up too."

"Yes sir," Nick said.

Ruth pitched three shutout innings. In the last of those innings he batted against Eddie Winters. Winters had drunk himself stupid the night before and was badly hung over. In spite of this he was able to get two swinging strikes on Ruth with a pair of dancing, tobacco-stained spitballs. And then he came in with heat.

Ruth swung and the bat made a vicious crack and the ball went up and up. "Holy Christ," said one of the rookie players, squinting and shielding his eyes with his hand. Far out in a field of furrows that soon would turn green with corn, the ball came down more than five hundred feet from home plate. Kids scrambled for it. As Ruth rounded second, he yelled, "Hey Summers, what was that, your changeup?"

Two batters later, Nick replaced Winters. He struck out the first of the men he faced, got the second to pop to short, and struck out the third. Two innings later, he found himself facing Ruth, who was now playing center field.

"Okay, rook, show me what you got," Ruth grinned,

46

cocking his bat behind his ear. He waved it slightly, almost imperceptibly.

Nick fired hard. The pitch was high, but Ruth went for it, missing. "Shit!" he said.

Nick threw a crisp quick curve, inside. Ruth lunged and missed.

The catcher called for a waste pitch, inside, high, but Nick shook it off. The catcher, a regular, looking angry, spat tobacco juice at the dust. Gritting his teeth, Nick reared back and let loose another fastball, this one low and tight. Again Ruth missed.

Nick almost laughed, he felt so good.

"Now there's a man who's gettin steady tail," Ruth said as he took the field.

That night, in the hotel dining room, Nick ate with Winters and two other rookies. At the table beside them, Ruth attacked platters of food without aid of utensils, drank beer after beer, belched loudly, bragged constantly, and pinched the blond waitress. After three mammoth wedges of chocolate cream pie he rose, a cigar in his teeth, and said, "Well, boys, I got a mouse to catch."

Nick went to his room. He emptied the ashtray and sat at the table and wrote:

Dear Alice,

Hot Springs is pretty nice. The hotel is great, with a beautiful lobby, good food and a nice-looking dining room. And the hot springs take all the aches and pains away—or so the players say, I haven't tried them yet.

The only bad thing—aside from the fact that you're not here—is they've put me in with George Ruth. You probably remember him. They call him "Babe," and he pitched for the Grays at the end of last year, in the pennant drive. Big guy, loud mouth, smokes cigars all the time. He's arrogant, dirty, selfish, crude, and thinks he's just great. And the thing of it is, he's right. He can do it all—pitch, run, field, and hit. Only twenty years old, a year younger than me, and he plays the game better than most of the veterans. And boy does he rub it in. Today he said to Smoky Joe Wood, the pitcher, "Hey, Joe, where'd the smoke go, up the chimney?" Wood's only twenty-six, but his arm is shot and he knows it. Three guys had to hold him back from slugging Ruth.

But I struck him out. He faced me once, and I struck him out on three pitches. I guess I ought to rub it in, but I won't, it's not my way. But this will be a long rookie year if I'm stuck with him all summer.

I'll write to you every night, as I promised. Right now I've got to get some sleep, since it's been a long day and I'm pitching again tomorrow. Say hello to your mother and Johnny for me and give them my best. I already miss you so much.

All my love,
Nick

He awoke to a thumping sound and a shriek and turned with a quick stab of fear in his heart, not remembering where he was. "Come on, Mouse, squeak for me," he heard Ruth say, and saw him there with the blonde in the hazy light of the lamp on the bedside table, pinning her up against the headboard. "Do it!" he said, thrusting, making the headboard smack the wall. "Eek, eek," the blonde said, her legs in the air, and the tall dark-haired woman who'd been with the blonde at the ballfield was lying beside her naked. "Yeah!" Ruth said, and let out a whoop, a rising train-whistle sound, then grunted and jerked and laughed. He spun toward the dark-haired woman and said, "Okay, your turn again."

"I can't," the dark-haired woman said. "Three times is enough, I *can't*."

"What? *What?*" Ruth roared. "I'm *payin* you, goddamn it! Here!" and a shower of bills filled the air.

"I can't!" the dark-haired woman said.

"In the mouth then."

"All right," the dark-haired woman said.

"Mouse, get up here an' help," Ruth said.

The blond-haired woman groaned and roused herself.

Nick fell back on the pillow and stared at the ceiling.

"Oh hell, now we woke up the rook," Ruth said. "Hey rook, you want some snatch?"

Nick's face went hot.

"My treat," Ruth said. "You can start with the mouse. Woop, woop, hey, doll—" He grunted and jerked again, and the dark-haired woman fell away. "I guess—I guess he don't want none. Hey, that was all right!"

The women were snatching the bills off the bed. With fists full of dollars, they gathered their clothes.

"What? You can't quit already! Come on, one more round."

"Tomorrow," the blonde said. The two of them went to the hallway, still naked. The door banged shut.

"Hey!" Ruth yelled, "get back here! Shit!"

He sat on the edge of the bed, his pale thick body slick with sweat, and lit a cigar. He took a few puffs, and belched. "You was dead to the world, keed, or I woulda let you join in from the start. Want a drink?" and he held up a bottle. "The bourbon here is the best."

"For God's sake, you're married," Nick said.

"Yeah?" Ruth swigged from the bottle. "I'm married an' where the hell is she, my steady stuff? In Boston, an' I'm here till April." He drank. "She wouldn't come down, wants to fix the apartment up." He smoked.

Nick shook his head. "Good God."

"But you ain't married," Ruth said, "an' tomorrow I'll get you somethin. You see that redhead up in the bleachers today?"

Nick didn't answer.

"Christ, now I'm hungry," Ruth said with a belch. "You ain't got nothin to eat, I guess."

"No."

"Not even some goddamn cookies?"

"Nothing."

"Shit." Smoking again, Ruth took a long swig of the bourbon. "Well, maybe *I'll* want the redhead tomorrow," he said, "and you can take Mouse. Take Busty, too, she'll let you—"

"Shut the hell up," Nick said

6

NICK WENT NORTH WITH THE TEAM, but two weeks later the Sox sent him down again. He swallowed his hurt, worked hard, did well at Providence and got a September call-up. When the Sox played in Philly early that month, Nick stayed with his mother, and after each game he went to see Alice. She worked as a clerk in a lumberyard but not on the weekends and came to the Saturday game, but Nick didn't play. Later that afternoon, as the two of them walked on Twentieth Street in the shadow of Shibe Park's right field wall a Packard screeched up with cigar-chomping Ruth in the driver's seat and Helen, his wife, beside him.

"Hey, rook, we're gone to the carnival, wanna come?"

Nick was ready to turn him down but before he could open his mouth Alice said, "The carnival! That sounds like fun!" and the next thing he knew they were riding in Ruth's back seat over cobblestone streets, the Packard jerking and belching like Ruth in rut.

"Some car," Nick said.

"Cost me a goddamn arm and leg," Ruth said, "but there's gonna be plenty more dough where that came from."

At the carnival, which was only a couple of blocks from the ballpark, they rode on a Ferris wheel, and Ruth was unusually well behaved. Then the wheel stopped with them at the top—and stayed there.

"We're stuck," Ruth said. "And you know what? I gotta go. If we don't get movin soon, there's gonna be some unexpected showers on those suckers down on the ground."

"Oh, Babe," Helen said.

Ruth took his seat again, grinning like mad, then started to rock the car. Helen let out a shriek. "Babe, stop it, don't do that!"

Alice tightened her grip on Nick's hand and he said, "Knock it off, it's not funny, George."

Ruth stopped. Still grinning, he leaned forward, clapping his heavy wide paw on Alice's thigh, above her knee, and said, "I hope I didn't scare you, keed."

Nick glared at him, shocked and seething. He had kissed Alice plenty of times and held her tight, but he'd never touched her thigh. And the next time he saw Ruth alone he said, "If you ever lay a hand on Alice again I'll bust your jaw."

"Yeah? You an' what army?" Ruth said, but his smile was thin, his lips pale.

Later that month, there was joyous excitement among Philadelphia's baseball fans. A great rarity had occurred: the Phillies had won the pennant and would play in their very first World Series—against the Boston Red Sox.

The Series would open in Philadelphia. Nick hadn't made the Series roster, but had tickets to all of the games—the two he'd been issued by the Sox and another pair that he got from Eddie Winters, who'd also been left off the roster and headed straight to Florida.

Nick was back at his mother's house and had already seen Alice twice. She managed to get time off from work for the first World Series game and so did her brother, Johnny. And Johnny contacted Jimmy Harriman, and he got time off too. So on Wednesday, October 8th, a sparkling day, the four of them took the trolley north to the Phillies' ballpark, Baker Bowl, which stood at Broad and Lehigh, six blocks east of the Athletics' field, Shibe Park.

Philadelphia Ball Park, home of the Phillies, was built in 1887, burned to the ground in 1894, and was reconstructed that year. It was given a new name, National League Park, but the fans soon christened it Baker Bowl, after the Phillies' owner, William Baker. Called "America's first modern ballpark" when it opened, it was now a hazard. In 1903, when Nick was nine, one of its grandstands had collapsed, killing twelve people and injuring hundreds of others. His father had never taken him there after that. Most people could never quite shake the feeling that to go to a Phillies game was to put one's life in jeopardy.

Baker Bowl had only eighteen thousand seats, most of them usually empty, since the Phillies were always so bad. It was not a great place to hold a World Series, to say the least. Even new Fenway Park wasn't spacious enough for the Series crowds, so the Sox were going to play their games at the larger Braves Field.

Nick's seats were fantastic: along the first base line, behind the Red Sox dugout. As he moved down the aisle with Alice and Johnny and Jimmy he suddenly saw that the woman three seats away from his was Helen, Babe Ruth's wife. She recognized Nick and Alice and said hello.

The game was quite gripping. The Phillies' pitcher was Grover Cleveland "Pete" Alexander, the best in the National League, with thirty-one wins and an earned run average of 1.28. The powerful highly–favored Sox only scored on him once in eight innings. Babe Ruth was not in the lineup.

But then, in the top of the ninth, with one away, he was sent to the plate to pinch hit—and grounded out. "That's okay, George!" Helen yelled. Ruth looked at her. And then he saw Alice and tipped his cap, and in spite of his failure at the plate and his wife right there, he gave her a grin—a grin designed to charm her and anger Nick—which it did. He fumed as he thought of Ruth's hand on Alice's knee.

The next Boston batter went out and the Phillies were winners, 3-1. "Well," Johnny said, "what a surprise. Maybe there's hope after all."

But the Sox won the next game in Philly, 2-1. Nick went by

himself since nobody else could get time off. He gave his spare tickets away to some kids on the street.

It was a special day: Woodrow Wilson was in the stands. This was the first time a president ever attended a World Series game. Europe was now engaged in a terrible war, and it was Wilson's job to keep America out of it. He was only five rows away from Nick, who couldn't stop glancing at him. He looked like a professor, not a president.

The Series shifted to Boston, where the Sox won both games by the same score they'd won the second game, 2-1. Nick didn't go there to see them, although he had tickets.

Game number five was back at Baker Bowl and again Nick went by himself. The Phillies lost, 5-4, ending the Series. Nick began working at Frankie's Garage the next day.

The following year he started in Providence again. Ruth quickly became the Red Sox' best pitcher, which made Nick hate him even more. Nick worked very hard at his craft, while Ruth didn't have to: he was a great natural talent, born with the gift.

Once again, Nick started the season well. He was called up in late July but didn't see much action. For the most part, he ignored George Ruth. When he thought of him touching Alice's thigh he still burned, but once when he mentioned the incident to her she said, "Oh Nick, he's just a big kid, he didn't mean anything by it, that's just how he is." "I don't like how he is," Nick said. He wanted to marry Alice but not until he was sure he would stick in the majors; so far he had only been used in relief.

The Sox won the pennant again that year and Ruth was spectacular in the World Series, pitching a shutout. Nick made the post season roster but didn't play.

But the next year, 1917, he had a terrific spring training and knew that his time had come. His fastball, roundhouse and drop were all sharp. He was also honing a new kind of pitch he had recently learned that completely confounded the

54

batters. His earned run average was miniscule and he was filled with confidence.

Then right before the season started, America entered the war that still raged in Europe. All men between the ages of twenty-one and thirty had to register for the draft. When Nick signed up he told the draft board the sooner they sent him to fight for his country, the better. Alice was frightened but Nick said, "I have to go, our nation's in danger, baseball is only a game. This is the war to end all wars, and don't worry, now that America's in it the Germans will fold real quick."

Johnny agreed with Nick and he volunteered too. When Alice wiped tears away at Broad Street Station as Johnny and Nick left for basic training, Nick remembered that happy time in Baltimore when she'd come to see him pitch his first game for the Grays. As the train pulled out and he waved goodbye he told himself he would fight just as hard as he could to end the war and be back for spring training next year.

He could never imagine that ten years would pass before he'd come home again, and that when he did, the world he had known would be gone.

7

NICK STAYED AT THE ROSE HOTEL on the money that Jimmy had given him, twenty bucks. He guarded it carefully, spending no more than he had to. He got a noon meal for free every day at the Paradise Mission down the street, bought day-old rolls from a bakery and every so often ate wonton soup in Chinatown for a quarter.

The name of the guy in the wooden booth at the Rose's entryway was Perley White, which made Nick think of teeth. But Perley's teeth were far from white, and false, and sometimes slipped when he talked. He was sixty or so and his face was round, with skin like lumpy dough. He worked for a Mr. Ingraham, who lived on the Main Line, far from the Rose, and owned a ton of rundown properties in town.

Perley gave Nick some heavy cardboard and glue to fix the hole he had punched in the flimsy partition. Nick promised he wouldn't damage the wall again, though he knew he really had no control over that. But now that cubicle number 26 was home sweet home he was trying to be more careful.

Perley not only collected money, he kept things in line. If somebody started a fight, it was his job to stop it. He had a pistol to scare away robbers but never used it for fights. Sometimes he had to call the cops, but he hated to do that since most of them wanted a payoff. A couple of times Nick stopped a fight, and Perley was grateful to him.

"I helped run the POW camp at the navy yard," he said to Nick one day.

"There was a POW camp at the navy yard?"

56

"You bet. We had a few dozen German sailors there. They were treated good—had a much better life than most of the people here at the Rose." He grinned, displaying his mottled false teeth. "I even learned to speak some German."

"Yeah? Well don't speak any to me. So what ever happened to those lousy bosch?"

"When the war was over we let 'em go. Most of 'em went back home, but a few of 'em stayed right here and got their citizenship."

"What? Those guys who wanted to kill us are U.S. citizens now?"

With a shrug Perley said, "They wanted to kill us ten years ago, but not anymore."

Nick simply nodded and Perley said, "You fight in Germany?"

"No, just in France."

"Where?"

"I can't remember."

On his thirty-fourth birthday Nick treated himself to a bowl of wonton soup and a fresh sweet roll. He couldn't remember his birthdays at St. Luke's. Had the staff held parties for the patients? Probably not. As he ate the roll he thought of the birthday cake his mother used to make for him, a hot milk sponge with orange glaze icing: his favorite cake, and he'd never taste it again.

He had gone to his mother's grave the day after he met with Jimmy. He'd taken the trolley up Ridge Avenue to Mount Vernon Cemetery, and a guard had directed him to the place where he saw his mother's headstone next to his father's, both of them crowned with snow. Numbed by a heavy sadness he took the trolley back to Columbia Avenue, then briskly walked to where Alice lay, in Monument Cemetery. *No!* he screamed to himself as he looked at her stone. Curling his hands into fists he thought, *This should never have happened! If not for George Ruth, it* wouldn't *have happened!* He fell to his

57

knees in the powdery snow and wept.

Sick to his heart, he took the trolley to Market Street and wandered around for hours thinking about his mother and Alice and feeling a bitter fury when his mind returned to Ruth.

Though the Rose Hotel was bug-ridden and filthy, compared to the mud and rats of the trenches, it was heaven. But it was a den of thieves. Nick couldn't leave anything there because someone would steal it. He bought a toothbrush and comb at the five and dime on lower Market Street and kept them in his coat. But he had no place to stash a razor, soap and brush, and a barber was too expensive, so he grew a beard. It reminded him of his time at St. Luke's and he vowed to shave it off just as soon as he could.

Each night he would listen to snores and coughs and the nightmare shouts of sick and troubled men, most but not all of them old. Many times he himself was the one who was shouting about imagined battles or raging about Babe Ruth: Babe Ruth, the killer of Alice. Babe Ruth, who deserved to die. *Walk it out, walk it out* he would say to himself when he woke to the thin winter dawn with his mind a tangled confusion of worries and fears.

And each day he would do it: walk miles in the bitter cold, trying to lift the cloud he was living under or, at the very least, keep it from getting darker. He tried booze twice but it only made things worse. At times when he walked, that frightening sensation that he was dissolving, fading away, would arise and he'd stare straight ahead and walk faster, as fast as he could.

Sometimes he'd walk past the Chinese wall and watch the trains coming and going. He'd think of catching one to somewhere, maybe out West, far from this town and all its bitter memories, but he wasn't ready for that.

Sometimes a song would start up in his head and keep going and going. Most of the time it was "Oh, Johnny, Oh,

Johnny," over and over and over again, making him picture his good friend's grisly death. Sometimes it lasted for hours, all day long. Why did his mind keep repeating a song he hated, keep torturing him like that? As punishment? For what? His killing had been to save his country—that's what he'd thought at the time. Did he need to be punished for that? Or for failing to save Johnny's life even though he had tried his best? He kept telling himself that the war was over, far in the past, he was safe—but he wasn't safe from his mind.

During his walks he kept wondering why, after all those years of wandering lost in a fantasy world he'd come back to this real one again. He decided that maybe there was no reason. Maybe it had just happened.

Most days he would end his walks at the brand new public library at Twentieth and Vine. It was quiet and warm and they had an extensive collection of old newspapers.

The first day he went there he looked through a lot of old summer sports pages, but couldn't find what he wanted. He read about some of the baseball games, especially those featuring Ruth.

He read about the 1918 World Series, where Ruth had pitched a shutout in game number one and had also excelled with the bat. He had heard about that in France. He hadn't heard about the 1919 Series, how Shoeless Joe Jackson and other Chicago players had fixed it. He had been in St. Luke's when that happened, cut off from the outside world. In the older papers he came across names he recognized but in the more recent papers he seldom did. Most of the players he'd known in his day were already gone from the game.

He was startled to see the name "Winters" in some of the recent Philadelphia A's box scores. Eddie Winters? Still playing? He'd drunk like a fish when Nick had roomed with him and usually pitched hung over. Maybe he'd sworn off booze and saved his career. Or maybe this was a different Winters.

Maybe, but it was the same old Ruth, incredibly famous

now. There were stories galore about him. And finally, after two days of searching, Nick found what he'd been hoping for.

The photo showed Helen and Ruth at brand new Yankee Stadium—"The House that Ruth Built"—four years ago. Ruth was holding his daughter, Dorothy, age three. Nick looked at the child's face and saw Alice: same eyes, same nose, same chin. Of course Ruth had been the one, he was sure of it now. Luckily for the kid, she'd turned out to look like her mother and not her father.

He kept searching the papers and found lots of photos of Ruth, but no more of Dorothy. And no more of Helen, either; Ruth had a new companion:

"The Sultan of Swat paid a visit to St. Vincent's Hospital yesterday, and residents of the children's ward forgot their ills, at least for the moment. The kids were in awe as the Babe, accompanied by his friend, Claire Hodgson, talked about hitting his sixty home runs last year and signed autographs."

Nick examined the photo. That same stupid face, just older, uglier, wider, that same dumb grin. And the kids were thrilled. Another story claimed that the Babe had rescued an invalid boy from death's door by saying he'd hit a homer for him, and then had made good on his promise—twice. The papers made it sound like for crippled kids, a trip to a ballpark where Ruth was playing equaled a trip to Lourdes.

The Sultan of Swat, the Bambino, could do no wrong. In 1920 he crashed his car in a ditch outside Philly. The papers reported him killed, but he turned up fine. In 1925—only thirty years old—he collapsed from "indigestion and influenza," was thought to be close to death, but again survived.

The war that killed Johnny and ruined Nick's mind and arm—Babe Ruth had survived that, too. He'd been married to Helen, and married men were exempt from the draft. When Nick had signed up to keep the world safe from the savage Huns, to keep it safe for his mother and Alice, to keep it safe for democracy, Ruth had said with a laugh, "Hey, don't get your ass blowed off, and have fun, keed."

Oh he'd had fun, all right. He'd lost his sanity, lost his girl, lost his best friend and his pitching arm, and Ruth had grown famous and rich. Nick had come back to a world that held nothing for one who had kept it safe, and Ruth was a king. That ignorant, cowardly slob was the king of New York—of the whole U.S.A., as a matter of fact. But he'd made a mistake, a fatal mistake. He'd touched Alice. Touched Alice until he had killed her, and now he would have to pay.

Nick's face felt hot; his ears started to ring. All at once it was perfectly clear to him why he'd come back to this world.

He'd come back because Alice had called him back. She wanted him to make Ruth pay for what he had done to her. And he wanted to do it. He wanted to do it with all his heart and he knew that he *had* to do it. He would never be fully healed until he did. He would never be truly himself again, be *whole* again, until he made Ruth pay.

Suddenly an angry voice started up in his head. It said: *Kill him, kill him, kill him!*

The words were so loud and clear it was almost as if someone else in the room had said them. But nobody else was in the room except for a young man taking notes at the other end of the long oak table where Nick was sitting, and an elderly woman slumped in a chair by the door who looked half asleep. *Kill him!* the voice said again as Nick looked at the man at the table whose lips didn't move. Shaking, Nick jumped up quickly, startling the man, and hurriedly left the building, his thoughts on fire.

It was obvious to him now. Why hadn't he seen it before? He would heal his mind by avenging Alice, by killing Babe Ruth. He didn't know *how* he would do it but he would. He swore he would.

The day was overcast and raw with a threat of snow, and the air held the tang of burning coal. He walked quickly east twenty blocks past the Rose Hotel to the Delaware River, afraid of his anger, hoping to tone it down with exercise,

61

fearful of what it might do to his fragile mind. He didn't hear the voice again, but his anger didn't abate.

In an empty lot by the river he picked up a stone. He held it a moment, feeling its weight and its bone-biting cold, then threw it against the wall of a warehouse that stood about fifty feet off. It hit with a smack and a puff of white dust. He picked up another stone and threw.

No good. His arm was no damn good, that's all there was to it.

He continued to throw and his arm was powerless, stiff; it began to ache. He remembered his days with the Red Sox, the way he could hit the catcher's mitt at will with blazing speed.

He threw the last stone with all of his strength as he thought of Babe Ruth—*I'll make him pay!*—and a jolt ripped his shoulder. The stone hit the wall with a sharp cracking sound. On the corner, in front of the warehouse door, a guy yelled, "Hey! Cut that out or I'll call the cops, you bum!"

Nick walked away.

8

Nick CONTINUED TO READ the old newspapers, trying to close the gaps in his life, and they set his mind to whirling. He knew he would never catch up.

While he had been lost in his madness, President Wilson, who'd ordered the war, left office in 1921 and died in 1924. Nick remembered him in his seat at Baker Bowl in the 1915 Series, stiff and professorial. His successor, Republican Warren Harding, also died—a year before Wilson—of a heart attack. He'd been president for just two years, but in that brief time had allowed his cronies to pull off some really sweet deals at taxpayer expense. His pals had cleaned up—as Rockefeller, Ford and the rest of the rich had cleaned up because of the war. But not just the rich had grown richer: the average Joe was doing swell too.

Harding's replacement was Calvin Coolidge, "Silent Cal," drab but honest—or so most people believed. "I never got hurt by anything I didn't say," was one of his remarks. And, famously, "The business of America is business." A guy named Hoover was sure to extend the Republican reign in the fall election; in this red-hot economy—stocks had been rising for eight straight years—the Democrats had no chance. Hoover claimed in his speeches that poverty would disappear from America, that the country was headed for permanent prosperity. The guys at the Rose Hotel would be happy to hear that, Nick thought.

He read about natural disasters, "acts of God": earthquakes, tornadoes, hurricanes, tidal waves, floods, across the globe.

But the most destructive act of all was war, an act of man. Nothing could beat that for ruining human beings. *And we bring that horror on ourselves*, he thought. It was hard to believe. Some duke somewhere had been shot and a ship had been sunk and half of Europe had exploded. Madness! And why had America entered the war? Had we thought that the Huns would invade us? It made no sense.

A story in one of the papers said that a total of eight and a half million troops had died in the war and twenty-one million more were wounded. Next came a figure that made Nick laugh: seven million, seven hundred fifty thousand, nine hundred forty-five were missing. How had they ever come up with such an exact number? What a joke! Well, joke or not, it was wrong. It should be nine hundred forty-four—he had been found. He knew that a lot of the soldiers who'd never been found had been blown to tiny bits that were eaten by rats. How many civilians had been killed? He couldn't find that figure anywhere. What battles had he fought in? He couldn't remember.

He read about prohibition, how mobsters controlled the liquor business, ran speakeasies everywhere and were filthy rich. He learned that women were now allowed to vote, which didn't surprise him; things had been heading in that direction for years before the war. He read about Charles Lindbergh flying alone across the Atlantic—to France, the place where Nick had lost himself and hoped he would never see again. "Lucky Lindy." Well, some men were lucky, like Ruth and Lindbergh, and some were not. And most were not lucky forever.

Often while reading the papers Nick's thoughts wandered off: to the war, his days with the Red Sox, his mother, Johnny, and most of all to Alice. When they wandered to Alice his sadness was overwhelming, his rage at Babe Ruth white hot. *He must pay for his crime,* Nick would think as the noises would start in his ears. *He must die, he must die, he must die.* Then a terrible pressure would fill his head and he'd walk and walk.

Sometimes he walked to the heart of the city, through Rittenhouse Square, past gleaming hotels with well-dressed people coming and going through brass-rimmed doors; past theaters, insurance companies, swank grocery stores. He'd look in the windows of fancy shops, their plate glass windows filled with opulent displays. He remembered a lot of these places from years ago, but there were a lot of new ones too.

Everything seemed so normal. *Too* normal. There wasn't any constant excitement, no having to be on guard each minute for fear of being killed. He knew this was how things should be, but the tension instilled by the war hadn't totally died, and everyday life seemed bland to him.

The city was far more prosperous now than back when he'd joined the army. For one thing, the number of restaurants was greater. He'd walk past them slowly, envying the lucky diners. He and Alice had eaten a really swell dinner in town on her birthday once, but he couldn't find the place. Maybe it didn't exist anymore.

He'd walk through the big department stores—passing by counters laden with sweaters and shirts and candies and books and household goods—in order to thaw out his frozen hands and face and use the toilets, attracting stares from suspicious female clerks and snooty floorwalkers. No wonder they stared. Catching sight of himself in a full-length mirror he thought of a line from Shakespeare he had memorized at Girard: "Yon Cassius has a lean and hungry look. He thinks too much. Such men are dangerous."

One sunny afternoon with a slight touch of spring in the air he stopped in front of a sporting goods store on Market Street and looked at the dense display in the window. The fishing rods made him think of good times with his father; the baseball gloves made him think of his days in the game; the ice skates made him think of Sundays with Alice; and the rifles made him think of the war—and of killing Babe Ruth. It was suddenly all too much and a wave of dizziness hit him.

65

He turned away and braced himself against a wall for several minutes before heading back to Skid Row.

When he was a kid he had walked through Skid Row with his father one day on their way to a plumbing supply store. Unshaven desperate-looking men came staggering up to them begging for change and his father completely ignored them. Nick asked him why. "They're drunks," his father said. "They have no discipline, and this is what they get. While they were drinking, I was working, and why should I waste my hard-earned money on them?" They were nothing but bums, his father said. Nick figured his father would think *him* a bum if he saw him now. He was damaged goods, one of the surplus people that nobody needed or wanted and wished would disappear.

Some of the younger men who lined up on Vine for their Paradise Mission noontime meal had been in the war. Some of them were missing hands or arms or legs but Nick knew all of them were missing something in their heads that could not be seen. Some of them were drunks and some were not. He stood with them every day in the cold and rain and snow and almost none of them ever spoke about the war. Some of the men were very sick and some were plainly crazy, but not quite crazy enough to be sent to a place like St. Luke's; they were out of the world to a certain degree, but still in it. One old guy with wild white hair who everyone called "Einstein" spouted mathematical theorems. No one could tell if they made any sense or not. Another guy, "Longfellow," constantly chanted poems. "Walt Whitman," he would say, "lived right across the Delaware in Camden. The good gray poet! A wonderful man! I used to take the ferry there and visit him. He'd had a stroke and could hardly walk, but he never gave up, he never stopped writing until he died. 'I depart as air,' he said. That's how he spoke of his death, 'I depart as air.' Now his ghost roams the city alone."

As Nick stood in the dreary line each day he constantly wondered: Why did these men keep going? They'd hit

66

bottom, but still hadn't quit. Did they still have hope? Did they think that something would happen to change their fate? Or were they simply afraid to die? Did some of them hear voices the way he did, or have horrible waking dreams?

One of those dreams struck hard while he was in line at the mission. He looked at the guy in front of him, who was missing an ear, and found himself back in France again in a small damp quiet town that had suddenly exploded. He was running for cover when Cogswell, a guy he hated, was hit by a shell and splattered against a storefront. When the image died, Nick found himself down on his knees on the sidewalk. Somebody helped him back onto his feet. Another time he was sitting in Washington Square and a fire engine went screaming by, sending him into a wall of black smoke and the cries of the wounded. He awoke from the incident sick to his stomach, ears ringing, sparks skittering through his eyes.

He called these episodes memory-dreams and felt he was at their mercy. A sight, a sound, or something that somebody said could touch them off like a match ignited black powder. They could come anytime, anywhere, there was no way to keep them from coming. And he knew they would never disappear till he made Ruth pay for Alice's death.

Every day at the Paradise Mission, rain or shine, a guy they called Stubby, a man about sixty with short gray hair and long fingers, would move down the line selling fat cigarettes for a penny apiece. Stubby lived at the Rose Hotel. Each afternoon he would wander the city streets, collecting discarded butts, and back at the Rose he would tear them apart and roll new cigarettes. Most of the men at the Rose were beggars, but Stubby had a genuine source of income. He always tried to sell a cigarette to Nick though Nick told him every time, "I don't smoke."

It was Stubby who'd helped him onto his feet when he had the bad memory-dream about France. "You okay, pal?" he'd said. "You want a smoke?"

"No, I'm okay, just hungry," Nick had said.

That was the only time he'd fallen, but people fell nearly every day, and sometimes it was Nick who helped them back up.

He rarely spoke to anyone in line, but someone would speak to *him* sometimes. A hobbled guy named Rusty—because of his carrot-colored hair, no doubt—once asked, "You in the war?"

"I was."

"Where?"

"I don't remember."

"I was in Belleau Wood. Wrecked my knee and live on a government pension. I could still work, I can drive a car, but nobody's willin to give me a chance. They look at the way I walk, and—forget it."

"That's rough," Nick said.

"And Silent Cal vetoed the Soldiers' Bonus Act."

"Yeah, I read about that."

"So what's your problem?"

"Well—" Nick began, but a loud burst of speech from the front of the line cut him off: "He that is without sin," yelled the creaky voice, "let him first cast a stone!"

"Jeremiah," Rusty said. "He quotes the good book mainly to himself but sometimes something sets him off, and then watch out. He hears these voices, hears God telling him to do things. Really sad."

"Uh-huh," Nick said, and wondered: If his voices didn't stop, would he be on Skid Row forever?

At a junk shop on South Street he rummaged through dusty boxes. He bought only things he could keep on his person. He picked up a penknife for a dime, handy for sharpening pencils or slicing cheese or fending off troublemakers. It felt good to carry a weapon again, it felt right. He bought a wallet and a banged-up wristwatch that still kept time.

Monday through Saturday Nick walked everywhere, entering stores sometimes and spending hours in the library, but Sundays were hard because of the Blue Laws; everything was closed—except for churches. The Blue Laws had been in effect in Pennsylvania for over a hundred years. In the old days amusements of any kind had been banned on the Christian Sabbath. Even "excessive travel" had been forbidden. George Washington, before his days as president, had been arrested for it. These days the rules were not as strict, but businesses were not allowed to operate on Sundays, including the baseball business.

Nick wasn't much for religion, but usually went to a church on Sunday mornings for warmth since it took the Rose half a day to heat up. His parents had believed in God but hadn't gone to church and neither had he. Alice had, but Nick only went with her once; he hated the ritual. But now he was glad there were so many places to go where he could escape from the cold.

The Reading Terminal was another such place; the trains still ran on Sundays. So Nick would sit for hours there reading a paper that someone had tossed or a library book he had borrowed—or brooding over Alice's death, seeing her headstone over and over again in his mind and thinking about how to kill Babe Ruth.

Each Monday, right after his lunch of soup and day-old bread at the Paradise Mission, he took a communal shower there in a clammy concrete room. Then he rolled up his socks and underwear in his shirt, put his pants and shoes and overcoat back on, and walked a couple of blocks in the bitter cold to a Chinese laundry on Race Street. For a quarter the laundry washed the items, drying them on a gas contraption and pressing the shirt. Nick would wait on a bench in the little anteroom till the job was done.

Often to get back to Vine Street he'd cut through the park that it bordered on, Franklin Square, named for Benjamin Franklin, whose grave was nearby. Men were sleeping on benches there with newspapers wrapped around their shoulders like shrouds. Some days they were covered with snow and the snow, if it wasn't perfectly fresh, was covered with soot. These were the vagrants who didn't have money enough for even the cheapest flophouse. At least he was luckier than they were—thanks to Jimmy Harriman. He wondered what this square had been like in Franklin's day, and what Franklin would think of it now.

After a month at the Rose he came down with a terrible cold. It kept getting worse and worse. His cough racked his chest and his face was flushed. Some men at the Rose who had coughed a lot died and he wondered if he had their same disease.

One day at the laundry a terrible fit of coughing seized him. The Chinese man behind the counter, who looked to be maybe twenty, asked, "Have you seen anybody about that cough?" He spoke perfect unaccented English.

"Can't afford it," Nick said.

"There's a remedy that might help you," the young man said. "It won't cost much."

"How much?"

"Fifty cents."

"I'll take it," Nick said.

The guy pushed a curtain aside and entered an adjacent room. Nick could see shelves full of bottles in there and an ancient-looking man with a pointed white beard at work at a cluttered table. Soon the young man returned with a little box. "Two teaspoons of this in a cup of hot water three times a day," he said. "Let it steep for five minutes. "Keep taking it till it's gone."

Nick paid the man for the box and his clothes and went back to the Paradise Mission. You could only get food at noon but coffee and tea were available all day long and he chose the tea. He opened the Chinese box, took two large pinches of what it contained, stirred them into his tea and drank it down. Its bitterness puckered his mouth. Then he went to his mattress and slept.

That evening he drank some more of the special tea and slept again. In the morning he felt much better, not hot and flushed, and three days later his cough was gone. But the cough sent the fire-and-brimstone preacher, Jeremiah, to meet his maker, and Nick knew he had to get out of the Rose Hotel.

9

NICK FINALLY FIGURED OUT how to kill Babe Ruth—kill him in front of thousands, yet do it invisibly, with a good chance of not getting caught. The idea came out of the blue on a blustery afternoon as he walked past Independence Hall.

He'd been feeling okay in body and mind and had gone to Frankie's Garage to try to get work, but learned that Frankie had moved away years ago. Which was just as well, because now that he had his plan worked out he needed a job near Shibe Park, which stood on the north side of Lehigh Avenue at Twentieth Street, a pretty good distance from Frankie's.

He went to a filling station on Lehigh and told them what he could do, but they didn't have any openings. He tried another garage a few blocks away with the same result, and at every other place he tried—a grocery store, a hardware store and a foundry among them—he had no luck.

But then one sunny frigid afternoon in early March he saw a sign, "Dishwasher Wanted," in the window of the Home Plate Café, a hole in the wall that he'd passed by several times before. The place was on the south side of Lehigh, a couple of blocks off Broad Street, closer to Baker Bowl, where the Phillies played, than it was to Shibe Park. He went inside. Nobody else was there except for a chunky, middle-aged bleached-blond waitress behind the counter.

On the wall behind her head a sign said, "Yuengling's Ice Cream," which Nick found jarring.

Yuengling—pronounced Ying-ling—had always been a beer

when he was growing up, but now—because of prohibition?—
it was an ice cream? Beside this sign was a sandwich list: Ham
.15; Cheese .15; Ham & Cheese .25; Bacon & Egg .25;
Hamburger .25; Chicken .25; Tuna fish .25, and several more.
They served oatmeal, and eggs any style with bacon or ham
or sausage with toast. You could also get "Billy's Famous
Chili," meatloaf, Greek stew, and the special "Home Plate of
the Day." Today's was spaghetti and meatballs.

Nick told the waitress—"Shirley" her nametag said—that
he'd seen the sign in the window. Shirley said wait a minute
and disappeared through the door to the kitchen. Soon she
was back with the owner, a short fat balding suspicious-eyed
guy named Sid.

"You ever washed dishes before?" he asked.

Nick thought about lying, but then said, "No."

"It's hard work."

"I like hard work."

Nick was very aware that the guy was sizing him up, and
hoped that he didn't look too bad. His overcoat, which he
always kept clean, covered the same clothes he'd worn since
they set him free. Each morning he buffed up his well-worn
shoes with a rag. But he didn't have any scissors to trim his
beard, and it looked a bit wild.

"It's more than just washing dishes," Sid said. "It's cleaning
up after hours and stocking shelves." He paused for a couple
of seconds, peering more closely at Nick, then added, "And
maybe a little bit more than that. It's night work, five in the
afternoon until midnight each day except Sunday and pays
you nine bucks a week plus you get your supper."

"I'm interested," Nick said.

"Well stop in at four tomorrow," Sid said, "and I'll show
you the ropes." Then he went to the kitchen again.

Everything worked out well the next day. A different
waitress named Doris was there, hard-looking and thin, but
she seemed nice enough.

Sid went over the job with Nick in the kitchen, where he

met the night cook, Louie Makous, an older, solid, swarthy man with graying hair, black whiskers and huge stubby hands. "Hard work," he said in his thickly accented English. This puzzled Nick. Yesterday he'd been the only customer and today he'd seen only three. "At night, completely different," Louie said.

Now that Nick had a job, he could rent a room. He needed to rent one on Twentieth Street, across from Shibe Park's right field wall, but none were available now, so he took one on Bancroft Street, behind the café. It was shabby and small and cost four dollars a week; a lot of money, but that was the best he could do for the moment.

Since he had his own room with a lock on the door, he could buy a few things—impossible while he stayed at the Rose Hotel.

At a church sale near Rittenhouse Square he found a carryall bag, a pair of gray pants, three shirts, a pair of shoes, a towel and a tan windbreaker. Since this was the best part of town it was all good quality stuff. He felt like a minor philanthropist: in addition to helping himself, he was helping the church with some needed repairs to its steeple. He bought more socks and underwear at Gimbels department store on Market Street. At the junk shop on South Street he'd gone to a while ago he found a shaving cup and a pair of scissors. He bought a razor and blades and soap and brush at the five and dime.

In the hallway's bathroom he cut off his beard and shaved, then soaked in the tub. What luxury! He thought of the muddy trenches in France, when he hadn't bathed for weeks at a time and lice had feasted on his scalp. He thought of the slimy showers at the mission. How had he bathed at St. Luke's? He couldn't remember. He must have been seen by a dentist; his teeth had fillings that weren't there when he joined the army. How he got them he didn't know.

The soaking completely relaxed him. He toweled himself dry and put on his brand new underwear and one of the shirts

74

and the pants. Fresh clothes, his own room, and a job. He felt renewed.

Then sudden tears sprang to his eyes, he didn't know why. Sometimes black sadness just came out of nowhere. Alice, his mother, the war...he never really knew what triggered it, he only knew it was always there waiting—the same way the memory-dreams were waiting. His thoughts would begin to slide, take a slippery shift, and disturbing sensations would start to swell, rise up through his stomach and chest and throat, and he'd feel himself disappearing, becoming a ghost. He would take deep breaths, bang his fists on his thighs or start walking to make the sensations stop, hoping to God he would never slide back all the way.

When he went to the Home Plate the next afternoon, Louie didn't recognize him without his beard. Then he shouted, "Ha!" and laughed. After that, he let him in on the café's secret.

He opened a door at the rear of the kitchen and Nick saw a well-stocked bar on his left. It was thirty feet long or so with a mirror behind it. There were tables across the room near a door that led out to the side alleyway. A piano was standing between this door and another door that led to the storeroom. "This is the real business," Louie said. "You got any objections?"

Nick said he didn't, and Louie said good. He said that the speakeasy's business was decent during the week but on weekends it was tremendous: that's when the colored trio played jazz and the couples came to dance.

"Alcohol illegal," Louie said. "America! Can you imagine that in Europe?"

Nick had a sudden brief flash of himself at an outdoor café somewhere—in Paris? "No, I can't," he said.

"Dumb," Louie said. "What does it get you? Bad booze and gangsters. But the booze here is good—not that I ever drink it."

Nick went back to the kitchen and sat on a stool and ate a big platter of Louie's Greek stew—the best food he'd eaten since his release from St. Luke's. Along with the stew he ate some bread—with butter! He couldn't remember the last time he'd eaten butter. It tasted fantastic! Then Louie gave him a small dense piece of pastry. It was sticky and sweet and very delicious. Nick said, "Did you make this?"

"My niece Alena makes it," Louie said. "Everyone calls her Al. I live in her house down town. She's a saint, good lookin too, but not married, I don't understand it." He shrugged. "I take the Broad Street trolley to work every day but soon I'll be able to take the subway. Fast! I'll get some extra sleep."

Nick ate more of the pastry. "So what do you call this stuff?"

"Baklava."

"It's great."

"Al's a wonderful pastry cook," Louie said, his eyes fastened on Nick. "If only she could find a husband!"

Nick swallowed the last of the sweet and said, "Uh-huh."

When the speakeasy opened, he found it hard to keep up with the stream of glasses from the bar. There were dishes, too, primarily from the bar but a few from the little café, which stayed open till nine. "Hard work!" Louie said. "But you get used to it."

Louie worked like a demon with swift efficiency, turning out burgers and sandwiches, doling out bowls of stew. When Nick dropped a glass and broke it, Louie didn't yell at him, he just said, "Kick it under. Take care of it later." And when ten o'clock came around he said, "Break time. You get fifteen minutes. You don't take it now, you'll miss it, so get goin."

Nick made his way through the crowded bar and into the storage room. He sat on a wooden box there for several minutes but pictured the dishes piling up and returned to the kitchen. Louie looked at him, heavy black eyebrows raised, and then just shrugged.

The bar closed at midnight. After Nick finished cleaning up,

76

Louie said, "You did good!" and gave him a slap on the shoulder. "You're gonna be fine."

Nick smiled. It was good to hear somebody say that—even if it only applied to washing dishes. "I hope you're right," he said. He was thoroughly beat, and couldn't imagine what the workload was like on weekends.

The following night, a Friday, he found out. When he came in that afternoon he met the colored trio: Slomo on sax, Tubby on bass, and Henry, who played piano and sometimes sang. They seemed like good guys, always smiling and joking around. "Reefer," Louie said. Nick wondered if that might cheer him up but he was afraid that he might get addicted, as Johnny had gotten addicted to opium pills.

The place was soon jammed with dancing couples; the bartenders worked nonstop and so did Nick. All of the couples were white, and all night long no Negroes came through the door. Nick wondered where the band members lived, but he didn't ask them. He had read in the papers that teams from the Negro leagues played at Shibe Park sometimes, and he knew that there wouldn't be any whites at those games, just as there wouldn't be any Negroes when the A's were playing. Philly was split in two when it came to race. All cities were.

When Nick passed the bar on his way to the storeroom to take his break, he heard a grinning customer say, "The niggers are really hot tonight."

Nick wanted to paste him one. How could the colored put up with the constant insults? How could they stand being always shut out of things? They could only live in certain neighborhoods without fear of reprisal. They weren't allowed to attend Girard College, the school he had gone to. In the army they had been kept apart from the whites. They had to have separate baseball teams. Down South they had separate toilets. How could they live with discrimination day after day after day? How did it feel to wake up every morning and think once again: *I'm colored.* Slomo and Tubby and Henry

77

apparently hadn't heard the jerk's "nigger" remark. Or maybe they had; maybe they just ignored that kind of stuff, they'd heard so much of it. Maybe they were so high on reefer they didn't care. Whatever, they just kept smiling and playing.

The work never ceased, but Nick was adjusting, finding a rhythm, and after the cleanup he wasn't as bushed as he'd been the night before. He was still plenty bushed, just not as bad. But he liked the steady repetitive work, it kept him from thinking. It was almost as good as walking for doing that.

He reported each day at four forty-five, ate a platter of Louie's terrific food or the chili made by the day cook, Billy Milligan, and then washed dishes till after twelve with only that one short break at ten. Once he finished the dishes he'd wipe off the tables and mop the floor and go to his room exhausted. But often he couldn't sleep or would sleep just a couple of hours and wake in a sweat with his heart pounding hard from a dream of the war or thoughts of revenge against Babe Ruth, and then he would leave his room and walk the dead night streets.

He would walk past the looming dark hulk of Shibe Park where he once had played and by rights should be playing now, and a bitter sadness would claim him and then a dark anger. Ruth played inside these walls. *He's on the inside of everything,* Nick thought, *while I'm on the outside.* He was working like crazy for just over four hundred dollars a year and had read in the papers that Ruth was hauling in seventy grand—for six months of hitting a ball with a stick. He thought: *If my mind hadn't failed, I'd have come back to Philly and married Alice. I'd have made the majors. I would have my own house by now and maybe a couple of kids. I would have some money.* Well no use thinking about all that, and in daylight he usually didn't, but deep in the night, he just couldn't help it. And he'd walk till his legs started aching, then go to his room and sleep until after noon.

A bakery across the street from the Home Plate Café sold

day-old rolls for a penny apiece and Nick would buy three of them after he washed and dressed. They would hold him until his free supper at work. After he ate them he took the same walk every day, the walk he took on the nights when the terrors seized him: up Lehigh Avenue to Twentieth, turn right and walk to Somerset. Some people called the neighborhood North Penn while others called it Swampoodle, nobody seemed to know why.

The houses on Twentieth Street were a lot like the house he'd grown up in: modest two story places with four wide steps going up to a porch and, on the second floor, bay windows. He knew that some of these houses let out rooms, but a rent sign never appeared.

Shibe Park's right field wall—just twelve feet high—stood across from these houses and during the baseball season the homeowners rented their roofs to fans. The infield looked far away from up there but the view of the outfield was good. Nick figured it had to be good from the second floor windows, too.

When Nick was a kid he had gone to games with his father a number of times at Columbia Park, the A's small field on Twenty-Ninth Street. Then in April of 1909 the A's new home, Shibe Park, opened up. It was labeled "America's first modern baseball park"—the same thing that Baker Bowl had been called decades earlier. Nick and his father watched games that month and again in early June from grandstand seats, but another game they wanted to see was sold out. So they walked to Twentieth Street—which was lined with trees in those days but not now—paid someone a dime apiece and climbed a ladder that went through his open bathroom skylight and onto his roof. A couple of drunks had fallen off roofs back then (not when Nick and his father were there) and now when he looked up he saw that a safety railing had been installed the entire length of the block. He wondered what a roof seat cost today and thought: Maybe soon I'll find out.

10

ON A FREAKISHLY HOT AFTERNOON at the end of March Nick reported to work and found Louie leaning against the refrigerator. Frowning, Nick said, "You okay?"

"Sure, sure, I just didn't get much sleep. Bad dreams. And this heat's a killer. What the hell's wrong with the weather these days, it's all messed up." He pointed to the ceiling. "One stupid fan! We need two, three! I told Sid that, but—" A buzzer over the door to the speakeasy cut him off. "You got here just in time," he said.

Nick opened the door, crossed the speakeasy, empty now, and went to the storeroom. Its shelves were stacked to the ceiling with boxes and bottles and cans. Nick opened the heavy door to the wide back alley.

A broad-shouldered man in a derby hat was standing there chewing a toothpick. A paneled truck stood behind him with "Dougherty's Milk, Eggs, Cheese," on its shiny white side in red letters.

Nick said, "Hi, Mack."

"How's it goin, Nick?"

"I can't complain." That's what you said when you were a normal person, which he was pretending to be.

"Pretty steamy for March."

"I can't wait until August," Nick said. Then the door of the truck opened up and the driver got out. He stood there a second, looking at Nick, then said, "Well I'll be damned."

"New man on board," Mack said. "You know him?"

"Rusty!" Nick said with a laugh.

"I told you that I could still drive."

"Well isn't this great. So you out of the Rose?"

"Yep, got me a room in Fishtown, not too far from Dougherty's. Been on the job for a week now and love it. I don't only drive, I help unload stuff, too. So let's get goin."

The three of them carried eight boxes out of the truck and into the storeroom.

"So boss man Grady still hasn't kicked up a fuss," Nick said.

"I guess he has bigger fish to fry," Mack said, handing Nick the bill. "Sal Mario and Sid go way, way back and that's why Mario's here instead of Grady. But hell, Grady's rakin it in all over North Philly, so why should he really care if the dagoes step over his line?"

"Guys like him never get enough—of fish or anything else," Nick said.

"Gotta go," Rusty said. "We're runnin behind." He limped to the truck and got inside and Mack took the passenger seat.

"Stay cool, guys," Nick said. "Great seeing you, Rusty."

"See you again soon, Nick."

The truck pulled away and Nick closed the door to the storage room. He unpacked two boxes containing eggs, milk, cream and butter and put all the stuff in the large white fridge, then opened the other six boxes. Two of them held rye whiskey—"brown"—two held gin, one held bourbon and one held scotch. He took two bottles of gin to the bar and put them under the counter, then went to the kitchen again to help Louie.

After another couple of weeks went by, one of the bartenders, muscular, tough-looking Alex, gave notice and Sid asked Nick if he'd like to take Alex's place. It would mean a three dollar raise plus tips—practically Easy Street—and Nick jumped at the chance. But he knew that the job consisted of more than just tending bar.

"Sometimes a customer gets a bit rowdy," Sid said.

"Sometimes he needs to be taken outside to cool down. That was Alex's job. Charlie and Jake are too soft for that kind of work, but you fought in the war, right?"

"Right," Nick said. He had talked about it a little to Louie, who'd served in the Spanish-American War with Teddy Roosevelt—or so he claimed.

"Any hand-to-hand combat?" Sid asked.

"A little."

"You think you can handle being a bouncer?"

"I'm sure of it."

Sid slapped his shoulder. "Good man."

Sometimes when Mack and Rusty made a run they had a quick bite to eat in the little café and joked with genial married Shirley or single hard-edged Doris. It was Doris who told them Nick's job was changing. Before Sid could put the "Dishwasher Wanted" sign back in the café's window, Rusty—whose last name was Bridges—found Nick's replacement, a guy who had just left the navy and moved into Rusty's building. His name was Gus, he was muscular, tall, with short blond hair and looked like a German but wasn't— his last name was Olson. "His father's a Swede," Louie said to Nick, "but his mother's a Greek!"

As soon as Gus started washing dishes, Nick started tending bar, a task that was totally new to him. The easy part was learning to mix the drinks; the hard part was dealing with customers. The two guys who worked beside him, Charlie— forty-eight, short, red-faced, smiley—and Jake—thin, sallow, fifty-two, with hound-dog eyes—had a smooth calm way about them and patiently listened to everyone's stories, happy or stupid or sad.

Nick became fast and accurate with the drinks but hated to hear the stories. A lot of people loved blabbing about their problems, but Nick wasn't like that and didn't respect those who were. It had been hard for him to open up to the psychiatrist, and he never completely did. And it was hard for him to listen to others telling their tales of woe, but he tried his best to feign interest. If the tale was supposed to be funny, he forced a smile.

Most of the Home Plate's customers were well behaved. On the few occasions when somebody had to be removed, Nick handled the job efficiently without getting really rough. One hot sticky Friday a big foul-mouthed fool really stirred up his rage with "nigger" talk and he wanted to tear him apart, but he kept himself in check.

Some of the same guys showed up nearly every night: "Happy Ernie," a thickset balding middle-aged fellow who never smiled; pale-faced Jackie "Gloom and Doom" Dodd, a radio addict whose mouth was thin and tight; "Shrimpy" Petrullo, a shade under five feet tall but with a voice like a bullfrog; "Iron Mike," a dark wiry guy who had worked on the railroads; "Butterball" Saleski, a chubby upbeat fellow who seemed to have never worked at all; and "Hesitant Harvey," who could just about speak until he'd downed a few. All of these regulars drank for hours, trying to forget the world, while Nick was working as hard as he could to remember it. He didn't drink at all anymore. Now that he'd thought of a plan to make Ruth pay, nothing would stand in the way of it—not drink, not women, nothing. When flappers tried to flirt with him he politely brushed them off.

While Friday and Saturday nights were the wildest, the Home Plate was busy all week. The country was rich and kept getting richer. Lots of people had cars and radios and fancy clothes and big houses with fine furnishings; they could afford to go to nightclubs and theaters and take vacations and eat at high-class restaurants. People like Jimmy Harriman.

Jimmy had missed the war and had made a fortune in stocks; he was set for life. And his head hadn't been messed up. Jimmy had told Nick to stop by again any time, but Nick couldn't do it. He just couldn't stand to look at all that happiness. Jimmy's leg was worse but that was the only thing bad in his life as far as Nick could see. As for himself, he felt that even if he had a life like Jimmy's, he wouldn't be right.

For Charlie and Jake every night was a party. For Nick, it was just an ordeal to get through, a way to get by; the patrons' fun intensified his gloom. On his ten o'clock break he would go to the storeroom and shut the door and sit on his box with his hands on his ears to block off the joyful noise.

Nick worked very hard and Sid was pleased. He had to work hard to keep horrible thoughts from invading his mind. But at night in his dreams the thoughts and strange feelings would rise from the darkness again and he'd walk and walk.

The A's opened their season on April 11th at home against New York. Spring was now underway in Philly; the pale green leaves on ailanthus and gingko and buttonball trees were starting to open up. But the air was still quite cool.

The Yanks and their "Murderer's Row," led by Babe Ruth, were heavily favored to win the pennant again, as they had the year before. In the bar, Shirley's husband, Vince, a balding middle-aged guy with a fringe of red hair and puffy eyes, took bets on the games—on all of the games in both leagues. He worked for Sal Mario, Louie said, and Mario headed a South Philly mob. Mario pushed Vince to hit up the big boys, high rollers, but Vince would take bets from anyone, no matter how small they were. Lots of people placed bets, including the cops that Sid paid off, but Nick didn't bet; he saved every dime he could.

Nick didn't go to the opening games. Shibe Park was sold out and he hated crowds; they gave him a hollow dark feeling deep down in his stomach, he didn't know why. When he'd played for the Sox he'd loved crowds, the bigger the better, but not anymore. And he wasn't ready to see Babe Ruth. Not yet.

The A's lost both of the Yankee games, then played a pair with Washington and lost them too. In the box score of one of the games Nick saw the name "Winters" again.

On Thursday, an off day for the A's, the saloon was half full when a rawboned man with a tanned lined face came through the door. Nick instantly recognized him. The man walked up to the bar and leaned his elbows on it. Nick went over to him. "Eddie."

The man frowned suspiciously. "Yeah?"

"Nick Hudson."

The man gave a little jerk of his head and said, "Jesus Christ."

"Good to see you again."

"Nick, Jesus, how... I heard you was killed in the war."

"No, I just went away somewhere. I'll tell you about it sometime, but not here."

Eddie Winters was shaking his head. "I don't believe this."

"I see you're still playing."

"Yeah, for the A's. And you—?"

"I hurt my arm a long time ago."

"In the war?"

"Yeah."

"Was you shot?"

"No, something else happened, I don't know exactly what."

"Hey, that's too bad."

"So what can I get you?"

"A double brown. So how'd you get here? Where you livin?"

"Around the corner."

"You married?"

"No."

"You went with that good lookin girl, what was her name?"

"Alice."

Nick set the drink in front of Eddie, who took a big gulp, then wiped his mouth with the back of his hand. "Alice, yeah. So it didn't work out."

"She died."

"Oh, Christ, that's terrible, Nick."

"Spanish Flu."

"It killed so many."

85

"Are you still single?"

Eddie laughed. "A skirt would have to be crazy to marry me."

"Where you living?"

"On Twentieth Street, near Somerset."

"I'd like to get a room there too."

"To watch the games?"

"That's right."

"My room's in back so I don't have to look at the field, I see enough of it durin the day. But we're gonna be good to watch this year."

"If you say so. What happened this week? The Yanks I can understand, but Washington?"

"I know, but we'll straighten out real quick, you wait and see."

"I hope."

"We're playin the Yanks again tomorrow up in New York, two games, and we're gonna take 'em."

"I hope."

"You struck Ruth out in spring trainin once."

"You remember that."

"Who could forget it? He always hammers me. And he still laughs about it."

"What a bastard."

"He sure is." Eddie finished his drink. "Well listen, I gotta get goin, we catch an early train tomorrow. See you again soon, this is my favorite hangout."

When Eddie left, Charlie came over to Nick. His flushed round shiny face wore a constant smile and people called him Jolly Cholly. "You know Eddie Winters?" he asked.

"From long ago."

"Did you used to play ball?"

"A little."

"In the majors?"

"Yeah, but just off and on for a couple of years."

"No kidding. Well that's really something. You'll maybe

86

know some of the other players who come here. A bunch of them come here, even Babe Ruth."

"Is that right."

"Yep, a couple of times a season. He's a real joker, and generous, too. He tips you great, and he gives everybody cigars."

"Big deal," Nick said. "It would take you a hundred years behind this bar to earn as much dough as he makes in six months."

This remark didn't put the slightest dent in Charlie's steady smile. "He's worth every penny he makes, in my opinion. He's a great ballplayer and a really swell guy."

"Maybe I'll meet him someday," Nick said.

11

THE A'S WON BOTH OF THEIR GAMES in New York, as Eddie had predicted, then came back home to face the Boston Red Sox, Nick's old team. The Sox were all strangers to him now but he went to see them anyway.

He paid six bits for a general admission seat. When he went through the gate he felt overwhelmed: the echoing shouts of the scorecard vendors in front of the dark green walls he remembered so well, the smell of cigar smoke, the hundreds of fans going every which way buying hot dogs and drinks and finding the concrete ramps that led to their seats made his head spin with all he had lost, and the sadness he always carried deep down began to rise.

He walked to the left, away from the entrance, hoping to get a seat far down the third base line where there wouldn't be so many fans. But the Sox were good and the season was new and chances were that the game would be sold out.

He made his way up a ramp, and the field and the soft spring sky opened wide before him, a manicured green oasis deep in the heart of the harsh industrial streets of North Philly. A memory rush and the beauty of it made him catch his breath.

He took an aisle seat in a row that was almost empty. But people kept pouring in, and gradually the seats to his left were filled. At least no one could sit on his right. He could get out fast if he had to.

Soon the stands were packed. People were talking loudly and happily, eating and smoking and drinking sodas. No beer, of course—prohibition. But even before prohibition there hadn't been any beer in Shibe Park. The father of Connie Mack, who managed and partially owned the A's, had been an alcoholic, and Mack had promised his mother he'd never drink. He wouldn't let his patrons drink either, or his players, but Eddie Winters and some of the others did, behind his back. Mack had stated, "Old Man Booze has put more men out of the game than all the umpires together."

Nick looked at the soft blue sky and the right field wall and saw that the rooftops on Twentieth Street beyond the wall were also packed—except for one, in the middle of the block, which held a single person in a chair. He wondered who that person was and why he had the entire roof to himself. He wondered which house Eddie Winters was living in.

Now the game was about to begin. A guy in a black business suit strode onto the field, held a megaphone up and shouted the names of the catchers and starting pitchers.

The players' uniforms had no numbers, but Nick knew the lineups from reading the papers. He also recognized two of the A's as they took the field. Tris Speaker was in center; he had been on the Red Sox in 1915 when Nick was new to the team. Ty Cobb, the former Tiger, was in right. When Nick had played, these men were in their prime, among the best, but now they had come to the end of the road. They had both been accused of being involved in a crooked gambling scheme, and Connie Mack took pity on them and signed them. People said he was hurting his pennant chances by giving them so much playing time, that Mule Haas and Bing Miller should start every game instead.

But today, even with Speaker and Cobb in the starting lineup, the A's looked dominant. The league's best pitcher, Lefty Grove, mowed the Boston batters down, and "Bucketfoot" Al Simmons, the left fielder, Jimmie Foxx, the hotshot rookie playing third, and "Black Mike" Mickey Cochrane, the catcher, all had big hits. Maybe the A's really *would* give the Yanks a run for their money this year as

Winters thought.

As Nick watched the game he ached to be out on the mound, zeroing in on the catcher's mitt, excluding all thoughts except thoughts of the game. He still found it hard to believe that ten years had flown by and his time on the playing field was gone forever.

He got through the first five innings okay; the crowd surrounding him made him feel slightly uneasy but not claustrophobic. But then when the sixth inning started he glanced at the right field stands and received a shock.

He saw Germans. Germans in uniform over there, at least a dozen of them. He squinted and blinked and yes, he was sure of it, there they were, the Huns! The ones who had been released from the POW camp and their comrades, sitting right there!

His pulse beat hard in his neck. He looked at the bright blue sky and the brick row houses beyond the right field wall, saw that guy on the rooftop sitting alone, took a long deep breath. He looked back at the right field stands again and the Germans were gone.

A tightness swelled in his chest and throat and he broke into quick cold sweat. That terrible feeling that he was dissolving began and he rose abruptly and hurriedly left the park.

As he walked past the boys on the street who were waiting to chase foul balls, he wondered how his eyes could have fooled him so badly. A trick of sunlight and shadow? But he'd seen Johnny dead in a ditch on Broad Street, a siren had made him think he was back in the war... Would this terrible stuff never end? He quickened his pace and told himself, Walk it out!

At Shibe Park, the A's were at bat in the sixth. And up on the roof of the row house across from Shibe where the lone figure sat, a woman appeared. She was tall, with broad shoulders, high cheekbones, brown hair pulled back in a bun, and luminous light brown eyes. She went to the chair and

90

said, "Willie, it's time to leave."

The boy in the chair, who was nine years old and small for his age, with the same brown eyes as his mother and prominent ears, frowned under the peak of his blue baseball cap. "But Mother," he said, "the A's have two runners on and only one out."

His mother let out a sigh and said, "All right, we'll wait till the inning ends."

It ended quickly, thanks to a double play, and Willie said, "Drat!"

"Okay, here we go," his mother said. Leaning over, she lifted him up and slung him across her shoulder. She walked to the hatch in the roof and slowly and carefully backed down the steps to the hallway. She paused there a minute, and Willie began to cough. She waited until he stopped and then carried him down the stairs to the first floor hall.

She deposited him in a wicker wheelchair that stood at the foot of the steps. He wheeled himself into the parlor, crossed the rose-colored flowery rug, passed the upright piano, and went to the large front window. He looked out the window, across the porch and across the street to the back of Shibe Park's dark green right field wall. "I wish I could have stayed," he said, "but at least they were winning big."

His mother said, "I hated to have to bring you down, but the sun is very strong today."

"It didn't feel that strong."

"But it is."

Willie looked sulky. "Well, anyway," he said, "the A's play twenty-one of their next twenty-three at home."

"You'll have plenty of chances to see them."

"Yes. But I hope I can watch the whole game sometimes."

"When the sun's not so strong, you will."

"Yes," Willie said. Then he wheeled himself up to the piano and started to play some Bach, which his mother was thankful for. When Willie felt really good he often played something light by Chopin. When he was angry, he chose something

91

dark by Beethoven. When things were going relatively well, he usually played Bach.

Suddenly the sound of shattered glass came from somewhere upstairs, then a man's voice hollered, "Oy!"

"Not again," Willie's mother said.

Willie's eyebrows went up. "I wonder who hit it."

"Poor Mr. Cohen."

"I hope it was one of the A's," Willie said.

The shooting range sat in a broad brown field near the Delaware River in South Philadelphia. It was owned by a dark stubby guy named Angelo who kept his weapons locked in a small brick shed with a metal door. Nick chose an old familiar friend: an army surplus Springfield. He wondered how many Huns it had killed.

"You ever shoot one of these babies before?" asked Angelo as he handed the rifle to Nick, and Nick nodded. "Was you in the war?" "I was," Nick said and he started to sweat. "I got a couple other customers like you," said Angelo. "They love this gun."

Nick had last held a Springfield more than nine years ago; he could hardly remember it now. The battles were all just a blur and yet every so often a scene would jump out at him crisp and clear. Johnny suddenly bolting up out of the trench with his Springfield, screaming and running straight into his death was one of those scenes. It came back at least once a day. And other horrors rushed back at him too, tearing at him, staggering him, giving him weak sick panicky feelings he hated and feared, but he no longer felt he could push them away or walk them away or sleep them away. The psychiatrist said you could talk them away but he didn't believe it.

When he aimed at the target the Springfield felt much too heavy. In the war his rifle had been like a part of him; now it seemed foreign. His heart began racing, he started to shake, and his hands began turning numb. He got the bull's-eye in his sights but then tiny black dots began dancing in front of his eyes. He lowered the rifle and took a deep breath.

He hadn't had any memory-dreams for a while now: those episodes that kidnapped his mind, jolting him out of the present and into the past, making him live the terror all over again. He hoped he had seen the last of them, but feared that he hadn't. He felt that the darkness was always there waiting to claim him; felt he could tumble back into its depths and be lost again, maybe forever this time.

Another deep breath and another. And then when he raised the rifle again, while his heart was still quick in his ears, his hands felt okay and the spots in his eyes were gone.

When he squeezed the trigger, the sharp report and kick brought a new rush of sweat. He had missed the target completely.

"Little rusty, huh?" said Angelo.

"Looks that way," Nick said.

Over the next several weeks Nick went to the range twelve times. The first few times he felt dizzy and weak but forced himself to shoot. And the more he shot, the stronger he felt. He saw Johnny again every time but it wasn't as bad as before. And slowly his old skill came back. He could hit the bull's-eye with regularity now at a hundred yards. Which was good enough. Plenty good.

One hot May day he said to Angelo, "If I wanted to buy a Springfield, where could I get one?"

"You don't like my Springfields?"

"They're fine, but I might like to own one."

"Why? You plan to go huntin this fall?"

"I was thinking about it."

"I can rent you one."

"I'd rather have my own."

Angelo shrugged. "I got mine at Goldstein's on Washington Avenue, but it was a while ago."

"I'll probably never do it," Nick said, "but I was just wondering."

12

DURING THE A'S LONG HOME STAND a number of players showed up at the Home Plate's bar. Eddie Winters was there at least once a week, and one time a couple of Cleveland Indians appeared. Eddie ignored them; it was against league rules for players from different teams to fraternize with each other. The Indians made some disparaging comments about the A's on their way to becoming staggering drunk, and Nick led them out to the curb and into a taxi that whisked them away before one of the rougher A's fans had a go at them.

The bookie, Vince, did a bang-up business each night; he solicited just about everybody. Jake and Charlie never bet—bets were for suckers, they said—and Nick agreed. But Eddie Winters placed bets on the A's, who were doing better as time went on. "If I could get my spitter to work again I'd be on Front Street," he said to Nick. That meant he'd be really good.

The spitball had been banned in 1920; Nick had read about this in the library's papers. He'd never thrown a spitter, but it was Eddie's bread and butter pitch and he was still allowed to throw it; those who were using it when the ban came down could continue until they retired. "Not many of us left," said Eddie morosely one night as he sat at the bar. "But mine don't dance like it used to, I don't know what happened. I use the same chew I always did, the grip's the same. How can a pitch betray you like that?"

A pitch? Nick thought. How can your *mind* betray you?

Eddie had said he would let Nick know if a room turned up on Twentieth Street, but Nick walked that block every day to check for himself. The chances of finding the room that he wanted were slim, but he had to keep trying.

On May 24th, the Yanks came to Philly to play six games: doubleheaders on Thursday and Friday, then a Saturday single game. They would have a day off while the A's went away for a Sunday game with Washington, then play the A's once more on Monday. The A's couldn't play at home on Sundays because of the Blue Laws.

On Saturday Nick gave a short, cigar-smoking man on Twentieth Street a quarter—four bits less than he'd paid for a grandstand seat at Shibe—and climbed up a set of outside steps to the roof of his house. It was already crowded with people standing or sitting on makeshift bleachers. Most of the fans were men wearing hats or boys wearing caps but there were some women too. Everybody was white.

Nick understood the big Saturday crowds, but not the big weekday crowds. How did people find time to attend these ballgames during the week? Did they all work at night, like him? Were they retired? Unemployed? So rich that they didn't have to work?

People kept coming up onto the roofs, and soon they were full—except for the one on his left, the one with the single chair that he'd seen from the grandstand during the Red Sox game. And now he could see that the person who sat in that chair was a boy.

He was wearing a dark blue baseball cap and frowning at the field, and to Nick he looked rather frail. The roof he sat on was sectioned off from adjacent roofs by wooden railings. It was strange to see all those crowds on the other roofs and this roof totally empty except for this boy.

Another boy, this one about thirteen, weaved his way through the mob on the south side roof, a tray filled with cups of popcorn and lemonade hanging around his neck. He was doing a bang-up business. The boy in the chair softly waved to him once and said something Nick couldn't understand, then gripping the chair's arms firmly again he turned back to the field.

The A's left the dugout and took their positions. The team had lost three of the first four Yankee games and their fans were riled up; they raised their fists as they cheered. Miller and Haas were playing instead of Speaker and Cobb today, and that would surely help. As Miller jogged out to right field, Nick watched him intently. He was sixty or seventy feet from Nick when he stopped and turned towards home plate, and before he did, Nick was able to see his face.

Rube Walberg was pitching for the A's and got the first two batters out. Then his nemesis, Babe Ruth—after pausing to touch the crippled batboy's back—stepped up to the plate. Ruth had hit four home runs off Walberg the year before.

Nick stared at Ruth, a flood of anger rising in his chest. There he was, the great hero, the Sultan of Swat. His stomach was bigger than Nick remembered—not surprising, considering how he stuffed himself—but his legs looked thinner. From this far off, Nick couldn't see his features. He took two strikes then smacked the third pitch high and deep to right. Bing Miller turned and ran in Nick's direction. He disappeared behind the wall but Nick knew from the shift in the roar of the crowd that he'd made the catch. He saw Ruth stop just short of first and head for the dugout.

The Yanks took the field. Ruth trotted to right, and now Nick could see his ruddy wide face and his stupid grin, and he felt another rush of rage.

The Yankee pitcher, Wilcy Moore, was sharp, and the game moved quickly. Nick watched Ruth bat two more times. He drove in a run with a single but didn't homer.

Every so often Nick looked at the boy in the chair. When the A's got a hit he would push himself up just slightly then settle back down again.

At the end of the sixth, Nick left. The high May sun and

strong emotions were draining him, and tonight the café would be packed. It always was on Saturdays.

The A's lost the game—this made four out of five to the Yanks—and the Home Plate regulars, all of whom followed baseball, agreed that Connie Mack's team, while excellent, was just no match for New York. "What an outfit," Butterball Saleski said from his perch at the end of the bar. "Power, speed, defense, pitching... You'd have to be crazy to bet against them." Happy Ernie agreed: "The A's are good enough to win most years, but not this year, not with the power the Yankees have." And Hesitant Harvey said, "M-maybe if Ruth and G-Gehrig get hurt the A's have a chance, b-but otherwise, f-f—" "Forget it," chimed in Iron Mike, who had the annoying habit of finishing Harvey's sentences.

The joint was jumping, roaring with voices and layered with cigar, pipe, cigarette and sometimes reefer smoke. The reefer often, but not exclusively, came from the boys in the band. The sports and their glittering painted ladies were having a grand time out on the floor, dancing with abandon to the jazz. Nick envied them—their energy, their life, their spirit. He never felt like dancing anymore, and knew he'd never feel like it again.

It was just after ten when Babe Ruth appeared at the door with a dame on each arm, laughing in that raucous way Nick knew so well and smoking a cigar.

A shock went through Nick's body, then a surge of rage. Here he was, right here, Babe Ruth, the married man, the German who'd escaped the war because married men were exempt, cheating on his wife again—which was very old news, but now he was also cheating on his girlfriend, Claire.

The knife Nick used to cut up lemons, limes and oranges lay on the bar in front of him, and he wanted to run up to Ruth and plunge it into his neck. But that would be far too easy and far too foolish; his plan was much better than that. This man who lived on a grand stage must die on a grand stage too, it

97

was only right.

Nick was sweating like mad. He told himself to calm down, but his hands were shaking as he sliced a lime.

He gritted his teeth as Ruth bellied up to the bar and stood right in front of him. Blowing a cloud of smoke Ruth said, "So what'll you broads gonna have, tell the man."

One of the women was short and blond and heavily made up. "Brown on the rocks," she said in a girlish voice. The other one, a brunette with big eyes said, "Yeah, me too." "Same here, keed," Ruth said, "and make it a double."

Trembling with anger, Nick fixed the drinks, thinking, *keed.* Ruth called everyone that. The only name he could remember was his own. It used to drive his teammates nuts.

Nick slid the drinks across to him and his women. Ruth felt in his pocket and tossed a bill onto the counter. Nick went to make change but Ruth said, "Keep it, keed," then frowned and said, "You look kinda familiar. You work here last year?"

"No," Nick said. Then somebody pushed his way up to Ruth with a paper and pen in his hand. "For my boy, okay?" he said. "His name is Joey."

As Nick watched Ruth signing the paper he wondered: What does it feel like to be like him, to be loved and admired by millions of people? They didn't just love that you hit home runs, they loved *you* as a person—or who they thought that person was. What did it feel like to have all that money and fame when you put your head down on your pillow at night? Money and fame had never driven Nick; all he'd wanted to do was play the game he loved as well as he could, at its highest level. Still, he couldn't help wondering what it was like to be in Ruth's shoes.

Somebody else came up and The Babe signed again, then waved off two other autograph seekers. "That's all for now," he said as he lit up a fresh cigar, then he started to dance with the blonde. Nick wondered if he'd learned to flush a toilet yet.

As he watched Ruth dance, Nick thought: *Just one of many.* Plenty of ballplayers cheated on their wives. They were gone for three weeks at a time in various cities and most of them weren't angels. But in Nick's playing days he'd respected the ones who were.

Charlie and Jake saved Ruth's seat at the bar and when he came back he was sweating hard. He gave more autographs, and Nick wondered what *that* was like—having people hound you every minute, everywhere you went. He himself would hate it; it would be like an iron weight around his neck. They even told Ruth what to write: "Good luck." "Best wishes." "To my pal." He was in an expansive mood and turned no one away.

"You know what I like about this place?" he said to Jake. "It's like the dive my parents used to run in Baltimore, not fancied up, you know? They had eight kids, and six of them died. I ever tell you that before?"

"Yes, Babe, you did," Jake said.

"Yeah, me and my little sister Mamie are the only ones who made it. I don't know how Mamie feels, but while I'm still alive I'm gonna *live!* Gimme another double, keed."

Jake poured the drink. Then a massive square-headed guy with a jutting jaw came up to Ruth and said, "Big man," and Ruth looked puzzled. "You want me to write that?" he said. "Where's your paper?"

"Oh, so you think you're funny?" the man said, sneering.

Nick had been keeping an eye on this guy all night; he looked like a German, a mean one. He'd gotten real tight early on and was now obnoxiously drunk. He gave Ruth a poke on the shoulder and said, "You ain't so great."

Nick was tempted to let Ruth handle this situation by himself, but dealing with jerks like these was part of his job. He came around from behind the bar and took the man's elbow. "Okay, buddy," he said. "It's time to go home."

"Getcher hands off me, punk," the guy said loudly.

Nick forcefully steered him through the crowd, thinking, *Nobody touches Babe Ruth except me, you creep, he's all mine.*

When they reached the door the guy took a wild swing at

99

him and missed. Nick put his leg behind the guy and gave him a shove, sending him into the alley on his back. The guy was slow getting up; his eyes looked glazed. "Get lost," Nick said, and returned to the bar.

Ruth kept ordering drinks—for himself, his women, and various patrons. God only knew how much money he spent, and everyone loved him for it: the patrons and Jake and Charlie and Sid, the boys in the band... By closing time he could just about walk. Tomorrow the Yanks had off, so he wouldn't play. But he could if he had to, and better than those who had gone to bed early and slept all night; he'd done it plenty of times when Nick was with the Sox. Ruth had the constitution of a bull and would probably live to be a hundred no matter how much he abused himself. Unless he had some kind of...accident.

As he left the bar, his female companions holding him up, he looked back at Nick and said, "Thanks for snuffin that lunkhead, keed. Say, don't I know you from somewhere...?"

The A's went to Washington, lost, then returned to Philly and lost to the Yankees again. Then they started a month-long road trip. They would not return until June 27th—to play the Yankees again.

Each day, Nick walked down Twentieth Street, which was quiet and empty now that the A's were gone, but no rental signs appeared in the windows there.

13

THEN ON JUNE 21ST, a muggy Thursday, he finally saw it: "Second Floor Room For Rent."

He walked up the four wide wooden steps of the porch and rang the bell. Inside, a piano was playing. The piece was familiar to Nick and he liked it a lot but didn't know its name; he'd never paid much attention to music. It stopped and he waited.

A shadow moved behind the double door's etched glass and then the door's left half came open.

The woman standing there was about his age. She was very attractive, tall, with clear brown eyes and brown hair pulled back in a bun. No makeup, as far as Nick could tell. She was wearing a long yellow dress. "I saw your sign in the window," Nick said.

"Come in," the woman said.

Nick stepped into the vestibule. It had dark green tiles halfway up the walls; the plaster above them was brown. He followed the woman into the hall, which was painted a pale bluegray, and her dress against this background seemed to glow. A rolltop desk was standing against the wall, and down at the hall's end, Nick saw a kitchen stove. Past the desk, a flight of stairs began. On his right, through a wide doorway, he saw half of a parlor: a sofa and coffee table, a bookcase, and a card table up against one wall.

He heard a soft squeaking sound then and a boy in a wicker wheelchair appeared in the doorway—the boy Nick had seen on the roof. No cap on his head and his brown hair was shaggy but short. He was holding a baseball. *Tiny Tim,* Nick thought.

The woman said, "The room fronts on Twentieth Street. It's not as quiet as the room in back, but if you're a baseball fan, you can watch the games from there."

"I'd like to take a look at it," Nick said.

He followed the woman up the stairs. Her posture was very erect; *sturdy*, Nick thought.

At the landing, a door was open part way and Nick saw a dressing table and chair and framed photographs on a wall. In the hallway he saw a bathroom. "You'd share this with one other person," the woman said. She walked past a door that was closed and then opened the door at the end of the hall.

The room was twice the size of the one Nick was living in now. It was sunny and cheerful, papered in pale blue vertical stripes. It contained a bed with a blue bedspread, a nightstand with a clock, a dresser, a two-seat sofa, and a round wooden table with two chairs under it next to a large bay window. Nick went to the window and looked outside—at Shibe Park's right field wall and, above it, an excellent view of the playing field. "I'm interested," he said.

The woman nodded. "I rent by the month," she said. "You have to pay in advance, and the rate is twenty dollars."

"That's fine," Nick said. He looked at the empty playing field again and thought, *It couldn't be better.*

"My name is Anna Shuster," the woman said and Nick thought: *Shuster, a German name*, and felt a quick surge of anger. He almost considered not taking the room and then thought, *No, to rent from a German is perfect.* "And I'm Nick Hudson," he said.

"So where are you currently living, Mr. Hudson?"

"Not far from here, but my room is quite small and I'd like something bigger."

"And what kind of work do you do?"

"I wash dishes at the Home Plate Café."

"I know the establishment," Anna said, and Nick sensed

disapproval in her tone. "Ballplayers go there."

"That's right."

"I don't rent to ballplayers, they're untrustworthy."

"I believe it."

"And I don't allow smoking."

"I don't smoke. So when can I take the room?"

"On Saturday. I'll need five dollars up front."

"That's fine."

Nick followed her down the stairs. He was wondering what her husband did—or if she had a husband.

The boy was still there in his wheelchair, still holding his baseball. Now Nick could see a piano across the room and near it, on the wall, a painting of some boaters on a lake. "This is Willie, my son," Anna said. "Willie, this is Mr. Hudson, he's taking the empty room."

"Hello," Willie said.

"Hello," Nick said, and thought: *Willie. Probably named after Kaiser Wilhelm.* He said, "Are you the one who was making the music?"

"Yes."

"What was the name of that piece?"

"*Fur Elise.* It's by Beethoven."

"You played it very well."

"Thank you."

Anna sat at the rolltop desk and brought forth a book of receipts. Nick took out his wallet and gave her a five. She wrote a receipt, tore it out of the book, and handed it to him. "Thank you," she said, and the baseball that Willie was holding slipped out of his hands, hit his leg and rolled over to Nick.

With his left hand, his pitching hand, Nick retrieved it. This was the first time he'd held a baseball in more than ten years. It felt different, lighter and tighter than what he remembered. Jimmy was right: they had changed it. It had a few smudges and scuffmarks and a signature: Mule Haas. He turned it around in his hand a few times and then gave it back to the boy. "An official American League ball," he said.

"That's right," Willie said. "It was hit by Mule Haas, a homer. It went through Uncle Sol's window, the side part, and landed right next to him on his sofa. He was reading the paper and said that it scared him to death. He laughed when he gave it to me. It didn't really scare him to death but he died anyway. The A's had to buy a new window for us. I like Mule Haas, but Bucketfoot Al is my favorite A."

"Al Simmons," Nick said.

"Uh-huh. He lives up the street in the Conwells' house."

"Is that right."

"Uh-huh. Sometimes when I'm out on the porch I see him walk by and I wave to him—and he waves back."

"That's great."

"It is. But he sleeps too late so Peanuts Sullivan has to wake him up in the morning. Peanuts is older than I am but smaller. He has a condition, like me, but a different one. He got Al Simmons to sign a ball for me, and Al got Mule Haas to sign this one."

"Wonderful."

"It is. Even though Peanuts is little he runs real fast and when balls are hit over the wall he gets a lot of them. He sells them to people or turns them in for free tickets. Bucketfoot Al's real name is Aloysius Szymanski, not Al Simmons. How's come some people change their names?"

"Maybe their real names are hard for people to spell."

"I bet that's right. Are you a baseball player?"

"No."

"You kind of look like one."

"Well I'm not."

"Do you like baseball?"

"I like it okay."

"You can see the games from your room. Uncle Sol watched them all the time. But the best place to see them is up on the roof."

"Uh-huh."

104

"My mother won't rent to baseball players because they get drunk. Do you get drunk?"

"Willie, that's rude," Anna said getting up from her desk.

"I'm sorry," Willie said. "But another baseball player, Eddie Winters, he lives down the end of the block, when he doesn't do good in a game he gets drunk and starts yelling."

"All right, that's enough of that talk," Anna said.

"He's not very good anymore."

"That's too bad," Nick said. "Well, listen, I have to get going. I'll see you Saturday."

"With the balance of the rent," Anna said.

"With the balance of the rent."

After Nick left, Willie swung his chair around and wheeled himself into the parlor. "I like Mr. Hudson," he said. "I wish he played baseball, though."

"Well, I don't," Anna said walking into the room.

"I really miss Uncle Sol. He told me those stories about long ago when he was a boy in Austria."

"Uncle Sol was a very nice man."

"Yes. How's come he died?"

"Willie, how many times have you asked me that?"

"I know, but I don't understand what attacked him."

"I told you before, that's just what they call it."

"But it was inside him, so did he attack himself?"

"Of course not."

"Did I attack myself? Is that why I have my condition?"

"You know very well you were born with it."

"Well will something attack me and kill me when I get old like Uncle Sol?"

"You won't be old for a long, long time."

"But when I am."

"Probably not."

"I didn't like how they put Uncle Sol in the ground."

"That was only his body, not his soul," Anna said.

"I know, but I still didn't like it."

105

They now heard halting footsteps on the stairs, and after a minute a woman appeared in the hallway beside the desk. She was elderly, hefty, and garishly made up, with orange hair and bright red lips and spots of rouge on her cheeks.

"Good afternoon, Flora," Anna said.

"Good afternoon," the woman said in a piercing, quavering voice. "Did you rent the room to that young man?"

"I did."

"I hope he's quiet."

"He'll have to be, or I'll ask him to leave."

"Sol was so quiet."

"Yes, he was."

"A pity he died. He was such good company. What's this man's name?"

"Mr. Hudson."

The woman nodded. "That's nice, a nice name. Some of the names these days are so hard to remember, especially the Polish ones. And the spelling? Im-POSS-ible! All those Zs and Ks. Well, I'm going out for my constitutional now."

"Can we play cards later?" Willie asked.

"I'll see how I feel."

"Don't walk too far in this heat."

Flora smiled. "I won't."

When she left, Willie rolled himself up to the large picture window that looked onto Twentieth Street and Shibe Park's right field wall. Two boys his age were having a catch in the street. They were wearing short pants, but he always wore long pants since sunlight might damage his skin. Peanuts Sullivan always wore knickers; he said that they made him run faster. Willie knew both of the boys in the street, they went to the Saint Columba School, but school wouldn't start again till September. He didn't go to school at all except at home. He looked at the baseball in his lap. "I hope Mr. Hudson is friendly," he said.

"I'm sure he will be," Anna said. "As long as you don't annoy him with too many questions."

"I won't," Willie said, then rolled himself up to the piano and started to play—Chopin's *Polonaise Opus 53 in A Flat Major*—which meant that his mood was mellow. It was a lively, good-spirited piece, one of Anna's favorites, and she was glad that he was playing it.

She sat on the sofa, feeling immense relief. The room would start bringing in money again, money she sorely needed. Mr. Hudson did not have a very good job, but seemed pleasant enough. As long as he paid his rent on time and acted decently, as Sol Cohen had, that was all she cared about.

Willie stopped playing. He said, "The A's come home next Wednesday. I just can't wait."

"They've been gone a long time," Anna said.

"As soon as they get back, they play the Yankees. I hope they murder them."

"Willie, that is not nice language," Anna said.

14

THAT SATURDAY, JUNE 23RD, Nick moved to Twentieth Street. All he had was his carryall bag, his overcoat—slung over his arm—and a roll of canvas containing the Springfield rifle he bought right after he found the room.

He mounted the steps of the porch and rang the bell. Anna opened the door. "Good afternoon, Mr. Hudson."

"Good afternoon," Nick said, and followed her into the hallway.

Willie was parked in the parlor doorway. Nick wondered how long he'd been waiting there to observe this momentous event.

"Hello, Mr. Hudson," he said.

"Hello, Willie."

"Is that a fishing rod?"

Nick didn't know what he meant for a second, then realized: the roll of canvas. "Yes, that's what it is," he said.

"Can you show it to me?"

"Willie, please," Anna said, "Mr. Hudson is busy now, he has to get settled in."

"Drat!" Willie said.

His mother scowled at him, then said to Nick, "Your room is unlocked. When you come down to pay your rent, I'll give you your keys."

Nick nodded. "Okay." He was looking across her shoulder at the piano that stood near the large front window. In the room's right front corner a small lamp sat on a table and next to it was a treadle sewing machine.

"I'd like to go fishing someday," Willie said. "I never did."

"Well maybe we can work that out," Nick said, and started up the stairs.

In his room he set his bag and the roll of canvas on the bed, hung up his coat in the closet, and went to the large bay window.

He parted the center section's curtains. The lower sashes of all three sections—left side, right side, center—were raised, and all had screens. The top sashes had no screens and were closed. He looked across the street to the baseball field.

He didn't see how he could miss. At the shooting range he had hit targets much farther off than this with ease.

He left the room, closing his door, and a woman was there in the hallway. She was seventy-five at the very least. Her hair was brilliant orange, her lips were cherry red, and circles of rouge inflamed her cheeks. Give her a funny hat and some floppy shoes, Nick thought, and Barnum & Bailey would snap her up. "You must be Mr. Hudson," she said in a high-pitched voice.

"That's right."

"I'm Flora Cavendish, the other tenant here. We'll be sharing the bathroom."

"So I've heard."

"Mr. Cohen, the man who used to rent that room, was a very fas-TID-i-ous person."

"That's good."

"Are you fas-TID-i-ous?"

"You might say that."

"I'm up very early and usually out of the way by seven."

"Uh-huh."

"Do you play a radio?"

"I don't have a radio."

"Mr. Cohen did, but he kept it low."

"I don't plan to get one," Nick said. "Anyway, I work at night." Anticipating more from Mrs. Cavendish he added, "At the Home Plate Café, washing dishes and cleaning up."

"I know the place. Baseball players go there."

"Yes, they do."

"The trouble with front rooms on Twentieth Street is that sometimes balls come through your window. It happened to Mr. Cohen more than once. The last time, it scared him to death. And now he's dead, poor soul."

"A shame."

"He loved baseball. I can't see it myself, grown men in funny outfits running around in the heat and hitting a ball with a stick."

"It does seem kind of silly," Nick said. "And just think of how much they get paid for doing that."

"It's out-RAGE-ous!"

"Indeed."

Mrs. Cavendish smiled. "I'm sure you'll enjoy it here, it's a real family atmosphere."

"That's nice."

"Willie is like my grandson, the grandson I never had. He calls me Aunt Flora. He used to call Mr. Cohen Uncle Sol."

"So I've heard."

"He'll probably be calling you Uncle Nick before too long."

"Could be," Nick said. He wanted to ask her: *Where is the kid's old man?* but didn't. He said, "Well, listen, Mrs. Cavendish, I have to see Mrs. Shuster now."

"A pleasure to meet you, Mr. Hudson. And please, call me Flora."

"And you call me Nick. I'll see you later."

Anna was at her hallway desk. Nick took out his wallet and gave her the rest of the rent. She thanked him and wrote a receipt. He liked the look of the hair on the back of her neck and suddenly wanted to touch it. Except for hugging Mrs. Hill, he hadn't touched a woman in over ten years. He took the receipt along with his keys. "The small one is for the front door and the big one is for your room," Anna said.

"I won't be coming in until after one most nights," Nick said.

"The Home Plate stays open that late?"

"Until midnight. We do a good business, especially on weekends."

Anna frowned. "Really. Each time I walk past the place, it seems pretty empty."

"Sometimes it is, but at other times it's quite busy."

Willie was still in the doorway and asked: "When do you think you'll go fishing, Mr. Hudson?"

"Willie, please," his mother said, "don't pester Mr. Hudson."

"I'm not pestering, I just want to know."

"I haven't really thought about it," Nick said. "I'll tell you when I decide."

"Do you like the A's?"

"I do."

"On Wednesday they come back home for three games with the Yankees. I'm going to watch from the roof. You can watch from your room, but it's better up on the roof."

"How do you get up there?"

"The people who owned this house before us built some steps, and Mother carries me up."

Nick looked at Anna, who said, "He's not very heavy. Not heavy enough, as a matter of fact."

"If you'd like me to give you a hand with that, just let me know," Nick said.

He went back to his room and locked the door. He pulled the table and chairs away from the window then parted its curtains and lowered the center section's bottom sash, covering the screen. He tried to lower the upper sash but it was stuck; it probably hadn't been opened in quite some time. He banged on its sides with his fists till he got it to move. Its pulleys were badly in need of oil and squeaked as it descended. At least its cords didn't break; they looked pretty old.

A warm breeze washed over his face from the open

window. He pushed the curtains back into place, leaving a gap of eight inches or so, and then went to the bed. He unrolled the canvas that lay there, picked up the Springfield, and went to the window again.

Keeping the rifle's barrel a few inches back from the window, he flipped the rear sight up and aimed at the ballpark, focusing on right field. He held steady a minute, then lowered the rifle again. He had only fired it once, right after he'd bought it, at the tiny range behind Goldstein's army surplus store. It was a beauty, as good as the one he had carried during the war. He pushed its sight down and ran his hand over its stock and suddenly pictured himself in a sweltering trench, facing the onrushing Germans. He flushed with hot sweat and put the gun down on the bed.

He rolled it back up in the canvas and set it in the bottom drawer of the dresser that stood against the room's south wall. He opened the carryall bag, put his socks and underwear in the top dresser drawer, then hung up his windbreaker, shirts and pants in the closet and set his extra pair of shoes on the closet floor.

Reaching into the bag again he took out a five round magazine and five extra bullets, far more than he needed if things went right. He put them in the bottom drawer beside the rifle, then took out the only remaining things in the bag: two rectangular sheets of lead he had found in the South Street junk shop; they had come from the roof of a house that had been torn down. He laid them on top of the bullets.

He would stand well back from the window, the curtains parted a bit as they were right now, and no one would see the rifle. He would wait until one of the A's hit a long drive to left and the crowd was roaring, all eyes on the soaring ball—including those of the Yankee fielders—and then he would fire. Nobody in the stands would hear the shots because of the roar they were making, and then they would see Ruth suddenly fall to the ground. They would probably think that the stomach condition that hit him a couple of years ago was acting up again. But he wouldn't move, and the trainers would hurry across the field to him and maybe the umpires too and the truth would be known and they'd carry him off the field on a stretcher. The fans would be stunned. The police would be everywhere.

Nick wouldn't see all this; he'd have no time to admire his handiwork. As soon as the deed was done he would wrap the sheets of lead around the Springfield and roll it up in the canvas. He would go to the Delaware River by trolley car, unroll the canvas and heave the gun out in the water as far as he could. He'd throw the extra ammo out there too. Then he'd head downtown to the sporting goods store he'd seen on Market Street, buy a fishing rod, wrap it up in the canvas and ride back to Twentieth Street, where all would be chaos. If Willie or anyone else asked him where he had been he would tell them that he had gone fishing.

He'd act totally shocked. Someone had shot and killed Babe Ruth on the playing field during a game? What kind of a monster would do such a thing, and why? He was more than a monster, he was a madman, Nick would say, and all would agree. Had they caught the fiend? he would ask. Not yet? Did they have any clues as to who he was? Oh, he'd play it up big.

He was worried about the noise the shots would make. The crowd as they yelled wouldn't hear them but what about people down on the street or up on the roofs or in the house? Well, they'd probably think they'd heard a car backfire—until they saw Ruth on the ground.

The cops would figure out that the shots had come from one of the houses and would grill everybody. By then the lead-wrapped gun would be sunk in the Delaware's mud. Nick knew he'd be one of the likeliest suspects—anyone with access to a second floor front room on Twentieth Street would be—but no one could prove a thing.

The cops were clever though. They would no doubt discover that years ago he had known Babe Ruth—had even roomed with him once. "That's true," he would say. "And he

113

was a great man, a wonderful man. Why anyone would want to harm him I can't imagine." And the cops would not believe him. They had to arrest somebody, and since he was a veteran who knew how to shoot a gun and had known the victim, they'd question him over and over and maybe get rough, beating his back with a rubber hose the way they did the colored men they interrogated. He vowed that even if they did, he wouldn't talk.

But if somehow they managed to trip him up? His life was over anyway, so what did it matter? He sniffed as he thought: *If they catch me, I'll be world famous, front-page news—as the man who murdered Babe Ruth.*

He would hate that—and wouldn't be able to live with it. And *wouldn't* live with it. They would say he was crazy, a maniac: the nine years he'd spent in a madhouse would prove it. So instead of murdering him they would lock him away again, this time for good. But he'd fool them; madhouse beds had sheets.

If he wasn't caught he would stay on at Anna's for months so as not to arouse suspicion. He'd continue to work at the Home Plate Café, leading his regular normal life. Then when things had cooled down he could leave. But leave for where?

He looked out the window again and thought: *An easy shot.* And if he succeeded he'd finally be healed. But if he was caught they would claim he was crazier than ever.

His plan was not original. He'd realized this a while ago. In 1909, Shibe Park's inaugural year, someone had threatened to shoot the Tigers' star, Ty Cobb, from a house on this street. Cobb had spiked the A's Frank Baker badly, and angry fans swore they would take revenge on him the next time he came to town. He happened to come right after Nick's father died, when baseball was far from Nick's mind, but now after all these years he remembered this. There were so many crucial things he'd forgotten about the war and about St. Luke's that might be lost forever, but he could remember those threats against Ty Cobb. It seemed ironic that Cobb was now playing

114

at Shibe—as one of the A's.

He pushed the window's top sash up again then raised the bottom sash. The breeze flowed over the screen and rustled the curtains. He lay on the bed where a dead man had lain not long ago, and slept for over an hour.

It was Saturday night and the Home Plate was swinging. The painted young ladies were laughing and flailing their arms, the long strings of pearls around their necks swaying from side to side.

"All tryin to be Clara Bow," Charlie shouted above the noise.

Nick frowned at him. "Who?"

"Clara Bow, The 'It' Girl, don't you go to the movies?"

"Not often," Nick said.

As he worked he was hardly aware of the flappers; his mind was fixed on Anna Shuster and her son. She hadn't mentioned a husband and the boy hadn't mentioned a father. Was Anna divorced? Was her husband dead? And what the hell was wrong with that scrawny kid?

He forced himself to concentrate on the customers, to respond to their small talk. A lot of it concerned the A's, who were thirteen games behind the Yankees now with half the season gone. The three game series starting on Wednesday was crucial, all agreed. If the A's could sweep the Yanks, they would still have a slender chance at the pennant. If they lost all three, they were doomed.

A couple of Phillies players were present tonight. They sat at the end of the bar, eyeing the ladies, and they looked beat. They had split a twin bill with the Giants at Baker Bowl this afternoon, but their team was already hopelessly out of the pennant race. Nick had never played on a terrible team. He thought it must be hell.

Vince went from place to place soliciting bets on games. He took money from Happy Ernie, Iron Mike and Butterball, and then came up to Nick. "Want to give it a shot?"

"No thanks,"

"Just a little one? Just a buck?"

"I don't have a buck to spare," Nick said.

It was then that a short compact young man with thick black greased-back hair came up to Vince, took his arm and pulled him aside. Nick had seen this guy in the place a couple of times before.

"Slick Dominic," Charlie said. "A Scorpion, and he packs heat."

"A scorpion?" To Nick he looked like a well-groomed rat.

"That's the name of Sal Mario's gang," Charlie said.

Nick was aware that Vince worked for Sal, the racketeer who supplied the Home Plate's booze. Sal had come to the speak a couple of times since Nick started tending bar. Jake had pointed him out: a beefy sharp dresser of fifty or so with dusky jowls, thick eyebrows and a sneering smile. "There's a rumor that Vince is skimming bets," Charlie said. "I hope not, those boys play rough."

Tough guy, Nick thought as he looked at Dominic. How tough would he be with shells going off all around and the air filled with bullets and poison gas?

The rat let go of Vince's arm and gave him a pat on the back. Vince smiled weakly, and Dominic made his way through the crowd and out the door.

When Nick walked back to Anna's house at one-fifteen the streets were deserted. The streetlamp in front of her porch cast a wide ring of light on the sidewalk and shined on the ballpark's wall.

The lamp on the little table that Nick had noticed earlier glowed in the window, seeming to welcome him. He climbed the steps to the porch and used the key to the door for the very first time.

The house was dead quiet. When he locked the door behind him the sound seemed loud.

He now knew that Anna and Willie slept in the dining room

116

with a fabric partition between them. He could see that their door was closed. Their bathroom was in the shed past the kitchen, which also held a laundry tub and a wringer washing machine. Anna had said he could do his wash there if he wanted to. She did all the linens once a week and did Flora's wash for a dollar.

Nick mounted the stairs and one of them creaked in the silence. When he reached the landing he heard loud snoring coming from Flora's room.

He went down the hallway and unlocked his door and crossed the room in the light that came from the streetlamp. He looked at the wall and the ball field beyond it, totally black, and thought of the rifle that lay in his dresser drawer. *The fishing rod.* If the kid had a father, wouldn't he take him fishing? That's what fathers did, right? That's what *his* father had done.

He took off his clothes and lay back on the bed. But even though he was exhausted, he couldn't sleep.

15

NICK'S DREAMS WERE NUMEROUS, woke him often, and he ended up sleeping late. When he came downstairs, Flora was at the parlor's card table playing a game of solitaire. "You were very quiet last night when you came home," she said. "I didn't hear you at all, and I thank you for that."

"I usually don't make a racket at night," Nick said.

"Thank heavens!" said Flora. "My husband, Harold, was terrible on that score—and many other scores. He'd go out and drink and consort with women and come home after I'd gone to bed and slam things around. An im-POSS-ible situation. My attempts at reform were completely fruitless, I finally had to admit that he'd never change, and I walked away. He was a tippler and phil-AND-erer through and through."

The front door came open and Anna and Willie appeared, the boy in his wheelchair. They were wearing their Sunday best.

"And how was church today?" Flora asked.

"Uplifting," Anna said.

"As it should be."

"I thought it was boring," Willie said as he wheeled himself into the parlor. "It's always boring."

"You will appreciate it more," Flora said, "when you get older."

"Then how's come you don't go?"

"I talk to God right here."

"I wish I could do that too," Willie said. He turned to Nick.

118

"Mr. Hudson, do you go to church?"

"Not usually."

"How's come?"

"I used to go when I was a kid."

"Was it boring?"

Nick smiled. "Yes."

"Willie, go change your clothes," Anna said.

"Okay. And after I do, can we play cards, Aunt Flora?"

"It's time for lunch," Anna said.

Nick's lunch and supper were in a bag upstairs: two sandwiches from the café—an egg salad on white and a ham on rye. He always got up too late to eat any breakfast. If he wanted to buy something else today to go with the sandwiches, tough: nothing was open on Sundays—no restaurants, cafés, diners, grocery stores—because of the Blue Laws. *Religion,* Nick grumbled under his breath as he went back up to his room.

There wasn't any breeze today and the room was hot and close; it felt like a storm was coming.

Nick had taken a soda bottle from work and filled it with water and put it on his nightstand. He took a long drink from it now, then sat the table in front of the big bow window looking out at Shibe Park. The stands and the field were completely deserted because it was Sunday. In ballparks in other cities games would be played today, but not in dear old Philly.

As Nick started in on the ham on rye, a wave of anxiety struck. When he finished the sandwich he drank again, then sat there staring at the field. He suddenly needed to walk, and he left the room.

He went down Twentieth Street to the patch of green on the other side of Lehigh Avenue, Reyburn Park, usually called the Square. Some kids were playing ball on the diamond there. He'd heard that a semi-pro team called the Wildcats used that field in the evenings. Scouts from the A's and Phillies watched their games sometimes and had actually signed a

119

couple of sandlot players. He remembered his sandlot days and that time Jimmy Harriman had talked about, when he'd had twenty strikeouts against North End.

Seized by a terrible sense of loss he walked under leaden skies for blocks, out to the cemetery—the one where his parents were buried. He found their graves and stood there sadly looking at them and then he began to think of Alice's grave. He turned away and walked again and the rain finally came. By the time he got back to the house he was thoroughly drenched.

As soon as he came through the door he smelled something delicious. Roast beef?

Willie was at the piano and didn't look up as Nick mounted the stairs to his room and his supper, the egg salad sandwich.

The rain lasted till early morning, when thick humid heat replaced it. Nick went to the shooting range and practiced for almost two hours in the sweltering glare.

"I guess you didn't buy no Springfield yet," said Angelo, "or you'd be usin it." He mopped his sweaty forehead with something that looked like a rag but was no doubt his handkerchief.

"I decided against it," Nick said. "I decided I couldn't afford it."

"You still plan to do some huntin?"

"I'd like to. I'll have to see."

"If you bagged a deer, would you know how to dress it?"

"No."

"Then what would you do with it?"

"I don't know."

"There's this meat locker over on Christian Street, they'll dress it and keep it for you. Venison is sure good eatin, you ever try it?"

He had. He remembered: In a forest in France a doe had appeared out of nowhere and one of the soldiers shot it. They dressed it and cooked it and wolfed it down.

"I did eat venison once," Nick said. "It was very good." He tried to remember more about that forest, where it was and when he was there, but nothing else would come.

He lifted the Springfield slowly and aimed at the target again, imagining it was Ruth. He did this every time he shot. He clenched his jaw and squeezed the trigger and hit the bull's-eye again for the eighth straight time.

Nick practiced the next day, Tuesday, too, another scorcher, and was just as sharp. In the Home Plate that night the customers talked about how the Athletics were not at all sharp; they had just lost four in a row to Washington, which was only a so-so team. "They better step it up tomorrow against the Yanks," said eternally pessimistic Jackie Dodd as he swallowed the last of his beer, "or their season is cooked."

Nick slept very little on Tuesday night. A lot of the time he sat on the edge of his bed in the light coming in through the window, seeing himself at that window the next afternoon with the Springfield in his hands.

At eleven A.M., when he started downstairs, the house was rich with the odor of baking. On Monday he'd run into Flora again in the hallway and commented on the aroma.

"Anna bakes three times a week," she said, "for Leewright's Grocery on Somerset Street. She sews for people too, does whatever she can to make ends meet. A war widow's pension doesn't go far, especially with Willie's medical bills."

"Oh...no," Nick said, absorbing this. "I'm sure it doesn't."

When he reached the foot of the stairs, Willie was parked in the parlor doorway. He was wearing a white tee shirt with dark blue horizontal stripes that made him look like a prisoner—which, in a way, he was. His hair was now convict short. *Mother at work*, Nick thought. A barber was out of the question, of course, because of the expense.

"Are you going to watch the A's play the Yankees today?" Willie asked.

"I don't know yet," Nick said. "I have a few things to do."

"You can watch from your room, but the roof is better."

"You told me that before."

"Oh, yes, that's right, I did. Do you think you'll go fishing today?"

"Maybe, I'm not sure."

"If you do, will you take me along?"

"Not today. Some other day."

Now Anna came down the hall from the kitchen and said, "Good morning, Mr. Hudson."

"Good morning, Mrs. Shuster." She looked suddenly different because of what Flora had told him.

"Willie, you can practice now that Mr. Hudson's awake."

Nick shrugged. "The music won't bother me," Mrs. Shuster. "Willie can practice any time."

"We didn't want to disturb your rest."

"That's very thoughtful of you, but really, it won't disturb me. I enjoy Willie's playing. He's very good."

"He is," Anna said. "He has a fine teacher who comes every Monday. He's from the Curtis Institute."

"Sorry, but I don't know what that is," Nick said.

"It's an excellent music school that was started four years ago by Mrs. Bok."

"I see," Nick said. He wondered who Mrs. Bok was, but didn't ask.

"Professor Shultz, my teacher, says I have good hands," Willie said. He held his right one out. "Look at my fingers, how long they are."

Nick nodded. "Curveball hands."

"What?"

"With fingers like those, you could throw a good curveball."

"How do you know that?"

"I read it somewhere."

"Oh. But I'll never throw curveballs—or fastballs either. I'll never play baseball."

"Maybe someday."

"I don't think so, I have a condition. But I'm really good at piano, and if the condition doesn't attack my fingers, someday I'll play in Carnegie Hall."

Suddenly he began to cough. His face turned red and his mother frowned. When he stopped he cleared his throat and said, "I'd like to call you Uncle Nick, Mr. Hudson. Would that be okay?"

Flora had been right on target. "That would be fine," Nick said. "You can call me just plain Nick if you want to."

"But that's not polite."

"That's right," Anna said. "Uncle Nick is better."

"Whatever you want," Nick said. "Well, I have to get going now. See you soon."

He left the house and walked up Twentieth to Somerset, turned left, and entered Leewright's Grocery Store.

He had been in the place before, back when he'd looked for work, and remembered Mr. Leewright, a wiry, thin-faced, impatient man whose movements were quick and jerky. When Nick had asked if he needed help, Leewright's "No!" was loud and brusque, as if the question had insulted him.

The wall behind the store's oak counter had shelves that rose up to the ceiling and held an amazing array of cans and boxes and jars: soups and soaps and syrups and cereals...tons of stuff. On the counter itself Nick saw a display of muffins and squares and an apple pie. A card said, "Baked goods by Anna." He bought two blueberry muffins.

He took them to the Square and sat on a bench and ate them. They were far and away the best he had ever tasted. Even better, he had to admit, than his mother's.

It was close to noon and the day was really warming up; the air hung heavily in the trees. He looked at Shibe Park's ornate corner turret, wondering what went on behind its windows. Must be offices up there, he thought. Well whoever occupied those offices and whoever bought tickets down at the turret's base would get their money's worth today. And Babe Ruth would get what he deserved—in front of thousands. In spite of

123

the steamy heat the thought of it made Nick shiver.

When you killed somebody in war the act was put in a special box and not called murder, but that's what it was. He had already murdered many men, so what was one more? Men who had killed in the war were everywhere, all over the country. It was strange to think about all those murderers trained by the government roaming around on the loose like that. *Murderers like me*, Nick thought. We're trained to kill and then are supposed to forget about it. And some did. But some obsessed about it, had nightmares about it, some died too young or—like him—were never quite right in the head because of it. All of the countries that fought in the war had men like that. Someone in one of those countries had murdered the husband of Anna Shuster. Nick wondered where and when it had happened. He wondered if the killer was still alive and if he was right in the head.

In his mind he saw Willie and thought: *A condition.* What kind of condition? Could anything cure it? What kind of a God would give something like that to a kid?

Number 54 trolleys kept coming from east and west, clanging their bells and disgorging fans eager to see the mighty Yanks with the great Babe Ruth do battle with their A's. They flooded the sidewalk beside the turret, and soon its doors swung open. Nick's stomach cramped. He wondered how he'd been able to eat those muffins, even as good as they were. His throat was sour. He left his bench and walked back to Twentieth Street, where all the parking spaces were now filled.

In his room he lowered the bay window's upper sash. The curtains were limp in the muggy heat. He went to the dresser, opened its bottom drawer and took out the Springfield. Took out the clip and inserted it and his hands started shaking. He went to the window, flipped up the gun's rear sight and aimed at the field.

People were filing into the stands. He wondered if he could

hit somebody all the way across the diamond, over by third base. In the war he had hit distant targets but now he couldn't remember how far away they'd been.

He sat by the window in one of the wooden chairs, his rifle resting against the sill. The Yanks were taking batting practice now. Ruth came to the plate and smashed one high and deep in Nick's direction. It cleared the wall and he heard it hit something somewhere down the block. When he stood up and looked at the street he saw kids running after it. He thought of how Willie missed out on stuff like that.

He sat down again. The heat was damn near unbearable now and his forehead was covered with sweat. He wiped it off with his handkerchief—and somebody knocked on his door.

He jumped up, grabbed the Springfield, and shoved it under the bed. Then he went to the door.

It was Flora. "Nick," she said, "I'm sorry to bother you, but my window is stuck. I wonder if you could help me raise it."

He went with her down the hallway to her room. Her window looked out on Anna's brick courtyard and fence, the alley, and the backs of the houses the next block over, on Opal Street.

Anna had planted a garden in that courtyard. On its right hand side was a bed of flowers in glorious bloom, and a vine of some sort with round green globes—a melon?—was climbing the fence on the left. Nick's mother had always planted a garden back when they'd had their house, Alice had planted one too, and Nick recognized a number of Anna's flowers: day lilies, evening primrose, rose campion. The sadness began to rise and he quickly looked back at the window.

The center sash had been raised halfway. Nick grabbed it, jiggled it, freed it and lifted it all the way up.

"Oh, wonderful," Flora said. "Today we need every bit of breeze we can get, this atmosphere is absolutely ENervating."

"You have a broken sash cord, Flora."

"*Five* broken sash cords," Flora said. A small electric fan hummed busily on her table; she plopped down heavily in the chair in front of it. "The side windows don't work at all. I guess I should ask to have them repaired, but that costs money that Anna doesn't have. And I don't either. Thank you so much for your help, I'm truly grateful."

"Glad to do it," Nick said, thinking: *What a nice guy I am. Perfectly normal, perfectly sane. Flora will surely attest to that.* He went back to his room and locked his door.

The game was already underway; the Athletics were in the field. Nick took the rifle from under the bed and stood at the window. Bing Miller was playing in right for the A's again today. Nick aimed at his head. He had Miller right in his sights—and then he didn't.

Miller had taken a step to his left and Nick remembered: outfielders don't stay still. Between pitches they move around, flip their gloves off their wrists and on again, they look at the grass, they look at the sky, they look at the people in the stands. Why hadn't he taken that into account?

The first two Yankees grounded out and then Ruth popped to short. The A's left the field and the Yankees replaced them. As Ruth trotted out to right he was flashing his big crowd-pleasing grin, making Nick's hatred boil: *He killed my Alice! Killed her!* Acid rose to his throat. When the big man stopped and turned to face home plate, Nick took up the rifle, gritted his teeth and aimed.

It occurred to him then that he was a sniper. Snipers were very valuable in wars but nobody liked them: they were sneaky, dirty. But hadn't the colonists beaten the British largely because of snipers?

Nick started to shake all over now. In the war men who shook didn't last very long. He had shaken the first few times he killed, but had gotten over it. You had to, or you died. And after a while he'd actually started to like the rush of excitement he felt as he went into battle. He'd always liked the rush when he walked to the pitching mound at the start of

126

a game, but it didn't compare to the rush of war, where the stakes were a matter of life and death. And then at a certain point in the war it had hit him, he didn't know why, that it was wrong to like this feeling. It was wrong to look forward to killing. He was turning into a murderer, and it was wrong.

He tried not to think about this as he followed Ruth's movements in his sights, waiting for one of the A's to hit something high and hard to left, for the crowd to erupt with noise. The gun was feeling heavy and his arms began to ache. No breezes came in through the window; he was sweating profusely. He wondered how hot it was out on the field. Across the diamond, Connie Mack stood on the dugout steps in a shirt and tie. When Mack had quit playing years ago and become a manager, he had shunned a uniform and adopted formal clothing. God, Nick thought, the man must be dying of heat out there.

The A's, just like the Yankees, went down in order. Nick lowered the rifle, set it against the windowsill, sat down in his chair and wiped off his face with his handkerchief.

Every time Ruth took the field, Nick aimed at his head. The big man was restless, taking a step or two forward or backward or pounding his glove with his hand. Nick kept hoping for one of those deep drives to left, but it never came.

At quarter to five the game was still going, but Nick had to leave for work. He rolled the rifle up in the canvas and put it away in the dresser drawer, then went downstairs. Anna was hard at work at her sewing machine and didn't notice as he went through the hallway and out the door.

As he walked down Twentieth Street a roar arose from Shibe Park. *Probably something hit to left,* he thought.

In the Home Plate an hour later, Iron Mike arrived with the news that the A's had suffered their fifth straight defeat and Ruth had homered. Jackie Dodd claimed that the Athletics' season was finished, while Hesitant Harvey and Shrimpy Petrullo were of the opinion that this was no more than a bump in the road, albeit a rather substantial one. Nick wondered what they would think if they knew that tomorrow the great Babe Ruth, the Colossus of Clout, the world famous Bambino, would play his last game.

16

AGAIN NICK HAD A TOUGH TIME trying to sleep. When he got back home from work his room was stuffy and hot, but that was the least of it. Over and over again as he lay in his bed he pictured himself at the window, aiming the Springfield. Dripping with sweat, he wished that he had a fan like Flora's to move the stifling air.

When finally he drifted off he dreamed of a spring training field in Arkansas years ago, when he had been young and strong. He was on the mound pitching when suddenly the sky began to roar with planes and bombs began to fall. The infield exploded and searing hot pain tore his arm—his pitching arm.

He came out of the dream with a jolt and his arm was throbbing. He flexed his aching fingers. He thought of his gun in the dresser drawer and the task ahead. He drank from the bottle of water that sat on his bedside table then lay on his back staring up at the ceiling for over an hour. This time when he dreamed, he was talking to Alice. "I'll make it right," he was telling her. "Believe me, I'll make it right."

He awoke to the sound of Willie playing. His music this morning was soft and slow. As Nick descended the stairs it stopped and then Willie was there in the doorway in his chair. "The A's lost yesterday," he said.

"I know," Nick said.

"I hope they win today."

"Me too."

"It's hot. Maybe too hot for me up on the roof."

"Yeah, you have to be careful."

"Are you going to watch the game?"

Nick realized where this was heading and said, "I don't think so."

"Oh. I thought I could watch it with you, maybe. In your room."

"Someday," Nick said. "But not today."

"That's what you said about fishing, too."

"Well, that's how it is."

"Drat!" Willie said.

Nick went to Leewright's Grocery again, but all of Anna's baking had been sold the day before. "People can't get enough of the stuff," Leewright said with a scowl. "I sure wish she had the time to make more."

Nick bought a banana. Back when he lived at the Rose Hotel he had placed a banana beside his mattress, looked away, and when he'd looked back it had seemed to be smiling at him. The openings in his shoes had seemed to be screaming at him too. Thank God he wasn't that bad off anymore. This banana was just a banana, and wasn't smiling. But his pitching arm was just as bad as back at the Rose Hotel. Earlier, it had hurt from his dream, but now it just felt limp. He sat in the Square and ate the banana and then went home.

The house was quiet. He didn't see Anna or Willie. He thought that they might have gone out to the back porch hoping to get some air. A feeble breeze was coming from the east.

He climbed the stairs. Flora's door was wide open and there she was, in front of her fan at the table. "Hello, Nick," she said. "I thought yesterday was bad but today's even worse. What a scorcher!"

"Terrible," Nick said.

It was bad that her door was open. She'd see him leave with the roll of canvas—provided he was successful. He told

130

himself not to worry about it, she'd think he was going fishing.

In his room he looked out at the empty field. And he knew it: today was the day, he felt it in his bones.

Right from the start, the Yanks jumped all over the A's. Nick followed Ruth's head with his rifle each time that he took the field but the moment was never good; the crowd didn't make enough noise. He was starting to doubt his intuition. After the first four innings his stomach hurt and his shoulders felt stiff.

Then it happened. With two men on for the A's in the fifth, Jimmie Foxx hit a deep drive to left and the ballpark exploded. Like everyone else, Ruth was watching the flight of the ball. *This is it!* Nick said to himself. *Right now!* Shaking all over, sweat soaking his forehead, he gritted his teeth and fired—precisely as Ruth took a step to his right—and the bullet missed.

Another quick rush of sweat and he fired again—as Ruth bent forward, his hands on his knees, as if he were looking for something down on the ground. He suddenly straightened and batted the air with his hand, and then turned to his right as Meusel, the Yank's left fielder, made a spectacular leaping catch of the drive by Foxx.

It was out number three and the crowd went silent. Drenched with sweat, feeling suddenly drained, Nick gritted his teeth. *Goddamn it!* Both bullets had missed by just a hair, whizzing past Ruth and burrowing into the earth. Nick set the rifle against the sill, his heart pounding hard in his ears. His pitching arm felt numb.

He sat in his chair, wiping sweat from his face with his handkerchief. If he didn't kill Ruth he would never get well. The horrible feelings and memory-dreams would never let go, he would never be fully healed. And he had to do it for Alice, he had to! He banged his fist hard on his thigh. *Goddamn it! The perfect opportunity, and I blew it!*

131

He had hoped to take care of Ruth in the early innings, head to the Delaware with the gun, buy the fishing rod, come back to the house and report to work on time. But now if he waited around to try again and succeeded, he would be late for work. That wouldn't look good. People would wonder why he was late today of all days when he'd never been late before.

He could only hope that tomorrow would give him another chance. Tomorrow's game was the last one the Yankees and A's would play at Shibe Park this year. If he didn't succeed tomorrow... *I have to!* he told himself. *I just have to!*

The final score was Yankees 10, A's 4. Things looked bleak for the A's; this was their sixth straight loss. In the last few weeks they had gone from fifteen games above five hundred to a game below.

At work, Nick heard that Eddie Winters had pitched in the eighth and the Yankees had roughed him up. "Won't be showing his ugly mug around here tonight," Charlie said with his usual smile.

But the guy who did show his ugly mug was Babe Ruth. He came in laughing and smoking with just one woman this time, a buxom broad with crow-black hair. "Hey, keed," he bellowed to Jake, "double browns for me and the lady!" Then he started to pass out cigars to the great delight of the customers at the bar.

"Babe, I heard you punished the ball today," said sloe-eyed, olive-skinned Jake.

"Yeah, I done pretty good," Ruth said. "Them A's pitchers ain't as hot as they think they are."

He ate a few pretzels that sat on the counter. "You wanna know somethin?" he said to Jolly Cholly. "Shibe Park has bees."

"You're kiddin."

"Like hell I am. One of them was after me in the outfield, after my head. I batted it away and musta killed it, it never come back. Sometimes they live in the ground, in holes, but I didn't see no holes. They oughta look into that, them things can hurt."

As Nick listened to this, he wondered what Ruth would have been if he hadn't played ball, didn't have his incredible talent. A bartender, like his old man, Nick decided. *A bartender like me, and no one would ever hear of him—as they'll never hear of me. But because of his talent his name will live on for decades. And if I succeed tomorrow and they catch me, my name will live on too—like John Wilkes Booth's.*

Ruth kept joking around and spinning self-flattering tales, most of them laced with profanity, and Nick was thinking: *By rights, you should be in a morgue tonight, not here in the Home Plate cheating on Claire again. Drink up, tomorrow you might not be so lucky.*

The small lamp was glowing behind the parlor curtains as Nick climbed the steps of the porch. As always, the house was quiet as he left the vestibule.

But tonight something was different: Willie was there in his wheelchair beside the piano, one side of his face in shadow. He was wearing pale blue pajamas.

Stepping into the parlor Nick said to him, "What are you doing up at this hour?"

"The pain is bad tonight. I can't sleep."

"Does it often hurt like that?"

"No, only once in a while."

"Where does it hurt?"

"In my bones. Especially my elbows and knees, but everywhere."

"Do you take something for it?"

"I do, Mother gives me some aspirin. It helps a little but won't take it all away."

"That's tough."

Willie nodded. "What works best is music. When I play the piano I go far away to a different world. I see mountains and forests and rivers and beautiful skies and I can forget the pain

133

for a while. Sometimes the music I play is sad, but it's a good sadness that makes me feel better. It comes through my fingers and arms and into my heart. But I can't play at night, I'd wake everyone up, so I read instead."

"And that helps?"

"It does. I can go far away on books, too. Not as far as on music, but pretty far. Right now I'm reading *Great Expectations*. Do you like Charles Dickens?"

"I haven't read a lot of him," Nick replied. "In school I read *A Tale of Two Cities*."

"That's not like his other books," Willie said. "I don't like it too much."

"I read *A Christmas Carol* too."

"Tiny Tim," Willie said. "He has a condition, like me. It's a pretty good book. But you should read *Oliver Twist* and *David Copperfield* and *Great Expectations*. They're all about children too, children without any fathers, like me—and sometimes no mothers, either. David and Oliver get in big trouble but things work out fine in the end. In *Great Expectations* the boy is Pip. I think things will work out okay for him too, but he's in big trouble, he's helping a convict escape."

"That sounds exciting."

"It is."

"Those are pretty long books."

"They are, and when I get tired of reading I look at my baseball cards. Would you like to see them?"

"Sure."

Willie rolled into the hallway and down to his room. He returned with a packet of cards secured by a rubber band, wheeled himself up to the card table, took off the rubber band and spread out the cards. Nick sat down beside him.

"These are the Yuengling Ice Cream cards," he said. "Mother doesn't let me eat ice cream too much so I don't have very many. There are sixty cards in the set. I hope I can get them all, but I probably won't."

The cards didn't look so hot to Nick; they were black and

134

white. When he was a kid his father had smoked cigarettes, three packs a day, and in 1909 they came with brightly colored cards. Nick had saved more than a hundred of them by the time his father dropped dead of a heart attack that summer. The doctor had warned him numerous times about his cigarette habit. "Animals," he had said, "are not designed to breathe smoke," but his father paid no attention and the cigarettes killed him. After that, Nick put the baseball cards away in a box in his closet and never looked at them again.

"Some of these players are from the National League," Willie said. "I never see them 'cause I never watch the Phillies."

"Well, you aren't missing much."

"I know they're not too good, but I'd like to see the other teams in the league. I'd like to see this pitcher, Carl Mays." He slid the card over to Nick and said, "He did something really bad—he hit another player in the head and killed him. Ray Chapman, his name was. He was the only player to die from being beaned."

"I didn't know about that," Nick said. He had played on the Red Sox with Mays, who was an angry, tight-lipped man.

"That tragedy changed the game," Willie said.

"In what way?"

"Now, whenever a ball gets dirty, they have to take it out and put a new one in. They say that Chapman didn't see the ball because it was so dirty."

"Huh," Nick said. In the games he'd watched, he'd been struck by the number of times the ball was replaced. Back when he'd played, the same ball was used the entire game. It not only got dirty and harder to see as the game progressed, it got softer and harder to hit for distance. Using new balls all the time was surely a major reason for the rise in homers and averages.

Willie was frowning. He said, "If you kill somebody like Carl Mays did, is it murder?"

"No."

"How's come?"

"He didn't mean to kill him, it was an accident. You have to mean to kill somebody for it to be murder."

"Oh," Willie said. "Well how's come people have to die?"

"Everything living has to die," Nick said. "That's part of the deal."

"Part of God's plan, my mother says."

"That's as good an explanation as any, I guess."

"I hate that plan," Willie said. "And how's come parrots and giant tortoises live longer than people?"

"How do you know they do?"

He nodded towards the bookshelf. "My *Book of Knowledge* says so."

Nick saw it, a lineup of dark blue volumes. He also saw Dickens, Twain, Jules Verne, Zane Grey and Thomas Bailey Aldrich. "I don't know why parrots and tortoises live so long," he said, "but most animals have much shorter lives than we do."

"Yes," Willie said. "They're not so lucky. He frowned. "Some trees live for hundreds of years. Does God like trees more than he likes people?"

"Maybe," Nick said. "They don't give him anywhere near as much trouble."

Willie smiled just slightly then picked up another baseball card and said, "I'd like to see this player too, Gabby Hartnett, he's on the Cubs. The Cubs are good, I hope they meet the A's in the World Series." He gave the card to Nick, who examined it and then placed it back on the table.

"I saw a World Series game two years ago," Willie said.

Nick frowned. "You did?"

"Yes. A Negro League World Series game. Two of them took place at Shibe. Two teams named the Giants played each other. They were both very good. How's come the colored players can't play in the majors?"

"It's hard to explain."

"It doesn't seem fair."

"It isn't."

"Some of the neighbors wouldn't rent their roofs to colored people for those games."

"It figures."

"My favorite player was Double Duty Radcliffe, but there aren't any cards of colored players."

"No."

"It's too bad," Willie said. He looked at the table again and said, "My favorite card of all is this one. It's not a Yuengling card, it's a Babe Ruth Candy Company card." He pushed it over to Nick.

Good God, Nick thought, *the bastard even has his own candy company!*

The photograph showed Ruth at bat and said, "'Babe' Ruth Knocked Out 60 Home Runs in 1927. His Candy Helped Him." Nick sniffed. "His candy helped him. Do you believe that?"

"I do. The candy is full of sugar, and it gave him energy."

"It probably gave him cavities, too."

"I hate the dentist," Willie said.

"Everyone does. So why is this your favorite card? You told me you hate the Yankees."

"Yes, I do, but I love Babe Ruth. He's the best baseball player ever. Last year he hit sixty home runs and it looks like he'll hit even more this year. He hit one today, I saw him. The ball went all the way over to Opal Street."

"So I heard."

"I hope I can get him to sign a ball for me someday, it would help me get better."

"What?"

"That's right. The Babe can make sick children better. He goes to hospitals and does it all the time. If I could get a ball from him or meet him and shake his hand, it would cure my condition."

Nick didn't respond to this. Willie added, "I wrote to him three times at Yankee Stadium, but he didn't answer."

"He must be terribly busy."

"Yes," Willie said with a nod, "that's what Mother says too." He frowned and said, "I wish he was my father, then I'd *have* to get better. And it would be really swell to have a famous father. He has a daughter, her name is Dorothy, I read it in the *Inquirer*." He pronounced the name of the paper the Philly way, *Inkwire.*

Nick thought of the photo he'd seen in the newspaper back in the winter. He wished he could meet the child—Alice's child—but didn't see how it was possible.

"She's really lucky," Willie said. "It would be great to have a father who played in the major leagues.

"Maybe not," Nick said. "Ballplayers are gone from home a lot."

Willie thought about this. "Well, yes," he said, "I guess that's not so great. And I wouldn't want Eddie Winters to be my father. He didn't pitch well today and got real drunk and started hollering in the street."

"Not very nice," Nick said.

"It's upsetting and Mother hates it. My father wasn't a ballplayer, he was a teacher. He was killed in the war before I was born, in France. He was very brave."

Nick nodded. "I'm sure he was." In his mind he saw Johnny again.

"He killed a whole lot of those dirty Germans. He was a hero."

"Your mother told you this?"

"That's right. Were you in the war?"

"I was."

Willie widened his eyes. "Did you kill any Germans?"

"I did."

"Then you're a hero too."

"No, just a soldier. That's what we did."

Willie looked a bit crestfallen. "Oh," he said. "It wasn't murder, was it?"

"No."

138

"But you meant to kill them and you said—"

"It wasn't murder," Nick said, "it was war," and he felt a sudden cramp in his stomach. He said, "When you were up on the roof today did you hear any noises, like popping sounds?"

"Like cars make, you mean?"

"That's right."

"A few, but they weren't real loud."

Nick nodded.

"Did you hear any in your room?" Willie asked.

"A few. So how are you feeling now?"

"Better. My bones don't hurt as much."

"Then you better go get some sleep. That's what I'm going to do."

"Okay," Willie said. "I'll see you tomorrow."

Nick went upstairs to his room. He sat on his bed in the glow of the streetlamp and held his head. He thought of the rifle in his drawer. He thought of Willie's Babe Ruth card. *Now what?* he said to himself. *For Christ's sake, now what?*

17

Nick sat on the edge of his bed and stared at the sliver of streetlight that slashed the ceiling and ran down the wall. He was dripping with sweat. The air in the room was completely dead.

He was picturing Ruth at the bar with his latest floozy, smoking and laughing and drinking, the Sultan on top of the world, and again his anger surged.

But to kill Ruth would devastate Willie. To see his hero die a violent death would cause him incredible pain. For God's sake, it might even worsen his damned condition, whatever it was. And even if it didn't, what would he think of the peaceful, prosperous world he lived in after that?

Nick suddenly thought of the millions of other children who idolized Ruth, some of them sicker than Willie. How many kids in this country had pictures of Ruth on their bedroom walls? What would the death of their hero do to *them?* Amazingly, he had never thought of that, he had only thought of himself. He had suffered far more than his share of nightmares and fear and hurt, did he want to inflict that kind of suffering on children? Of course not.

But he had to. He had to kill Ruth for Alice—and for himself.

He clenched his jaws and held his head. He had to kill Ruth, that's all there was to it, and had to stop thinking about its effect on others.

But he couldn't.

He stripped to his undershorts and lay down in the

140

smothering heat. The image of Willie holding his Babe Ruth card wouldn't leave him alone. He turned away from the windows then back again. He angrily punched his pillow. But who was he mad at? Himself? Yes, for being unable to sort things out, for being that stupid. His thoughts were a hopeless jumble; he needed sleep.

But sleep would not come. Thoughts of Willie and Ruth and Alice kept hounding him, getting him nowhere. Then finally he slept in short bursts, dreaming briefly and waking again with his heartbeat quick in his neck.

"President McKinley has been shot!"

Nick awoke from a four A.M. dream with this cry in his ears—and remembered:

He was seven years old. His mother had answered the door to find her next door neighbor, Mrs. Babcock, standing there to deliver this dreadful news. The president had been shot at the exposition in Buffalo, Mrs. Babcock said, but he was doing well and was sure to recover.

Nick had been stunned. To think that someone could actually shoot the president! He knew it had happened before. In school he had studied the shooting of President Lincoln— the first time he'd ever heard the word "assassination"—and another president, Garfield, had also been shot, but those killings were far in the past. He hadn't thought something like that could happen *today*. It scared him and gave him a sick tight feeling deep in his stomach. "A lunatic," his father had said. "Nobody but a lunatic would do such a horrible thing."

When days later they heard the news that McKinley had died, tears rolled down his mother's cheeks. Nick hadn't felt sad for the president, but he *had* felt sad for his mother. "What is happening to this country?" his father had said and Nick had lain awake for hours that night with the frightening thought that if someone could shoot the president, anyone could be shot: his mother and father and he himself could be an assassin's victim. He had thought that the world was safe

141

for his family but it was not. The impact of that murder had lasted for years, bringing him daytime worries and horrible dreams.

Now he sat on the edge of his bed and thought: *assassin*. It was a dirty, ugly word. And that's what he hoped to be, an assassin. The consequences of his act would be as great or even greater than if he killed the president. It was obvious that more people liked Babe Ruth than liked Calvin Coolidge. Coolidge might hardly be missed, but Ruth...

Nick remembered this too: the jury had not agreed with his father that McKinley's killer was a lunatic. They didn't put him away in an asylum, they gave him the electric chair. And today almost no one remembered his name; unlike Lincoln's killer, he wasn't famous.

Nick kept sitting there on his bed, mulling this over. And as dawn touched the window curtains he thought: *If Alice hadn't died, what then?*

If she hadn't died, he would never have known about her affair with Ruth. He would never have known that she'd given birth, for she'd never have kept the child no matter how much she might want to. The responsibility of caring for it would be an incredible burden given her circumstances, and the scandal and disgrace would ruin her life. Helen, Ruth's wife, had wanted a child but couldn't have one, no one knew why, so Alice would give her the baby and people would never know where it came from unless Ruth told them, and why would he ever do that?

Then Nick started to wonder: Had Ruth made Alice pregnant on purpose so Helen could have a child? It was possible, even probable, and the more Nick thought about it, the more he was sure it was true. Ruth got the child that Helen wanted, but something went terribly wrong and Alice died. But her death had been accidental, so was Ruth to blame for it?

Alice had probably left her job when she knew she was

142

pregnant and stayed with her mother out of sight till the baby was born. If she hadn't died she'd have given the baby away to Ruth and gone back to her normal life. Today she would probably be married to someone who'd never learned of her times with Ruth, never known she had given birth. Or maybe she wouldn't be married. Maybe she'd still be waiting, hoping for a miracle—her lover's return from the war.

But she *had* died. If not for Ruth she would still be alive, so he *was* to blame. But Alice was also to blame. It was hard for Nick to believe, but Alice had slept with a married man, committed adultery. Innocent Alice! Had he gotten her drunk? No matter how it had happened, it had happened. So her death was partly her own fault, wasn't that right?

Nick stood. He went to the brightening window and parted the curtains. The ballpark's stands were emerging from morning mist. Yes, Alice was partly to blame. And since that was so, did Ruth deserve to die for what he had done?

Maybe instead of killing him, Nick told himself, I can maim him. Maybe ruin a knee so he can't run, can't stand at the plate. Take him out of the game forever, as I have been taken out of the game. Maybe that would be punishment enough. It might even be a greater punishment than death. If you died, you knew nothing. If you lived and lost what you loved the most, that would be torture.

Sports fans were fickle. One day's hero was the next day's bum. Nick had observed this transformation a number of times. In one instance, a pitcher who'd won twenty games three years in a row, a darling of the crowd, had rapidly declined and become the target of their wrath. The cheers had turned to raucous boos. How fantastic to see this happen to Ruth! And once he left baseball, he would be lost, it was all he had ever known.

But hitting his knee while he moved around on the field, or even his hip, his thigh... You'd have to be really lucky to pull that off. And even if you did, and Ruth couldn't play anymore, people would no doubt sympathize with him. It

143

might even add to his legend. No, wounding him was a bad idea, there had to be some other way...but what?

He started to pace the floor. Everything was too complicated, he couldn't sort things out. And now he was thinking: his mental collapse had taken place nine years ago, long before he had known about Ruth and Alice. Since Ruth hadn't caused his breakdown, why would taking revenge on him help stop the voices and memory-dreams? Maybe it would only make things worse, lead to *more* obsessive thoughts and nightmares. And Alice...Alice was gone forever, nothing he could do would bring her back. She was not looking down at him from some heaven somewhere, passing judgment on him, he didn't believe in any of that kind of stuff. So how could he say that he wanted to harm Ruth for Alice when Alice didn't exist? He wanted to harm Ruth because he hated him, that was the truth of the matter. But how would it help anything?

Around and around went his thoughts in the heavy heat. He sat down on his couch and lay back, sapped of energy, filled with confusion. He was starting to drift to sleep when he suddenly smelled the wonderful comforting fragrance of Anna's baking. *Today must be Friday*, he thought.

In the hallway Flora said, "You're up so early, weren't you able to sleep last night?"

"Not very well."

"You need an electric fan. It makes a tre-MEN-dous difference."

"I'm sure it does."

Flora took a deep breath. "Doesn't the house smell heavenly? It's cinnamon buns today, my favorite. Have you tried them yet?"

"Not yet."

"She always gives me one and asks for my opinion. Of course they are always superb. Maybe I can convince her to make you a taster too."

"That would be great."

"They're gone by now. Morris, the man from Leewright's, comes by early to pick them up. Amazing how the fragrance lingers here on the second floor."

"Sure is," Nick said. He was suddenly starving.

At Leewright's he bought two cinnamon buns and ate them in the Square. My God but they were good! When he went back home, Willie was at the piano; the tune that he played was brisk. He caught sight of Nick in the hallway and stopped.

"How you feeling?" Nick asked.

"Pretty good. After I talked to you I was able to sleep."

"I'm glad to hear it."

"Can you look at some more of my baseball cards?"

"Sure."

When Anna entered the parlor she seemed surprised to see Nick sitting with Willie at the table.

"We're looking at his cards," Nick said. "I hope it's okay."

"It's okay," Anna said, but she didn't sound pleased. She went over and sat at her sewing machine.

Willie said, "If you get all sixty cards and turn them in, they give you a gallon of ice cream free."

"No kidding," Nick said. It sounded like a racket: no one would ever get all sixty cards because Yuengling would hold one back.

"But I'd rather have cards than ice cream," Willie said. "I look at them all the time."

"I used to collect cards too when I was a kid," Nick said.

"You did? What happened to them?"

"We moved and they disappeared."

"I hope we don't move," Willie said. "I like it here, I like to watch the games. But Mother says if we moved out West, the air out there might make me better. That's what Dr. Fletcher told her."

Nick looked at Anna, who was threading her sewing

145

machine, and said, "Really."

"The city air is bad for those with lung problems," Anna said.

"I'm sure."

"I'd like to see the West," Willie said. "I've read about it in Zane Grey, all the cowboys and roundups and everything, but I don't want to move there."

"Even if we wanted to, we couldn't," Anna said. "We don't have enough money."

"And we don't have enough for an operation, either."

"No, we don't."

Nick frowned. "What kind of an operation?"

"On my lungs," Willie said. "If I get a lot worse I might need one."

"Please, let's not talk about that," Anna said.

"Okay," Willie said. "It might never happen, right?"

"That's right."

Willie looked at his cards. "Mr. Leewright told Mother that Fro-Joy ice cream is giving away a six card Babe Ruth set in early August. Each day of the week you get a different card when you buy a cone. I guess I'll have to buy a cone each day."

"I'm afraid not," Anna said.

"But ice cream is good for you," Willie said. "It builds strong bones. I saw it in the newspaper ads."

"You have to watch out for ads," Anna said. "They aren't always true."

"How do you know?"

"Experience."

Willie turned to Nick. "We don't buy Fro-Joy from Mr. Leewright," he said. "We buy it from Blinkey's ice cream cart. He comes every day, but I'm only allowed to buy one cone a week, on Friday."

"Even that is too much," Anna said.

"But I really do want those cards," Willie said. "Six different Babe Ruths!"

Nick's stomach tensed. He pictured himself at his window again, aiming his gun at Ruth. A pressure began to build in his chest; his ears started to ring. *Stop, stop!* he told himself. *Do something! Get busy!*

He said, "Flora's big window is giving her trouble again, Mrs. Shuster. She has a broken cord. The sash either sticks or won't stay up. Her side windows need cords too. I'll fix them if you want me to."

Anna said, "That's a very kind offer, Mr. Hudson, but I have a handyman who does that kind of thing. I don't expect my tenants to work for me."

"Stanley the Handyman," Willie said. "He doesn't always come when you want him to."

"I'll be happy to do it," Nick said, and the noise in his ears was louder.

"Well—"

"I'll do it," Nick said.

Willie suddenly started to cough, and Anna sighed.

18

BUT NICK FELT TOO SHAKY to fix the windows now. Instead he went out to the little backyard and took deep breaths. The pressure in his chest began to fade but his ears still rang. He looked at the vine on the fence, saw a man climb the stairs to the roof two doors away. Inside again, he went to his room and closed the door.

He walked to the window and looked outside at the playing field. In the course of just a few hours his world had turned upside down—because of a crippled kid.

There were already plenty of people in the stands. He looked at them milling around out there and wondered about them. Most were good people for sure but some were bastards, bigger bastards than Ruth. So maybe they too deserved to die. *What the hell am I thinking?* he said to himself, and suddenly realized: Almost since the day he had left St. Luke's six months ago, his life had been fueled by hate.

Hate had driven him into battle during the war; he had wanted to kill every German he saw. That hate had never completely left him, even after all those St. Luke's years, and he'd transferred it all to Babe Ruth.

And what kind of a way was that to live—on hate. In the army and baseball he'd come across people who did just that, but was it how *he* should live? Maybe that's what had finally broken him years ago—hate. It certainly wasn't Babe Ruth who had done it.

He looked out the window, sweating heavily, feeling lost. If he buried his hatred and didn't harm Ruth, what would he

148

live for? What would he live for if he *did* harm Ruth? His thoughts were whirling and scattered again but finally he said to himself: *For God's sake, can't I just live?*

Countless others had suffered injustice, had seen what they loved destroyed and had kept on going, so why couldn't *he*? If a woman who lost her husband to war and gave birth to a crippled child could keep on going, couldn't *he*? If that child, who lived with almost daily pain, could keep on going... How could he hurt that child and countless others by killing Babe Ruth?

He realized now: he couldn't. Killing Babe Ruth would be like killing Santa Claus.

But the urge to harm him was lodged deep inside like a poison. He still felt that Ruth must pay—just for going to bed with Alice, something that he himself had never done. She'd asked him to hold off until they got married. Then he went to war—and she went to bed with Ruth! Committed adultery! Yes, but not until years had passed. By then she was twenty-five and was sure he'd been killed. Who knew what her mind had been like by then—after his death, her brother Johnny's death...

He went to the dresser and took out the Springfield. At the window again he aimed at the crowd in the stands, at random heads. "A lunatic," he remembered his father saying and remembered his mother's tears. He let out a breath and lowered the rifle again. He rolled it back up in the canvas and put it away.

He would try to sell it. Someone who came to the Home Plate would probably want it.

He sat at the table, looked out at the field. So what was he going to do, let Ruth get *away* with what he'd done? He couldn't, it wasn't right! If he could make the death look accidental—a car crash, something like that—Ruth's fans would be saddened, but not destroyed the way they would be by a murder. But how could he ever pull off such a thing? It seemed impossible. Well maybe if, instead of harming Ruth,

149

he could make him fail—fail at a crucial moment, in front of the entire baseball world, in front of Willie, maybe *then* the poison would disappear. But he didn't even know how to do *that.*

He stared out the window, confused as ever. If he wasn't going to take revenge on Ruth, what was the point of staying in Philly? But where would he go? Montana? Had his buddy who came from there survived the war? Did he still live there? Nick only knew one thing for sure: before he lit out for some other place—if he did—he would go to see Jimmy again and pay back that twenty he'd borrowed. He'd never feel right if he didn't. That generous act was one of the kindest things that anyone had ever done for him. It had probably saved his life.

He kept sitting there, staring at nothing, trying to sort things out—then heard a noise in the hallway and knew what it was.

He opened his door and saw Anna with Willie slung over her shoulder. She was taking him up to the roof to watch the game.

"Mrs. Shuster," he said. "Here, let me carry him."

"I can manage," she said, not turning around. "I do it all the time." With her free hand she opened the door to the steps leading up to the roof.

Nick saw that the back of the door held a hook with a ring of keys. "Please," he said. He was next to her now. "I'm going up there to watch the game too."

Willie widened his eyes. "You are?"

"I am."

Nick lifted him off Anna's shoulder before she protested further and transferred him to his own. "It's no problem," he said. Willie was lighter than he'd anticipated.

"I check on him every hour," Anna said.

"No need for that with me up there," Nick said. "But I'll have to leave for work before the game's over."

"All right," Anna said. She watched Nick start up the steps, then turned away.

Willie said, "You're strong, Uncle Nick."

"Not as strong as I used to be."

"Like when you were in the war?"

"That's right."

Nick opened the hatch and went onto the roof. The makeshift stands on either side were filling up. Nick went to put Willie in his chair but Willie said, "Wait, the rag."

"What?"

"The rag under the chair. I have to wipe off the soot."

Nick leaned over and picked up the rag. "Here, I'll do it," he said. He wiped the chair clean, still holding Willie, then set him down. "Thank you," Willie said.

Across the way, Shibe Park was almost full and the game was about to start. "Grove's pitching today," Willie said. "I bet the A's win."

"They at least have a fighting chance," Nick said, "but there's no guarantee." The day he had found the "room for rent" sign on Anna's house, Grove had been beaten in New York four to nothing by journeyman pitcher Hank Johnson. Nick remembered it well because several of the Home Plate regulars had bet on the A's and were in a foul mood.

"I like it up here but the air isn't really fresh," Willie said. "That soot on the chair?" He turned to the north and pointed. "Look over there."

Nick saw the chimneys of several factories spewing black smoke. "Not good," he said.

"And we have to breathe it," Willie said. "Sometimes I cough real bad. And it's worse in the winter 'cause people burn coal to heat their houses. We even do that ourselves."

The game began. Nick stood beside Willie, his hand on the back of his chair. When Babe Ruth came out of the dugout and went to the on deck circle, Nick felt a rush of anger. The pressure in his chest surged up again. *I tried to kill Santa Claus,* he thought. *A vulgar, lecherous, stogie-smoking Santa Claus who instead of bringing you presents cures your ills.*

Ruth swung his bat a few times and then knelt in the circle. The Yankee's batboy came over and knelt beside him. Nick saw himself in his room with his gun.

"You know who's really lucky?" Willie asked.

"Who's that?" Nick said. *This goddamn ringing, when would it stop?*

"That batboy, Eddie Bennett. He's not really a boy, he's a man, but he has a condition that keeps him small. It doesn't slow him down like my condition does, he's a hunchback."

The name was familiar to Nick; he'd read a story about the guy in one of those library papers. He was not just the Yankees' batboy, he was their mascot. "The A's used to have a batboy mascot like Eddie years ago," Nick said. "As a matter of fact, they had two of them, Louis Van Zelst, and later, Hughie McLoon."

"Were they hunchbacks?"

"They were."

"Did the A's rub their humps, like the Yankees do with Eddie?"

"They did."

"They think that it brings them good luck," Willie said. "And Eddie's the first one to shake their hands when they cross the plate. I'd love to be a mascot. You get to see all of the games, even the ones on the road, and you get to know all of the players. I could probably be a batboy too if I wasn't slow. It would be so great."

It was now Ruth's turn to bat. He rubbed Eddie Bennett's hump, then stood up and strode to the plate.

As he fouled off the first two pitches a leathery voice from deep in the stands proclaimed him a bum. Nick was amazed by how loud the voice was.

"That's Harry the Huckster," Willie said. "He goes to almost every game. He doesn't just yell at the other teams, he yells at the A's sometimes if they don't play well. Mr. Mack has threatened to have him locked up for disturbing the peace."

Nick laughed—and Ruth struck out. Nick wondered what Grove had thrown him.

The A's scored first but the Yanks fought back quickly. Pennock, the Yankees' pitcher, was as sharp as Grove. At the end of the fourth, with the game still tied, Willie asked, "What school did you go to, Uncle Nick?"

"High school?"

"Yes. Where you read *A Tale of Two Cities.*"

"Girard College."

"I know that school, it's very good. I could go there because I don't have a father, but Mother doesn't want me to." He frowned. "Didn't you have a father?"

"He died when I was fifteen."

"You were almost grown up."

"I'm sure I thought so."

Willie frowned again. "I never even met my father."

"That's too bad."

"It makes me sad. Did you like Girard College?"

"Very much."

"I think Mother should let me go there. But she says I shouldn't go to any school, even the one in our neighborhood, because it's too tiring and I'll get germs. That's why she teaches me at home."

"And what do you think of that?"

"I like it okay, but I don't get to be with other kids except for Scootie Mulroney, who sometimes plays cards with Aunt Flora and me. He lives next door. He's the kid selling lemonade over there." He pointed. "Mother says most other kids are ruffians, but—"

His words were cut short by a sudden loud roar from the crowd. Al Simmons had crushed a ball to left; higher and higher it went towards the stands. *Perfect moment to shoot,* Nick thought, and he looked at Ruth, who was watching the flight of the ball with his hands on his hips, standing perfectly still. Then it hit him: when he was trying to kill Ruth yesterday, Willie was right above him, sitting right here, right over his head.

He'd known that—yet hadn't thought about it at all. *My*

153

God, he told himself, *I'm as self-absorbed as Ruth!*

The crowd was cheering wildly now as Simmons circled the bases. "I think we're going to win!" Willie said.

At the end of the inning Nick said that he hated to leave but needed to get to work.

"Drat!" Willie said. "I like having you watch the game with me, it's good to have someone to talk to."

"There will be other games," Nick said. "I'll see you tomorrow."

He went down the steps to the hallway and stopped for a minute to look at the keys on the back of the door to the roof. There were four of them, one for the bathroom and each of the bedrooms, he figured. The third bedroom door was always locked; he had tried its doorknob a couple of times, curious to know how large the room was. Now that he had access to its key, maybe he'd find out.

He went down the stairs and into the kitchen, where Anna was cleaning the stove. "Mrs. Shuster, I'm leaving now," he said. "It's a tight game, he'll probably want to stay till the end. He hasn't coughed at all."

"Thank you so much for your help, Mr. Hudson," Anna said. "It made me feel more comfortable to have someone up there with him." She smiled then, and Nick felt a sudden warmth expand in his chest and the pressure begin to subside.

As he walked to work the last of the pressure dissolved and so did the noise in his ears.

He went through the Home Plate's café door instead of the speakeasy door. As usual, practically no one was there. Two middle aged men sat at the counter, drinking coffee and talking to Shirley, and a couple of kids, a boy and a girl about fourteen, were eating ice cream at a table. As always, Nick wondered if anyone knew what went on past the kitchen. He went up to Shirley and said, "When you sell ice cream, do any of the customers leave their baseball cards behind?"

"Oh sure," Shirley said with a smack of her gum.

"What do you do with them?"

"Throw them away."

"Could you save them for me?"

"Anything for you, Nick," Shirley said.

As always, he ate in the kitchen with Louie working beside him. "I'm gettin too old for this," Louie said, "but I ain't rich, so I gotta keep goin. I'll probably die in this kitchen."

"Before you do," Nick said. "Give me your Greek stew recipe, okay?"

In the bar he heard that the A's had beaten Babe Ruth and the Yankees, 6 to 4. Iron Mike and Hesitant Harvey had both won their bets and were in a good mood. Nick kept wondering how he could make Ruth fail but couldn't come up with anything. He thought of Willie watching the game on the roof and remembered the smokestacks belching black. He thought of something that Willie had said to him shortly before he left for work: "If my mother gets married again, I hope she doesn't marry a tippler and philanderer the way Aunt Flora did."

"You know what those words mean?" Nick had asked.

"Of course. A tippler means a person who drinks too much, like Eddie Winters. Philanderer means a man who goes around with other women when he's married. Mother would not like that at all."

"I'm sure she wouldn't," Nick had said.

He let Jake and Charlie know that he had a rifle for sale. "It's a Springfield, really nice. I was doing some target shooting but got bored with it."

It was Friday night and packed as usual. The colored band was hard at work and couples filled the floor, among them Butterball Saleski—who had also won his bet—and his wife, Irene, who was toothpick-thin, with short straw-colored hair. At the piano Henry belted out a hit from the previous year called "Ain't She Sweet?" making Butterball grin and making Nick think of Alice again. He mixed drink after drink and poured beer after beer, expecting at any moment to see The

Bambino walk through the door. But the Yankees were heading back to New York tonight and the big man never showed up.

19

THE SENATORS CAME TO TOWN for just one game. The Athletics won it, 7-4, then went to New York for a doubleheader and lost both ends of it to the dreaded Yanks. They came back home for six straight games with the Red Sox: a doubleheader on Monday, a single game on Tuesday, another twin bill on Wednesday—the Fourth of July—and another single game on Thursday.

Willie was finishing up his piano lesson on Monday when Nick came downstairs. The fragrance of Anna's baking still hung in the hallway. The piano teacher, a strict-looking older man with a trim gray beard and moustache, was reviewing some of the finer points of the piece that Willie had just finished playing and Willie paid close attention. "I'll remember that, Professor Shultz," he said. "I'll practice it that way."

"Willie, you are a gem," said Shultz as he rose to go. "Most of the children I work with are merely pupils. *You* are a student."

Anna gave him a brown paper bag and Nick knew what was in it; Flora had told him that Shultz got paid in muffins. He said hello to Willie and Anna and Flora—and Professor Shultz—then hurried to Leewright's, hoping the muffins were not all gone.

He was in luck—there were just two left—and he sat on a bench in the Square and savored them.

The first game of the doubleheader started early, right after Anna served lunch, so Willie didn't have time to nap. Before

Nick went to the roof with him he said, "I have something for you," and gave him the baseball cards that Shirley had saved. There were twelve of them.

"Wow!" Willie said. "Where did you get all these?"

"From a friend at work. I can probably get more, too."

"Nifty!" Willie exclaimed as he spread them across the kitchen table. "Tris Speaker, he's an A. He used to be an Indian. One time he got hit in the face with a ball and it cut him open. He got sewed up and went back in the game. He's tough."

"I guess," Nick said. He had suddenly thought of a soldier who'd had two fingers blown away and kept on fighting. He was pretty sure Speaker had served in the war.

"Here's Gabby Hartnett, I have him already," Willie said. "But I don't have these other ones. Oh, wait a minute, I do have George Burns... Here's Joe Dugan, a Yankee! This is great! Thanks a lot, Uncle Nick."

"You're welcome. Now see, if you knew other kids who collected cards, you could trade your doubles with them."

"Yes, that would be good, but I don't know other kids except for Scootie Mulroney and Peanuts Sullivan, and they don't care about cards. They play real baseball games, not just card games the way I do."

"Well maybe you can make them care."

"I doubt it," Willie said.

The A's split the doubleheader, winning the first game and losing the second. Willie was only allowed to watch the first game because he had missed his nap and the sun was strong. This was fine with Nick. After five or six innings of baseball his interest waned. He'd become restless and sometimes the pressure would start in his chest and he'd think he was going to faint. On Tuesday, light-headed, he left the game—which the A's also won—at the end of the sixth. As he went to his room Johnny suddenly shouted *"I'm dead!"* in his ear as if he were right there beside him. His hands went cold, but the voice did not return.

The Home Plate was closed on the Fourth of July. When Nick came downstairs at eleven that morning he heard distant band music playing.

"A parade!" Willie said. "Let's go see it, Mother!"

Anna pushed Willie's chair through the hallway and onto the porch and Nick helped to grapple it down the steps. Anna asked Flora to come but she said "I'd love to, but I can't. My rheumatism is acting up and walking is ex-CRU-ciating. I'll watch it pass by from the porch."

As Nick and Anna and Willie started toward Lehigh the sound of the band kept increasing. Most of the houses on Twentieth Street were flying American flags.

At the corner they joined the crowd that had gathered and soon the parade appeared with a soldier up front, the pole of a huge flag propped in a holder around his waist. Nick saluted, along with most of the other spectators, Willie included. The band in white uniforms trimmed in gold marched briskly by, clashing symbols, followed by ranks of soldiers who waved and smiled at the crowd.

And now Nick remembered: shortly before he was shipped overseas he was in a parade in New York. And that's when he'd been on a subway train; he had taken it to Fifth Avenue. Ranks of soldiers in brand new uniforms had filled the entire street, and cheering crowds had packed the wide sidewalks, waving their tiny American flags. He had felt so strong, so confident, so proud of what he was doing to save America, the greatest country in the world. It had never occurred to him then that other countries might feel that *they* were the greatest.

The band was playing something familiar. Nick didn't know its name, but it made him think of a booklet his classes had used in grammar school: "War Songs for School Rooms." They'd sung a selection from it every day. That and tales of the glorious exploits of Teddy Roosevelt in Cuba had set him up good.

This parade was like a big party. Most of the soldiers weren't kids and were wearing medals on their chests. Nick wondered how many of them had fought in the war to end all wars and had killed other people. He wondered how many had not gotten over it yet. Some veterans in wheelchairs passed by and received the biggest cheers of all, but Nick thought of the soldiers who weren't here, the ones who'd been brutally damaged in body and mind and lay twisted and mute in their lonely beds and heard no cheers. Nick wasn't proud of the killing he'd done even though it was necessary, but these folks certainly seemed to be. He knew he could never bring himself to take part in a war parade.

He glanced at Anna. A teardrop was coursing down her cheek, and he had a sudden urge to wipe it away.

Willie, entranced by the show, never noticed his mother's tears. The marching stopped and three of the soldiers fired their rifles at the sky. Willie covered his ears with his hands. The shots made Nick think of the Springfield back in his room and his legs felt weak.

The parade moved on and kids ran after it and soon the music faded out. "Wow, that was really nifty!" Willie said.

"Yeah, glorious," Nick said.

"You were a soldier," Willie said. "You could be in that kind of parade. Do you still have your uniform?"

"No, I don't."

"What happened to it?"

"I don't know," Nick said, and wondered if it still existed, maybe in an army surplus store.

He went to the roof again with Willie that afternoon. When the first game ended, Anna told Willie he needed to take a second nap if he wanted to stay up late to see the fireworks. Nick felt tired and bruised, as if he had been in a fight, and decided to lie down too. Now that his plan to kill Ruth was finished, he felt lost. He still hated the bastard and wanted to get him but still didn't know how to do it.

At nine that night as darkness fell and a full moon rose above Shibe Park, Nick carried Willie back up to the roof and helped him into his chair. The kid talked endlessly about the A's as Anna and Nick stood beside him. The A's had won both of their games today, which made four out of five against the Sox. "And I bet they'll beat them tomorrow too," he said. "Then after that they're here for seventeen more games, and I'm going to watch them all. They're really getting good."

People were jamming the roofs on both sides, looking south to where the fireworks would appear. These roofs had supported thousands of baseball fans for almost twenty years and as far as Nick knew not one of them had collapsed. It seemed remarkable.

At nine fifteen the fireworks began with a silent expanding umbrella of yellow and green. "How lovely," Anna said as orange embers burnt themselves out in the blueblack sky, but Nick began feeling uneasy and started to sweat. Two beautiful starbursts followed, red and purple, throwing their colors across the upturned faces of the crowd. Then a brilliant white flare near the moon burst apart with a loud sharp echoing crack and Nick was clutching his Springfield and running, running right into the Huns who had killed his best friend and were trying to kill him too. He fired wildly as screaming shells split the black night sky, then he hit the deck and kept shooting again and again. And then Anna was saying, "What's wrong, Mr. Hudson? What's happening?" And Nick on his knees now could hear himself distantly saying, "It's nothing, I'm fine," as Willie was staring down at him with shocked wide eyes, a spray of bright orange and blue exploding behind his head.

Nick shakily pulled himself onto his feet, then turned and stumbled to the hatch and down the steps and locked himself in his room.

He turned on the nightstand lamp and shut all the windows and closed the curtains and lay on his bed. Gasping for breath with his heart banging hard, he pressed his hands over his ears to block out the fireworks noise.

I will never be right, he thought. *It will always be with me, I'll always be crazy.* His skin was drenched and his heart kept pounding. *I don't want to live anymore!* He felt a quick sinking sensation and took his hands down from his ears and sat up. He stared down at the rug. Then he heard a sharp rap at his door.

Go away! he said in his head. *Go away, go away, go away!* But the knocking persisted.

He got up and opened the door and Anna was there. "What is it?" she said with a look of alarm. "Do you need a doctor?"

He shook his head. "These memories of the war come back sometimes like vivid dreams. It's like I'm really there again."

"I've heard that can happen," Anna said. "It must be dreadful. Is there anything I can do? Can I get you some water?"

Nick looked at the nightstand beside his bed; his water bottle was empty. "That would be good," he said.

Anna came into the room, took the bottle, and went down the hall to the bathroom. She came back and gave him the bottle, now full. He thanked her and took it and drank.

"Do these episodes happen often?" she asked. "It's been so long since that horrible war."

"Not to me," Nick said.

They sat at the table together. He told her about his lost time, about how he'd been trying his best to catch up since his nightmare ended. He told her that he had created a whole different world in his head, that he'd thought he was in a prison camp but had actually been in St. Luke's. He told her that while he was there his mother had died of the Spanish Flu and his girlfriend had died of consumption. As he spoke he heard distant explosions.

Anna quietly listened to this with a look of concern, and after he finished she said, "I can't imagine what it's like for you."

"I'm just one of thousands," he said. "And you're another. Willie told me his father was killed in France."

Anna nodded. "At Belleau Wood, June 1918. I was seven

months pregnant and thought I would die or go mad."

"But you didn't," Nick said. "You didn't break down the way I did and send yourself into a fantasy world."

"Are you blaming yourself for that?"

"Who else should I blame?"

"Nobody. It simply happened."

"It didn't happen to you."

"And I don't know why. Maybe because I was pregnant. I told myself that I had to be strong for my child. Then Willie was born so small and weak and I couldn't afford to dwell on myself anymore. I stayed with him every minute until he pulled through. Then after his crisis passed the Spanish Flu struck and I was afraid we'd both catch it. We didn't, thank God, but my parents did and both of them died. Then my husband's parents died and my best friend died. Death and more death, it was horrible, horrible. Willie and I were the only ones left. There were times when I felt like dying too, but I had to survive for Willie."

"You're a brave woman, Mrs. Shuster."

"My faith gave me strength," she said. Then looking straight into his eyes she said, "Please call me Anna."

"And you call me Nick."

"Nick," she said. Then she added, "I knew there was something distressing you."

"How could you tell?"

"The first week you stayed here you shouted out in your sleep sometimes. Willie and I didn't hear it downstairs, but Flora told me. 'Something terrible has happened to that man,' she said. I think she was scared."

"Poor Flora. I'm sorry, I didn't know I was doing it."

"You haven't recently, and of course she knows you better now."

"She's okay?"

"She's fine."

It was quiet outside; the explosions had stopped. "I need to get Willie," Anna said.

"I'll get him."

"Maybe you better stay here."

"No, I'm okay."

"We'll both go then."

"I probably scared him to death."

"You scared *me* to death."

"That's apparently one of my better skills," Nick said. "First Flora then you and Willie. I'll try my best not to do it again." As they went to the hallway he asked, "Exactly what is Willie's problem, anyway?"

"Nobody really knows. He was just born sickly, and very small—he only weighed three pounds, four ounces. At one point they thought that he might have an abscessed lung but it turned out not to be true. Our doctor says he could still develop an abscess in the future. I certainly hope he doesn't, it would require surgery."

The fireworks had ended and the rooftop crowds had dispersed. Willie was staring at empty Shibe Park looking very worried.

"Was the ending spectacular?" Anna asked.

Willie nodded. "Yes." He turned to Nick. "Are you all right?"

"I'm fine."

"How's come you fell down?"

"I don't know. It just happened."

"Did you hurt yourself?"

"No."

"That's good."

"Well, let's get going, pal," Nick said, and hoisted him up.

"Are you going to watch the A's play the Red Sox again tomorrow?"

"A few innings. I have to work in the afternoon."

"I love it when you watch with me. You know so much about baseball."

"Lots of people do," Nick said.

The A's won again the following day and things were looking good for them. But not for Eddie Winters.

At the bar Happy Ernie said, "They bring Winters in with a five run lead in the ninth and he almost blows it. Back-to-back doubles and a walk. Mack oughtta dump the guy." Shrimpy croaked his agreement and Harvey added, "He's all w-w-w—" "Washed up," said Iron Mike, completing the sentence for him.

Nick kept hoping that Eddie wouldn't appear, and he didn't. He also kept hoping that Eddie would not get blotto in some other hangout or all by himself because of his bad performance.

But as soon as Nick walked onto Twentieth Street, shortly past one in the morning, he heard the commotion. It came from the end of the block, near the streetlight down there, a steady loud stream of swearing. A man leaned out of a window and yelled "Shut up! Shut up!" Nick broke into a run.

Eddie Winters was pacing with lurching steps in front of the house where he lived. He let loose another vulgar blast and Nick said, "Eddie! Pipe down, or somebody's going to call the cops!"

"Let 'em call," Eddie said. Then looking at Nick, the streetlight catching his furrowed forehead he said, "Who are you?"

"It's Nick."

"Nick. My old buddy. My dear old roomie. I'm finished, Nick."

"Eddie, let's go to your room."

"I'm no good anymore."

"Come on, let's go," Nick said, and took his arm.

He helped Eddie up the steps and onto the porch. "Whoa, steady," he said, "or you'll bring us both down."

The door to the house was unlocked. Nick led staggering Eddie through it and closed it behind him. "You on the team again?" Eddie asked.

"No, I'm not on the team."

"You should be. You're good. You struck Ruth out."

"Up we go," Nick said.

He managed to get Eddie up the stairs and into his room and guided him to his bed; Eddie flopped on it, bouncing, and lay on his back. "I'm finished," he said.

"You're not finished. Now get some sleep."

"Game tomorrow."

"No, Eddie, tomorrow's an off day. You have a doubleheader Saturday against the Indians."

"Another goddamn doubleheader," Eddie said. "Are they trying to kill us?"

"You can rest all day tomorrow."

"I'm finished, Nick, it's all over."

"No, Eddie," Nick said.

Then it suddenly dawned on him how he could make Ruth pay. Not with his life, or a ruined knee, but he'd pay, all right. "Eddie," he said, "you're not finished, you just need a new approach, a new pitch. I can teach you one."

"I'm too old for that."

"No you're not. Now listen: how would you like to get Babe Ruth and get him good."

"I'd love it!"

"Okay then, we'll talk about it the next time I see you."

"Talk," Eddie said. "We'll talk." His eyes looked slightly crossed as he stared at the ceiling.

Nick waited till Eddie fell asleep and then left the room, closing the door behind him.

He wanted to see the size of the middle bedroom—it would be the same size as the one in Anna's house since every place on the block was identical—but its door was also closed. It was certainly big enough to rent, however: somebody in it was snoring.

166

20

IN MARCH OF 1917 the Red Sox played a preseason game with an all-Negro team called the Arkansas Crows. The Crows had a left-handed pitcher named Flapjack Jackson, who, legend had it, survived on a diet of nothing but pancakes and coffee. Tall and sinewy, with sleepy eyes, he'd been playing forever, or so it seemed. Nobody knew how old he was; estimates ranged from thirty-five to fifty-five, and Flapjack wasn't saying. When anybody asked him, he simply grinned, displaying a gold front tooth in the upper right side of his jaw.

On this particular warm spring day, facing the Red Sox, Flapjack was astounding. He mowed the opposition down with slow methodical efficiency, striking out Ruth three times, making him look pathetic. But Ruth on the mound was also great and the Crows didn't have a run either.

By the seventh, the Red Sox' tempers were frayed. Several rookies were in the game in place of the regulars, but even so, for a bunch of coons to be showing them up like this was hard to take. What the hell was this Jackson throwing, anyway? It wasn't that fast, but whatever it was, nobody could hit it. It seemed that—just for a second—the ball would disappear on its way to the plate.

At last, in the bottom half of the seventh, a rookie named Swift blooped a single off Jackson, but Flapjack picked him off right quick with the slickest move to first you'd ever see. His next pitch came in high and tight, just missing the batter's head, and the batter, another rookie, a big blond guy named

Blundin, charged the mound.

Jackson just stood there holding his arms out and saying, "Mistake, mistake," but Blundin was having none of it. He came full force at Jackson, who turned and covered his head with his hands.

And that's when Nick sprang from the bench and tackled Blundin, pinning his arm behind him. The giant tried to shake Nick off but Nick held him fast. "Cool down, big boy," he said as Blundin continued to struggle and holler curses. Jackson walked off toward his bench and after a few more minutes Nick let the hothead go and that was the end of it. Both sides agreed to terminate the game.

The Red Sox players walked back to the Hotel Majestic. All except Nick, who went to the Crows' old broken-down bus. He approached Flapjack Jackson, who nodded and said, "You saved me a scuffle, man. Coulda been some big trouble you hadn't did that."

"What were you throwing?" Nick asked. "Your strikeout pitch."

"Thass what I call my ghost," said Flapjack. "Now you see it, now you don't. An then you do again."

"I'd like you to teach it to me."

Flapjack grinned and his gold tooth made an appearance. "Well see, thing is, it's my own invention I don't teach *no* one." He paused for a moment then cocked his head to the side. "However, considerin you saved my life, in your case I'll make an exception. Course, showin you *how* to do it don't mean you gone be *able* to."

He took his ball out of his glove and said, "It's like this," and showed Nick the grip. "But see, you don't break your wrist, you keep it straight and let the ball roll off your fingers. This way. Go out on the field an I'll throw you some."

Nick went to home plate. Jackson walked to the mound, went into a windup and threw. The ball came straight then amazingly vanished then reappeared again where you didn't expect it. It was like you went blind for an instant and then

168

when your sight returned it was too late to swing. Flapjack threw another dozen times with the same result. "You try it now," he said.

He went over the grip again and they switched positions. The grip made the ball feel strange to Nick. He threw. "Not bad, but you're breakin your wrist a little," Jackson said. Nick tried again. Each pitch was a little better, more natural. "You're gettin the hang of it, now what you need is practice. Keep that wrist real straight." The bus had been idling for a while and somebody shouted from one of the windows, "Hey Flapjack, we're hungry, man, let's get goin."

With a goodbye wave to Nick as he walked off the field Jackson said, "Thanks again for your rescue, man. You practice hard and maybe I'll check you out again next year."

"I hope so," Nick said.

He could never have guessed that when next year came he'd be far from Arkansas, far from spring training, fighting for his life in a forest in France.

A few days after Nick escorted pie-eyed Eddie up to his room, Eddie appeared at the Home Plate already pretty well tanked. During the four game set with Cleveland he hadn't been used at all, but this afternoon, with the Athletics leading the White Sox ten to one in the first of another doubleheader, Mack had put him in at the end of the game. He had given up two quick runs. "I'm cooked," he said to Nick as he sat at the counter and drank his rye. Some guys on the stools beside him were laughing and joking around as he mournfully looked at his glass.

Nick poured a draft of lager and slid it across to a customer; some foam slopped over the rim of the glass. He said to Eddie, "Remember a guy named Flapjack Jackson?"

Eddie kept looking down at his drink. "Flapjack Jackson. Sure, tall colored guy."

"That's right."

"I heard he's still pitchin down South."

169

Nick smiled. "No kidding."

"That's what I heard. So what about him?"

"He taught me his strikeout pitch. I was starting to get the hang of it when I joined the army."

"Yeah?"

"I could teach it to you."

"Nah, I'm too old for that."

"How old you think Flapjack is?"

"A hundred, but what's it to me?"

Nick mixed a drink for a customer, forcing a smile. He turned back to Eddie. "You got any dough saved up?"

"Hah," Eddie said.

"So if Mack lets you go, what will you do?"

"I don't know."

Nick was thinking about his new plan. Ruth had looked like the world's biggest fool as he'd helplessly flailed at Flapjack Jackson's pitches. If Eddie Winters could learn the ghost, Ruth would look like a fool again. Not only that, someone could make big money by betting against the Yanks and Ruth when Eddie was on the mound. And that someone, Nick thought, is *me*. By failing, Babe Ruth would be working for *me,* making money for *me*, and wouldn't that be delicious! A lot of things would have to go right for the plan to work, but it was worth a try. First, Eddie had to cooperate.

Nick said, "Eddie, listen to me. If you learn Jackson's pitch you'll be able to keep on going, maybe for years, the way he has. You'll be able to put some money aside, play the stock market maybe. Everyone wins, it's a sure thing these days."

"There ain't no such thing as a sure thing, Nick."

"Okay, I'll grant you that, but you'll save your career. You should give it a shot. Let's do it."

"Pour me another one," Eddie said.

"No, Eddie, I won't. The first thing you have to do is cut down on your drinking."

"Come on, Nick, pour me another one."

"Did you hear what I said? Do you want to end up down on

170

Vine Street?"

Eddie was staring at his glass. "It's so damn humiliatin'," he said. "I used to be good."

"Real good," Nick said. "And you can be good again— better than ever."

"Hah!"

"Let's give it a try."

Eddie shrugged. "Okay, what the hell."

The following morning, while Willie was at the piano, Nick told Anna he'd like to fix Flora's windows. Anna protested, but Nick said he liked that kind of work and asked if she had any tools. She told him that yes, there were some in the cellar.

He turned on the light and went down the steps. The cellar walls were brick and looked recently whitewashed. The floor was also brick and was spotless. A clothesline was coiled on a hook—the winter clothesline. He thought of the two other clotheslines he'd seen in the back yard yesterday, crowded with wash, and then thought of the gardens there, the one near the fence on the right filled with flowers, the one on the left with that vine that was maybe a squash or melon. He thought of Anna taking her dustpan and scraping up horse manure out on the street to use on these little gardens. The woman never stopped working.

A coal bin and cast iron furnace stood straight ahead. Nick pictured Anna in wintertime shoveling coal at the mouth of that furnace, then banking the fire. He saw a water meter and a gas hot water heater. And he saw what he'd come down here for, a well-stocked toolbox there on the workbench against the north wall. Some shelves held cans of paint and boxes of screws and nails and hinges and other hardware. Nick wondered if Willie had ever been down here to see all this stuff.

He looked around and found four saws: rip, crosscut, hacksaw and coping. He wouldn't need any of those today. He found a hatchet, a plane, and a brace and bit. He wouldn't need those either. He took the toolbox upstairs.

In the kitchen he said to Anna, "I couldn't find any sash cord, do you know if there's some around?"

"There probably isn't," she said. "But Martin had all kinds of things down there so I'm not really sure."

"He must've been very handy."

"He could fix anything," Anna said.

Willie's music had stopped. Nick found him playing cards in the parlor with Flora. "If you're not going to be in your room for a while," he said to her, "I'll fix your windows."

"Oh that would be grand!" Flora said dramatically, throwing her hands in the air.

Willie grinned at his cards and then slapped them down. "Gin!" he triumphantly cried.

In Flora's room Nick pried the sash bead away from one of the windows, removed the sash and measured the length of cord he would need. Then he walked to the hardware store where he'd tried for a job months ago. As the clerk measured out the cord, Nick thought of how desperate he'd been in the winter. And he realized how much he'd improved since then.

He hadn't heard voices or had any panicky feelings recently. He hadn't had any crying jags. He was sleeping better. If the memory-dreams would quit he would be in good shape. Maybe he'd been completely wrong about what it would take to be healed.

Back at the house the card game was over. Flora was reading a magazine on the sofa, and Willie was staring outside at some kids who were roller-skating and skillfully skirting the clumps of manure that Anna would certainly harvest. Nick thought of his own early years, how different they'd been from Willie's: he had always been running and jumping and skating and riding a bike. He said, "Want to give me a hand with the windows?"

Willie's face lit up. "Sure!"

Nick carried him up the stairs to Flora's room, placed a

chair near the window and set him in it. As he worked on the cords, he had Willie hold the edge of the sashes to keep them from falling over. Willie seemed to enjoy this task and took it quite seriously.

The toolbox held a copper oil can and Nick oiled all of the window pulleys, including those in his room. It also held a bottle of rubber washers, so after he finished the windows he carried the chair and Willie into the bathroom and worked on the faucet that started to drip a couple of days ago.

"How's come you know how to do all these things?" Willie asked. "Are you a handyman, like Stanley?"

"I learned from my father, he was a jack of all trades," Nick said. He was thinking that if his father hadn't smoked so much, he would probably still be restoring old houses and doing odd jobs. "Do you know what a jack of all trades is?"

"Someone who knows how to fix lots of things?"

"That's right."

"My father was one of those jacks," Willie said, "that's what Mother told me. I want to be one of them too when I grow up."

"You're already on your way."

"I'll be a jack of all trades and a concert pianist."

"Good combination," Nick said.

He finished the faucet job, closed up the toolbox, slung Willie over his shoulder, returned the chair to the bedroom and went downstairs.

As he put Willie into his wheelchair he heard a loud noise from the kitchen and went down the hall.

Anna was turning the crank of a grinder attached to the kitchen counter. She stopped when she saw him.

"What's this?" he asked.

"I'm grinding red wheat into flour."

"You make your own flour?"

"It has more nutrients than the store-bought kind. It's better for Willie."

173

"Well isn't that something. No wonder your bread's so good. It makes that store stuff taste like nothing. And you know what I saw at Leewright's the other day? Bread that's already sliced!"

"Who would ever buy that?"

"Lazy people."

She smiled. "So how did your work go?"

He told her what he had accomplished.

"Wonderful," she said. "But I still feel guilty about you doing all that."

"Don't," Nick said.

Her pocketbook hung on a peg near the door that led to the bathroom. She went to it, took out her change purse. "How much was the sash cord?"

"Forget it."

"I insist," Anna said, but Nick waved her off.

"You'll have lunch with us then," she said. "It's the least I can do."

"That would be great," Nick said.

Flora paid extra to take all her meals with Anna and Willie, and so she was present at lunch. The four of them sat at the round wooden kitchen table. A vase full of garden flowers—pink mallow, white phlox, and red sweet William—sat at its center. Alice had grown these very same flowers. Sweet Alice. Nick took a long deep breath.

Anna served what she called Danish pancakes, made from her freshly ground flour, slathered with butter and drizzled with real maple syrup. Nick wondered what Flapjack Jackson would make of *these*. They were absolutely fantastic.

Anna and Nick drank strong black coffee, while Flora and Willie had tea. "I love coffee, but can't drink it anymore," Flora said. "It keeps me up all night. How did I get so old?"

"Oh Flora, you're not old," Anna said.

"What would you know?" Flora said with a laugh. "You're still a child."

Turning to Willie, Anna said, "What do you think, am I a

child?"

"Of course not!" Willie said. "*I'm* a child!"

Nick said, "Danish pancakes, I've never had them before. Are you Danish, Anna?"

"My parents were."

Nick was silent a moment. He frowned at his plate, then said, "And your husband..."

"His father was German and his mother was Dutch."

Nick nodded. He took a bite of his pancake and chewed it slowly. "That third bedroom upstairs," he said. "I guess it's pretty small compared to the others, but isn't it big enough to rent?"

"It's my storage room," Anna said. "These houses don't have attics and the cellar gets damp at times, so that's where I store the things I'm not presently using."

"Oh. I thought it might bring in some extra money."

"Extra money is always welcome, but it won't come from there."

"Well how about renting your roof to baseball fans like the rest of your neighbors do?"

"I don't want to do that either."

Nick shrugged and poured himself more coffee.

After the meal was over, Flora made her ponderous way upstairs; she was eager to see how her windows worked. Nick followed her into her room, and she tried the center sash first. "Smooth as silk!" she exclaimed. She tried the side windows. "Wonderful! What a difference this makes! Thank you so much!"

"You're quite welcome," Nick said. He paused for a moment then said, "Were you in the theater, Flora?"

She laughed. "Heavens no, why do you ask?"

"While I was working I noticed the photographs on your walls—Sarah Bernhardt and other actresses—all of them signed."

"Oh, they were customers of mine. For years I was the women's clothing buyer at Wanamaker's, and I had the most

MAR-velous clientele. Whenever they wanted something special they could count on me to procure it. I found several exquisite robes for Sarah. What a delight she was! You must have noticed the poster, too."

"I did." It showed a woman—Bernhardt—with her hands on a very large jar of some kind; Nick thought it quite beautiful.

"That's the poster that Mucha created for *La Samaritaine*," Flora said. I first met Sarah when she starred here in that play back in 1911, creating all the stir."

"What kind of stir?"

"A large contingent of Christians rallied at City Hall in an effort to keep the play from being staged. They said it was blasphemous, sacrilegious. But Sarah paid no attention to any of that and the show went on. Imagine! She'd played that part in Paris years ago without any fuss at all. Well, that's the difference between the cities of Paris and Philadelphia."

Nick was looking at the poster now and frowning: *La Samaritaine*. "Metropolitain," he said in a quiet voice.

"I beg your pardon?"

"I was there," he said.

"In Paris?"

"Yes." The memory was very dim. "It was during the war. I can't remember how long I was there or how long I stayed, but I was there. I remember the streets smelled of coffee and cigarettes. Water constantly ran in the gutters. I remember the Metropolitain, the subway train."

"La Ville de Lumiere!" Flora said. "The City of Light! I always wanted to go, but fate would not cooperate."

"A shame," Nick said. He was thinking that his mind was a lot like that tricky pitch, the ghost, riddled with blind spots. But the blind spots were filling in; his past continued to expand. He said, "Is Sarah Bernhardt still alive?"

"Oh no, she died five years ago. She's buried in Paris, in Pere LaChaise. She used to sleep in a coffin to prepare for some of her roles, and I wonder if that's the coffin they buried her in. A truly a-MAZ-ing talent! Even after she lost her leg to gangrene at the age of seventy-one she kept on going. Did you know that she once had a show of her paintings and sculptures here, right here in Philadelphia?"

"Really."

"Yes, she was an artist, too, and a very good one. Too bad you never saw her perform."

"It is," Nick said. He had only seen one professional play in his life, with Alice, at the Walnut Street Theater, and he hadn't liked it. "Well, glad you're happy with the windows," he said. "Let me know if you have any trouble with them." He started toward the hall when Flora said, "Wait a second, I want to tell you something. Close the door."

Nick pushed it shut and came back to Flora. Her fragrance was suddenly overpowering. "That storage room," she said in a confidential tone. "It was Anna's husband's study. When he died she locked it and no one has ever gone in there again, other than herself. That's what Sol Cohen told me, he came to live here shortly before I did."

"You've never seen it, then."

"I never have. I don't even know how big it is, but it doesn't matter, she'd never think of renting it. Willie is almost ten, an age where he'll want more privacy, but I guess that room is off limits."

"Too bad."

"Indeed," Flora said. "Her husband's death was such a tragedy! She was twenty years old and pregnant, and then when Willie was born he was terribly frail. She had to rent out rooms in order to keep the house, but not that room."

Flora paused for a moment then said, "She goes there sometimes late at night, I've heard her. She thinks I'm asleep but I've heard her go in there and close the door. She stays there quite a while then goes downstairs again. Martin was killed a long time ago, but I don't think she'll ever get over it."

"There are some things you never get over," Nick said. "They're like scars deep inside you that won't go away." He felt suddenly foolish and said, "Well, Flora, I'm sure I don't have to tell you that."

Flora threw up her hands and said, "Scars! Do I have scars!"

21

THE A'S WON NINE of their last eleven games at home then left on a long road trip. Nick had seen parts of those contests with Willie up on the roof, and there had been plenty to cheer about. In one of the games, the first of yet another twin bill, twenty year old Jimmie Foxx hit the longest blast Shibe Park had ever seen, a ball that cleared the left field stands. Willie had gaped in amazement and Nick had said, "There's a boy with a future."

On that very same day, Babe Ruth hit his thirty-ninth homer, putting him nine games ahead of his record-setting pace of the year before. But the Yankees were not doing well. One of their pitchers suddenly couldn't find the plate, another fell gravely ill, and another one's arm went dead. Their seemingly insurmountable lead was shrinking. They were now only eight games ahead of the A's, who were coming on strong.

Nick had worked on the ghost pitch with Eddie for more than a week before the A's took off. He didn't want Anna and Willie asking him how he knew Eddie Winters—Anna was so dead set against ballplayers—so he'd go to the diamond in Reyburn Park by himself and Eddie would join him shortly with a ball and an extra glove—a lefty's glove. Eddie was a lefty, same as Nick. When they finished a session, Eddie would go home first and Nick would follow ten minutes later.

The first time they went to the park Nick took the mound and had Eddie stand at the plate. As they tossed the ball back and forth to warm up, Nick tried to put something on it but couldn't. He wondered: did Willie's legs feel the same way his arm felt? They probably felt worse. "Okay," he finally said, "let me give it a try." He held the ball with Flapjack's grip, wound up and threw.

Eddie spat some tobacco juice onto the ground. "Just looked like a changeup to me," he said as he tossed the ball back.

"It's been a long time," Nick said. He threw it again and again with the same result and then suddenly realized his mistake: he was keeping his wrist straight but wasn't releasing the ball at the proper point. He made the adjustment and threw and the ball struck the heel of Eddie's glove and rolled all the way to the backstop. "Whoa," Eddie said, "what was that?"

"Did it look like it disappeared for a second?"

"Sure did, and then when I saw it again it was lower than I expected."

"I'm getting the feel of it now."

The next pitch also bounced off Eddie's glove. "That's a helluva pitch," Eddie said, "but it'll be hell on a catcher, too, worse than a spitter or knuckler."

Nick laughed. "The catcher will get used to it because he'll see it so often. But the batter won't."

He threw it a few more times and Eddie managed to catch it. He shook his head. "How come you never used this beauty back when we played together?"

"I learned it just before I went to war and never had the chance to try it out. Okay, now it's your turn, come here."

Eddie walked to the mound. Nick showed him the grip and release point and Eddie said, "Reminds me of old Chief Bender's nickel change."

"You know how to throw a nickel change?"

Eddie laughed. "Chief Bender's a coach now and one time I asked him to show me his famous pitch. He did, but I never could get the hang of it."

"The nickel change is great," Nick said, "but the ghost is

180

even better. With the nickel change the batter sees a red dot on the ball. With the ghost he sees *nothing*."

He reviewed the mechanics again with Eddie then went behind the plate. "Okay," he said, "give it a shot."

Eddie threw and the pitch didn't work. He threw a few more failures and moaned again that he was too old to learn something new. Nick said, "You told me you wanted to get Ruth good, right?"

"Did I?"

"That night when I helped you up the stairs."

Eddie spat brown juice. "You helped me up the stairs? I don't remember."

"My God. Well you do want to get him, don't you?"

"Hell yes."

"Well this is the way to do it."

Nick showed him the pitch again and went back to the plate. After another dozen throws and plenty of spitting and cursing, the ghost finally made an appearance. "All right!" Nick said. "All you need now is repetition."

By the end of the week, Eddie had pretty well mastered the ghost's fundamentals but still had trouble with control. Nick told him to practice the pitch with Cy Perkins, the Athletics' backup catcher, while the team was on the road, but figured he probably wouldn't.

"Don't show it to anyone other than Perkins," Nick said. "Don't talk about it, don't say how you learned it. Keep it a secret."

"Will do," Eddie said.

He hadn't shown up at the Home Plate since Nick said he had to stop drinking, and there hadn't been any more shouting episodes in the street. Encouraging signs, but Nick was afraid that when Eddie was off in distant cities his dry spell would end. However, a few days after the A's left town he saw in the paper that Eddie had pitched an inning against the White Sox and hadn't allowed a hit. He wondered: had he tried the ghost?

On Willie's tenth birthday Anna baked a chocolate layer cake, and at two o'clock, when Willie was up from his nap, she invited Nick and Flora into the kitchen to share it. They sat at the table and Willie blew out the candles with one huge face-flushing breath and made a secret wish, and then Anna sliced into the cake.

After Nick took his first bite he said, "Anna, you are the world's best cook."

She laughed. "And how would you know that?"

"I've bought your bread and muffins and cinnamon buns at Leewright's and I've eaten your Danish pancakes. I can't imagine anyone making better stuff than that."

"Well," Anna said, blushing slightly, "I must say, I'm flattered."

"Just telling the truth."

"Nick's right," Flora said. "You are the best."

"Yes, Mother, you are," Willie said.

"I suppose this means you'll all want a second slice," Anna said.

"Just a small one for me," Nick said.

Flora opened her pocketbook, took out her change purse, came up with a couple of dollar bills. "Willie, this is for you on your special day," she said.

Willie smiled broadly as he took the money. "Thank you very much, Aunt Flora!"

Nick got up from his chair. "Excuse me a minute," he said, and went down the hall and up the stairs.

He came back with a box wrapped in yellow paper. "I have a present for you too," he said.

Willie tore off the paper and opened the box—and took out a baseball glove. "Wow, this is really swell!" he said. "Thanks, Uncle Nick!"

"You're welcome. Now look, I was thinking that if you aren't too full of cake, we could go down the street to the Square and have a catch."

Willie looked at his mother. "Can I?"

182

Anna was frowning, but said, "I suppose so."

"Swell!" Willie said.

Nick had Willie wheel himself to Reyburn Park. Anna was always afraid that Willie would get too tired and tended to push the chair when they went out, but Nick thought she babied him too much.

The park was only a half block away from the house, but Willie was breathing hard when they reached it. And that was good, Nick thought. He needed the exercise.

The glove was in Willie's lap and a baseball was nestled in it; an unsigned, scuffed-up ball, not one of the autographed balls. "So Willie, you ever used a glove before?" Nick asked. Willie shook his head no.

"It needs to be broken in, and the way to break it in is to use it. And when you're not using it, keep your ball in it. Here, throw me the ball."

Willie threw and Nick caught it. "Hey, pretty good," he said. He moved away ten feet. "Put your glove on," he said, and Willie did. "Good. Ready? Here we go."

He tossed the ball softly, underhand. Willie stuck out his glove and the ball struck its heel and bounced onto the grass.

Nick retrieved it. "Ready?" He threw again. Same result. "Drat!" Willie exclaimed.

"Don't worry, you'll get it," Nick said.

After another three tosses, Willie managed to catch the ball. "Good job," Nick said. "Now after you catch it, close your right hand over it so it won't fall out and you're ready to throw."

They kept going, and Willie broke into a grin each time he caught the ball. "This is fun," he said.

"Of course it is. And you're using the very same ball that the big leaguers use."

"That's right, I am. And I bet I could catch the ball better if I could stand up."

183

"I'm sure you could."

"I can stand up a little."

Nick frowned. "You can?"

"If you help me."

Nick went to the wheelchair. "I stand when I go to the toilet," Willie said. "Mother helps me at the door, then once I'm up, I'm on my own."

"You mean you can walk to the toilet?"

"Yes. It's only a couple of steps."

"Well isn't that something," Nick said. "Okay, up we go."

With Nick's support, Willie got to his feet. He was shivering, trembling, but said, "You can let go now."

Nick did. Willie took a few shaky steps and then collapsed. He made a face.

Nick helped him up. "Did you hurt yourself?"

"Not really, but it's kind of hard to walk on the grass."

"Want to give it another try?"

"Okay."

This time Willie went two steps further. When he fell he was fighting for breath. As Nick helped him into his wheelchair he said, "Does your mother know you can do this?"

"No. I never walked this far for her."

"Well listen, let's keep it a secret for now. We can practice, and then when you get real good, we'll surprise her."

"You think that I'll get real good?"

"I'm sure of it. Look at all you've learned today. You've caught a real major league ball and you've taken six steps."

"Yes," Willie said.

"What you really should do is roll your chair up to Somerset Street and back a few times every day to build up your wind."

"Will you watch me if I do that?"

"Of course."

"Okay then, I'll do it."

"Good. And remember now, don't tell your mother about

184

how you walked today, and someday we'll really surprise her."

Back at the house Nick went up to his room. Willie rolled down the hallway and into the kitchen and drank a big glass of water.

"So did you have fun?" Anna asked.

"I did. I caught the ball zillions of times."

"That's wonderful."

He rolled to the bathroom door and pushed it open. Anna came over and helped him stand. When he walked the few steps to the toilet his legs were shaking as always and yet he felt stronger than usual.

Back in his wheelchair he went to the living room. Kids were playing a game in the street with a pink rubber ball. It was a game like baseball but they used their fists to hit the ball and they didn't have any gloves. He knew he was lucky to have a glove and a baseball too. But the kids on the street were really lucky because they could walk.

He turned away from the window then and went to the piano. As he stared at the keys he thought: *I will walk someday. I will practice and practice, just like I practice piano, and I will walk.*

Then he thought of his birthday party, the wish he had made. He could never tell anyone what he had wished, or it wouldn't come true. He had not wished that he would get better or that he could walk. What he'd thought when he'd blown out the candles was this: *I wish Uncle Nick was my father.*

22

Each hot steamy midsummer morning, Nick guided Willie's wheelchair down the wide steps of the porch and watched as he rolled his way up the sidewalk to Somerset Street. At first it was all he could do to go to the end of the block, turn around, and come back to the house again. But pretty soon he was able to do it twice, then three times, four times, and then he was going past his house to Lehigh Avenue and back. After a couple of weeks he was able to do the house to Somerset to Lehigh trip four times.

On his trips he often encountered kids in the street. He knew a few of them—like super ball hawk Peanuts Sullivan and super popcorn salesman Scootie Mulroney, who'd played gin rummy with Flora and him a few times—but he didn't know most of the others. Some of them would say hi to him, he'd say hi back, and that was it. But after he finished his exercise he would sometimes sit on the porch in his wheelchair and talk with them.

Nick was pleased about this and thought that Anna was too, but she never said. She admitted that Willie's increasing endurance impressed her, but said she was worried, too. She feared that the vigorous exercise might put too much strain on his delicate system and lead to a collapse. "I won't run him into the ground," Nick assured her. "Just little by little is all we do."

He fixed a number of other things around the house: more sash cords, a worn out light switch, a clogged-up drain in the bathroom, a couple of rotted fence boards. Anna invited him

186

to her Sunday dinners and he accepted gladly. The café's sandwiches were good, but Anna's meals were superb.

If it wasn't too hot and not raining and Willie was feeling good, Nick would have a catch with him in the Square. Willie's arms were much stronger because of his wheelchair exercise, and he could get out of the chair on his own. In the games of catch he sometimes got hit in the shoulders or chest and he winced but never cried. Nick cheered him on as he practiced his walking; on a good day he'd take twenty steps. Willie was thrilled, and of course Nick was too. It was almost time for Willie to show his mother what he could do.

The A's would be back pretty soon for a long home stand and Willie could hardly wait. But before that, another exciting event would take place: Fro-Joy Cone Week.

It would start on Monday, August 6th, and with every cone you bought that week you'd get a Babe Ruth card. Each day the card would be different. "I have to collect them all," Willie said to his mother, who stood at the sink scraping carrots.

"Willie," she said, "you know you are only allowed to have ice cream on Fridays."

"But this is a special week. And anyway, Fro-Joy is good for kids."

"According to them."

"Uncle Nick, if I get a cone one day and you get one the next day and Mother gets one the next day it means that I'll only eat two cones and I'll have the whole set of cards."

"You have it all figured out," Nick said.

"Can we do it?"

"And who's going to pay for all those cones?" Anna asked.

"I will—with the birthday money I got from Aunt Flora."

"It's going to be pretty hard to watch us eat those cones when you don't have one yourself," Nick said. "Especially when you're paying for them."

"I won't mind."

"Well, I guess so then," Anna said.

So on Monday, when Blinky the Ice Cream Man turned his cart onto Twentieth Street, ringing his irresistible bell, it surprised him to see Willie waving him down from his porch. "A Monday cone for you?" he said. "What is this, some kind of a special day?"

"A special *week*," Willie said. "I'm buying a cone every day because of the cards."

"Ah-hah," Blinky said.

Blinky was part of the neighborhood's rhythm. Snuffy Simpson, the paperboy, led off each day, tossing his tightly folded *Inquirers* onto the porches. He was followed three times a week by Milton, the milkman, who clopped down the street with his horse-drawn wagon. Soon after Milton came Randolph, the butter and egg man, who smoked bitter-smelling cigars; Augie, the ice man, strong as a bull; and Harry, the huckster, whose leather-lunged yell could wake the dead. Warren, the mailman, a short peppy red-headed guy who constantly whistled came morning and afternoon, and Blinky, the ice cream man, appeared every day except Sunday some time after one P.M.

Blinky, whose given name was Maurice, a skinny young guy with a white uniform and a white peaked hat, was an entrepreneur and inventor. He had fashioned his cart from a huge tricycle to which he'd attached a box lined with cork insulation. He would pick up a block of ice from Augie each day before noon and then fill up his box with treats he bought wholesale the same as the grocery stores did. He would pedal like mad from street to street ringing his bell and the kids would come running. He had a condition that made him jerk and blink a lot but didn't slow him down. And now as he mounted the steps and took Willie's nickel and gave him a cone and a card, he twitched his shoulders and blinked three times and said, "Well I guess you know if you get all six of these cards you can trade them in for a genuwine autographed picture of Babe Ruth."

"I know," Willie said. He was staring intently at the card, a headshot of Ruth. Under the picture it said, "George Herman ('Babe') Ruth." "He's the best baseball player in the world!" Willie said, and Blinky, even though he was an A's fan, didn't disagree.

The fact of the matter was, though, the Wizard of Wham had not been performing well for weeks; his average had dropped and his home run output had shrunk dramatically. His past had been peppered with various ailments, and people were starting to wonder if he was again in the grip of some kind of affliction. Without the force of his thundering bat, the Yankees continued to slide.

With pressure from Nick, Anna relented and let Willie eat the cones Tuesday and Wednesday. "Look Mother," he said, as he happily took a long lick of vanilla, "it says it right here on the cards. 'Fro-Joy builds bone and strength.' And it's full of 'youth units,' too."

"Whatever they are," Anna said.

"They must be like vitamins," Willie said. "Milk has vitamin D." He turned to Nick. "Did you know you can also get vitamin D from the sun?"

"From the sun?" Nick said. "Where did you ever hear that?"

"I read it in the *Book of Knowledge*. Vitamin D's real good for you. It cures rickets."

"Well you must get a lot of it up on the roof."

"I do. And I think it helps my condition." He took another lick of the cone. "If ice cream's bad for you," he said, "how's come we like it so much?"

"It must be a part of God's plan," Nick said, and Anna shot him a look.

Willie now had three cards. Number 2 was "Look Out, Mr. Pitcher!" and number 3 was "'Babe' Ruth's Grip." "So *that's* how he holds his bat!" Willie said. "I can't wait to see what the other cards are, it's so exciting. And tomorrow the A's come home and play the Senators!"

Actually, the A's were already home, and on Wednesday evening, while Nick was at work, Eddie Winters came through the door.

"You guys are really clicking," Nick said.

"But I ain't," Eddie said.

Nick frowned. "From what I read in the papers, you did okay."

"At first, but then I stunk. I gotta learn that pitch you were tryin to teach me. I tried to practice it with Cy but forgot the grip. That's why I came here tonight, I don't want no drink, I want you to work with me again."

"You been cutting back on the booze?"

"Not a drop the whole time I was gone."

"Good man. So when do you have to report to the field tomorrow?"

"Noon."

"Well come to the house at ten and I'll be waiting. With a friend."

Willie practiced piano for over an hour the following morning, beginning at nine. At ten, with his glove and his ball in his lap, he sat on the porch in his wheelchair. Nick sat beside him on the steps.

"Maybe he's not going to come," Willie said.

"He better come," Nick said. He had gotten up more than an hour early and hadn't eaten anything. His stomach was hollow.

"Well how's come you know him anyway?" Willie asked.

"He eats at the place where I work."

"And he wants to practice his pitching with you?"

"Yes. I said I would do it."

"Oh," Willie said with a puzzled look.

Another ten minutes went by before Winters appeared on the porch at the end of the block. "I had a little problem I had to take care of," he said coming close. He was wearing his baseball glove and holding another, which he gave to Nick.

He spat a stream of tobacco juice into the gutter and glanced at Willie. "We ready?"

"All set," Nick said. "My friend Willie Shuster is joining us."

Willie was staring at Eddie; he seemed transfixed.

Nick smiled. "Well here you are," he said, "a real major leaguer."

"I know," Willie said.

Nick bumped the wheelchair down the steps and then Willie took over. "Who's pitching today?" Nick asked.

Eddie and Willie both said, "Earnshaw," and Eddie laughed. "You know your baseball, kid. You're right, it's Earnshaw, and he's hot."

"Al Simmons is my favorite A," Willie said. "He lives on this street and sometimes I see him walk by." Then his face clouded over as if he had made a tremendous mistake and he added, "But I like you too, Mr. Winters."

"Call me Eddie."

"Okay, thank you, I will. I like you too, but I don't have a baseball card of you."

"That's because there ain't none."

"Why not?"

Eddie laughed again. "That's what *I* want to know."

They crossed Lehigh Avenue, entered the Square and went to the baseball field. By the time they got there Willie was breathing hard and soaked with sweat.

On the mound Nick showed Eddie the grip and the motion again and then went behind the plate. Eddie threw a few warmup tosses then said, "Okay."

He spat some brown soup and then threw the ghost. "The wrist," Nick said as he tossed the ball back. "Right," Eddie said, and threw again.

"That's it," Nick said.

Before the next pitch, Eddie's hand traveled up to his mouth and Nick shouted, "Eddie!"

"Oh, geez," Eddie said, "I forgot, it's such a habit." He

191

wiped his hand on his pants.

Nick had warned Eddie not to use spit. Any stain on the ball could spoil the ghost effect. But Eddie had thrown his spitball for so many years that he needed constant reminding.

"Sorry, Nick, I'm ready now," he said.

"You have to remember, Eddie."

"I know, I know."

They practiced for half an hour and Eddie kept getting better. By the time they quit, the pitch had a decent dip and was going where Eddie wanted it to the majority of the time. "Not bad," Nick said, and Eddie grinned. "Old Flapjack Jackson," he said.

"You throw so *fast*," Willie said.

"Nah, this is slow stuff," Eddie said. "You want to see fast, watch Grove."

"We'll practice it every day," Nick said.

"It's a deal. You want to switch places and throw a few?"

"And why would I want to do that?"

"For old time's sake."

Nick laughed. "I want to throw some to Willie."

Willie got out of his chair and Nick walked off a dozen feet or so and tossed the ball—overhand this time. Willie caught it and threw it back.

"Good going," Nick said. He threw another dozen times and Willie only dropped two. "Hey, Eddie," Nick said, "why don't *you* throw a few to Willie."

Eddie took the ball and threw. It bounced off Willie's glove. "A little softer," Nick said.

Eddie threw again, and this time Willie caught it. "There you go," Nick said. "Now you can say you caught a ball that was thrown by a real major leaguer."

"*Two* real major leaguers," Eddie said.

Willie looked at him. "What do you mean?"

"He never told you?" Eddie said. "Me and him played on the Red Sox together."

Willie just stood there, his arms at his sides. Then turning to

192

Nick: "You played on the *Red Sox*?"

"A long time ago."

"Wow!" Willie said.

Nick laughed—but he wanted to throttle Eddie. "Want to practice your walking?"

"Sure!" Willie said. He was grinning from ear to ear.

He went about twenty-five feet before falling and stood up without any help. He was shiny with sweat. "Terrific," Nick said. "Now we better go home and get something to drink."

Nick parted ways with Eddie in front of the house. They agreed to meet the same time the next morning.

Nick took the baseball glove into the house and hung it on one of the hallway's coat hooks. He hung Willie's beside it. The hallway was filled with the fragrance of freshly baked bread and Nick's appetite kicked in hard. Willie rolled himself into the kitchen, where Anna was taking loaves out of the oven. Nick followed and stood in the doorway.

"Mother, guess what," Willie said. "Uncle Nick was a baseball player."

Setting a loaf on a wire rack Anna said, "I seem to remember he told us he *wasn't* a baseball player."

"He's not anymore," Willie said, "but he used to be. He played for the Red Sox—with Eddie Winters. I met Eddie Winters today, and he wasn't drunk, he was nice. He threw me a ball and I caught it."

"Wonderful," Anna said. She placed a second loaf of bread beside the first. "Now get yourself some water, your face is flushed."

"And Uncle Nick is teaching him a new pitch," Willie said as he wheeled himself up to the icebox. "It's called the ghost."

"How interesting," Anna said.

Willie opened the icebox door and took out the water bottle. The water was boiled. Anna would not let him drink water straight from the tap; she thought it might give him a bug. "Why don't you pour Uncle Nick a glass," she said.

193

Willie did, and gave it to him, then filled his own glass.

Nick took a drink of the water and said, "Your bread smells wonderful, Anna."

"Is that a hint that you'd like a sample?"

Nick smiled.

Anna sliced off the end of a loaf and handed it to him. "The butter is there on the table," she said.

"Anna, you are too kind," Nick said.

Willie finished his water, put the glass on the counter, then turned and frowned at Nick. He said, "Babe Ruth used to play for the Red Sox a long time ago. He was a pitcher."

"That's right," Nick said. He spread butter across the bread.

Willie's eyebrows went up. "Did you know him?"

Nick nodded. "I did."

"Wow!" Willie said.

23

THE SESSION WITH EDDIE went well the next morning. The trees in the Square were heavy with heat and cicadas were whining as Willie stood watching, bracing himself on the back of his chair. Yesterday afternoon he had gotten another Fro-Joy Babe Ruth card, which he'd left at home on the nightstand beside his bed. It was "Ruth is a Crack Fielder."

"I don't know about that," Nick said when he saw it.

"You don't think he is?" Willie asked.

"I've seen better."

Eddie was throwing the ghost with confidence now. His control was good and the dip was sharp. "Try it today in the pen and see what Perkins thinks," Nick said.

"Will do," Eddie said, and spat some tobacco juice onto the grass.

"You guys were terrific yesterday," Willie said. The A's had beaten the Senators eight to three.

"And we're gonna be even better today," Eddie said. "Grove's pitching."

"I can't wait to watch it," Willie said.

"Let's do some walking," Nick said.

Willie walked from the mound to home plate and almost back again before his legs buckled. "You're doin great, Skipper," Eddie said. "Good work," Nick said, and Willie grinned.

When they got back home Nick said, "I think this might be the day to surprise your mother. You want to try?"

195

"Okay."

Nick pulled the wheelchair up onto the porch and Willie wheeled into the house. At the end of the hallway Anna, as usual, was working away in the kitchen.

"This is the perfect time," Nick said. "Give it a shot."

Willie pushed himself out of the chair. He stood there a couple of seconds, getting his balance, then started to walk. "Mother!" he said.

Anna turned from the stove and stood motionless, looking astonished. "Willie!" she said as he kept advancing with slow and careful steps.

He made it to her with ease and she reached out and gathered him into her arms. "Oh Willie, how wonderful!"

"We've been practicing," Willie said, breathing hard. "Uncle Nick has been helping me out in the park every day."

"What a great surprise."

"And my legs don't hurt when I do it. They used to hurt but now they're stronger."

"I'm absolutely thrilled."

Willie was beaming. "I think I might get all better someday," he said, then he suddenly started to cough. He sat at the table and Anna brought him some water.

He drank, but the coughing resumed. When it finally subsided he said, "Do you think I will get all better?"

"I do," Anna said. She looked at Nick, who stood at the edge of the hallway. "It's lunchtime," she said. "Will you join us?"

"I'd love to," Nick said.

Anna had bought a bushel of Jersey tomatoes from Harry the Huckster and also a bushel of peaches. What she didn't use fresh she would can. Now she sliced some tomatoes, spread mayonnaise on some bread and made sandwiches. They all drank iced tea, and after they finished the sandwiches each of them had a peach and a homemade cookie. Then Willie went in for his nap. Nick dried the dishes as Anna washed them.

196

"How long has this walking been going on?" she asked.

"Ever since we started playing catch. He told me he could walk a few steps so I asked him to show me. We took it from there."

"It really is quite amazing."

"I think he's going to beat this condition, whatever it is."

"He very well might," Anna said. "But if he needs an operation to help him beat it, I don't know what I'll do. It's hard enough making the mortgage payments and paying the taxes on this house."

"Let's not think about operations," Nick said. "But I think you should reconsider renting your roof. If you rent to just twenty people, you'll make five dollars each day that the A's are at home. That would help you a lot."

"But wouldn't all those shoes damage the roof? I don't want it to leak."

"It's tar and gravel, very tough. And I can make bleachers like those your neighbors have. They distribute the weight and get people off their feet."

Anna did not look convinced. "I hate the idea of all those strangers tromping through my house," she said.

"I'd keep an eye on them."

"But you'd have to leave for work before the game was over."

"Not every day."

"Most days."

"You're right. But most people behave themselves. We wouldn't allow them to drink. And you know what? Willie could sell them popcorn up there. The kid next door does it, and lemonade, too. There's a kid down the block who even sells hot dogs."

Anna shrugged. "I don't know. I'll have to think about it some more."

"Please do."

One thirty came and went, then one forty-five, and Blinky

the ice cream man still hadn't arrived. Willie wanted to see the game, which started at two, but didn't want to miss his Fro-Joy card. He asked his mother if she would buy his cone for him today.

"And what am I supposed to do?" she said. "Stand out on the porch and wait until Blinky shows up?"

"You'll hear his bell. Mother, please, won't you do it for me?"

Anna sighed. "By the time I take the cone up to the roof in this heat, it will be half melted."

"The card's the important thing, you can eat the cone."

Nick carried Willie up to the second floor. At the foot of the steps that led to the roof he said, "Want to give it a try?"

Willie looked anxious. "I guess."

"I know you can do it," Nick said.

Setting one foot on the lowest step, Willie grabbed onto the railing and started up. The going was painfully slow, but he didn't quit. At the fourth step he faltered but Nick was behind him and kept him from slipping. Willie pushed open the hatch that led to the roof and sunlight poured in, then he tumbled out onto the gravel. He was gasping.

"Good job," Nick said. "Really good."

Willie rested a minute then stood up and walked to his chair. The other roofs were already full and some of the people had turned to watch him. One of them, a chubby cigar-smoking fellow, grinned and gave him a thumbs-up sign. Willie was grinning too. Nick wiped off his chair and Willie sat down. Nick stood beside him, holding the back of the chair.

Lefty Grove was hot right from the start and the Senators looked pathetic. By the end of the fifth, Nick's interest waned and his mind began to wander. He stretched; looked around at the crowds on either side. He looked at the factories blocks away, spewing their deadly smoke.

The afternoon sun was coating the houses on Somerset

Street with a golden light and one of them caught Nick's eye. The upper sash of one of its windows was gleaming so brightly it made him squint.

Something disturbed him about that window, that blinding sun. He seemed to remember another window just like that, far off, the sun on it just like that on a hot afternoon. Then somebody on the roof to his right, standing against the wooden railing, said, "He's just a kid."

The words went spiraling through Nick's head. Then the rooftops exploded with sudden loud cheering, his skin went hot, and the gunfire came from the second floor window. Its top half was blazing with sunlight. "Strike him out, Hudson!" the captain yelled.

Nick stood, pulled the pin out and threw the grenade and it shattered the bright upper sash. A few seconds later the house spewed debris with a mighty roar.

They waited a minute and all was still. "Let's go!" the captain said and they ran to the house, ran into the fading smoke, their weapons ready.

At the top of the stairs they found only one body lying there, soaked in blood. "Oh Jesus," the captain said, "he's just a kid."

He was maybe fifteen, and the top of his head was gone. Nick had killed many others but this one was different. *A kid. Just a kid.*

Then the arm that had thrown the grenade began burning, and then it went numb. And the next thing he knew he was outside again on the ground looking up at the smoking sky and the captain's face. "Hudson," the captain said, and his voice was soft and thin.

Nick worked his mouth but no sound came out. The world was dull and far away. He was back on his feet and slowly walking; someone was holding him up so he didn't fall. His feet were numb, his legs were numb, his entire body was numb. *Johnny,* a voice in his head kept saying, but the man who was holding him up wasn't Johnny, the man who was holding him up was a Hun. He tried to break free but a bunch of them grabbed him and pinned his arms back. "No!" he shouted. He thought of the boy on the floor with the top of his head blown off and now it was Willie. "No!" he yelled again.

"Uncle Nick!"

He saw the roof's gravel and found he was down on one knee holding onto the chair and his cheeks were wet with tears.

"Uncle Nick, you're crying."

"No," Nick said. He was wiping his eyes. "I felt dizzy, that's all, the sun..."

"It's very strong today. You need a hat."

"Yes," Nick said. He saw the boy dead on the floor of the house and this time it wasn't Willie.

All of those years had gone by and he hadn't remembered that boy. He pushed himself onto his feet and held onto the chair. His heart was racing; he took a deep breath; in spite of the heat he felt cold all through. "What's the score?" he managed to ask.

"Six to nothing."

"You want to keep watching?"

"No, it's too hot. I want to go see if Mother got my card."

Nick stood at the foot of the steps feeling dizzy as Willie came slowly down from the roof. When he reached the hall, he insisted on going the rest of the way on his own. It seemed to take forever as he held the banister and set both feet on each step. As he eased himself into his wheelchair next to the rolltop desk, he was winded but smiling.

"Good job," Nick said. And then, still feeling weak, he went up to his room.

Willie rolled to the kitchen, picturing Nick kneeling down on the roof—and crying. He'd said that he hadn't been crying but that was a lie.

His mother was busy at the sink. She said, "You're back early."

"It was too hot up there," Willie said, and he saw the Fro-Joy card on the tabletop. "The A's had a big lead anyway, they were going to win." He rolled himself up to the table. "Thank you for buying the cone for me," he said. "What flavor did you get?"

"Strawberry," Anna said.

Willie picked up the card. It showed Ruth batting and said, "Bang! The Babe Lines One Out." He put it back down on the table and frowned.

"Is something wrong?" Anna asked. "It's not the right card?"

"It's right."

"Then what's the matter?"

"Nothing."

"You seem tired."

"I'm not," Willie said.

He wheeled himself out of the kitchen and into the parlor and started to play the piano: Liszt's *Liebestraum Notturno III*, a piece that always calmed him when he felt upset. He was just on the verge of finishing it when Nick came down the stairs.

"Uncle Nick—"

"I can't talk now, I have to get to work," Nick said. "I'll see you later," and he hurried out the door.

24

"So THIS EARHART WOMAN flies across the ocean the other day and Agnes gets all pumped up," said Iron Mike, shouting above the noise of the Friday night crowd. "Women are equal to men now," she tells me. "They vote, they fly, they're liberated. Then she tells me she wants me to buy her a new Frigidaire. Well if you're so liberated, go get a job to pay for one, I said, and leave my money alone."

"D-d-d-dames," said Hesitant Harvey. "B-Butterball t-told me that his old l-lady wants a F-Frigidaire too."

"Earhart!" Mike said. "And the thing of it is, she didn't even pilot the plane like Lindy, she was a passenger. 'Next time out, she'll pilot,' Agnes says, and she's probably right." He drank some beer. "Speakin of Butterball, where'd he get to, anyway, he ain't showed up for days."

"Didn't you hear?" said Charlie. "He didn't pay off his last bet in time and Slick Dominic roughed him up—broke one of his fingers."

"N-no!" said Harvey. "That b-b-b—"

"Bastard!" said Iron Mike. "They shoulda shot *him* instead of McLoon."

Nick couldn't focus on conversations. When customers tried to engage him he mainly just nodded and smiled. He couldn't stop thinking about that memory-dream he'd had on the roof: how he'd thrown that grenade and killed that boy, some unfortunate German kid who'd been caught in the final days of a hopeless campaign. But then when he heard the name "McLoon," these obsessive thoughts broke apart. He turned to Charlie. "What's Mike talking about? Who's this McLoon?"

"You didn't hear?" Charlie said. "Hughie McLoon, the A's old mascot. They gunned him down last night."

"The hunchback! But why?"

"He got caught squealin to the cops, tippin them off about hootch. Nobody knows who did it yet."

"I hope it wasn't Grady."

"You and me both," Jake said, his eyes more worried than ever. "We don't need none of that stuff around here."

Nick shook his head. "God, Hughie McLoon," he said, and thought: This is something Willie doesn't need to know about. He mixed a customer a drink, then started to think of the German boy again.

After all of the many horrors he'd seen, that was the one that finally broke him and sent him down into darkness. And after the darkness lifted he found that the war that had ended nine years ago hadn't ended for him; he kept fighting it every day. The memory-dreams had never stopped and maybe they never would. He could never feel at ease because of that.

Two veterans were at the bar tonight and both of them were drunks. Hopscotch had lost a leg at Belleau Wood and Duckie had lost an eye at Meuse-Argonne and wore a pirate patch. Nick wondered if they still had nightmares about the war, if they had any memory-dreams, but he'd never ask. He knew about their campaigns because of the papers he'd read, but he didn't remember if he had fought in them. He wondered if he had fought beside these pathetic heroes—or beside Anna's husband.

The dancers were having a grand old time and the guys at the bar were mellow. The floor was a sweating, pulsing mass so crowded that people kept bumping and rubbing against each other, increasing the fun but restricting the kind of dance they could do: no varsity drag or Charleston, at least for now.

Nick was not having fun. As he kept making drinks he could not tear his mind away from his memory-dream, how

203

the boy in that dream had turned into Willie. He thought of the German boy's parents and wondered if they were still living.

On his break he went to the storeroom as usual and sat on his box. With his left hand he wiped the sweat off his forehead and suddenly noticed something: his arm felt different.

The storeroom's back door was open because of the stifling heat and Nick went out to the alley. Under the one small streetlamp there he wound up and threw a phantom ball three times—and yes, his arm felt different all right, it actually felt pretty good. *I'm kidding myself,* he thought. *It's another dream, let's see what tomorrow brings.*

The next morning, another hot one, he went to the Square with Eddie and Willie.

Willie was in his wheelchair; his legs were hurting today. He hadn't told his mother or anyone else about the dream he'd had last night. He was playing right field for the A's, Babe Ruth hit a high hard drive to right center, and Willie took off like a rocket. He ran so fast he was practically flying, leaped, caught the ball, came down hard on the grass—and woke, his legs in pain. They had hurt ever since.

Eddie's cheek bulged with tobacco. He spat on the ground and said, "How bout that Amelia Earhart, ain't she somethin?"

"My mother went to school with her," Willie said.

Eddie's eyebrows went up. "You're kiddin."

"It's true. Mother told me she wanted to be a nurse back then, but now she's a flier."

"She certainly is. She's one brave woman."

"Yes. But Mother had to leave that school. Her grandfather lost all his money, and he was paying for it."

"Oh. Tough luck."

Preoccupied, Nick didn't comment on any of this. He hoped that Eddie didn't mention McLoon. When they reached the Square he said, "Did you show the ghost to Perkins?"

"Yep."

"So what did he think?"

"He said that he'd never seen anything like it."

"Is that good or bad?"

Eddie laughed. "I just might give it a try when Mack sticks me in next time."

At the diamond Nick said, "Let's do it," and went to the plate.

Eddie spat some tobacco juice, threw, and the ghost was sharp. "Perfect," Nick said. And then when he tossed the ball back to Eddie his arm felt quick and light. He hadn't been dreaming last night in the alley.

They practiced for half an hour and Nick couldn't keep from smiling. No doubt about it, his arm had changed, it had some *life*. "Good job," he said to Eddie. "Now let me throw some to you."

They switched places. Nick used his fastball grip, wound up and let go. "Hey," Eddie said, "you got some zip on that one."

Nick laughed. He threw for another fifteen minutes. His arm wasn't strong yet, but it could get strong, he knew it.

Eddie Winters was shaking his head in disbelief. "Man, what happened to you?"

"I don't know."

"You ought to keep practicin."

Laughing again, Nick said, "For what? You think Mack will take me onto the team?"

"No, but the Wildcats might. And those players get paid, you know."

"They play in the evenings," Nick said, "and that's when I work."

"Oh, right."

As they went back up Twentieth Street Eddie said, "I got a surprise for you, Skipper, a late birthday present."

"You do?" Willie said. "What is it?"

"You're goin to the game today. I got two tickets for you and your Uncle Nick."

"Oh, wow! I've never been to a game before!"

"You can park your wheelchair right in the aisle behind the backstop, I've got it all squared away."

"That's great!"

"If your mom wants to go I can get her a ticket too, but I hear she don't like baseball."

"No."

Nick said, "We'll have to leave before the game ends, Willie. I have to go to work."

"I know, but that's okay."

"Eddie," Nick said, "that's swell of you. I hope we get to see you pitch."

Eddie grinned. "If I do," he said, "maybe I'll try the ghost."

Willie looked dazzled by Shibe Park's bustle and noise. Nick guided him through the haphazard patrons and down the aisle between the packed stands.

Eddie Winters was there on the other side of the chainlink backstop. "So what do you think, Skipper, close enough for you?"

"It's great!" Willie said.

The game began and Willie looked totally awed. Both of the pitchers threw with such speed that the ball made a hissing sound as it crossed the plate. Willie could scarcely believe that someone could hit a ball that was thrown so fast, but sometimes they did. He saw all of his heroes up close—Foxx, Cochrane, Simmons, Miller, Haas—heard them question the umpire and grunt when they missed a pitch. Saw them spit brown tobacco juice into the dust, heard them pepper the air with curses when they struck out.

Nick bought Willie a box of Cracker Jack; it had a tiny metal dog inside. "I'd love to have a real dog," Willie said, "but I'm not allowed to because of my condition. Its fur would make me cough."

"That's a shame," Nick said. He was sure that a dog would be great for the kid.

At the end of the sixth he told Willie they had to leave. He hated to, but he needed to get to work. He'd hoped to see Eddie pitch, but both of the starters were still going strong and the game was close.

Out on the sidewalk Willie said, "That was really swell."

"Sure good of Eddie to get us tickets," Nick said.

"I'll say. How's come he calls me 'Skipper'?"

"Because he likes you."

"Oh. I like him, too," Willie said. "Then he frowned and said, "I'll never be a baseball player, it's all too fast."

"It doesn't look as fast when you grow up," Nick said. "And you know something? Not one of those guys you watched today can play the piano as good as you. And you're only ten years old."

"Yes," Willie said. But he was thinking about his dream, about how he'd run so fast and jumped so high and caught the screaming drive that was struck by Babe Ruth, the greatest baseball player in all the world.

The next day was Sunday—no game because of the Blue Laws. Nick practiced again with Eddie while Anna and Willie went to church, and Eddie did better than ever. "You're ready to use it," Nick said, and Eddie agreed.

When Nick got home he found Willie playing gin rummy with Flora. "Guess what," Willie said. "I asked Mother if we could go on a picnic today and she said yes. And you're invited and so is Aunt Flora."

"But I'm not going," Flora said. "My rheumatism is on the RAM-page again."

"But maybe the sun and fresh air would help you feel better," Nick said.

"I need more than sun," Flora said. "I need dry. Philadelphia is so danged humid!"

Nick went to the kitchen, where Anna was making sandwiches. "You heard the plan," she said. "Are you going to come?"

"Of course."

They didn't take Willie's chair. Nick helped him manage the trolley car's steps and the three of them rode to Fairmount Park, Anna with her picnic hamper beside her. In addition to sandwiches, cake and lemonade, it contained Willie's glove, Nick's glove, and a ball. The other times Willie had taken the trolley it was for dental appointments, which he dreaded, but today he found the ride enjoyable.

In the park they sat at a picnic table and ate their lunch. It wasn't so hot today and was pleasant under the trees as they watched people strolling by, some of them hand in hand, some of them smoking, some of them pushing baby carriages. As they ate, Willie said, "How's come you quit pitching, Uncle Nick?"

"I went into the army."

"But when you came out?"

"I wasn't the same."

"What do you mean? Did you hurt your arm in the war?"

"That's right."

"But it's better now, isn't it? Yesterday Eddie said you were throwing good."

"I was doing okay, I guess."

"If my legs can get better your arm can get better, isn't that right?"

"I guess so," Nick said.

He had a catch with Willie, and then Willie said that he wanted to go to the river. It was a pretty good hike, so Nick carried him piggyback most of the way. The three of them crossed the car-busy East River Drive and went to the riverbank, where a couple of fishermen had cast their lines into the murky swift water. This was illegal under the Blue Laws; even fishing was banned on Sundays. But since money wasn't involved, the ban was rarely enforced.

"So when are *you* going fishing, Uncle Nick?" asked Willie.

"Not on a Sunday," Nick replied. "Fish aren't allowed to bite on Sundays."

Willie squinted. "You're teasing, right?"

"Have these fishermen caught any fish?"

"They just haven't been lucky."

"Maybe. Or maybe fish don't even live in this river."

As Willie kept watching the fishermen, Anna and Nick sat down on the grass beside each other. "He's doing so well," Anna said. "And he's grown up so much."

"It happens."

"I really appreciate how you've helped him."

"I know you do. But he's helped me, too. He's taken me out of too many thoughts about myself. We've helped each other, and it's been fun." He paused for a second then said, "Do you ever have any fun? Do you ever go out anywhere? To plays or concerts or lectures or things like that? I watch a game nearly every day that the A's are in town and while I'm doing that you're cooking or cleaning or washing clothes or weeding your garden. It makes me feel guilty sometimes."

Anna laughed and said, "Guilty? Why? You've fixed a number of things in the house and saved me time and frustration and money. No other tenant has ever done that."

"Okay, but you know what I mean. You ought to enjoy yourself more."

"I don't have the time for that."

"You should make the time. Now listen, there's this movie I heard people raving about at work. It's the first real full-length talkie. It's playing on Broad Street. Why don't you go see it with me."

"I…"

"Come on. It's supposed to be really something, I'm sure you'd enjoy it. You can have Flora stay with Willie and we can go. I'm definitely going, and I'd love to have your company."

"I'll think about it," Anna said. She was looking at Willie, checking to see that he didn't stray close to the water; the treacherous Schuylkill had claimed the lives of even the strongest swimmers. Satisfied that Willie was safe, she looked back at Nick and asked, "How did your arm get hurt during the war?"

He shrugged. "It wasn't really my arm that got hurt, it was more than that."

"I know. That time on the roof on the Fourth of July...and again the other day."

"Willie told you."

"He did. It frightened him. He told me that you were crying."

Nick looked down at the grass.

"If you don't want to talk about it, don't," Anna said, "but I think it might help."

Nick took a deep breath. He looked out at the river. "I killed a boy," he said. "A German boy, he was no more than fifteen years old. I threw a hand grenade into a house. It turned out that he was the only one in it."

"Oh Nick, how horrible."

"Toward the end of the war the Germans were desperate and started recruiting kids. We didn't know that until later. It was after I killed that boy that something went wrong with me. I know that now. I know it because of the dream I had up on the roof. Remembering seems to have helped me. My arm feels better."

"That's wonderful."

"Yes. But I hate those dreams."

"Maybe that was the last of them."

"Maybe. But I've thought that before, and the next thing I know, I have another one. Sometimes I think that I'll never be right again."

"I felt that way too after Martin died and Willie was born so sickly."

"But your faith got you through that bad time."

"It did."

"It's wonderful to have that."

"You have no religion."

"No."

"My faith makes me feel that I have some control over things, but I'm probably fooling myself. Even with prayer and doing our best, things can go terribly wrong."

"For sure," Nick said. He looked out at the river again—and saw Willie coming toward them with jerky steps.

"Mother!" he yelled. "Uncle Nick! One of the men caught a fish! Come look!"

Anna and Nick stood up and followed Willie, and there in the grass was a catfish, six inches long at the most. "Look, isn't it great?" Willie said.

"A real whale," said the fisherman with a grin.

"See, fish *do* live in this river," Willie said. He frowned. "How's come they're called catfish?"

"Because they have whiskers," Nick said.

"How's come they have whiskers?"

"I think maybe they feel things with them."

"Is that why cats have whiskers?"

"I guess."

"Well how's come other fish don't have whiskers?"

"Willie, you got me."

"Oh. So when are *we* going to try and catch some fish?"

"Any day now," Nick said.

25

THE NAME OF THE MOVIE was *Lights of New York*, and it was amazing: the voices of the actors were coordinated with their lips! On the trolley ride back to Twentieth Street Nick said, "Talkies are the wave of the future," and Anna agreed.

"So you're glad you came?" he asked.

"I am."

"I detect some hesitation in your reply."

"It's just that—"

"You never leave Willie alone—and you're worried."

"Yes."

"I'm sure he's just fine."

"I'm sure you're right. There's another thing though."

"What's that?"

"People are going to talk."

Nick smiled. "About us taking a walk together? They won't even notice."

"They'll notice all right. Especially Mrs. Watkinson and Mrs. Brady. "

"So let them talk," Nick said.

As they walked up Twentieth Street the porches were empty and none of their lights were on. Anna said, "That poor man in the movie. Having to do all those terrible things for that bunch of mobsters. I'm glad I don't live in New York."

"People like that are everywhere," Nick said. "Even here in the City of Brotherly Love, believe it or not."

"I found the story upsetting."

"Me too," Nick said, but he didn't say why. In the movie a

couple of barbers unwittingly buy a shop that fronts for a speakeasy. The entire time he was watching the film he felt guilty.

When they entered the living room Willie was playing gin rummy with Flora. He said, "Was the movie good?"

"It was," Anna said.

"The people in it really talked?"

"They really did."

"Wow! I want to go see it!"

"It's not for children."

"Drat!"

"But soon there will be a whole lot of talkies and some of them will be for kids," Nick said.

"I hope so," Willie said. "Maybe they'll make one about *Tom Sawyer*. Or one about *Kidnapped* or *Treasure Island*."

"They probably will."

"Or maybe they'll make one about Babe Ruth, a long one. He'll tell you how to hold a bat and hit and run and throw. I've never heard him talk. It would be so great!"

"Wouldn't it though," Nick said.

"Flora, you should go see it," Anna said.

Flora threw up her hands. "Oh no, I'd find it too STIMulating. I saw *The Phantom of the Opera* with Lon Chaney and it kept me up all night. If he had talked, I wouldn't have slept all *week*!"

Anna and Nick both laughed.

Eddie Winters got into a game where the A's were blowing away the Senators. He used the ghost and struck out the side. Nick and Willie were cheering him on from the roof.

In the Square the next morning he said, "I got it down good. Cochrane was really impressed, and he don't impress easy."

"Terrific," Nick said. "Now what we need to do is stretch you out."

He had Eddie pitch for fifteen minutes, rest for a bit, then

213

pitch again. They spent over an hour at it. Willie watched patiently, standing for most of the time.

"Feels good," Eddie said. "I'm bushed, but it feels real good."

"We'll take a day off and then do it again," Nick said. "And we'll just keep doing it until you're strong enough to pitch nine innings. By the time you play the Yankees again you'll be more than ready."

"I hope."

"You will be. What you have to do now is convince Mack to let you start one of those games. Have Cochrane tell him what you can do. Even better, show him."

Eddie looked doubtful. "I don't know, Nick. For him to start me against the Yanks... He probably won't even use me in relief against that gang."

"Relief isn't good enough, Eddie, you have to start one of those games."

"Why is it so important to you?"

"I'll tell you some other time. Just believe me, it is."

As Nick was tying his apron on that night, Jake said to Charlie, "Mob war, wait'n see."

Nick said, "What are you talking about?"

"I guess you didn't hear," Jake said. "Someone shot Danny O'Leary last night while he was in bed with his girlfriend. Payback for killin McLoon. The war has begun."

O'Leary was one of the city's most famous gangsters. Nick thought of *Lights of New York*. "That's all Philly needs," he said.

"It'll come to us, right here, we won't escape," Jake said.

Charlie smiled and shook his head. "Jake, you always imagine the worst."

"Cause it always happens!" Jake moaned.

Willie was all worked up about the Yankees series, which was still several weeks away. Each morning after piano practice he spread his Fro-Joy collection out on the card table,

214

along with some Yuengling cards. He had forty-two of the latter, thanks to Nick. He'd developed a ritual in which he pitted a Ruth card against a Yuengling. Nick didn't understand how Willie decided who won but the kid was completely absorbed in the game. For kids like him, Nick thought, you could probably just sell the cards without any ice cream or candy. He wouldn't be surprised if it came to that someday.

Willie had written to Ruth again; again he'd received no reply. Every day, he would eagerly wait for Warren the mailman's morning and afternoon visits. Every day, his hopes would be dashed.

"He's just so busy," Anna said.

"But I've written four times."

"Well maybe you'll still get an answer. We'll see."

Willie was totally focused on Ruth. It was starting to grate on Nick's nerves. The kid talked about Ruth when he played gin rummy with Flora. He put a Ruth card in his tee shirt pocket—"for luck"—when he practiced walking. On the roof as he watched the games he incessantly talked about Ruth: "He went into a slump but now he's hitting homers again and I bet he'll hit more than sixty." "I bet he could hit one all the way over to Nineteenth Street." "I bet he'll set a record for homers that no one will ever break." It set Nick's teeth on edge.

Eddie Winters threw longer sessions with Nick to increase his endurance. He was coming along just fine. He'd been used in relief against the Tigers and Browns and hadn't allowed any hits—but he still hadn't talked to Connie Mack about starting a Yankees game. "He's really good now," Willie said. "He is," Nick said. "He's got that ghost ball working great." "But I bet Babe Ruth can hit it," Willie said.

At a workout when Willie was home with Professor Shultz, his piano teacher, Nick gave Eddie the silent treatment. Then once they got back to the house he said, "You know what I'm going to ask you."

Eddie looked sheepish. "Yeah, I know."

"Well?"

"No, not yet."

"Well how long are you going to wait? The Yankees series is coming right up."

"I know."

"You'll talk to him now, this morning, as soon as you get to the park."

"Eddie spat some tobacco juice. "Maybe."

"No, Eddie, not maybe. You'll do it."

"I'll try, but it ain't easy dealin with Mr. Mack."

"Come on! You've known the man for years!"

"Nobody really knows Mr. Mack."

"You'll talk to him, Eddie. This morning."

Again Eddie spat. "Say, what are you all riled up about? If I don't do it, I'm the only one who stands to lose."

"Maybe not."

"What's that supposed to mean?"

"Just talk to Mack, okay?"

"I'll try."

"Goddamn it!" Nick said. "Don't just try, do it!"

Eddie simply shrugged and walked away.

Furious, Nick went inside. In the hallway he angrily hung up his glove on the peg next to Willie's. Willie was watching him from his wheelchair. Frowning, he said, "Uncle Nick, are you mad at Eddie?"

"You bet I am."

"How's come?"

"It's hard to explain."

"Oh," Willie said. He rolled himself up to the table and started to play his Babe Ruth card game. "The Babe writes to other kids," he said, "why doesn't he write to me?"

"Because he's a jerk," Nick snapped.

Willie looked at him sharply. "What! He is not! He's the greatest hitter the game has ever known!"

"Maybe so, but he's still a jerk. And not only that, he's a

216

glutton, he eats like a pig."

"He has a big appetite."

"Like a pig's. Willie, listen, Babe Ruth is not what you think. He's a foulmouthed slob. And even worse than that, he's…he's a tippler and a philanderer!"

"That isn't true!"

"I knew the man, Willie."

"I bet you didn't! I bet that's a lie!"

"It's no lie, I was his roommate."

"You weren't!"

"I was, and I know what he's like."

"*I* know what he's like," Willie said on the edge of tears. "He helps crippled children get better. He hits homers for them. He visits them in hospitals. I've seen the pictures in the paper."

"It's an act," Nick said. "A publicity stunt to cover up all the bad things he does."

"You're lying again!"

"Why would I lie about something like that?"

"Because you're a liar! You lied about crying! You said you didn't do it but you did! And you said you'd go fishing with me and you didn't!"

Anna appeared in the doorway. "Willie, that's enough," she said. "Apologize to Uncle Nick."

"I won't!" Willie said. "He's saying these terrible things because he's jealous! Babe Ruth is the greatest ever and Uncle Nick—he can't even play anymore!"

Willie rolled back from the table and swept past his mother and down the hall into his room.

Nick stood there, speechless, and then he went out the door.

It was lunchtime, but Willie couldn't eat. Flora finished her sandwich and went upstairs but Willie just sat at the kitchen table, jaws clenched, his food untouched.

"Uncle Nick is just having a bad day," Anna said.

"He's a liar," Willie said. "Everyone knows that Babe Ruth

is the best."

"Uncle Nick knew him."

"I don't care!"

Willie stood up and went into his room and lay on his bed and cried. Then he stopped and stared up at the ceiling. Those bad things couldn't be true about Babe Ruth. But why would Uncle Nick lie about that?

He tried to sleep but he couldn't; his thoughts just kept going around in his head and his stomach felt sick.

At last he got up from his bed and went into the hallway. He heard his mother at work in the kitchen but couldn't see her. He went to the stairs.

Uncle Nick had lied to him about crying and fishing. And maybe about Babe Ruth, but he wasn't sure, and now he felt guilty. He thought that it wasn't right what he'd said to him, it wasn't fair. Maybe he couldn't play ball anymore but he'd fought the Germans the same way his father had fought them and kept him safe and his mother safe and had hurt his arm in the war while Babe Ruth had stayed in America. Uncle Nick was a war hero. Babe Ruth was not. Babe Ruth was a baseball hero but not a war hero. A war hero was more important.

And now Willie wished he could take back the words he had said. He wanted to watch the game with Uncle Nick this afternoon. He wanted to be friends with him again. He'd talk to him now and maybe things would be all right.

Slowly, gritting his teeth, he climbed the stairs, setting both feet on each step and holding the banister tight. When he reached the top he was wheezing and soaked with sweat. But his arms and legs were much stronger now and he'd done it; he'd climbed the stairs all by himself for the very first time and he thought: *What will Uncle Nick think of this? He'll be amazed.* He thought: *I'm going to get all better.*

Holding onto the banister, heart racing, he made his way down the hallway and knocked on Nick's door.

No answer. "Uncle Nick," he said.

Still nothing.

He knocked again, louder. He waited. Nothing. He tried the door. It was locked.

He's gone out, Willie thought. *He's not here.* Deflated, he stood there—then had an idea.

He walked the few feet to the door that led up to the roof, pulled it open, and grabbed the ring of keys that was hanging there.

Aunt Flora was in still in her room. Willie hoped that his knocking had not interrupted her after-lunch nap. He moved quietly, slowly, across the hall; found the key to Nick's room and inserted it into the lock. He twisted it and turned the knob and the door came open.

Through the large bay window he saw Shibe Park. Players were practicing on the field. The game would be starting soon.

He went to the closet and searched inside but didn't see what he was looking for. Some shirts and some pants hung on hangers. A pair of shoes sat on the floor.

He went to the dresser and pulled its top drawer open. Socks and underwear, a handkerchief, a few coins. The second and third drawers were empty. And then, in the bottom drawer, he found it: the roll of canvas.

He had asked Uncle Nick to show him the fishing rod several times but he never did. "Later," he'd always said. Well now he would finally see it.

He lifted the canvas out of the drawer. It was heavy. He didn't know fishing rods weighed so much. Frowning, he set the canvas down on the rug and unrolled it.

At the sight of the rifle he caught his breath. What was Uncle Nick doing with *this*? He gingerly touched its barrel and a shock traveled over his arm. A real gun! Quickly he rolled it up in the canvas again and placed it back in the drawer. He saw two sheets of metal lying there and, curious, lifted one up. Some bullets!

He was sweating profusely again. Not a fishing rod but a *gun*. Another lie. Uncle Nick *was* a liar, a terrible liar. He'd

219

lied about crying, about Babe Ruth, about taking him fishing—and about the fishing rod!

Willie felt hot all over, suddenly scared he'd get caught, and he left the room. He was shaking so much that the key wouldn't fit in the lock. Then it did, and he turned it, and hung it back up on its hook.

He had just started down the stairs when the door to Aunt Flora's bedroom swung open. "Why, Willie," she said with a startled expression, "what are you doing up here?"

"I...I came to see Uncle Nick."

"He's not here," Flora said. "My word, I had no idea you could manage those stairs by yourself."

"It's the first time I ever did it."

Flora's eyes were sharp. "Willie, tell me the truth now," she said. "Did you go into Uncle Nick's room?"

"No!" Willie said, then his conscience kicked in. *Now I'm a liar too*, he thought. Fresh sweat broke out on his forehead.

"It sounded as if you did."

"I didn't," said Willie, shaking his head. "I just...I wanted to see... I knocked on his door..."

Suddenly his right leg buckled. He lost his grip on the banister, opened his mouth in surprise—and then fell down the stairs.

"Willie!" Flora cried, rushing forward. "Oh, Willie!"

He lay in the first floor hallway, not moving. Flora went down the stairs as fast as she could and bent over him. "Willie!"

Anna came up from the kitchen, looking shocked. "What happened? Willie—"

"He fell down the stairs," Flora said.

"The stairs? But how—?"

Willie moaned.

"He must have struck his head," Anna said. "I have to call Doctor Fletcher. Don't move him, Flora."

She went to the rolltop desk and made the call.

The doctor's office was around the corner and he came right

away. A short, brusque, balding man with a black moustache, he placed his bag on the floor and examined Willie. "Possible concussion," he said, then gently carried Willie into his bedroom and placed him on the bed.

Willie started to stir. He groggily opened his eyes. "How are you feeling, sonny?" the doctor asked.

In a weak voice Willie said, "He lied to me again."

Dr. Fletcher looked up at Anna and said, "What's he talking about?"

"Something that happened this morning with one of my tenants."

"Let him rest, but don't let him sleep. I'll be back in an hour."

Right after the doctor left, Willie started to cough, and the coughing was deep and long.

When the doctor came back, he sat on the edge of Willie's bed, took a thermometer out of his bag, and placed it in Willie's mouth. He waited for several minutes and then withdrew it. "Just under a hundred and two," he said. He put the thermometer back in his bag and stood up. "Keep giving him plenty of fluids," he said, "and an aspirin every four hours. Take his temperature tonight and then call me to let me know how he's doing."

As Anna was showing the doctor out, Nick appeared. "What's happening?" he said as he stepped inside. "What was that doctor doing here?"

"Willie fell down the stairs. He might have a concussion. He's running a fever."

"He fell down the stairs? But—"

Flora was there in the hallway too and said, "He went up to your room to see you."

"He climbed the stairs?"

"That's right."

Nick hurried to Willie's bedroom. Willie lay flushed and motionless against the pillow, his eyes half closed.

"Willie," Nick said. "What happened?"

"I went up the stairs to see you."

"All the way up the stairs by yourself. That's great."

Tears were rolling down Willie's cheeks. And then in a soft weak voice he said. "You lied to me again, Uncle Nick. It isn't a fishing rod in the canvas, it's a gun."

26

WHEN NICK GOT BACK from the Home Plate after one thirty he found Anna sitting beside Willie's bed in the light of the little lamp.

"He's asleep," she whispered. "His fever went up a degree for more than an hour then dropped down again. But his cough has been worse."

"Well what does the doctor say?"

"He says to keep giving him fluids and aspirin." She took a deep breath. "Come with me."

They went to the hallway and Anna said, "Dr. Fletcher's afraid that he might have an abscess. He's thinking of having Dr. Spearman see him tomorrow. He's Willie's lung specialist." Tears suddenly came to her eyes. "He's talked about surgery before and now I'm afraid he'll recommend it."

"But maybe it isn't an abscess," Nick said. "A fall wouldn't cause an abscess."

"But it might reveal one."

Nick shook his head. "You shouldn't let this Spearman guy cut him. Specialists always want to do what they're trained for."

"It's out of the question anyway," Anna said. "I can't afford it."

"How much would it cost?"

"A lot. Maybe two thousand dollars."

"What!"

"That's right. It would mean a long hospital stay."

"But two thousand dollars! Only the rich could afford to

pay that much! Listen, Anna, you have to move. Get out of this dirty city and into some decent air."

"I can't afford that either."

"Sure you can. Sell this house and just move."

Anna sighed. "I'd be lucky to sell this house for enough to pay off the mortgage. And even if I did, where would I go?"

"Out West somewhere. The air is clean out there."

"Out West? I don't know anyone there. And Willie's doctors are here and he likes it here. He loves to watch the games."

"But maybe he could get better there. He'd love that more than anything."

"And what about Flora? I can't abandon her."

"I'm sure we can find—"

"Mother!"

Anna went to the bedroom. Nick stood in the doorway.

Willie was sitting up. "Mother, I'm hot again." His cheeks were blazing red.

"Let's take your temperature," Anna said.

It had risen again—by two degrees. She poured some lemonade from the pitcher that sat beside the lamp and had him drink, then gave him another aspirin. He swallowed it and looked at the doorway with heavy eyes. "Uncle Nick," he said.

"Hi, Willie."

"You lied to me."

"Willie, don't talk about that now. Just go to sleep. It's very late."

"But you lied."

"Tomorrow, Willie. We'll talk about it tomorrow."

Willie sank back on the pillow. He stared at Nick. Then he started to cough again.

In his room, in the light from his nightstand lamp, Nick sat on his bed with his head in his hands.

Willie's illness was all his fault. If he hadn't blown up about

Ruth, it would never have happened. Willie would never have climbed those stairs.

Nick got up from the bed and went to the dresser and opened the bottom drawer. It was obvious that the canvas had been unrolled.

He went up to the window; pulled the curtain aside. The streetlamp in front of the house made a yellow ring on the concrete sidewalk. He looked at the wall across the way. Above it Shibe Park was an empty black hole and suddenly baseball seemed meaningless, stupid. For God's sake, what if Willie died? He let the curtain go and looked back at the room.

One of the most requested songs at the Home Plate was last year's big hit, "The Best Things in Life Are Free." Maybe so, but some of the things that weren't the best—like surgery— cost a goddamn mint.

If he had enough money he'd give it to Anna so she could move out of the city. If the doctors were sure that an operation would cure Willie's lungs, he could pay for that. Now that his arm was alive again he could probably make extra money at semi-pro ball. The Wildcats played their games while he was at work, but maybe there was some other team... Anna could make extra money by renting her roof, but it would take years to scrape together enough to move or to pay for surgery. The only way to get big money fast was to make his plan to get back at Babe Ruth succeed. *Eddie*, he thought, *you have to come through for me.*

He sat on the bed for over an hour then went downstairs. Willie's door was still open. Nick looked inside and saw him sleeping heavily. The light from the little bedside lamp glowed on his crimson cheeks. Anna was sound asleep in the chair beside him.

When he went back upstairs he wondered how Willie had entered his room. The door had been locked, so the kid must have used the key that hung on the door to the roof.

In the hallway Nick went to that door, took the keys off the

225

hook, then crossed to the storage room. He found the right key and opened the door. He felt on the wall for the light switch, found it, and pressed the button.

A dim lamp went on. It sat on a desk across the room and was brass with a green glass shade. A floor-to-ceiling bookshelf took up the wall beside the desk. A brown leather easy chair sat in a corner, a floor lamp beside it.

Nick quietly closed the door and went to the desk and sat down. A photograph in a gilded frame was sitting there in front of him; it depicted a smiling couple: a much younger Anna Shuster and a handsome young man in an army uniform.

Nick looked at the bookshelves. They contained mainly history books: about the Ancient Greeks and Romans, the Middle Ages, the Reformation, the American Revolution, the Civil War. There were books on philosophy too, some on science, and quite a few works of literature: Balzac, Hugo, Dostoyevsky, Poe, Hawthorne, Wharton, Henry James... Everything was in order and perfectly clean. *My God*, Nick thought, *it's a museum.*

The desktop held a spotless green blotter; on top of it sat a cup full of pencils and pens and a bottle of dried-up ink. A stack of envelopes sat there too. Nick looked at the one on top. It was from Martin Shuster, U.S. Army, postmarked December 11, 1917, and addressed to Anna Shuster. Nick opened its flap and took out the letter. It said:

My Darling,

I was thrilled to receive your news that we will be having a child. What a marvelous Christmas present! If only I could be with you at this time of great joy.

I've already been thinking of names. If we have a son, I think my father's name, William, would be a good choice. If it's a girl we could name her Elizabeth, after your mother. Of course, you might have entirely different ideas. Please let me know.

I certainly hope the ruthless German murder machine is

stopped before our troops see action. But if it isn't, and I join the fight, I am confident that I will survive and one glorious day will be home again with you in our little house away from all this madness. And I hope that day will arrive before our child is born.

I was sorry to hear that your mother is ill and fervently hope she recovers soon. Please give her my love and best wishes. And darling, do take care of yourself. You are my entire world. I miss you terribly and constantly dream of the day when we will be reunited. I will continue to write to you every chance I get, and will keep the letters you send me close to my heart.

Have a wonderful Christmas. And may the world find peace in the coming year.

With all my love,
Martin

Nick folded the letter and slid it back into the envelope. He looked through the other envelopes. All were from Martin, addressed to Anna. He didn't open any of them. He put the one he had read back on top of the rest, then went to the hallway, turned off the light, and locked the door.

He left his door ajar and hardly slept. Sometimes he'd hear Willie's harsh deep cough and sometimes he'd hear Anna talking in comforting tones. He went down twice; Anna was awake both times and Willie was asleep. The second time Anna said, "His temperature's lower again."

"Good news," Nick said.

"But it's still not normal, and his cough's no better."

At six o'clock Nick got up. He checked in on Willie and Anna then went for a walk in the warm morning sun. He walked for more than an hour and when he came back, Doctor Fletcher was there.

"He's holding his own," Fletcher said. "I've brought you

227

some medicine for his cough, some codeine syrup."

"Is there anything more you can give him for fever?"

"Just continue the aspirin and fluids. If he wants to eat, give him oatmeal."

Willie woke up three times in the next three hours but didn't want food. He would take a spoonful of codeine syrup and drink some lemonade and go right back to sleep again.

Eddie Winters showed up on the porch at ten for his daily workout. He was smiling and jumpy, pounding his glove with his ball. "You're gonna love this," he said to Nick. "I finally got up the guts to talk to Mack, and guess what? It turns out he's had his eye on me for quite some time. He heard from Cochrane I had a new pitch and said that he wanted to see for hisself how I threw it. He was a catcher a million years ago, and damned if he can't still catch. I threw him the ghost a dozen times and his face was as stiff as stone. I thought that he didn't like it—then he said he would give me a start in the third Yankees game!"

"That's terrific, Eddie!"

"Yeah—and scary."

"Come on, you're practically unhittable with the ghost."

"If I throw it right."

"You will."

"I hope." He frowned. "Where's Skipper?"

"In bed with a fever. He fell down the stairs and hit his head. The doctor was scared it might be a concussion, but now he doesn't think so. He thinks it's his old disease acting up again."

"Hey, that's too bad."

"I'll say. And I'm the one responsible for it."

"What? What do you mean?"

"He was going on and on about Ruth again yesterday and I finally lost my temper. I told him that Ruth was a bum and he got really mad."

"And that made him sick?"

228

"Not exactly. Later on he went up to my room. That was the first time he'd ever climbed all those stairs and it took a lot out of him, I guess. I wasn't there, I'd gone out for a walk to calm myself. So he started down the stairs again and that's when he fell."

"But that ain't your fault."

"Yeah, Eddie, it is. He would never have gone to my room if I hadn't blasted Ruth."

"Hey, Nick, don't blame yourself for that. Look at the good stuff you've done for the kid. If it wasn't for you, he wouldn't be walkin the way he is."

Nick was quiet a minute then said, "I can't go to the Square today, Eddie."

"You want to stay here with Skipper."

"Yeah."

"Okay. Can I see him sometime?"

"I'll ask Anna. Not now, though."

"Okay."

When Eddie walked back up the street Nick went inside. He passed the bedroom where Willie was sleeping and went to the kitchen, where Anna was cutting up celery. He said, "How's he doing?"

"He's not coughing as much, which is good, it tires him so. I guess the codeine helped. He won't eat oatmeal, so I'm making the vegetable soup he likes so much."

"Good. I'm going out for a while if you don't mind."

"Why should I mind?"

"I'll see you soon," Nick said, and left.

He got off the trolley at Race Street and walked to the Chinese laundry he'd gone to back in the winter. The same young man was behind the counter. At first he didn't remember Nick but after a couple of minutes he did. Nick described Willie's symptoms. The young man nodded and said that he thought he could help. "How old is this boy?"

"He's ten," Nick said.

The young man went through the curtain behind him and soon returned. "He's formulating it," he said.

Nick sat on the bench where he'd sat in the winter waiting for his laundry. He thought of how sick and despondent he'd been back then. After about ten minutes the ancient man with the pointed beard pushed the curtain aside and handed the young man the same kind of box that Nick had been given months ago. "One teaspoon of mixture soaked in a cup of hot water for five or more minutes and taken three times a day before meals," the young man said. "Can it hurt him?" Nick asked. The man shook his head. Nick paid him, thanked him, and left.

Placing the box on the kitchen table in front of Anna, Nick said, "Back in the winter when I was sick a herb concoction like this stopped my cough and cured my fever too. At least I think it did."

She frowned doubtfully at the box.

"The Chinese doctor says it won't hurt him," Nick said. "I think you should try it. It's a tea."

Anna went to the sink and ran water into her kettle. She placed it on top of a burner and lit the flame. Then turning and looking straight at Nick's eyes she said, "Why do you have a gun?"

He caught his breath. "Willie told you."

"He entered your room without permission. That was wrong and he knows it. But yes, he told me he saw your gun. So why do you have it?"

Nick started to sweat. He said: "I was doing some target practice before I came to live here. It's a hobby of mine."

"Well why did you tell us the gun was a fishing rod?"

"I was afraid you wouldn't rent to me if you knew the truth."

"You were right, I wouldn't have. I hate the idea of having a gun in the house."

"I'm trying to sell it," Nick said, then changed the topic.

230

"Do you have any honey?"

"I do."

"The tea is really bitter, so put some in it."

Willie was awake when they went to the bedroom. He scowled at Nick.

Anna gave him the tea. After the first small sip he made a face. "I hate this," he said.

"It will help your cough."

Willie screwed up his face and drank some more. He didn't look at Nick. Nick left the room and went upstairs and didn't go back to see Willie again before he went to work.

Shortly after six, the doorbell rang. It was Eddie Winters. "Hello, Mrs. Shuster," he said, "how's Willie doin?"

"A little better."

"Can I come in for a minute? I have somethin for him."

"Just for a minute."

They went to the bedroom. "Eddie," Willie said.

"Hi, Skipper. How you feelin?"

"Better."

"Great."

"How did the A's do today?"

"Not so good. We lost."

"Did you pitch?"

"Two innings and gave up one hit, no runs. Struck two guys out."

"Did you use the ghost?"

"Yep."

"Good," Willie said. Then he started to cough.

Eddie waited until it subsided then said, "Hey Skipper, 1 brought you a present." He reached behind him, into his back pants pocket, and brought out a baseball cap. It was white with pale blue seams and a pale blue peak. It had no lettering on it.

"An A's cap," Willie said. He was clearly pleased, but his voice didn't have any strength.

"It's the real thing, Skipper. We all have some extras, you know, and this one's yours."

Willie took it, turning it over in his hands. "Try it on," Eddie said.

The cap was too big, but, "Better too big than too small," Eddie said. "You'll grow into it."

"Thanks," Willie said. "It's great." Then he started to cough again.

"Well I better get goin," Eddie said. "I don't want to tire you out."

Willie kept coughing. When he stopped he took a deep wheezy breath and said, "Thanks again, Eddie."

"Don't mention it, kid. You get all better now."

"I'm trying. Eddie?"

"What, Skipper?"

"Was Uncle Nick really Babe Ruth's roommate?"

"He was, a long time ago, on the Red Sox. I was there."

"So you knew him too. Babe Ruth, I mean. You know what he's really like."

"I do, but let's not talk about that now. You get some rest."

In the vestibule Eddie said to Anna, "He seems to be doin pretty good."

"He's improved quite a bit."

"Terrific. I guess Nick don't get back from the speak until after one, right?"

Anna didn't reply for a second and then said, "What?"

"From work."

"You said 'the speak.'"

Eddie suddenly flushed. "What was I thinking? I meant the café."

"Yes, not until after one," Anna said.

"Well, too late for me after pitchin today, I'm kinda wore out. I'll catch him tomorrow." He opened the door.

"Thank you so much for your gift to Willie," Anna said. "He's thrilled."

"He's a great kid," Eddie said, then added with a laugh,

"and probably my biggest fan. I'll see you later." He turned away and went down the steps of the porch.

Anna closed the door. She stood in the vestibule, frowning, then went back to Willie. He had fallen asleep again with the A's cap still on his head.

27

DR. FLETCHER HAD ALREADY GONE by the time Nick came down in the morning. At the foot of the stairs, the baseball gloves that hung on the hooks by the door—the one Nick had borrowed from Eddie, the one he had bought for Willie—caught his eye. He stared at them for a second, took a deep breath, then went down the hall.

The door to the bedroom was open and Willie was sitting up reading—*Green Mansions*—and looked pretty good. On the bedside table an eggnog was halfway gone.

"Hello," Nick said.

Willie lifted his head and said softly, "Hi."

"Hey, where did you get that A's cap?"

Willie had worn it all night in his sleep and continued to wear it. "From Eddie." he said. "He came to see me yesterday."

"You look like a major leaguer," Nick said. Willie smiled just slightly.

In the kitchen, Anna was kneading some dough. Nick said, "He's looking better."

"He *is* better," Anna said, not looking up. "Dr. Fletcher said that his lungs are much clearer. He's not going to call Dr. Spearman."

"Well what do you know. Did you tell him about the Chinese tea?"

"I didn't dare."

Nick laughed. "Maybe it's working and maybe not, maybe it's just his time to get well. Or maybe it's the A's cap. Did you give him more tea this morning?"

"I did." Anna pushed hard at the dough with the heels of her hands, turning it over, then said, "Nick, where do you work?"

He laughed again. "What? You know where I work."

"Is it just a café?"

He frowned. "Why are you asking me that? Do you think that it's something else?"

"I think it's a speakeasy."

Nick hesitated a second then said, "You're right, it is."

"So you lied again."

"I did. Again, I was afraid if I told you the truth you wouldn't rent to me."

"You lied about the fishing rod and you lied about your work. How many other lies have you told? Did you lie about the war? The insane asylum? About playing ball with Babe Ruth?"

Nick shook his head. "No, Anna, I didn't." He suddenly thought: *My God, what if she knew the truth about why I have the gun?* He could never tell her that truth. Not ever.

Her lips compressed, Anna pushed at the dough again.

"Anna, listen, you have to believe me. I wasn't in very good shape when I came here, I needed a better place to stay than the one I was living in, so yes, I lied about the fishing rod and my work, but not about anything else."

She kept kneading the dough. Without looking up she said, "I'm not sure if I trust you anymore."

Nick's mouth tightened. He didn't speak, just turned abruptly and went down the hallway and up the stairs.

He came back with the roll of canvas in his hands. Brushing by Anna, he hurried past the bathroom, across the porch and yard, through the gate and into the alley.

He unrolled the canvas and took out the rifle. Holding it by the barrel he smashed it against the fence with all his strength. "There!" he said, gritting his teeth, and swung again. "There! There!" and the stock split apart and the trigger and bolt went

235

flying. He dropped the bent barrel and leaned on the fence, his chest heaving.

Then Anna was there beside him. She looked at the fragments of gun scattered over the alleyway's bricks and said with alarm, "What's happening? Why did you do this?"

"I'm crazy," Nick said, his breath coming hard. "And I'll always be crazy."

"No."

"Oh, Anna," he said, and now he was holding his head. "Why isn't there some kind of medicine, some kind of herb…something to help me shut out the darkness for good."

"You're doing it," Anna said. "You're getting better."

"I'm sorry I lied to you, Anna, I just wasn't right in my mind. I know that it's no excuse, but—please, forgive me."

"Nick…let's go back in."

She held out her hand and he took it. They crossed the yard together, crossed the porch, then heard the doorbell ring, heard Willie call out, "Mother!"

They went to his bedroom.

"Someone's been ringing the doorbell a lot," he said, and his voice sounded almost normal.

Anna went down the hall to the door. It was Eddie, holding a ball and glove. He was smiling, but looked concerned. "So how are things goin?"

"Okay," Anna said, but her voice was thin.

"Can I see Willie?"

"Come in."

Nick was there in the hallway, next to the bedroom door, and Eddie said, "Nick, you all right?"

"I'm fine."

"Yeah? You look kinda funny."

"That's nothing new."

Eddie laughed. "Can we practice today?"

"Sure."

"Good. Let me say hi to Skipper."

He went to the bedroom. Willie was sitting up, wearing his

236

A's cap, his book on his knees. "Hi, Eddie."

"Hey, lookin good, kid. Lookin real good."

"I'm feeling better."

"Great."

"The A's cap makes me feel stronger."

"Terrific. One of these days you'll be strong as Foxx."

"He's really strong," Willie said. "He can lift bags of wheat that weigh two hundred pounds as if they were feather pillows."

"Foxx the ox," Eddie said. "He could lift me over his head and throw me into the garbage can!"

Willie laughed.

"Listen, Skipper, you keep gettin better and soon you'll be out in the Square again with us."

"Okay."

Eddie went to the hallway, where Nick was waiting, his borrowed glove on his hand.

On the porch Eddie said, "He's gonna be fine, I bet. I was kinda worried there for a while."

"You and me both," Nick said.

As they walked to the Square Eddie spat some tobacco juice into the street. "Nick, listen, I have a confession to make. I let the cat out of the bag last night about the speak."

"I know."

"I guess Anna was pretty sore."

"She was sore, all right. But we're working things out."

"That's good."

Eddie threw for a half an hour in the park and looked real sharp. And then Nick threw.

"Hey, take it easy!" Eddie said. "You're almost as fast as you were with the Sox. You'll break my hand if you keep it up, this ain't no catcher's mitt."

Nick laughed. "Lefty catcher's mitts are pretty hard to find."

When they finished, he said, "There's something I have to do. Drop my glove off at Anna's and let her know that I won't

237

be back for a while, okay?"

"Will do," Eddie said.

Nick left the trolley at Second Street and walked to the sporting goods store. As he went through its door he thought of his plan of shooting Ruth, throwing the gun in the river, then buying a fishing rod here and wrapping it up in the canvas. It was clearly the scheme of a madman.

He looked through the rods and reels and made his selection; purchased some hooks, some small lead sinkers, some red and white bobbers. The clerk wrapped everything up in brown paper and, smiling, Nick went back home.

Willie was out of bed, in the parlor with Flora, playing gin rummy, still wearing his baseball cap. "I got you a get well present," Nick said as he entered the room, and gave Willie the package.

Eyes bright with anticipation, Willie demolished the wrapping. "A fishing rod! Wow! This is great!"

Nick put it together, then handed it back. Willie gave the reel's handle a turn; it emitted a series of clicks. "Thank you so much!" Willie said. He looked at the sinkers and hooks and bobbers then said, "I'm sorry I went in your room without your permission."

"I understand," Nick said. "You wanted to show me you'd climbed the stairs."

"Yes, but not only that, I wanted to apologize—for calling you a liar."

"Well, the fact of the matter is," Nick said, "I did tell a few whoppers."

"But I lied too. About going into your room."

"Everybody lies sometime."

"I guess," Willie said. He looked at the rod again. "So when can we go fishing?"

"As soon as you're all better," Nick said.

Three days later they were sitting beside each other on the bank of the Schuylkill River. Willie was wearing his A's cap; he almost never took it off.

It was nine o'clock in the morning, an ungodly hour for Nick, but they didn't want to miss the start of today's game against the Red Sox, so they had to get an early start on the fishing trip. The day was supposed to be very hot, and they could feel it coming.

Nick showed Willie how to attach the hook and lead and bobber to his line and how to cast. It took him some time to catch on; Nick had to undo a number of snarls—"bird's nests"—in his line. "Nice and easy," he said, "use your thumb as a brake," and at last Willie got it.

For bait they were using dough balls made out of Anna's stale bread. They had made them at home in the kitchen, enough to fill up an old tin can. In addition to the tackle and bait, Nick had brought along an old *Inquirer* to wrap fish in. As he set it on the ground, he saw an article that startled him: fifteen nations had just agreed to a treaty outlawing war. Incredible! And Germany had been the first to sign it! But could something like that ever work?

More than an hour went by and Willie got no bites. Neither did the only other angler, an elderly colored man who was using worms. He'd been fishing for almost three hours, he said, and had only had two nibbles.

"Looks like we picked the wrong day," Nick said.

"It's kind of boring," Willie said.

"Fishing is often boring, but that's how it teaches you patience," Nick said.

His father had told him that. Most of the time when he'd fished with his father they'd come up empty-handed. Sometimes they hooked a carp or a catfish, a sunny or two, or maybe an eel or a sucker. Nick didn't like to fish nearly as much as his father did, but even if they didn't catch anything and he was bored, he liked spending time with his father and seeing him happy. As he looked at Willie intent on the

239

bobber, the spot where his line met the water, he hoped he was having fun and thought: *If Dad hadn't smoked so much he'd probably be here with us.*

The colored man finally called it quits. "Lady Luck is not bein kind to me," he said. "You fellas want the rest of my worms? There's only three."

"Sure," Nick said. The dough balls were constantly pulled apart by the river's powerful current.

The old man dumped his worms on top of the remaining dough balls and Nick thanked him.

"Maybe they gone work better for you than they did for me," the man said smiling.

He walked away, and Nick took a worm from the can and taught Willie how to thread its soft body onto his hook.

Willie frowned. "But doesn't that hurt?"

"Worms don't feel things the way we do," Nick said.

Willie looked unconvinced as he watched the speared worm wriggle and twist. He cast it into the water.

Another half hour went by with no bites, Nick hoping that Willie would hook at least *something*, maybe a little sunny. His mind was eased by the flow of the river, the heavy green boughs of the trees on the opposite shore. He looked at some buildings over there and thought of how lucky he was to have this moment, to live where he lived, to be with this boy in this moment of peace. He thought of the other river and how had had planned to throw his rifle into it. The remains of that rifle still sat in the trashcan that stood on Anna's back porch.

"How deep is this river?" Willie asked.

"I don't really know," Nick said. "Maybe twenty or thirty feet."

"So why do we fish on its top?"

"Because that's where the best fish are."

Willie was down to his last worm now. He gingerly threaded it on by himself and cast it off. As it hit the water he asked, "Do they drown?"

"After a while, I guess," Nick said. "Sometimes you see

240

dead worms on the sidewalk after a heavy rain. They drowned."

"Yes," Willie said. "Do worms have noses?"

"Maybe just mouths," Nick said.

"Do they have brains?"

"You got me on that one."

"Well are both of their ends the same?"

"I don't think so."

"Oh."

They sat there quietly. Nick's mind began roaming again. He was starting to think he should look for another job—as an auto mechanic, maybe, or maybe he'd do some carpentry work on his own, as his father had. He was drifting off, when suddenly Willie shouted, "Uncle Nick!"

His rod was bending and jumping around like mad. Nick sat up straight. "Hold it tight!" he said.

"I got one! It's pulling hard!"

"Hang on!"

The line shot straight out and Nick said, "Give me the rod."

Willie handed it over. Nick loosened the drag and handed it back. "We'll give it a little line and let it run," he said. "Just keep on holding tight."

The line went slack for a second and Nick was afraid that the fish had escaped. "Pull up on the rod," he said.

Willie did and it started to jump again. "Start reeling in," Nick said. "Here, let me tighten the drag."

The fish was losing strength and Willie kept reeling. Nick wondered what it could be. It was pretty big, but didn't act like a catfish or carp. For a second they saw a silver flash in the water and then it was gone. A carp would flash gold, not silver. "Keep reeling," Nick said.

"It's hard," Willie said. His hand seemed stuck; his face was flushed and covered with sweat.

"Let me have it a minute."

Nick took the rod, kept reeling, and soon Willie said, "There it is!" and the fish was out of the water and flopping

241

around on the mud. Nick grabbed the line and pulled the fish onto the grass.

It kept flopping. "Wow!" Willie said. "It's big!"

"Striped bass!" Nick said. "Incredible! And you caught it. Good job!"

"It's beautiful!"

"It sure is. Won't your mother be proud?"

"Yes," Willie said, then he suddenly frowned. "Will we eat it?"

"Of course."

"Oh."

"Don't you want to? You don't like fish?"

"I do, but…"

"But what?"

"Oh, I don't know."

Soon the fish stopped flopping and Nick wrapped it up in the paper. He put the bait can into a trash barrel next to a picnic table and then, with the fish in one hand and the rod in the other, he went with Willie across the park to the trolley stop.

They walked slowly. Willie looked bushed; he was breathing hard. "Is it a boy or a girl fish?" he asked.

"I don't know yet. We'll know when we cut it open."

"Oh. When it dies will it go to heaven?"

"That's something to ask your mother."

On the trolley the fish gave another kick. "Still alive," Nick said. "That's good."

When Nick unwrapped the fish on the kitchen table, Anna was astonished.

"Willie's the one who caught it," Nick said. "Imagine that. My father spent his whole life trying to catch one of these and never did, and Willie gets one his first time out."

"Beginner's luck," Anna said.

"It was hard to pull in," Willie said.

"They're real fighters," Nick said. "Like Willie."

Willie smiled.

Nick cleaned the fish at the sink. He cut off its head then slit its belly and pulled out the entrails and suddenly thought of a horse on the ground somewhere, its side blown open, a cart wheel spinning, then thought of something worse: a guy named Lake had been hit in the stomach— He felt a bit dizzy and stopped for a second to take a deep breath.

"Is this like an operation?" Willie asked.

Nick looked at him, telling himself that the past was gone, this was only a fish, here, now. "Oh, no," he said, "this is worse than an operation, much worse. You've seen your mother do this, haven't you?"

"No," Willie said. "The fish we buy at Leewright's have been cleaned. The chickens too. Morris does it."

"Oh," Nick said. He pulled the roe out of the mess and said, "It's a girl fish, these are its eggs."

"So many," Willie said.

"Uh-huh. And they're good eating."

"You can *eat* them?"

"Sure. They're great with scrambled eggs."

Willie looked highly skeptical.

Nick scaled the fish with the knife and washed it off. He wrapped the head and guts in the paper and put it out back in the garbage can, pushing the lid down tight so cats couldn't get at it.

They ate some lunch and after Willie napped they went to the roof to watch the Red Sox game. It was terribly hot, the sun glaring off the gravel, not pleasant at all. But the A's played fantastically well and won by a score of 14-2.

This gave them six wins in their last seven games. At the end of June they had trailed the Yankees by thirteen games but then in July they got hot, winning twenty-five games and losing just eight. They kept up the torrid pace in August while the Yanks cooled off, and now they had actually caught them. The four game Yanks-A's series next week in New York was critical—could decide the pennant race. After two games on

243

Sunday the teams would take Monday off, and then Eddie Winters would pitch game three on Tuesday.

As Nick walked to work he kept wishing that he could be at that Tuesday game. He was certain that Eddie was wishing the very same thing.

28

AFTER FISHING AND WATCHING the game on the blistering roof Nick was pretty well bushed, but he had no time to slack off. It was Saturday night and the place was as busy as ever—and hotter than hell. On his break he went to the alley but even out there the air was incredibly thick and still; it was like breathing through cheesecloth.

When he went back behind the counter, Vince arrived. As Nick mixed a drink he said to him, "I want to place a bet."

Vince squinted. "You? Since when are you a betting man?"

"I thought I should give it a shot. It's probably the only bet I'll ever make."

"So what is it?"

Nick gave the drink to his customer. "I want to bet on the A's to win game three of the Yankees series."

Vince laughed. "Forget it. I got some inside information on that game."

"Oh?"

Vince lowered his voice. "Mack's gonna let Eddie Winters pitch."

This startled Nick. How in the world had Vince ever found that out? He seemed to have the dope on damn near everything. "You gotta be kidding."

"My sources are very reliable," Vince said. "Everyone knows that Winters is through, but I guess Mack's desperate now that Earnshaw's hurt. Nick, you don't want to bet on that game."

"Yeah, I do," Nick said. And then he explained *how* he wanted to bet.

Vince stared at him. "You've lost your mind. You know what that means? If you lose, and you will, you'll owe a fortune. Where would you ever get that kind of dough?"

"I'm not going to lose."

Vince shook his head. "Nick, listen to me. The guys I front for are not nice guys. If you don't pay them off you're in big trouble. I mean *big* trouble. Remember what happened to Butterball? And all he owed was fifty bucks."

"I can take care of myself."

"No, Nick," Vince said. "I'll take your bet—a small one— on another team and another game, but not on the game you want. Stay away from the Yanks. The Babe was asleep for a month and a half, but now he's awake again, and—" He suddenly stopped. "Well speak of the devil, look who's here." He nodded toward the door.

Sure enough, there he was, with a mile-wide grin on his pudgy face and a statuesque redhead on his arm. "A finger of brown for the lady," he said coming over to Jake as he chomped on his stogie. "And a draft for me."

"Comin right up," Jake said, and set to work. "But Babe, what are you doin here tonight? The Yankees ain't in town."

"Car problems," Ruth said as he smoked his cigar. "Me an the lady here was toolin along Route One on our way to New York and the damn thing up and quit on me. Not even a year old yet and it quits. Got towed to a garage and they said it would take three hours to fix. I figured I might as well spend the time in a place I like, so I grabbed a cab and came down here. I'm starvin, you got Greek stew tonight?"

"Of course."

"I'll have it." He turned to the redhead. "What about you, keed, you wanna try it? The cook here's terrific."

"No, just a burger for me," the woman said.

Jake went to the kitchen window and gave the orders to Louie. When he came back Ruth said, "Well at least I made it past Wawa this time. You ever hear of what happened in Wawa?"

"Everybody heard of it," Jake said. "It made the front page of all the papers."

Ruth laughed. "That's right, it did." He turned to the woman again. "You ever hear of it, keed?"

"No, Babe, I never did."

"Yeah, you're too young. Well see, this was back in 1920. I was drivin Route One pretty fast with some people I knew and I went off the road and smacked a tree. We all went flyin, but no one got hurt. Well, some got a little bit hurt, not bad, we were pretty damn lucky. But some of the newspapers said I was killed!" He laughed again. "Imagine that! I wasn't even scratched! The next day I played terrific. This happened in Wawa, just outside Philly. Wawa, what a name!"

Ruth ate three bowls of stew and had two beers with every bowl, then downed two slices of chocolate cream pie. He smoked and laughed as guys came up to him to tell him how great he was and ask for his autograph.

At break time, seething, Nick went to the storeroom, stood on the little stepladder there and took down a paper bag from the topmost shelf.

In the bag was a baseball. As he'd started out for work two weeks ago, a high pop foul came flying over the grandstand roof behind home plate. It hit the street hard and bounced into the Square. The kids who hung out on the sidewalks went scrambling for it, running in front of the trolley car, making it screech and clang its bell. Nick gave the winner, lightning-quick Peanuts Sullivan once again, a quarter for it. At work he put it in a bag and hid it away in the storeroom, hoping that Ruth would show up again, and now he had.

Nick went back to the bar with the ball in his hand and said to Jake, "Get him to sign this for me, will you?"

"Why don't you do it?"

"I can't."

"How come?"

"I just can't. Now listen, get him to sign it 'For Willie.'"

A few minutes later Ruth ordered a round of drinks for everyone and Nick and Jake and Charlie all set to work. Jake put Ruth's drink in front of him along with the ball and a fountain pen. "'For Willie,' Babe," he said.

The big man scowled. "For who?"

"For Willie. A friend of mine."

Ruth laughed and picked up the pen. "Any friend of yours is a friend of mine," he said, and signed the ball.

Jake gave it to Nick, who put it under the counter to let the ink thoroughly dry. Later, he stuffed it into his pocket.

Ruth kept drinking and shooting his mouth off until the garage called to say that his car was ready. "Get me a cab, keed," he said to Jake and Jake went to the storeroom, where it was quiet, and made the call.

Ruth was bleary; his face was sagging. He said to his female companion, whose name was Trixie, "My mother hated me."

"Oh, Babe, I'm sure she didn't," Trixie said.

"I'm sure she did. I know she did. She stuck me away in that school…"

After Ruth left, Nick approached Vince again and he finally gave in. "It's suicide," he said. "Don't expect me to bail you out, I can't do it."

"I don't expect anything."

"When you lose you have maybe a week to pay up—if they're in a good mood. And they're never in a good mood."

"I told you before," Nick said, "I won't lose."

But back in his room he couldn't sleep. He sat by the window, the light of the streetlamp striking his curtains, a small breeze pushing them into the room and then sucking them out again. He thought of the striped bass Willie had caught, and Willie's amazed expression. He thought of the baseball that Ruth had signed sitting across the room in his dresser drawer. And he thought of Eddie Winters. All he needed to do was throw the ghost the way he was throwing it now and all would be fine.

Nick wasn't sleepy at all and kept sitting there watching the empty street, just thinking. If everything fell into place, he would have enough money for Anna to pay off her house. He'd convince her to move away from the city. She had to, for Willie's sake. For her own sake, too. But if things went wrong and he lost the bet, he would have to leave this house and this city for good—or at least for a very long time. He tried not to think about that, but he sat at the window for hours.

In the morning, while Anna and Willie were off at church and Flora was up in her room, the doorbell rang. It was Eddie.

Nick went out to the porch. Eddie said, "I'm catchin a train for Washington soon, but I had to see you first. I'm nervous about that Yankees game."

"Come on, you'll do fine," Nick said. "Nobody's ever seen what you're going to throw them. Unless they faced Flapjack Jackson somewhere along the line."

"Ruth did."

"Yeah, and how did he do against him?"

"I'm not Jackson."

"You're throwing his pitch real well."

"For a couple of innings, yeah, but this will be for a whole damn game—the biggest game of my life. If I do good, Mack will sign me again for next year. If I don't do good, I'm finished."

You and me both, Nick thought. "Eddie," he said, "you're throwing great. You're gonna knock 'em dead."

"I sure hope so. If the games were here at home and I had you to practice with I'd sure feel a whole lot better." He shook his head. "They're tryin to kill us again. Four doubleheaders this week! The first one's tomorrow in Washington, then a single game, a two day break, then twin bills Friday and Saturday in Boston—then another one Sunday in New York!

Six games in three days! Then Monday off and it's my turn to pitch on Tuesday if Mr. Mack sticks to his plan. I hope our guys ain't all wore out by then."

"Tough schedule," Nick said.

"Well, nothin we can do about it," Eddie said. "If we have a rainout they'll probably make us play a tripleheader!"

Nick laughed—as Anna and Willie appeared at the end of the block up by Somerset Street.

"I'm here to say goodbye," Eddie told them as they came near. "We end our season with twenty-three straight on the road, so I'm not gonna see you again for almost a month. I'm sure gonna miss you guys."

"We'll miss you too," Willie said.

"Keep walkin and throwin, you're doin great."

"You're doing great too—with the ghost."

Eddie grinned. "I just hope I can keep it up."

"You will," Nick said.

He and Willie shook hands with Eddie and wished him luck and he walked up the street to his room.

That afternoon, while Anna prepared Sunday dinner, Nick had a catch with Willie out in the Square. A thunderstorm had swept through the city at four A.M. and the air was less hot and humid than yesterday.

"So how did you like that fish last night?" Nick asked as he tossed the ball.

"I didn't eat any," Willie said.

"But why? I thought you liked fish."

"I do, but I just couldn't eat that one. She was kind of like a friend."

"I see," Nick said. "Will you want to go fishing again sometime?"

"I guess. I'm not sure yet. Maybe if I throw the fish back I will."

Nick was terribly restless. He couldn't stop thinking about his bet—and how anxious Eddie had been this morning.

"I sure wish those Yankee games were here," Willie said as they walked back home. "I could watch Eddie battle the Babe in game three. It would be so great. But Shibe Park's dead until next year—unless the A's win the pennant and we have the World Series here. I hate it when there's no more games to watch. It makes me sad."

"I have something that might cheer you up," Nick said as they entered the house.

He went to his room and retrieved the autographed ball from his dresser. Coming back to the parlor he said, "I got this last night," and he gave it to Willie.

Willie stared at the ball in silence a moment and then said, "Wow!" He looked up at Nick, his face shining. "But how did you ever get it?"

"The Babe's car broke down last night on his way to New York and he came to the Home Plate. I mentioned your letters to him and he said he remembered your name. He said he'd been meaning to write to you but he's just been so terribly busy—all those hospital visits and everything—so he signed this ball and told me to give it to you with his very best wishes."

"Wow!" Willie exclaimed again. "This is really nifty! Thank you so much, Uncle Nick!"

"I'm glad I could do it for you," Nick said.

29

On MONDAY NICK WOKE UP EARLY because of his worries. He tried to walk them away but they kept on dogging him. Eddie's big game was not till next Tuesday. It was going to be a long week.

Nick needed to get his mind off that game, and he thought of a couple of ways to do it.

In the kitchen, while Willie was practicing with professor Shultz, he shared one of these ways with Anna.

"Baker Bowl?" she said. "But it isn't safe! A section of its stands collapsed last year."

"Yeah, I read about that, but it's okay now."

"So they say."

"Tell you what. We'll sit at ground level away from the grandstands with nothing above our heads."

"But it was the lower level that fell apart!"

"It's completely repaired, I read about it, it's perfectly safe—stronger than ever."

Anna sighed. "Well, all right. But please, be careful!"

Right before lunch Nick said to Willie, "You told me you're sad when there aren't more games to watch. "Well, there are more games."

"What? What do you mean?"

"I mean the Phillies. They're playing the New York Giants this afternoon. Want to go?"

"Of course! I don't have any Phillies cards but I do have some Giants cards."

"Okay then," Nick said. "We'll do it."

After Willie got up from his nap, they started out. They walked slowly down Lehigh Avenue toward Baker Bowl, which was only six blocks from Shibe Park. At the Home Plate Café Nick said, "Here's where I work. Let's go inside."

As usual, few people were there: one man at the counter smoking and drinking a coffee and three little girls at a table enjoying their Yuenglings. "Shirley," Nick said, "this is the famous Willie Shuster."

"The kid I been puttin the cards aside for," Shirley said. "Pleased to meet you, young man." She extended her hand.

Willie shook it. "Thank you for saving those cards for me," he said.

"You're quite welcome."

"I have almost the whole set now. There are only three A's in it. Tris Speaker, Ty Cobb and Eddie Rommel."

"No Lefty Grove?"

"No."

"He comes here sometimes."

"He does?"

"Always orders an ice cream—and he gets a baseball card with it, of course."

This made Willie laugh.

"Would you like an ice cream?" Nick asked him.

"Sure!"

Willie chose chocolate and sat at one of the tables. Along with his purchase he'd gotten another card of Carl Mays.

A few more customers came and went as Willie ate. When he finished, Nick said, "Well, Shirley, we're off to see the Phillies."

"Why?" Shirley laughed. "What are they, fifty games out of first place?

"I wouldn't be surprised," Nick said.

Nick had last been to Baker Bowl twelve years ago during the Red Sox-Phillies World Series. He'd gone to the first of those games with Alice and Johnny and Jimmy. The park had been pretty decrepit even then, and now it was pathetic. The rot that had caused last year's collapse had allegedly been addressed, but it was clear that the place was ripe for demolition.

The ticket office was at Fifteenth and Huntington Streets. The last time Nick had come here, during the Series, a line of fans had stretched from the office up to Lehigh and around the corner all the way to Broad, but today the sidewalks were empty. Once he was inside the park Willie said, "It's so *small*."

In spite of the fact that there was a doubleheader today, most of the seats were empty. Shirley hadn't been joking about the Phillies: they actually *were* fifty games behind first place St. Louis.

The tickets that Nick had bought turned out to be for seats not far from where he'd sat with Alice twelve years ago, behind the first base dugout. He forced himself to short circuit the sense of loss he was starting to feel by jumping up and down on the wooden floor; it seemed solid and the seats didn't shake.

The Giants were finishing batting practice. Nick watched one of them hit a ball clear over the close but towering right field wall. A gigantic deodorant soap advertisement covered that wall: THE PHILLIES USE LIFEBUOY. The joke went: "And they still stink."

"They're very bad," Willie said, "but the Giants are good. They're only trailing the Cardinals by two games."

Batting practice concluded and there was a lull, then the managers came to the plate to confer with the ump. The Giants' manager wore a suit, the Phillies' manager a uniform. "Recognize the man in the suit?" Nick asked.

"It's John McGraw!" Willie said. "He's as famous as Connie Mack!"

"At least."

"I hope Carl Hubbell pitches," Willie said. "He's famous

too—and really good."

But instead of Hubbell the Giants' pitcher was Jack Scott, a guy who'd been kicking around for years. For the Phils it was Alex Ferguson, another journeyman.

Willie knew some of the Giants players: the outfielders Lefty O'Doul and Mel Ott and first baseman Bill Terry, whose card he had. The only Phillies player he knew was their young power hitter, Chuck Klein.

Nick kept trying to focus on the field, but it wasn't easy. He'd hoped this game would block out worries about that other game, a week away, but it didn't. He found himself thinking that right at this moment, a hundred and thirty-five miles south, the A's were playing a doubleheader with Washington.

There were plenty of hits in this game but hardly any runs. Chuck Klein did nothing in four at bats, but Bill Terry homered and the Giants won, 4-3. Ever since the Phillies won the pennant in 1915 they'd been dreadful. Nick wondered if they'd ever be good again.

He and Willie decided they wouldn't stay for the second game. As they left the park Willie said, "That was kind of boring, but thanks for taking me. I wonder how the A's are doing against the Senators."

Nick's worries were front and center again. "I wonder," he said.

At work he heard the distressing news from radio-addicted Jackie Dodd: the A's had lost both games of their doubleheader. Dodd also said that the Yankees had split their twin bill with Boston. So now the teams were even again.

On Tuesday morning Nick checked the newspaper's box scores and found that Eddie had pitched an inning in both of the Washington games and had not been scored upon. This brightened his spirits, but still didn't quell his worry. He needed another distraction.

Since the night that he and Willie had talked about the long life spans of parrots and tortoises, Willie had mentioned a number of times that he wanted to go to the zoo; he had never been. "Let's do it, all of us," Nick said to Anna. "The treat's on me."

To his surprise, she agreed without hesitation. She had wanted to go for quite some time, she said. So she packed a big lunch and she and Willie and Nick and yes, even Flora, took the trolley out to the zoo—the nation's first—which stood across the Schuylkill at Thirty-fourth and Girard. The ride on Girard made Nick think of Jimmy Harriman, and he promised himself to go see him one of these days.

The zoo shocked Willie with its stench ("It's quite o-DIF-erous today," said Flora), but it also enthralled him, as Nick knew it would. Here were all of the animals he'd read about in his *Book of Knowledge*. He loved the placid, constantly chewing giraffes, the camels, the graceful gazelles. The way that a hippo crunched up a whole cabbage tossed in his gaping mouth by a keeper amazed him. He viewed the big cats warily, as if not quite trusting the walls and the moats to hold them. The lions were lazing about on the rocks but one of the tigers was rapidly pacing as if propelled by rage, and so was a leopard, its eyes sharp and fierce.

The going was slow because of Flora, who needed more frequent stops than Willie did. One of these stops was across from Monkey Island, always a favorite of the crowd, full of hilarious action, and even after Flora had taken a good long rest it was hard to drag Willie away from there.

When Flora saw the zoo's gorilla, Bamboo, behind the bars of its cage, she said, "He reminds me of Harold, my husband. Something about his mouth and especially his posture. That's where Harold belongs—behind bars." She laughed. "No monkeying around for this big guy, there aren't any girl gorillas here."

In the reptile house they saw huge snakes that could squeeze you to death and tiny ones that could kill you with

256

poison. They saw beautiful polar bears swimming around on their backs and sea lions cavorting, and everyone felt that a swim would feel really good right now. They saw the parrots, who didn't look old but probably were, and a giant tortoise, who did look old and was as thrilling as a stone; his eyelids were the only part of him that moved. They ate their lunch across from the elephants, who were shoving trunkfuls of hay into their mouths, and then Flora bought them all Popsicles.

"A kid invented these by accident," said Willie, licking his lime. "He mixed up some soda powder and water with a stick and left it outside by mistake in freezing weather."

"I'm certainly glad that he did," Flora said. "It's very refreshing."

"That kid was only eleven," Willie said, "and I'm already ten! But you know what? He didn't really invent these things, it just happened."

"Just luck," Nick said.

"Yes," Willie said. "Just luck."

After another hour of wolves and hyenas and kangaroos and exotic birds it was time to go. Nick had thought that the zoo would make him stop thinking about his bet, at least for a while, but it hadn't, not in the slightest. He was obsessed.

As they got on the trolley car Willie said, "That was great. But do those animals like being there?"

"I'm sure they would rather be back in the wild," Flora said.

"Yes," Willie said, "they're kind of like prisoners, aren't they?"

The A's won that day's game with the Senators. The following morning Nick slept late and woke up thinking about his bet again. But at work he heard some news that made those thoughts evaporate.

Shirley went to the kitchen with him and told him that Louie had suffered a heart attack. She had found him on the floor beside the stove and called the cops, who took him to the closest hospital, Samaritan. Billy Milligan, the day cook, a gruff little freckle-faced leprechaun, was filling in for Louie, rushing around like mad. "Too hot in here!" he said. "We need more fans! I've told Sid that for years, maybe now he'll listen."

Charlie and Jake were gloomy behind the bar, but kept up a good false front, and so did Nick, the three of them waiting for word from Shirley, who'd gone to the hospital straight from work.

She returned with Vince a little after nine. "He was awake when we got there," she said, "but then he went right to sleep again. His doctor said things are touch and go."

In the morning, Nick went to the hospital. Louie was propped up in bed with tubes in his arm and his face was slack, his whiskers very black against his pale skin.

"You'll get through this," Nick said. "And don't worry about the café, Billy's doing a great job filling in. He found a guy who can give him a hand until you get back."

"I ain't gettin back," Louie said in a husky voice. "I'm done with the Home Plate. I'm seventy, Nick."

"Well what are you going to do?"

"I'll go back to my room at Al's and rest up, and once I'm feelin good, who knows? Maybe I'll just take it easy the rest of my life."

"Hard to imagine you doing that,"

"It's time. I'll cook for Al, of course. One way or another, things'll work out."

"If there's anything you want, just ask."

"I don't need nothin. They're treatin me good here."

"Okay, but I mean it, just ask."

Nick went to see Louie the next three mornings, and Louie looked better each day. His room was now filled with flowers. Other people from work were often there: Charlie, Jake, Doris and Sid. Vince was there too a couple of days but Shirley couldn't make it until she got off from work in the afternoon.

On Friday, when Nick was there alone, Louie said, "You asked me what *I* was gonna do, so what are *you* gonna do?"

"What do you mean?" Nick said.

"You ain't gonna tend bar forever, I hope."

"I don't know."

"You should do somethin better than that. You told me you used to fix cars."

"I did, but I couldn't find work in that field."

"You should give it another try. More and more cars all the time and they all break down. You'll never starve. Cooks never starve either, they always get work."

"I'm a terrible cook."

"Too bad. But I think Gus might make a good one. He helps me out sometimes. He has the knack."

"He's a swell kid," Nick said. "But you sure you don't want to come back to the Home Plate?"

"Never. I've worked enough. What I want to do next, when I'm strong enough, is go to Greece. I want to see the Aegean again before I die. My brother Mike, he waited too long and died three years ago. As soon as I'm better, I'm goin."

"I'll miss you, Louie. Thanks for all the help you've given me—and for all the Greek stew."

Louie smiled. "The recipe's in my head, but I'll write it out for Gus and he'll give you a copy."

"That would be great."

Louie smiled again. "You know what Sid told me yesterday? He's givin me a little bonus for all the years I slaved for him. That's what I'm gonna use to get to Greece."

"Sid's a good guy," Nick said.

"He is. Now if only he'd install more fans—" He turned his head. Rusty Bridges was there in the doorway. "Boyfriend," Louie said.

Nick frowned. "Boyfriend?"

"You didn't know he was goin with Al?" Louie said.

Nick grinned. "I didn't know."

"Yeah, for a couple of weeks now," Rusty said.

"Well what great news."

"Louie might be my uncle one of these days."

"You'll never starve."

To Louie, Rusty said, "You're lookin much better."

"I'm feelin much better too. They might spring me tomorrow."

"Let's hope."

Rusty stayed for another ten minutes then said that he had to get going and left with Nick. On the sidewalk he said, "Al feeds him some of her great baklava when he gets home, he's gonna be fine."

"For sure," Nick said.

"So guess where I went yesterday," Rusty said. "To the Rose. It seems like a million years ago since I lived there."

"Same here. So why'd you go back?"

"To see Perley."

"How is he?"

"Okay, but he fell down and broke two teeth in his upper plate. He don't have the money to get it fixed, so he talks kinda funny."

"Too bad."

"Yeah. I ran into Longfellow there, he's still blabbin about Walt Whitman."

"He always will."

"Stubby's still sellin his smokes."

"Uh-huh."

"And oh yeah, Einstein died."

"I'm not surprised. He must've been close to ninety."

"No, only seventy-six."

"You're kidding."

"That's what they tell me. Now listen, I have some news. Things are really heatin up between Grady and Mario, it's gettin a little scary. We may not be able to bring you your hootch anymore, but we'll still bring your butter and eggs."

"And you'll stop in for Billy's chili."

"I love the stuff!"

"Good luck with Al."

"She's a wonderful girl," Rusty said. "And what a cook!"

Nick was out back replacing the board he'd cracked when he slammed the fence with the rifle, and Willie was taking it in from the little back porch. He said, "His heart attacked him. Like Uncle Sol's heart."

"He's doing much better, though," Nick said. "He's going to Greece."

"That's far away. I'd like to go there too someday. I'd like to see the Parthenon."

"Well maybe you will."

Willie frowned. "Do parrots and tortoises get heart attacks? Is that why they finally die?"

"I think they just die of old age."

"Oh. Is that a condition?"

"More or less."

"Kids never get heart attacks, right?"

"That's right."

Willie looked at the melon vine growing along the fence. The fruits were oblong, quite large now and turning yellow. "The melons are almost ready," he said. "They're very delicious, and good for your heart. They were my father's favorite kind, and Mother grows them every year, it helps her to remember him. I think if I eat a lot of them I'll live to be very old."

Nick hammered the new board into place. "You probably will," he said.

"You'll like the melons," Willie said.

"And live to be very old?"

Willie laughed, but then his expression darkened, as if a sudden cloud had passed over his feelings.

After their Tuesday win the A's had a two-day break, and it seemed to renew them: they went to Boston and ripped the Red Sox twice on Friday and twice again on Saturday, putting them up on the Yankees by half a game. Eddie Winters was used three times and surrendered just two scratch hits.

And now they would start their crucial New York series with yet another doubleheader—their third in a row.

The crowd for the Sunday games was unprecedented. According to the papers, eighty-five thousand people packed Yankee Stadium's stands and an estimated one hundred thousand more were turned away. Five thousand or so put their lives at risk by watching from the roofs of apartment buildings.

And the Athletics lost both games.

Nick and Willie were gloomy. The A's were now a game and a half behind. But the game that really counted for Nick was the next one, Tuesday's game, when Eddie Winters would pitch.

Late Monday morning, Nick and Willie came back from a catch in the Square when the telephone rang. This was a rare occurrence in Anna's house. With the phone to her ear she listened a minute then said, "Yes, he's here," and handed the phone to Nick. "Eddie Winters," she said.

Frowning, Nick took the phone and said hello.

"Nick, really glad I could reach you."

"What's happening?"

"Well, I'm kinda gettin cold feet."

"But why? I read that you did just great against the Senators and the Sox."

"I did, but I only pitched an inning each game. It's this whole game thing that's got me goin."

"Eddie, how many times have we been through this?"

"I know, but I just can't help it. Yesterday was murder. The Yanks beat up on old man Quinn real bad, and then in the second game they hammered Rommel too. They're hot, Nick, *really* hot. And the crowd! I never seen nothin like it! The noise was deafening. To play in front of that... I feel like

262

takin a drink."

Alarmed, Nick said, "You better not!"

A moment of silence, then Eddie said, "I wish you could be here with me, Nick. You'd give me my confidence back."

"Eddie—"

"What do you say? Can you come? If we could practice the ghost before the game it would mean the world to me."

"Eddie, listen—"

"Come on, Nick, do it for me. I'll pay your train fare and get you a real good seat at the game."

Nick broke into a sweat. "Let me think about this," he said. "Where can I reach you?"

"At my hotel. Today's an off day for us and I'm not goin anywhere. Here's the number." He gave it, along with the number of his room.

"I'll get back to you," Nick said.

When he hung up, Willie said. "Is something wrong with Eddie?"

"Just his nerves again," Nick said. "Listen, I have to go out for a while, I'll see you soon."

As he walked to the Home Plate his worries surged. Eddie had sounded incredibly shaky. If he didn't do well and the A's lost this game… He could not let that happen, he simply couldn't. He would have to go to New York to calm him down—and to keep him from drinking. He didn't see any way out of it.

He had never missed a day of work or been late since he'd started the Home Plate job. Sid was well aware of this when Nick asked to take time off to see a sick friend who lived miles away.

"So Louie's better, now somebody else is sick?"

"That's right."

"Heart problems?"

"No, something else, I don't know exactly what."

Sid squinted.

"I can probably still be here by eight," Nick said.

Sid nodded. "Don't worry about it. It's a Tuesday, we'll get by."

"What if somebody needs to be bounced?"

"Gus can probably pinch hit for you," Sid said. Then, with a little laugh: "If not, I'll get Doris to do it."

Nick thanked him, ordered a burger and coffee from Shirley, and after he finished eating he walked back home. When he got there, Anna was at her sewing machine and Willie and Flora were playing cards. "I'm going to New York tomorrow to see Eddie Winters," he said.

Willie raised his head sharply. "You are? Are you going to watch him pitch?"

"Of course."

"Oh, wow, can I go too?"

Nick looked at Anna. He said, "Let's talk for a minute."

In the kitchen he said in a quiet voice, "It would be the best thing in the world for him. He's never been out of this city. He's hardly even been out of this *neighborhood*."

"But New *York*," Anna said.

"He'll remember it his whole life."

She rolled her eyes. "I've only been there once. What a place. Just like that movie we saw."

Nick frowned. "Philly's just as bad, on a smaller scale. Come on, Anna, let him go, he'll be perfectly safe with me."

"I'm sure—unless..."

"Unless what?"

"Unless you have one of your spells."

Nick was silent a minute then said, "I haven't come close to one in weeks. But if you're concerned, why don't you join us?"

"I can't, I have to finish a dress for a customer."

"Really? You can't—"

"No, it's very important. It has to be done by tomorrow afternoon."

"Okay, but let Willie go. It will be such a great experience

264

for him. Yankee Stadium!"

Anna sighed. "Well...all right. But I'll worry the whole time he's gone."

"Of course you will, that's what mothers do. But we'll be back tomorrow night safe and sound. I guarantee it."

"Well, if you *guarantee* it," Anna said.

In the living room Nick said to Willie, "Your mother says you can go."

"Wow!"

"Let me call Eddie back."

Eddie answered the phone right away. "So?"

"We're coming."

"We? You mean Skipper, too?"

"That's right."

"Terrific!"

"Yeah. But how do we get to Yankee Stadium? I don't know New York. I was only there once for a short time, years ago."

"I'll meet you at Penn Station, right on the platform, and we'll go together. Hold on, let me check the schedule." There was silence a moment, a shuffling sound, and then: "A train leaves North Philly Station at five after eight and pulls in here at eleven. That's when I'll meet you."

"Okay."

"This is great! Thanks a million, Nick."

"We'll see you tomorrow," Nick said. "Go to bed early, get lots of sleep. And don't you dare take a drink!"

30

NICK AND WILLIE were too wound up to sleep well. In the morning they didn't feel like eating, so Anna gave them a paper bag with some day-old muffins in it.

North Philadelphia Station was not far away and the trolley car took them there quickly. Willie was wearing a short-sleeved shirt and his Athletics baseball cap. "You won't see too many caps like yours where we're going," Nick said.

He'd come home from the café at one, had slept thinly and woken at six. In the station's waiting room he felt groggy, but Willie was wide awake with excitement. Nick bought the tickets and then bought a paper but didn't read it. When their train was announced he felt a quick anxious twinge. He wondered what Willie felt.

Nick helped him onto the train, the first one he'd ever ridden. Nick hadn't been on a train since the day they had let him out of St. Luke's. He remembered how shocked he had been by the dresses the women were wearing. He smiled at that now.

Willie sat by the window. The seats filled quickly, a conductor cried "All aboard!" and the train began to move.

Willie looked out the window as blocks of row houses and factories rolled by. Nick asked if he'd like to read the funnies but Willie said no, and kept staring outside. As the train picked up speed Nick read the front page of the paper and then read the sports. The starting pitcher for New York today was Hank Johnson, a so-so player who'd been around for ages and was having a surprisingly good year. Nick remembered when, back in June, Johnson had shocked everybody by beating Lefty Grove. The paper said the Athletics' starting pitcher was yet to be determined.

After a half an hour or so Willie and Nick decided to eat their muffins, and after Willie finished he asked for the funnies. He buried his head in the page and every so often giggled. "I love the Katzenjammer Kids," he said. "They always get in trouble."

When the train pulled into Penn Station, Eddie was there to meet them on the platform just as he'd promised. "Am I glad to see you guys. You hungry? Want somethin to eat?"

They said no. Nick gave Willie a piggyback ride up the stairs to the grand concourse, which soared to the sky. Willie dismounted and Eddie led them across the vast floor to the exit doors. It was after eleven o'clock and the station wasn't too crowded at this time of day.

But the street was quite busy with people and fast moving automobiles and double-decker buses. "The subway we need to take is a block away," Eddie said. "Not far, but the sidewalks are crowded and New Yorkers move real quick."

Again Willie got on Nick's back, and the three of them started off.

New York had grown tremendously since Nick had last seen it years ago. The skyscrapers were astounding. In Philadelphia, developers had agreed not to build any structures taller than City Hall, which was 548 feet high, but New York had no such restrictions, and several buildings seemed to touch the clouds.

Nick managed to get a subway seat for Willie, and he and Eddie stood in front of him, hanging on the overhead straps and swaying as the train moved rapidly north. It was hot, the windows were open, and there was a musty electrical smell. Nick remembered this train from years ago, and remembered the Paris subway too, the way its lights kept flashing on and off. Philly's new subway had opened a week ago but Nick hadn't tried it yet. One of these days he'd treat Anna and

Willie and Flora to a ride.

This was Willie's first time on a subway; its speed and rackety screeching made him wince. At one point a sudden loud sound made Nick think of the war, but that's all it was, a thought.

The ride was half an hour long. At their stop there were more steps to navigate, and Nick had Willie climb up on his back again.

Out on the street Eddie said, "Well, there she is, Yankee Stadium." He laughed and added, "The House That Ruth Built."

It was absolutely gigantic. Willie stared at it goggle-eyed. It looked so modern compared to Shibe Park.

There were long lines waiting for tickets. Eddie laughed again and said, "All of them here just to watch me pitch. And I'll walk right past them now and they won't even know who I am. On Sunday some people waited in line for twenty hours! Imagine that! It won't be packed like that today, but there'll be plenty here."

They walked past a long line of waiting fans to a gate at the end of the block and then followed Eddie inside. He showed a guard his I.D card and said, "Friends of mine."

They walked up a small flight of stairs and suddenly saw the sky and the bright green grass. The stands were nearly completely empty, but players were on the field. "There's Al Simmons!" Willie said. "And that's Mule Haas!"

He had never seen the A's road uniforms before and they looked strange. Instead of an "A" on the front of the shirt a white elephant stood on its hind legs. "We're the enemy here," he said. Nick laughed and pointed to an older guy who stood near the right field wall. "Ty Cobb," he said. "If he gets in the game today it might be his very last one."

They followed Eddie down an aisle and stopped in front of the Athletics' bullpen; it was tucked away in the stadium's right field corner. Eddie reached into his pocket and took out his wallet. "I called the railroad and found out the price of your tickets," he said. "So here's the dough for that and some extra for lunch."

"For lunch?" Nick said. "You don't have to buy our lunch."

"Yeah," Eddie said, "I do. And here are your tickets to the game. For now, just sit right here. This ain't where you're gonna be when the game begins, but if anyone asks what you're doin here, just show them the tickets and say that you're waitin for me. I have to change into my uniform." He put a leg over the wall that separated the stands from the playing field, stepped onto a bench and then onto the field. Then he walked toward the A's dugout down by first base.

Nobody asked them anything as they watched players having a catch in the outfield and running sprints. Willie stared as if mesmerized. "That's Lou Gehrig over there," he said. "I have his card." "So it is," Nick said.

Soon Eddie was back, in his uniform with the elephant on it. He held out his hands to Willie and said, "Up we go, Skipper," and helped Willie over the wall and onto the bench and the field. Nick followed.

They went to the empty bullpen. Eddie had Willie sit on another bench then handed Nick a glove.

Eddie went to the pitching rubber and Nick crouched behind the plate. After a couple of warmup tosses Eddie said, "Okay, here she comes," and he threw the ghost.

To Nick's immense relief, it was sharp as ever. "Terrific," he said. "What were you worried about?"

"I just needed to hear that from you."

They kept going for fifteen minutes. Nick told himself, *I'm throwing a ball in Yankee Stadium. Sure never thought that would happen.* He was wearing blue gabardine pants, black wing-tipped shoes and a white dress shirt instead of a uniform, but still, he was doing it. "Okay, enough," he said. "The drop is super."

Eddie grinned. "Feelin good. Still nervous, but good." He pointed. "Now look, you see the dugout? Your seats are twelve rows behind it. Go get yourselves some lunch and I'll see you there. At the end of the game stay put and I'll come for you and we'll go back downtown together. It'll take me a while to shower and change my clothes, but don't worry, I'll show up."

Nick and Willie climbed over the wall again and went to a concession booth below the stands. They bought hot dogs and Coca Colas with Eddie's money then found their seats and ate.

Willie was reading the signs on the low outfield walls. A sign that started in left and spread to center said, "Ever-Ready Shaving Brush Can't yank ' em out." On the high walls up behind the seats he read "Cascades," "Fashionknit," "Van Heusen," "Bronx County Trust Co.," and "Aratex America's Best Soft Collar."

The Yanks were taking batting practice now and the stands were filling up. Nick was startled to see some colored faces here and there, something he'd never seen at Shibe Park.

Lou Gehrig stepped up to the plate and hammered a half dozen baseballs over the right field wall. He was followed by Ruth, who did the same. The sight was enough to make the strongest pitcher quake. Then the Athletics took their turn in the batting cage and Foxx and Simmons blasted some to left.

By the time batting practice ended, nearly all of the seats were taken, even far out in center field. Nick had read that the park had seventy thousand seats, but the papers claimed that eighty-five thousand had watched the Sunday games. Had fifteen thousand stood? It was hard to believe. Today's crowd wasn't as huge as Sunday's, but it was by far the largest that Nick had ever seen; Shibe Park had only thirty-three thousand seats.

Eddie finished his warmup tosses down in the bullpen, and now he began his slow walk to the dugout. When he got there he looked up at Nick and Willie and raised his fist, and they raised theirs in return. Then he disappeared into the dugout.

The managers—the Yankees' diminutive Miller Huggins and the A's Connie Mack, in his shirt and tie—conferred with the home plate umpire then went to their dugouts. The announcer, with his megaphone, came to home plate and shouted the names of the pitchers and catchers and then the Yankees took the field. The cry from the crowd was so great that it made the stands tremble, and Willie looked apprehensive.

"Noisy bunch, aren't they?" Nick said, smiling.

Willie smiled too. "Yes," he said, "but they don't have Harry the Huckster."

Out in right field Ruth was leaning forward, his hands on his knees. This position was sometimes a sign of fatigue, and Nick hoped that the Babe had caroused last night and was feeling punk.

The umpire yelled, "Play Ball!" and the game began.

Hank Johnson, the Yankees' pitcher, did not look good. He had trouble finding the plate and gave up a quick two runs. "Great!" Willie said. "I think we're going to win."

"Good start," Nick said. "But we still have a long way to go."

And now it was Eddie's turn to pitch. As he walked to the mound he looked like a man on his way to a firing squad. He threw the ball to Cochrane a dozen times then signaled that he was ready. He looked at the stands—at Nick and Willie. They raised their fists and he nodded.

His first pitch to Combs, the leadoff man, wasn't a ghost and was high. "Combs will take the next pitch," Nick said.

He did, and it was a fastball strike. The next pitch, a ghost, was also a strike. Another ghost fooled Combs badly and down he went. The crowd let out a groan as Willie yelled, "Yay!"

"That ought to help Eddie a lot," Nick said.

The next batter, Koenig, tapped the ball weakly to first, where Jimmie Foxx gobbled it up. Two outs.

And then it was Gehrig's turn. The big first baseman missed two ghosts then poked one softly through the hole between first and second. If batters hit the ghost, for the most part that's how they hit it: for little scratch singles or bloopers. "Too bad," Willie said. "Now here comes the big test," Nick said, and his heart seemed to skip a beat.

After rubbing the batboy-mascot's hump, The Babe stepped up to the plate. He jiggled his bat in a menacing way and stared at Eddie, and Eddie leaned over and stared right back. He tugged on his cap, looked down at the ground and then finally wound up and threw—the ghost—and Ruth took a mighty swing and missed.

Eddie wasted the next pitch, high and wide, then tried another ghost and Ruth missed again. Eddie kicked at the pitching rubber. Staring and stalling, turning the ball around and around in his hand, he seemed to take forever to wind up. At last he threw—and that was it for Ruth, he went down swinging. Once again the crowd moaned.

"Struck him out!" Willie said.

Ruth's swing had been awkward, off balance. Nick wondered again if he was hung over, but gave the credit to Eddie. "He still can't hit the ghost," he said. Things were looking good.

When the A's got another run in the top of the fourth on a Cochrane hit, things looked even better. Eddie had already struck out seven by the time Ruth batted again.

Again Ruth rubbed the batboy's hunch, but it didn't help. He lunged at the first pitch and missed. On the second pitch, he tapped a foul past Foxx. On the third, he struck out again. "Wow," Willie said. "Maybe The Babe's not the greatest after all."

Eddie kept mowing them down, but the next time Ruth batted he walked. No harm done; the men who followed him struck out. Going into the seventh the score remained A's 3, Yanks 0.

In the last of the seventh, Eddie walked two and gave up a run on another scratch hit. Nick wondered if he was tiring. This was the longest he'd pitched in years and the day was now brutally hot.

The A's didn't score in the top of the eighth, and then, in the last of the inning, Eddie began to unravel. He walked two more batters then gave up a double and two more runs crossed the plate. "Drat!" Willie said. Now the score was tied, 3-3, with a runner on second, two outs, and Ruth coming up.

Nick was hoping that Mack would take Eddie out, but he didn't. Nick's stomach was in a knot, sweat collected along his brow and he wiped it away with his fingers. Eddie looked up at the stands and Willie and Nick raised their fists again. "Come on, you can do it, Eddie!" Willie yelled, and the fans on both sides of him scowled.

Eddie looked at the runner on second, banged his spikes on the rubber, examined the ball. Then finally he threw the ghost and Ruth missed. "That's it," Nick said. "Just two more, Eddie, two more ghosts."

But Eddie's next pitch was not a ghost. He decided to throw a fastball instead and Ruth hammered it high and deep. The crowd gasped as it left the park—foul by a couple of feet. "Wow, close," Willie said.

Nick's heart was in his throat. What had Eddie been thinking?

Eddie walked off the mound, stood there a minute, went back to the rubber, looked down at the ball. Threw the ghost again and Ruth fouled it off, straight back. "One more," Nick said, clenching his fist. "One more." Again Eddie left the mound, looked up at the sky, came back, turned the ball around in his hand, kicked the rubber—then went to his mouth.

A shock traveled over Nick's chest. What was Eddie *doing*? "No!" he shouted. "Eddie, no!"

But Eddie, unable to hear him, leaned over and stared at Ruth. Then he wound up and threw.

From the instant Ruth hit it, everyone knew it was gone. It went higher and higher into the hot summer sky and vanished far over the right field wall as the crowd went wild. Ruth trotted around the bases with pigeon-toed steps as the crowd kept cheering while Willie and Nick sat silent, steeped in gloom. Eddie just stood on the mound staring down at the dirt as the hunchback mascot shook Ruth's hand before he crossed home plate.

Now, finally, after the damage was done, Mack sent a coach to the mound to take Eddie out. As Eddie walked slump-shouldered off the field he looked up just briefly at Nick, who shrugged. Then Eddie went into the dugout.

The score was now 5 to 3 in the Yankees' favor. If the A's didn't rally in the top of the ninth, Nick's life would be drastically changed.

The inning started well: the A's got a walk and a hit and Nick was optimistic. But a double play and a popup—by pinch hitter Ty Cobb—ended the game.

"Two bad for Eddie," Willie said as the fans streamed into the aisles. "Too bad is right," Nick said.

The two of them sat there for almost a half an hour, saying little. "What's Fashionknit?" Willie asked. Nick said he didn't know. "Cascades?" "I don't know. I know 'Van Heusen' though, it's the kind of shirt I'm wearing." Everybody was gone except for the cleanup crew.

Finally Eddie showed up. "Well, close, but no cigar," he said.

"Yeah close," Nick said. "I guess you were really tired."

"You bet I was tired. But I was stupid, too."

"What happened?"

Eddie spat some tobacco juice onto the stadium floor. "Goldarn it," he said, modifying his language because of Willie, "after I snuck that first ghost past him he yells out, 'Throw me another one of them crazy things, Summers, I dare you!' He made me so sore, it was just like the old days back in spring trainin'. I figure I'll cross him up with a fastball. Cochrane says no, try a curve, but my curve wasn't breakin the way I like, so I shake him off. Big mistake! My fastball was feeble and Ruth takes me deep, but foul. I get him again with another ghost and then, on that last pitch, I was so

274

nervous I went to my mouth—out of habit. And that was it, goodbye."

"You stained the ball and killed the ghost."

"It was so *stupid*," Eddie said. "I'm sorry, Nick. Next time, I won't let you down,"

"Next time," Nick said. He thought of the bet he had made and felt sick in the pit of his stomach.

"Ruth really gets my goat and always will," Eddie said.

"Mine too."

"What does that mean?" Willie said. "'Gets my goat'?"

"It means makes you sore," Nick said.

"I know, but why do you say 'Gets my goat'?"

"I have no idea."

"Skipper, you're the question man," Eddie said.

As they made their way out of the stadium Willie said, "There's something I'd really, really like to see."

"The Statue of Liberty?" Nick said.

"No. Carnegie Hall."

"I don't know where it is."

"I do. It's at Fifty-Seventh Street and Seventh Avenue."

"Hardly out of our way," Eddie said. "We can do it easy."

"Great!" Willie said. "Now I have to pee."

While Willie was in the men's room Eddie said, "Here's one good thing at least. Cochrane said Mack was impressed with the job I done, and he's pretty sure he'll sign me on for next season."

"Well that would be wonderful, Eddie. The ghost should keep you going for years."

"I don't know about that, I'm already pretty wore out. But if you hadn't taught it to me, I'd be cooked. It's one sweet pitch, and you know, I been thinkin. Now that your arm has some zip again and you know how to throw the ghost, maybe Mack would give you a shot. I could talk to him."

Nick shook his head. "No, Eddie. You can resume a big league career at thirty-four but you can't begin one at thirty-four. At least I've never heard of anyone who did."

Eddie frowned. "Well, yeah, me neither." His face brightened a bit. "Say, Skipper looks pretty good. He all over that stuff he had?"

"He's better, yeah. But I think he needs different air to really get rid of it all."

"I feel it myself," Eddie said. "I escape every winter, go down to this place in the Florida Keys, do some fishin and lay on the beach. Go swimmin. It's good for my arm. The winter air in Philly is full of coal soot, really bad. The windowsills turn black."

"I wish Anna would move, but she's dead set against it."

"She probably thinks she can't."

"That's part of it."

Willie was back. "Carnegie Hall, here we come," Eddie said.

They rode the subway and walked a bit and there they were, across from the famous concert hall. "I'm really *seeing* it," Willie said. "And someday I'm going to play there, I know I am."

"I bet you will, Skipper," Eddie said.

In Penn Station Nick said, "At least you got Ruth good a couple of times, made him look like a fool."

"But then he made *me* the fool," Eddie said, "—as usual. I won't have another chance at him again, after tomorrow's game we're done with the Yanks for this year. We're still on the road for the rest of the month so I'll see you when I get back. You keep walkin and practicin catch now, Skipper."

"I will," Willie said.

"Thanks again for comin up here to support me, sorry I didn't do better. But you know what? We may still catch those Yanks."

"Let's hope," Nick said.

"If we don't, we'll get 'em next year. Next year we're gonna be great!"

The train was waiting and Nick and Willie boarded and

276

took their seats. As they pulled away they waved to Eddie, and as he waved back Nick was struck with the sudden sad thought that he might never see him again.

On the train Willie slept the whole time. Nick carried him to the trolley, where he groggily woke up.

It was almost nine when they came through the door, and Anna was there in the living room waiting.

She bent down and kissed Willie's cheek and gave him a hug. "Did you have a good time?"

He nodded sleepily.

"Did the Athletics win?"

"They lost."

"Oh, that's too bad."

"It sure is," Nick said.

Anna stood up. Willie said, "I saw Carnegie Hall."

"That's wonderful!"

"It's big. And really beautiful."

"I'm so glad you got to see it."

"I'm going to play there someday."

"I know you are. Right now you need some sleep."

Willie nodded and gave a tremendous yawn.

Turning to Nick, Anna said, "Thank you so much for taking him."

"It was fun."

"Are you hungry?"

Willie shook his head, and Nick said, "No, just beat. Goodnight, Willie, see you tomorrow."

"Goodnight," Willie said.

Nick went up the stairs to his room, feeling sick to his heart.

31

Nɪᴄᴋ ᴅɪᴅɴ'ᴛ ɢᴇᴛ ᴜᴘ ᴜɴᴛɪʟ ɴᴏᴏɴ the next day. When he went downstairs, Willie and Flora were ending their game of gin and Anna called them to lunch. She invited Nick to join them, but he declined; he had no appetite. He took a long walk but it didn't help calm his mind.

At work smiling Charlie asked, "How's your sick friend?"

Nick finished tying his apron on. "Much better."

"Good. So's Louie. He went back home today."

"That's great. But I'll really miss him."

"We all will. Gus made his Greek stew yesterday and it was good, but a little different, I don't know why."

Nick smiled. "Not enough sweat in it, I guess."

"That must be it. Hey, listen, I got a customer for that gun of yours."

"Too late," Nick said, "I forgot to tell you, I already sold it."

When Vince showed up he went straight to Nick. "I warned you," he said. "And don't think Sid's gonna get you off the hook. He and Sal go way back, yeah, but Sid won't interfere with Sal's business. *Can't* interfere with his business. So what are you gonna do?"

"I don't know."

"Then I'll tell you. You're gonna hightail it out of this town just soon as you can."

"How much time do I have?"

"Not much." Vince shook his head. "By God, you almost pulled it off. One more Ruth whiff and you mighta done it, and wouldn't Slick Dominic be steamed. Uh-oh, speak of the devil."

He was over beside the door. Now he made his way through the crowd and came up to Nick. "Shot of bourbon," he said.

Nick poured him the drink. Dominic smiled and took a long swallow, then said, "I hear you placed a bet."

"That's right."

"I hear it was a big one."

"Right again."

"I hear you lost."

"Three hits in a row."

Slick Dominic narrowed his eyes. He tilted his head back and finished the rest of the bourbon. "When you plannin to pay?"

"As soon as I can."

"You have one week. After that, bad things will happen."

Nick wanted to strangle the little creep. "Okay," he said.

Slick Dominic walked away and went over to Vince, who nodded at everything he said. The hit man kept glancing at Nick as he spoke, then went out the door.

At break time Nick went to the storeroom. He thumbed through the phone directory there and dialed.

A woman answered. Nick said, "Is Jimmy there?"

"Who may I say is calling?"

"This is Nick Hudson."

A pause. "Oh, yes, I remember you." She did not sound thrilled.

"Is Jimmy home?"

"He is. I'm sure he'll be happy to speak with you, let me get him."

Nick heard a rustling sound and a tinny faraway voice and then Jimmy was on the line. "Nick! How's it going? I've been worried about you. I thought I'd hear from you long before this."

"Jimmy, I know, I'm sorry, I should have called."

"Are you okay?"

"I'm fine. I'd like to see you."

"Is anything wrong?"

"No, I just want to see you."

The line was dead for a minute, then Jimmy said, "Okay, sure. I'm out of town for the next two days, but how about Saturday afternoon? Around two or so?"

"That would be fine."

"Let's meet at my club, it's at Eighteenth and Walnut. I'll stand on the sidewalk until you arrive."

I'll be there Saturday at two," Nick said. "See you then, Jimmy."

He hung up the phone, then looked up another number, dialed, and was told that a train to Chicago left Philly at 6:25 each morning. Back in the bar he worked like a steady machine until closing time, trying not to think.

On Thursday he woke at his usual time, eleven, filled with anxiety, wondering how to kill the day. He went for a walk, and when he got back, Anna invited him to lunch. This time he accepted. He hardly spoke as Flora told stories about her days at Wanamaker's. "Those lovely murals on the walls? They were painted in France by a Philadelphian, Anne Estelle Rice. She took one look at Paris and never came home again!"

After lunch Willie napped, and when he got up Nick asked if he wanted to have a catch. He said yes and they walked to the Square.

The A's had won their final game with the Yanks and were two and a half games back with thirteen games to go. "No more twin bills unless there's a rainout," Nick said. "That will make Eddie happy."

"There's a good chance the A's will catch up," Willie said,

"and Shibe Park will open again—for the World Series!"

"Wouldn't that be great," Nick said, wondering where he would be if that should happen.

On their way back home they saw a guy pasting a colorful poster on Shibe Park's right field wall, right across from their porch. "Shibe *is* going to open again!" Willie said. "Tomorrow!"

The poster was for a carnival that would start on Friday and run through next Wednesday—with Sunday off, of course. As soon as Willie went through the door he told his mother about it. "You never let me go those other times," he said. "But can we go this time?"

"We'll see," she said.

"You always say that!" Willie grumbled.

In the morning he asked again and Nick, who had just come downstairs, said, "I can take him if you want." He hadn't been to a carnival since that time with Alice and Ruth and Helen. That one had not been in Shibe but several blocks away.

"Well, if you want to go," Anna said, "then I'll go too."

"I want to go," Nick said. It would be a good way to eat up some time.

So after lunch and Willie's nap, they walked to Shibe's main entrance—minus Flora, whose rheumatism was bad again. "This is on me," Nick said at the gate. Anna protested, but Nick insisted.

Inside, they walked onto the playing field. There were plenty of people wandering around, but no one was in the stands. "This is weird," Willie said. "It doesn't seem like the same place at all, but there's the pitching mound."

They went to it. The rubber had been removed. "This is where Lefty Grove stands!" Willie said. "George Earnshaw, too!"

And where I also stood, Nick thought. He looked toward home plate, thinking about what might have been, then walked away.

The carnival was set up in the outfield. At a concession stand Anna bought Willie some popcorn after refusing to buy cotton candy. The whirling musical carousel, sparkling with yellow lights and mirrors, stood before them and Nick was surprised when Anna decided to ride it with Willie. She sat sidesaddle on a pony that kept going up and down, and seemed to enjoy herself. When the ride was over she said, "I used to love carousels as a child—and still do." Her face was flushed—and very beautiful, Nick thought.

They saw a booth where you'd win a prize if you knocked wooden bottles down with a baseball and Willie said, "Why don't you try it, Uncle Nick?" So Nick bought a ticket and reared back and threw and blasted the bottles away with one pitch.

"Wow!" Willie said. "You're great!"

The concessionaire, wiry and wizened and wearing a porkpie hat, set up the bottles twice again and Nick again used just one throw to knock them down.

The concessionaire chewed on his toothpick and scowled as if he'd been swindled.

"Uncle Nick was a major leaguer," Willie said.

"Izzat so," said the concessionaire in a sour voice. "Choose your prize."

Willie chose a box that contained a put-it-together-yourself model plane made of balsa wood that would fly with a rubber band-driven propeller. Anna put it away in her purse.

Next up was a shooting range and Willie urged Nick to try that too. "You're a real good shooter, right? You had your own gun."

"I'm not in the mood for it," Nick said.

Willie frowned. "Well can I try, Mother?"

Anna said yes, so Willie hefted the little rifle and squeezed off a couple of shots that missed the slowly moving black silhouette of a bird. Nick saw himself at the bedroom window, aiming at Ruth, and turned away. Willie's last shot clipped a wing. "Well, at least I hit a piece of it," he said.

"Very good for a first try," Anna said.

Willie wanted to go on the Ferris wheel. He asked his mother and Nick to go with him but Nick said he wasn't in the mood for that either. So Anna and Willie got into their seats across from each other and Nick watched them going around and around. When the ride stopped with Anna and Willie up top, Nick thought of Babe Ruth's hand on Alice's thigh, a million years ago.

At a stand where you rolled a ball up a slope, trying to make it fall into a hole, Willie and Anna both played without success. Willie rode in a little red car that bumped into other cars and said he didn't like it much, the bumping hurt his legs. In a tent they all watched some acrobats fly through the air with amazing grace and then Nick said he had to leave, had to get to work. "But you two stay," he said, "there's more to see."

"No, that's enough," Anna said, and Willie said, "Oh, Mother."

On their way out they passed a tent with a stage in front of it and on this stage stood a huge fat woman in a skimpy skirt and a very thin man whose skin was tightly drawn across his bony ribs and hips. Another man dressed in colorful clothing was shouting at people to buy a ticket and go inside and watch the odd couple dance. Inside they would also see the bearded lady and the alligator boy, whose pictures were on the side of the tent. And they'd see the pinheaded dwarf and the girl with six toes on each foot.

Willie frowned. "They have *conditions*," he said. "People pay to see other people who have *conditions*?"

"Some people do," Anna said. "But we don't."

On the sidewalk Nick instantly noticed a car parked down the street with a slouching figure at the wheel: Slick Dominic. When he and Anna and Willie turned onto Twentieth Street, the car slowly moved away.

32

THE DAY NICK WAS GOING to meet with Jimmy—Saturday—was beautiful, with clear blue skies and a gentle refreshing breeze.

In the morning Willie assembled the balsa wood plane Nick had won and they went to the Square and flew it. Willie would wind its propeller tight and toss it up and off it would gracefully soar. And he'd chase it. Sometimes he'd actually *run*. A couple of months ago he could hardly walk, and here he was *running*. He almost never used his wheelchair now.

Back home Nick took a bath and dressed in his best set of clothes. He had no appetite, declined Anna's lunch, then took the trolley and brand new Broad Street subway into town. The subway was marvelous, smooth and fast and beautiful, nicer than its counterparts in Paris and New York.

Jimmy was standing on Walnut Street in front of his club when Nick arrived on the dot of two. He smiled and held out his hand and said, "Hey, Nick, you're looking great. How you feeling?" His right eye twitched.

"Just fine," Nick said, and shook Jimmy's hand. It was clammy, and Jimmy was dark around the eyes, as if he hadn't been sleeping well.

They went up the brownstone steps of the club, Jimmy limping, and through the massive doorway. The club's ceilings were high and its walls were dark polished mahogany. Thick bands of golden sunlight streamed through the tall wide windows.

Jimmy said hi to some men who were sitting in armchairs, smoking and reading the papers, went up a couple of steps and into a room that had just one table with four chairs around it. As soon as they sat, a waiter came over and asked for their order. Jimmy suggested iced coffee and Nick concurred. The waiter went off.

"Some place," Nick said. "It's almost as big as your house."

Jimmy laughed—half-heartedly, Nick thought—and said, "So...this is great."

"It is," Nick said, and asked about Jimmy's family. All were well, he was told, and then he said, "Jimmy, listen, you saved my life. That money you gave me got me through a really bad time."

"You should have come back to see us again," Jimmy said. "You should have come back and stayed with us for a while."

"I couldn't impose on you like that."

"Nick, we've been friends since the age of fifteen."

"Yeah, still..."

The waiter returned with the coffees.

When he left, Jimmy said, "So where are you living?"

"On Twentieth Street, across from the ballpark."

"Still hooked on baseball, I guess. People watch games from the roofs over there."

"I'm one of those people."

"You ever see Ruth?"

"I have."

Droplets of sweat had blossomed on Jimmy's forehead. Nick reached for his wallet and took out a twenty. "Jimmy, I owe you this."

"No, no," Jimmy said, and he pushed it away.

"I have some money now," Nick said, "and I want you to take this. You told me it was a loan and I'm paying you back."

"Nick, really, please, I'm doing extremely well—

"I'd feel better if you took it."

Jimmy breathed deeply then said, "Okay." He pocketed the

bill, looking down at the table. His forehead was glistening now and his mouth was twitching. He said, "Nick, listen, there's something I have to tell you." He looked up again with troubled eyes. "I couldn't tell you before, when we met at the house, I just couldn't bring myself to. I was afraid that if I did...well, I didn't know what would happen."

Nick frowned. "What is it?"

Jimmy looked at his glass. He lifted it slowly but didn't drink, then set it down again. Without looking up he said, "Ruth didn't get Alice pregnant, I did."

Nick stared at him. "What?"

Now Jimmy looked up. "That's right," he said, "I'm the one."

Nick pictured his bedroom on Twentieth Street, Shibe Park, and the gun he had smashed. "You," he said. It was almost a whisper.

Running his tongue across his lips Jimmy said, "Let me try to explain." He paused for a moment, then started again. "Alice took Johnny's death terribly hard and her mother...her mother seemed lost in a world of her own. I was worried about them both and often stopped by to see them.

"Then your mother received a notice that you were missing. Alice had been in touch with her and told me this, and the two of us went to see her. Alice was worried to death about you. Your mother was too, of course, but she was hopeful. Shortly before the notice came she and Alice had both received letters from you saying that all was well, and she was convinced you were still alive and would soon be found. Then the Spanish flu hit the city and took her. Then two of my good friends died of it. And then my dear Rachel died and I was overwhelmed with grief. Alice tried to console me.

"She volunteered at Pennsylvania Hospital, helping flu victims, and then, to my horror, she caught it too. Her mother never left her side and she managed to beat it. I bought their groceries and helped out however I could. It took Alice months to recover.

"She and I were both shattered. We'd always been optimistic people. We'd thought that the world was a decent place and science would just keep making it better. But the war had revealed the dark side of science, and the flu showed how helpless science was in the face of potent disease. In one week alone, forty-six hundred people died in this city, your mother and Rachel among them. And Alice had nearly perished too. She and I had looked forward to living long lives, but now we were totally changed. Johnny and Rachel were dead and we thought you were dead and we realized that we could die at any moment.

"We met every couple of weeks to comfort each other. Alice kept writing to you but never received a reply. Our sorrow and fear drew us closer and closer and one thing led to another and..."

He stopped; took another deep breath. "I always liked Alice—adored her, really, but she was yours. But now you were gone and we were both hurt and we needed each other so badly. And I'd come to believe that there was a reason that she had survived the flu. She had survived it to be with me."

"Jimmy..." Nick said. And that's all he could say.

"We kept seeing each other for over two years," Jimmy said, "but couldn't commit ourselves to marriage. We hadn't recovered from our losses and nothing seemed permanent to us. Then Alice got pregnant. She told her mother but didn't say who was to blame. Her mother must have known, of course, but Alice denied it was me. I said I'd arrange an abortion. She wouldn't consider it. I promised to marry her.

"The pregnancy was terribly hard from the start and got worse and worse. She had to quit work. She was living at home and was bedridden much of the time. Her mother called me as soon as she went into labor. I went right away and drove her to the hospital.

"The labor was long and painful and two hours after the baby was born Alice died. And that was the end of the world for me and for her poor mother too. She's never been really

287

right since then. Losing both of her children like that, and of course she had lost her husband years before. Sometimes I go to see her. I've never told her that I was the one who got Alice pregnant."

Nick just kept staring at him. Finally he said, "What became of the child?"

"Stillborn."

Silence. Jimmy looked down at his coffee then took a deep breath. "The grief that I felt was devastating. And the guilt, my God, the guilt. My mind was completely confused. I gave up my room and went back to live with my mother. I was useless at work, I couldn't sleep and I drank too much. I thought that I might do away with myself. One night I got stinking drunk and fell down a flight of concrete steps and reinjured my knee. It turned out to be a blessing. I needed an operation and that's when I met Jane. She was my nurse in the hospital. Without her, God only knows where I'd be right now. She saved my life."

"And it's a good life, Jimmy."

"Better than I deserve."

"If you say so."

"It is. I killed Alice."

Nick shook his head. "No, Jimmy, you didn't. Things happen, that's all. Don't blame yourself for that." He frowned at the table then looked up again, "But why did you tell me that terrible lie?"

Jimmy looked at his coffee but didn't drink. He said: "When I opened my door last winter and saw you standing there, I was stunned. You were like a ghost out of my past. You even *looked* like a ghost. It was clear that the years had been hard on you, that you weren't the Nick I had known. You had this look about you—something cold and dark and desperate.

"I was terrified. I had never told Jane the truth about Alice. I'd told her she died of consumption. Her mother and I had agreed on this story. When you told me you'd learned that she died giving birth, I suddenly felt that the past I had buried was rising up again and would ruin me. You looked dangerous, Nick, you looked mad at the world, and then when you told me you'd just been released from St. Luke's, I was terrified. I didn't know what you'd do if I told you the truth. I knew you would hate me, you might even harm me, my marriage might be destroyed. So I made up that Babe Ruth story. I didn't actually say that he got Alice pregnant but led you to think he did."

Nick pictured his room's bay window again, the playing field. He saw himself aiming the rifle. "You did," he said.

"I gave you the money and hoped that you'd come back again when I gathered my wits, so I could explain myself and tell you what really happened. But you disappeared. I didn't know where to find you. Then I thought it was best that you'd disappeared. I could keep my secret. My life would continue smoothly. But then when I knew I was going to see you again, I realized I had to come clean. It's been a tremendous weight on my soul and I just couldn't keep it inside any longer. So there it is, that's all of it, the truth."

Nick looked at his untouched coffee. "I don't get it," he said. "Why didn't you simply tell me you didn't know who the father was and the baby died?"

"I *did* say I didn't know who the father was—and you didn't believe me. Your eyes...I felt they were seeing right through me. It was like you'd come back from the dead to punish me. I had to come up with something else—"

"So you told me that lie about Ruth."

Jimmy's hands were quivering now. "I...see, Ruth's baby had come out of nowhere, it mystified everybody—his teammates, the sportswriters, everybody. And Ruth knew Alice, you knew very well what he was like— and the idea just suddenly came to me."

"But Jimmy, my God..."

"I know, I know, and I cursed myself for what I'd done and worried about it constantly. But I figured the chances that you

289

would cross paths with Ruth again were so remote—"

"Oh, is that what you figured?" Nick said, his voice rising with anger. "Did it never occur to you that I might want to kill the man?"

Jimmy winced as if he'd been struck. "It did. Not at first, but as time went on and I thought more and more about what I had told you, yes, it did. I kept hoping that you would come back and we'd talk, but you disappeared. When I lied to you I wasn't thinking straight. It was all so confusing and shocking."

"My God," Nick said. "And all this time I thought—"

"I know, I know, it was terrible of me," Jimmy said." He looked up at Nick and his eyes were moist. "If you won't be my friend anymore, I'll understand. But please, don't tell Jane."

"That's one thing you don't have to worry about," Nick said. "I'm leaving Philly. For good."

"What? Where are you going?"

"I can't tell you that."

"What's wrong? Are you in a jam? Can I help?"

"No more questions, okay?"

Jimmy nodded. "Okay."

"You have a good life and I'm glad for you, Jimmy. I'm not going to mess it up."

Jimmy produced a handkerchief and wiped his sweat-soaked forehead. "Nick, you're a good man," he said. He took a deep breath then said, "Now listen, here's some advice. If you have any money, don't play the market. Everyone's doing it—cab drivers, plumbers, you name it—but don't get involved. The whole thing's crooked, a house of cards, and it's going to crash. Believe me, I know what I'm talking about."

Nick sniffed a laugh. "Don't worry," he said, "I won't play the market. Well, listen, I have to get going. Say hello to your family for me. And maybe I'll see you again sometime."

"I hope so."

They stood and Jimmy said, "I just kept pushing my secret down every time it came up—and it kept coming up every day. I'd have done it forever, kept fighting it, kept it burning. Then you came along."

"But the fire's not out. You haven't told Jane."

"I just can't."

"I understand."

They shook hands. "Good luck wherever you go," Jimmy said.

"Good luck to you too, Jimmy."

As Nick rode the subway north, his conversation with Jimmy kept spinning around in his head. *All that hatred,* he thought. *All that hatred directed at someone who didn't deserve it. My God.*

But maybe, he thought, he had needed that hatred. It kept driving him forward day after day, might even have kept him alive—and reasonably sane. His obsession with killing Babe Ruth might have kept him from going over the edge into darkness again—as crazy as that seemed.

He thought of how easily he had fooled himself back then. He had seen the features of Alice in Ruth's little girl, was sure that the child was hers—and had been wrong. He broke into a sweat when he thought of how close he had come to creating a monstrous tragedy. Those bullets he'd fired at Ruth must have missed him by less than an inch.

It occurred to him then that if Jimmy had told him the truth from the start, he would never have moved to Twentieth Street, would not have met Anna and Willie. And would never be running away to a distant place he had never seen in order to save his life.

At work that night he felt terribly sad: this was farewell to the Home Plate Café—to Charlie, Jake, Sid, Billy, Gus, Shirley, Doris and all of the regular customers. The worst part of it was, he couldn't say goodbye, he had to just disappear without a word, or Dominic would be on his tail. When they wondered why he didn't show up for work on Monday, Vince would explain. But Vince wouldn't know where he'd gone. He himself didn't know where he'd go. He wouldn't decide until he was on that train to Chicago—and that was good.

33

AFTER WINNING THE FINAL Yankees game the A's had a much-needed two days off. Then Saturday they beat the Indians in Cleveland while the Yankees, in St. Louis, lost to the lowly Browns. So now the A's were only a game and a half behind in the standings. "They just might do it," Nick said at Sunday dinner.

"Yes," Willie said, "they might. And if they do, we'll have the World Series here!"

After he dried the dishes Nick asked Willie if he'd like to go out to the Square. He'd heard that the Wildcats were playing there tonight.

When they got to the diamond the game was already in progress. A cigar manufacturer sponsored the team and the games were free to the public. Technically, the Blue Laws still applied, but like those dealing with fishing they weren't enforced since money wasn't involved.

Most of the players on both of the teams were kids—eighteen, nineteen, twenty years old, but there were a few old timers. *Old timers like me*, Nick thought. *Guys who just couldn't give up the game.*

"These players are good," Willie said. "Will they play in the major leagues someday?"

"Maybe one or two of them will," Nick said.

"That's all?"

"That's all. Very few players make the majors."

"And very few pianists make it to Carnegie Hall."

"That's right. But some do. We just have to work as hard as

we can with the talent we have. Then luck takes over."

Willie frowned. "That isn't fair."

"Maybe not, but that's how it is."

"Well I'm going to practice even harder. I'm going to *make* good luck."

"That's the spirit," Nick said.

The Wildcats beat the Spiders, five to four in the last of the ninth on a very close play at home plate.

"That was really exciting," Willie said on the twilight walk home. "I hope we can come again."

"The Wildcats' season is over," Nick said.

"Oh, that's too bad. But you know what I'd like us to do? I'd like us to have a catch every day while Eddie is gone. Then when he comes back I'll show him how much I've improved. Can we do that?"

"Of course," Nick said, and felt awful. He wanted to let Willie know what was going to happen, but just couldn't do it.

At home Willie played the piano. Nick wondered where the music was taking him now: what forests he was seeing in his mind, what mountain peaks, what skies.

Flora had gone to her room. Anna sat on the sofa knitting a sweater for Willie and Nick sat in one of the chairs. At the end of each piece Willie played, Nick and Anna praised him. Nick wondered what someone who really knew about music would think of Willie's performance—someone other than Shultz, the piano teacher, who had to be biased.

After some brisk renditions Willie played something soft and slow that made Nick feel sad in his bones as the last of the light left the sky. He excused himself after the piece concluded and went upstairs.

In his room, with the lights off, he looked through the big bay window. The streetlight shone on Shibe Park's right field wall; above it, all was black. Nick thought of what Jimmy had told him yesterday about his appearance and actions eight

294

months ago and realized how far he'd progressed. He still didn't think he was totally healed, but he was a good distance back from the edge of the pit. And what had been the cause of this transformation? Vengeance? Something far from it, something he'd never imagined.

He went to bed, fell asleep for an hour, then woke from a dream of fishing with Willie out on a wide bright sea. He stayed awake for a couple of hours, slept again, then woke again. Then he couldn't get back to sleep.

At four in the morning he turned on the bedside lamp, got dressed, then took his carryall bag from the closet. There was little to pack, mostly the same stuff he'd come here with in June: some shirts, some pants, his extra pair of shoes. He had accumulated almost nothing but gained everything. He lay down on the bed again then heard a noise in the hallway.

He got up and opened his door just as Anna, wearing her white terry robe, was leaving the spare room. She heard him and turned. "Did I wake you?" she asked in a whisper. "I'm sorry. I'm trying to find something—"

"Anna," he said, "I need to talk to you."

They went quietly down the stairway and into the kitchen. The lamp that sat on the counter was softly glowing.

They sat at the kitchen table across from each other and Nick said, "Anna, I know why you go to that room, I've been in it."

She frowned. "You—"

"I know, I shouldn't have done it, but not long ago I took the key and went there."

She sighed and looked down at the table. Nick waited. She didn't speak and he thought that maybe she couldn't. Finally he said, "It's over, Anna."

She took in another deep breath and then said softly, "They told me that he was missing. Not dead, but missing, and I kept hope alive in my heart. Night after night I couldn't sleep. I prayed to God to let him be safe but time kept slipping away and I heard nothing, nothing at all. I began to accept, but not

295

completely. I tried to convince myself that if I kept his room exactly the way it was when he left for the war he'd return to me. It took a long time to admit that I was deceiving myself. But even though hope was gone, I kept the room intact.

"Then you entered my life and everything started up again. You told me that you had been lost for all those years, that nobody knew where you were all that time, and my hopes revived. If it happened to you, I thought, maybe the same thing had happened to Martin. Maybe he too was locked away somewhere, still alive but hurt in his mind, as you had been hurt..." She stopped. A tear was sliding down her cheek.

Nick was silent a minute. And then in a gentle voice he said, "No, Anna, it's over. It's over for both of us. He'll never come back and Alice will never come back. It's over."

Wiping the tear away Anna said, "I know."

He reached across the table and took her hand. He said, "I have to tell you something."

She looked at him earnestly. "What?"

"I'm leaving this city. This morning. Soon."

"But why?"

"Remember that movie we saw? 'Lights of New York'?"

"Oh, no."

"Yes. I did something foolish, I made a huge bet that I can't pay off and they're after me."

"Oh, Nick." She shook her head. "But I don't understand. You told me you never gambled."

"And it wasn't a lie. When I told you that, it was true. But then I did gamble—for the first time ever."

"But why? And why did you bet such a large amount?" She was quiet a second; she frowned. Then she said, "You did it for us, for Willie and me. That's why you did it, isn't it?"

"I did it for several reasons."

"But mostly for us."

"That's not important now. The important thing is, I have to get out of town."

"For how long?"

"Until things calm down. It may be a long time, I can't really say."

"Where will you go? Out West?"

He nodded.

She pressed her lips together hard and her eyes were suddenly wet with tears.

He gave her hand a squeeze and then withdrew. "I have to get going," he said. "My train will be leaving soon."

Back in his room he removed the sheets from his bed and folded them up. He then took a ten dollar bill from his wallet and put it on top of the dresser. He wished he could leave a lot more, but that was the most he could spare.

He went downstairs again with his carryall bag, his coat flung over his arm. Anna was wearing her yellow dress and standing in front of the parlor window, looking outside at the pale morning street. Nick set his bag and coat on the chair that stood in front of the rolltop desk and started across to her.

Then Willie appeared in the hallway. He was dressed in his blue pajamas and wearing his A's cap. "Why is everyone up so early?" he asked with a puzzled expression. "Why do you have that bag and coat, Uncle Nick? Are you going somewhere?"

"Uncle Nick has something to tell you," Anna said.

"What?"

"I have to leave Philadelphia for a while."

"But why?"

"Your mother will explain."

"Well when will you come back?"

"I don't know."

"Will it be a long time?"

"I don't know."

"Will it be forever?"

Nick went to him, knelt down and gave him a hug. "I'll be back," he said. "I promise, I just don't know when."

"But..." Willie said. "I don't want you to go. I want you to change your mind."

"I'd like to, but I can't," Nick said.

"Are you going far away?"

"I am."

Willie's lower lip trembled. "But we always have such good times together."

"I'll be back," Nick said. "In the meantime, when Eddie comes home from his road trip, you get him to play catch with you. And maybe you can both play catch with some of the kids in the neighborhood. And bat the ball too."

Willie nodded, fighting to hold back tears. Then quickly he turned away and went down the hall.

Anna came over to Nick and he took her hands; they felt hot. "Sell this house and move out West," he said. "Don't think you can't do it, Anna, you can. It would be the best thing for you and for Willie, too. Those magnificent mountains and forests he dreams about when he plays the piano are real out there. It can be a fresh start for you both. He might even see me play ball. I'll write to you and tell you where I am."

"I don't know," Anna said with a shake of her head. "I just don't think I'm ready for that."

Nick let out a breath. "Well if you decide that you don't want to move," he said, "I hope you'll let Willie go to Girard. It would do him a world of good."

Anna shrugged. "I—"

"It's not far away, you could visit him any time. He'll come home for the holidays—"

Willie was back. He was holding a ball and a fountain pen. "I want you to sign this for me," he said.

Nick took the ball. "But Willie," he said, "this is the one that Babe Ruth signed. I'll sign a different one."

"No," Willie said, "I want you to sign this one."

Nick took the pen and signed, then handed the ball and the pen back to Willie.

"I bet you were as good as Babe Ruth is," Willie said.

"Willie…"

"I bet you were," he said, and now the tears were flowing.

Nick gave him another hug. "Say goodbye to Aunt Flora for me," he said. "And say goodbye to Eddie, too. And walk with him every chance you get and play catch with him and get him to take you fishing."

Willie said nothing, just nodded.

Nick went to Anna and hugged her too. She felt so warm and wonderful, then she kissed him behind his ear. It sent a shock wave through his arms. "I'll write as soon as I get where I'm going," he said.

"And I'll write to you, Uncle Nick," Willie said, wiping his tears away.

"I'll miss your piano playing," Nick said.

"I'll practice real hard, and when you come back I'll surprise you with how good I am."

"I can't wait for that day," Nick said. "Okay, now I have to go."

He picked up his carryall bag and coat and went to the hallway, glanced at the baseball gloves that were hanging there, then went through the door, crossed the porch and descended the steps. As he walked down the street with the morning sun touching the top of Shibe Park's tower, Willie and Anna stood on the porch and waved. He waved back, turned the corner, and then the tears came to him too.

Slick Dominic's car was nowhere in sight. Nick fully expected to see it appear and pull up beside him, but no. Slick Dominic kept late hours; maybe this was too early for him. Nick fervently hoped so.

He caught the 54 trolley to Broad Street. There were very few people on it at this time of day. It went past the Home Plate and Nick felt a sudden quick pang in his heart. It passed a garage where he'd asked about work months ago, when he was in terrible shape. In the window he saw a sign: "Mechanic Wanted."

He took the subway into town. At Broad Street Station he bought an *Inquirer* for the ride. Its headline screamed: HUGE HURRICANE SLAMS FLORIDA; MORE THAN 3000 FEARED DEAD. He folded the paper and tucked it under his arm. He wasn't ready to read about tragedies now.

Once he was settled into his seat he turned to the sports pages. Each game was crucial for the A's if they hoped to catch New York—and he saw that they'd beaten the Indians, 7-1. But the Yankees had also won, so the A's hadn't gained any ground. Nick didn't find Eddie's name in the A's box score; he hadn't played.

The train started up and crept over the Chinese wall. Philadelphia was golden with morning light. Nick set the paper aside and watched the city disappear.

After Chicago he didn't know where he would go. It would be to a place entirely different from Philadelphia: Denver or Billings or Phoenix or Santa Fe...he didn't know. But he knew that wherever he went, cars and houses would need repair and there would be sandlot ball. He would save his money, play baseball again and be healed for good. And then he'd come back. Just as soon as he could, he'd come back. But while he was gone, what changes would take place? What would happen with Anna, with Willie?

With a heavy sigh, he picked up the paper and looked at its front page again. He started to read about the hurricane and then the right hand column caught his eye. It said: SIX KILLED IN NORTH PHILADELPHIA MOB SHOOTING.

"Six people were killed in a North Philadelphia shootout yesterday involving two of the city's most notorious criminal operations. The dead were identified as Thomas Grady, 52, Walter Malone, 36, and Charles Kelly, 41, of the Shamrock gang of Fishtown and Salvatore Mario, 48, Anthony Decco, 35, and Dominic Santana, 29, of the Scorpion gang of Southwark..."

Nick just kept staring at the page. And he suddenly felt

300

ecstatic, lighter than air. He wanted to run down the aisle shouting, but just kept sitting there with a grin on his face that he couldn't hold back.

He was not going to go to Chicago. Instead, he was getting off at the next stop, whatever it was, and taking the first train back to town. A subway ride, then the trolley would take him to Twentieth Street, to Anna and Willie and Flora. It would take him to the healing place, the place where he belonged and hoped to never leave again. It would take him home.

POSTSCRIPT

The 1928 Philadelphia Athletics were on the verge of becoming the greatest major league baseball team in history. See the articles "Really the Greatest Ever," by Larry Swindell, *Today, The Philadelphia Inquirer Magazine*, August 15, 1976 and "The Team that Time Forgot," *Sports Illustrated,* August 19, 1996.

Shibe Park, known in its later years as Connie Mack Stadium, was demolished in 1976, but the houses on Twentieth Street, where my characters Anna, Willie, Flora, Nick and Eddie—and Al Simmons—lived, still stand. For a description of what it was like to live in one of them back in the days when my novel takes place, see *Bleachers in the Bedroom: The Swampoodle Irish and Connie Mack,* by John Rooney, and *To Every Thing a Season: Shibe Park and Urban Philadelphia*, by Bruce Kuklick.

All of the games mentioned in *Gone from the Game* are accurate as to teams, place, date, and scores—with one exception. Can you find it?

I once worked for a physician who had been a patient for ten years in a mental hospital. That's where I got the idea for Nick's long stay in the fictional St. Luke's.

I got the idea for the "ghost" while watching a pitcher warm up before a Little League game. Each time he threw to his catcher the ball would vanish for a second. I was totally baffled—but when jagged lights appeared in my eyes I realized that the vanishing was in my head. I was having the first of my many visual migraines.

As a graduate assistant in speech pathology at Temple University, I spent a year working at Girard College and was impressed by the school and by the magnificent old houses on Girard Avenue.

When my father was in his late teens he encountered a former girlfriend downtown and asked her what she was up to. She said she had recently become engaged to a ballplayer from Maryland. His name was Jimmie Foxx.